WE

COULD

BE

HEROES

Also by Mike Chen

HERE AND NOW AND THEN
A BEGINNING AT THE END

MIKE CHEN

WE

COULD

BE

HEROES

mira

ISBN-13: 978-0-7783-3139-1

We Could Be Heroes

Mira
22 Adelaide St. West, 40th Floor
Toronto, Ontario M5H 4E3, Canada
BookClubbish.com

Printed in U.S.A.

For good friends

WE

COULD

BE

HEROES

1

THE WAY THE BANK teller shrunk back in fear captured everything.

After all, Jamie Sorenson was a villain.

Not just a villain. He was the Mind Robber. And he *terrified* the people of San Delgado. The mere whisper of his name summoned panic, and when he incapacitated security guards with a brain-stun (his own term, which he thought was quite cool), that panic made robbing a bank as easy as handing over a bag—or in this case, planting a backpack on the counter.

"Tell me, who do you love in your life? Husband? Boyfriend?" Jamie reminded himself to not assume. "Girlfriend? Child? Parents? *Who are they?*" he asked. He put a hand up, then dramatically turned one finger toward the bank teller. Her eyes widened, clearly aware of the modus operandi documented last year in the *San Delgado Times*: a front-page feature breaking down his robberies and "extraordinary ability to stun people into a frozen stupor or worse, blank the memories of witnesses." They'd even given him the name Mind Robber, though he'd added the eye mask and hoodie himself.

From the corner of his eye, he made sure the remaining bystanders hung on his every word.

"My…my…wife," the woman said with barely a whisper.

"Do you want to lose her?" He stepped forward, and as he waved his finger, she winced. "Erased forever? Your whole relationship lifted from your brain? Your mind—" Jamie took a deep breath "—*robbed* of the very things you love?"

"No, please, don't." The teller's lips trembled, and her eyes welled up. "We're in the middle of the in vitro process. We're going to have a family. Please, don't." With each word, her hands shook.

Focus, he told himself. To get out of here clean, he needed to keep everyone else quiet and scared.

Only one way to accomplish that: threaten the things that people held most dear. With the slightest flick of a finger, he peeked into the teller's memories. He needed a name as the coup de grâce. Images flew by, but about half of them had a woman—a woman with dark brown skin, black curly hair and a gracious smile. Probably her wife, but what was her name? Voices came through as he focused, and during a conversation about in vitro costs, he heard it.

Victoria.

"Then get the cash. Every register. And the safe. And no silent alarms. Remember, I can track what you're seeing. I know what you're thinking. The police can't help. *She* can't help you." Jamie hesitated, wondering if he should clarify that he referred to the Throwing Star. Given the context of things, it seemed unnecessary. Besides, better to keep with the personal stakes. "One wrong move and…" Jamie went with the educated guess. "Victoria is removed from your memory. Forever."

The woman's sudden sobbing confirmed his hunch.

He unzipped his backpack's main compartment, only for a

library book to almost slip out, a memoir from an ex-soldier who moved to Alaska to race sled dogs. *That* certainly wasn't threatening, and while maintaining eye contact with the bank teller, his hand pushed the book down to the bottom as discreetly as possible. He slid the backpack several inches toward her, and she complied, stuffing it with cash before taking it to the adjacent register. Across the room, the two bystanders—a woman who had been working at a nearby desk and a customer in a polo shirt—continued watching, silent with their hands up.

The second hand of the bank's large wall clock inched forward.

Jamie scanned the room, scowling to appear *extra* threatening, but really just a cover as he gauged the level of trust in the room. Everyone had a role to play: he was the villain, the aggressor, and they were the passive victims. If everyone stayed in those roles, his escape would be swift.

Jamie took a second, making sure he'd accounted for every step in his list. Couldn't be too careful these days, not with the police on his tail. Or the Throwing Star, San Delgado's resident vigilante, for that matter. He'd seen enough videos of her extraordinary beatdowns of common street muggers, and that didn't fit into his plans. Not one bit.

The money flowed in, clean and quick—in fact, it might have been the smoothest of his nine bank robberies so far. Though the bank teller was out of sight, he heard the distinct *thump* of bundled cash being tossed into the backpack. Seconds on the wall clock ticked by, a *click click click* that made each moment seem like hours.

Her footsteps returned to a normal pace as she approached her window. "Here," the teller said. "Please. Just go."

Jamie reached over, then pulled his arm back with a flourish before grabbing it. "You didn't trip the alarm, did you?"

"No. No, of course not."

"Are you sure?"

Though his abilities didn't come with a lie detector, the freshest memories were the easiest to read. He dove in and confirmed she told the truth.

"Yes," she said, nodding faster and faster. "Please, take it. I promise, I didn't do anything."

Jamie wrapped his fingers around the backpack's strap, giving a little twirl as he flipped it onto his shoulder. The weight of the bag awkwardly slammed into his side, taking his wind for a second. "Alright." He turned, putting his back to the three people watching him. "You've cooperated for now. Consider yourself lucky." He hesitated, counting to seven for an appropriate dramatic pause.

One.

They wouldn't remember this since he was about to wipe the encounter from each of their minds, but the security cameras would capture it, local news would broadcast it, and social media would discuss it.

Two.

The hashtag #MindRobber would boost his legend even further. Just the thought, the mere mention of him would generate fear in anyone he encountered.

Three.

Okay, it stroked his ego a little bit too. When you wake up in a dingy apartment without any of your memories, you really don't have much else.

Four.

His only other accomplishment at this point was returning library books on time and being a good cat owner.

Five.

Remember your lines. And a good American accent, practice makes perfect, he told himself. "The Mind Robber has spared you...this time."

Six.

Jamie adjusted his posture to make his big declaration before brain-stunning the two bystanders and the teller *and* removing the memories of this bank visit with surgical precision. Done, finished clean, in a mere ten minutes. He took in a breath to begin when the silence broke.

It wasn't a word of defiance. Or desperation, or despair.

No, this sound was a guttural *ungggh*, like something choked. Jamie turned, then his eyes widened in horror.

This was unexpected. Uncontrolled. The preparation, the scouting, the review of his plans, the speech rehearsal, and none of it ever accounted for this.

The other employee, the woman standing by the desk, clutched her chest, eyes shut and brow creased in pain. She dropped to her knees, then fell face-first onto the floor, her skull hitting the stone tile with a sickening crack.

"Oh my God," screamed the teller. "Wendy!"

The man in the polo shirt stepped over before stopping and turning to Jamie. "Please! Let me help her!"

What do I do what do I do what do I do…

None of the robberies had gone totally smoothly, but nothing had ever happened on this scale. Jamie froze, petrified as blood began to trickle from the woman's head onto the floor. All that preparation, the theatrics, the ridiculous cackling, it acted as crowd control so no one played hero or got hurt. But this was something completely different. "I, um…" He wanted to say something, something to make this alright. Why didn't he get the ability to reverse time, just a few seconds—seven seconds, precisely, to remove that stupid dramatic pause and just get out of there.

Run. He should run. Every instinct told him to get out of there—no, stun the remaining people, lift their memories, *then* get the hell out of there. Should he call 911 first? That woman, she was on the floor probably dying because of him, either from an apparent heart attack or the ensuing face-plant onto a solid rock floor. She deserved medical attention.

"We need a doctor!" yelled the bank teller.

Was Jamie a doctor? Maybe. At least in his previous life, the one that hid behind that moment of waking up about two years ago with no identity, no memories, no history. Did medical training linger somewhere in the void of his brain?

More importantly, could he even recall that type of information?

"Please!" the man in the polo shirt urged. "She needs help!"

"I know that!" Jamie yelled back, his English accent breaking through for a moment. Any cool resolve in his character was totally broken. "Are you a doctor?"

"No, I'm an engineer. We need to call an ambulance. Please!"

That man couldn't help her right away. Jamie raised his hand, flicked a finger and put the man into a stunned stupor, standing but looking blankly into the distance.

"Wendy?" the teller asked. "Wendy are you—"

She stopped short, now also under the influence of a brain-stun. Jamie's hands trembled as he tried to lift the memories of the robbery from each witness, but his own frayed nerves lacked the focus for such precision. He counted down from five again, a mental regrounding technique gleaned from self-help books for panic attacks, then he took out memory chunks from the event, enough to blur their comprehension. *Good enough,* he told himself. As he understood it, no memory wipe was one hundred percent anyway, some visual fragments always remained. Broad-stroke erasure would still limit their memories to snippets and flashes, nothing too damning. He took one last look at the teller's mind, then lost his breath.

He wouldn't need to call 911. The police would be here soon.

It wasn't totally clear—adrenaline ruined recall and retention to begin with—but one of the woman's most recent memories showed her clicking a button underneath her counter. Probably when Wendy fell.

Her bravery was admirable. So was her loyalty.

The injured woman remained prone. Should he sit her up? Check for a pulse? In movies, didn't they say *not* to touch someone after a potential neck injury? The police would be here soon anyway. He should get to safety fast.

Yes, that was it. Run like hell. Inconspicuously. Ambulances would arrive quickly. Jamie bolted to the breezeway door and nearly smashed his nose into it when he forgot that he'd locked it per his usual precaution of preventing public entry. He typed the keypad code he'd lifted from the guard's memory about thirty minutes prior and threw it open the instant it beeped.

The outer revolving doors of the San Delgado Bank branch seemed harder than ever to push, and midway through the turn, he remembered to remove his ridiculous eye mask and yank the hood off. As daylight hit the top of his head, he wondered if his sweaty face mask left indent lines around his eyebrows and his nose. Shaky legs brought him down the bank's cement stairs when the audible gasps of passersby caused him to pause.

He swiveled, ready to brain-stun whoever may have noticed him.

But they weren't looking at him. Instead, they all stared at the sky, pointing above the two-story bank.

"It's her!" he heard. "Out here! I thought she only came out at night!"

A child ran into his legs, his excitement pushing him straight past Jamie while repeating his mantra of "Look!" to anyone who might be in earshot.

Jamie followed the pointed fingers all the way up into the sky. Above the bank building, the sun backlit the silhouette of a hovering feminine figure.

"I can't believe it," someone else said. "She really *can* fly."

The Throwing Star.

Here.

Jamie put his hood back on and began walking as fast as possible, the heavy backpack filled with cash that bounced with each step.

Oh shit.

2

THE WAY THE BYSTANDERS pointed and stared said everything.

After all, Zoe Wong was a hero.

Not just any hero. With strength, speed, the ability to hover, even thermal vision, she was more than a person with extraordinary abilities. The local newspaper called her the Throwing Star after smartphone footage of her emerged on social media.

Zoe told herself that she was going to live up to the name. Even though her heightened sense of hearing picked up gasps and exclamations below her, only one thing sat in her mind: she was out to catch a bank robber.

The bank robber of San Delgado.

Zoe scanned the scene of the city's Banking District, hands outstretched at waist level. Air pulsated beneath her palms, keeping her afloat, though a slight burn crept into her shoulders and worked down to her biceps, her elbows, her hands.

Zoe had seen all of the security footage online about the Mind

Robber, read the endless comments about motive and identity. His first robbery started simple, barely a word out of him. But by the most recent one, he had a full persona complete with stupid catchphrases and a ridiculous eye mask and hood, his gestures becoming grander and more theatrical, seemingly *posing* for the security cameras.

Unlike her. Her attitude—nothing but business. Her schtick— beating the crap out of criminals *fast* (though she did consider adding a catchphrase since people were paying attention). Her outfit—purely functional. She couldn't exactly sprint at extraordinary speeds in yoga pants. She'd tried, and they tore right apart. Hence, black leather, each piece held together by interconnecting zippers that unintentionally looked like a silver star.

Zoe scanned through the mass of humanity on the ground, doing her best to tune out the sounds that simply wouldn't stop: a several-block radius of voices, the rumble and horns of cars filling up the streets, even the random dog barks in the distance. The wall of noise lacked clues as to where *he* might be. And the colors, a cloud of reds and whites and yellows, heat signatures of all types overlaid the people in her view. She'd learned to read some of it as intensity and emotion in people, though in this case it worked best sensing outlines at a distance.

Her arms burned, screaming to release the air and guide her down, but she persisted for several more seconds, observing the crowd as more and more people were drawn to her like a magnet.

All except one person, a silhouette in a hood and backpack— the *only* person walking in the other direction.

Got you.

She tilted her palms back to propel forward. But she failed to burst ahead the way she expected, and instead, her powers wavered, her hearing range fuzzied just a hair even when concentrating.

The hiccup forced her to rotate her body, catching herself before hitting the ground less gracefully than she would have liked, especially with a broad-daylight audience. She stood and realized she'd just managed to avoid colliding with a security guard who'd stumbled out of the bank while rubbing his eyes and holding his head.

"Sorry," she said to him. He looked up, then recognition flashed across his groggy face, and he started babbling. Zoe stopped him. "Yes, I'm her. Gotta go."

A quick turn and two steps forward got Zoe nothing but a mob of people, all pointing and screaming her way, everything amplified by her heightened hearing to a point where the simple digital *click* sound of a camera phone echoed like a train plowing through. From behind, someone spoke in a reporter voice while recording on his phone: "What appears to be a daring daytime heist by the Mind Robber has come full circle, as San Delgado's Throwing Star has arrived. This battle of the city's extraordinaries has got everyone's attention right here, right now."

A hero pushes forward, she told herself, and her legs churned before she leaped into the air, a soaring arc that drew dozens of eyes on her path across the sky.

The heels of her boots clunked on the asphalt, a few feet from the empty parking spot she'd intended, and thankfully right after a car had passed. A quick glance showed that this remained the clearest path, though she'd lost sight of the Mind Robber. Zoe pushed herself, and while she still moved way faster than the rubberneckers jogging down the street to watch her, it became clear that something dialed down her swiftness and power.

Of course, she knew what caused it. But she shook it off. She'd deal with that later.

The end of the block came fast, the looming shadow of the TransNational Building and the dimming afternoon sun taking away some of her long-distance visibility. But she kept pace, coming to the intersection and leaping.

About two stories straight up. Not her best jump, but enough altitude to locate the outline of a hood and too-large backpack.

She landed, keeping her eyes on the bobbing hood while he ran. His voice carried through the din of traffic and humanity, repeatedly saying "sorry" and "excuse me" to the people in his way.

At least he was polite.

She ran again, dancing between coming and going cars. But at the end of the block, he was nowhere to be seen.

Cars slowed, then pushed past, no longer gawking at the novelty of the Throwing Star. Even passersby did the same, people hustling home or parents crossing their street tugging on the arms of their young children. The children, though, still marveled at her; she told herself to wave at one little boy even though she was generally terrible with kids.

That was unfair. She was generally terrible with human beings.

Zoe reminded herself to focus, and she scanned again. Still no signs of the hood with the backpack.

"Sorry, excuse me" floated through the air. But where?

Zoe looked down.

Straight down. A Metro station.

Of course. She mentally kicked herself. "Got you this time," she said. "Asshole."

Old newspaper pages kicked into the air as Zoe rushed to the Metro entrance. She dashed down the stairs and hit a wall of people trying to beat the rush-hour commute all at once.

None of them seemed to care that the Throwing Star was right behind them. Shoulders bumped into her as men and women tried to ram forward, all too busy staring at their phones or looking at their feet to notice that the city's extraordinary vigilante stood *right there*.

Zoe was kind of offended.

"Sorry, excuse me," the Mind Robber said from way within

the station—the left platform. Gauging the gulf of people between here and there, Zoe flexed her palms flat and she pushed
hard against an invisible pressure, propelling herself upward.
The top of her head bonked into the ceiling. Dust that had ac-
cumulated probably since, well, the opening of the Metro decades ago, sprinkled on her head and shoulders, and Zoe tried
to ignore the odor of soot and garbage that came with it. Instead, she angled her palms to shoot herself forward over the
daily workforce, speeding past them toward the interchange at
the room's far end.

"Look out!" she yelled, loud enough to get people's attention,
and she tried to land without stepping on anyone's toes or bags
before dashing through the next intersection, her extraordinary
speed slowed by the sheer volume of people. The squeak and
groan of a train pulling into the station caught her ear, along
with the Mind Robber's nonstop apologetic refrain—still polite, but more urgent. She considered hovering again, as the
view from her five-foot-four-inch frame meant more necks and
shoulders than a clear view of the Mind Robber. Instead, she
chose force. "Stop him," she called out.

Apparently, that was the best phrase to grab people's attention. They hesitated and looked at her, then parted into a path
as they gradually realized the Throwing Star was chasing a bad
guy. The train doors opened and the Mind Robber hopped on
with the quickest of looks back her way.

Her path came to an abrupt end as a half-dozen people stood
in Zoe's way, staring blankly ahead.

He'd stunned them. Melted their brains or whatever he actually did.

Would he try to do that to her?

The train beeped and announced itself. "The doors are closing. Next stop, McCrimmon Square," the automated female
voice droned. Zoe vaulted over the static group and rushed to
the platform. The train started to roll, and with each of Zoe's

steps forward, it seemingly matched her acceleration and upped the ante.

Twenty feet. Then fifteen. If she pushed hard enough, maybe she could jump onto the back of the train, punch through the window and climb in that way. The Metro office would probably accept the cost of repair for catching the Mind Robber.

Ten feet. She prepared to go, hands primed to help propel her forward. Seven, six, five…

The world spun, then her head hit concrete. "Oof," she grunted, realizing that she'd stumbled and fallen, tripping on her own legs. Not a consequence of dueling with the Mind Robber, but her own less-than-ideal coordination.

The back of the train disappeared into the tunnel, its lights fading into black.

The Mind Robber got away.

"Are you okay?" a man asked, kneeling down and offering a hand.

She waved him off with a frustrated sigh, and though she didn't have extraordinary smelling, the scent of alcohol on her breath clearly came through. Ceiling dust from earlier had melted with sweat, creating a thin but very palpable and very gross grime on her head. To top it off, her left pinky finger was now mashed into a wad of gum.

She pushed herself off of the Metro station floor. A small crowd formed around her, staring, some taking pictures, and some talking on their phones. "Holy shit, dude, the Throwing Star is right here and she totally ate it while running."

Don't punch him don't punch him don't punch him.

"You look like you could use a beer," a woman in a business skirt and glasses said.

A beer. Problem was, she'd already had a drink. Six in fact, a whole pack that she'd noticed sitting in the hallway on her way up to her apartment's roof. The original plan didn't involve finding the Mind Robber, or even to drink all those cans. She'd donned her speed-resistant suit and pulled her FoodFast delivery polo shirt over it, en route to pick up an order from Noodle Tent. Sprinting atop buildings proved to be the fastest way to deliver food, making her the only person in San Delgado qualified to do such things. Her five-star rating probably topped the list of *Best Things About Zoe Wong*.

But then she saw the six-pack. And several rooftop beers later, her hearing picked up chatter about the Mind Robber. Suddenly, chasing after him—and possibly living up to the reputation the media had built up for her—seemed like a good idea.

Little did she know that the same thing that boosted her confidence also took away her speed and strength. Lesson noted.

"I'd love one," Zoe said, the *whoosh* of another coming train causing her hair to whip all around. "But I probably shouldn't."

As she made her way out of the station, a new problem surfaced: On which rooftop had she ditched her FoodFast polo shirt? Missing that Noodle Tent delivery put her five-star rating in jeopardy.

3

JAMIE STOPPED, CATCHING HIMSELF. He'd gone too far this time. Close eyes, deep breaths, count to five, and then open eyes to see the damage.

Damn it. He'd really done it. He looked at the grout brush, then the lines between the countertop's tiles, then back at the brush. Yes, he'd gotten the coffee stain out, but he'd also scrubbed too hard, wearing away some of the grout.

Twenty minutes ago, he'd arrived home, throwing his cash-filled backpack on the futon cushion. It landed with a thump, startling Normal out of her cat tuffet next to the window. And though he stopped to give Normal a calming pat, his instincts took over, starting with a meticulous cleaning of the litter box, then a complete vacuum of the small apartment. Then organizing his stack of library books into a preferred reading order, putting away the neatly folded clothes in the laundry basket, cleaning the pour-over coffee carafe and kettle before brewing a fresh cup. As it settled, he noticed some drips of coffee had been absorbed into the grout lines adjacent to his row of ceramic mugs, thus kicking off his quest for a completely clean and reset kitchen. All of the fear and concern and guilt from the day funneled into his end-to-end cleaning spree even though it wasn't Sunday, the day he typically reserved for getting his home in order.

But this. Flecks of dried grout stuck to the brush bristles, and Jamie squinted, examining them as if he tried to break into the memory of the synthetic fibers. He blinked when Normal mewed at him, snapping him back into the present. He had to slow down. He had to regroup. He'd gone too far this time, and though the counter looked clean, a closer examination showed a tiny degradation in the grout.

Damn it. Jamie blew out a sigh and surveyed the room.

So neat. So organized. In fact, it was nearly identical to when he'd woken up here, standing in the middle of a barely furnished apartment two years ago. On that morning, he had blinked as he came to, his eyes adjusting from blurry to focused, taking in the sun shining through the cheap tan drapes onto the futon in the middle of the living space. Once he'd realized where he was, it had dawned on him that he didn't know who he was. He'd walked methodically through the semifurnished apartment, looking for triggers. Coffee table, bread, water, sink, bed, toothbrush. He knew what those were, their purpose, but none offered clues about himself. Even the mirror produced zero recognition; he didn't know what history lay behind those eyes, what the story was behind the scar on his palm.

And now? What he wouldn't give for that blissful ignorance, free from knowing that the injured woman from today was all his fault.

How could he have been so stupid, so reckless?

As with each of his bank robberies, he'd taken his time, planned a strategy, even wrote out his script beforehand and memorized it. He still lacked in execution, but that was why he had checked out some acting books from the library. The whole goal, the entire focus was to get in and out as quickly, as cleanly as possible. That meant brain-stunning the people in the building in a very specific order under a very specific time frame, all while cackling like a cartoon character and reciting over-the-top lines in a not-quite-there American accent.

If he controlled the entire situation, then no one got hurt and he did his job.

Except when one of them had a medical condition.

Jamie cursed at himself, cursed his fake-it-till-you-make-it attitude, cursed the whole damn situation. Not once, not a single time had he ever considered the possibility of a medical issue.

He finally broke, forcing himself to move. A click on the remote control brought his small TV to life, flashing a news report about electrical surges throughout the city before turning to the bank heist. His fingers fumbled to hit the power button again, taking several tries before the screen thankfully went to black, leaving only the sounds of a hungry cat meowing to remind him that he hadn't given her dinner or her nightly treat of coconut water yet. Jamie set the grout brush in the sink, and obliged the demanding cat.

Seconds later, the room filled with a content rumbling of purrs.

But even Normal's happy noises failed to remove the trauma of the day. The sound of the woman's head hitting the tile. The sight of the blood pooling. The desperate cries of her coworker.

Don't think about it don't think about it don't think about it.

Onward. Next task: the money. He grabbed the backpack and headed to the bedroom. The backpack's large top zipper got caught as he tugged on it, and the stress of the day gnawed at his patience, skipping past his normal mode of meticulously fixing it and jumping right to forcing it free. On the underside of the zipper, the corner of a hundred-dollar bill clung in between the metal clasps.

Jamie sighed, a sound soon mimicked by Normal yawning at his feet. "You have no idea," he told the cat before reaching in and starting his post-robbery sorting process for cash.

A buzzing sound rattled the room, causing a handful of loose coins on the end table to dance; it broke his focus, jolting his shoulders and neck in surprise. From the hallway, he heard Normal's claws catch in the thin carpeting before dashing off to find a hiding spot from the abrupt noise.

He picked up the phone, heart pounding that it might be someone on his trail. But a glance at his screen caused a sigh of relief. Reminder: Support Group. San Delgado East Side YMCA. Six o'clock.

Right. The weekly support group—more specifically, San Delgado Memory Loss & Dementia Support Group.

Not that Jamie cared about the giant gap in his personal life, the big cloud of nothing stemming from the moment he awoke in this apartment all the way back to, well, his birth. Something pulled him away from those thoughts whenever he even approached the matter, like staring into a bright beam of light until the intensity forced his eyes away. Every time. That avoidance happened so frequently it felt instinctive at this point, skirting whatever that was and whoever truly stood behind the impenetrable fog.

It didn't matter. No, the support group was for learning more about memory loss in general, to guard himself from any *further* memories vanishing.

The irony of the Mind Robber dealing with all that didn't escape him.

He resumed unloading the cash, first putting the stacks by denomination from left to right, then counting and rubber-banding any loose ones complete with a Post-it note with the total on each makeshift bundle. In the closet sat a safe—something that had been absolutely terrible to get into his apartment. He pulled off the blanket hiding it and turned the dial. Left with *click click clicks*. Then right. Then left again.

It opened up, revealing a larger version of the stacks assembled on his bed. Jamie took new bundles, two at a time, and neatly set them in the appropriate spots, making each tower of cash grow until the backpack and the bed were clear of evidence. A notebook leaned on the cash; Jamie pulled it out and opened it to the ledger he'd crafted, filling out the columns with the latest tally of earnings, anticipated expenses, safety-net cash and overall savings.

At the top of that column was a little drawing he'd made of a palm tree and a beach. Based on today's earnings, he was nearly 80 percent to his goal. Depending on the size of each haul, a few more robberies—especially if he remembered to ask for the stacks of hundreds specifically—would provide enough financial comfort to retire on a tropical beach at a much lower cost of living. He'd read that the coffee in the Caribbean was excellent.

A comfortable permanence, as long as the Throwing Star didn't track him down. That further complicated things, and Jamie wondered if he'd jinxed it all by invoking her during his bank performance. He gritted his teeth.

So close to a fresh start for him and Normal, and he wouldn't let the Throwing Star jeopardize that.

Normal gave an urgent meow, which translated in cat speak to "Where is my bed?" Jamie folded the blanket exactly and draped it over the safe, then put a small cat tuffet back on top of it. A gray-and-orange blur zipped by, and in one leap, landed on the tuffet, turning his trail of crime and/or source of income into the world's most valuable cat bed.

Jamie exhaled, and his mattress bounced as he flopped on his back, eyes glued to the ceiling but brain refusing to shut off. One blink and he saw the woman fall again. Every time he closed his eyes, the image reappeared, except each instance seemed to intensify in its color and sound, the sheer vibrancy of his mind seemingly taunting him.

He could lift the memory out. He'd done it before as an experiment, including writing a note with steps and details as proof that he'd removed his immediate recall of the moment. It left him with what he presumed to be the same nausea that his victims experienced, and other than a few follow-up trials, he hadn't done it for any practical purpose.

A small price to pay to be relieved of the guilt.

Jamie raised his hand, this time pointed at himself, and he closed his eyes, digging deep to flip through his own memories. Bright and fresh, full volume and movement, no haziness or missing pockets of moments. One wipe and it'd be gone.

But what would that make him? A possible murderer without a conscience? He treated his villain persona and robberies as a job, an income. Not to hurt people, not with malevolence or sociopathic apathy.

No.

This memory had to stay.

Jamie lowered his hand.

There was a knock at the door, jolting him to his feet.

He closed his eyes and stretched out with his mind, sensing the ghostly silhouette of a single form at his door.

No one ever came to his door.

"San Delgado police. Is anyone home?"

The very idea of having law enforcement at his door caused Jamie's hands to tremble and a thin layer of sweat to form on his forehead. He could brain-stun the officer and run. He could dive into the officer's memories, see what happened, why he was here—maybe it was just a fundraiser for the Police Athletic League.

Another knock rattled the door.

If he brain-stunned the officer, that wouldn't exactly be inconspicuous. You couldn't just leave gawking, unresponsive police on your doorstep. And the officer's location was probably tracked by SDPD, which meant that lifting memories and sending him on his way would only lead to more trouble.

No, the only way out of this was through it.

Jamie took a deep breath, put on a baseball cap with a logo of the local San Delgado Barons hockey team, then marched to the door. He opened it halfway to find the very serious, very professional face of a plainclothes officer. Despite the fact that he stood shorter than Jamie, his sturdy build made him far more intimidating.

"May I help you?" Jamie held the door ajar. "Sorry," he said, native English accent in full display, "I have a cat that tries to get out if I open the door all the way." As if on cue, mews came from behind him and Jamie scooped up the pudgy feline. Mental note: she deserved extra coconut water tonight. "Be nice, Normal."

The detective tilted his head at the name, then chuckled, sunlight gleaming off the light brown skin of his shaven bald dome. "No problem. Sorry to bother you this evening. Detective Patrick Chesterton. I'm the lead on the Mind Robber case."

No reaction rippled through Jamie. Which was probably a reaction in itself. He waited, seconds stretching into vast chunks of time, and though he somehow managed to keep a polite expression on his face, the pounding in his chest might have given him away.

"We get anonymous tips all the time about the Mind Robber. Some people even claim to be him. But this one was very specific. And since we know he left on a train heading eastbound about ninety minutes ago, I thought I'd check it out." He glanced over his shoulder, eyes tracking past the courtyard and toward the parking lot. "Traffic is going to be hell getting back to the station."

Jamie told himself to laugh, though in a completely different way from the forced maniacal display of the Mind Robber. Calm, quiet, a little nervous—the natural kind of nervous anyone got when questioned by law enforcement. Normal must have agreed, as she continued mewing in his arms.

"Well, aren't you a nice cat?" the detective said, his voice softening. He reached up to pet Normal's round head, but the cat replied with a hiss. Before Jamie could stop her, she swatted at Chesterton. The cat kicked out of his arms, and Jamie turned to see a streak of pudgy fur dashing for the bedroom.

"Oh, I'm so—" Jamie stopped himself at the realization that the detective nursed a fresh scratch across the knuckles.

If they weren't going to get him for being the Mind Robber, what about assault via cat scratch?

"I'm so, so sorry. Normal usually loves strangers." That was a lie, or it might have been a lie. Normal never met anyone, regular or stranger, so the sample size on that remained small. "But she gets weird occasionally." That part was true. Jamie held up his hand, palm out. "See this scar across my palm? Normal got me good one time."

Flat-out lie: Jamie had no idea where that scar came from, though whenever he focused on it for too long, a strange mix of nausea and embarrassment would flood over him.

"It's okay," Chesterton said. "I had a cat growing up. They can be temperamental. I should know better than to do that. Anyway, the tip said that someone who fit the build and look of the Mind Robber was in this area. This block, actually." He looked Jamie up and down. If Jamie decided to risk it, he probably could have poked into the detective's memories and seen specifically what he was thinking, even the source of the tip. "Have you seen anyone who fits that profile?"

In the courtyard, Jamie caught sight of the old couple across the way trying to get their mini schnauzer puppy to obey commands. They looked over at Chesterton, then Jamie, and Jamie offered a reassuring wave. Despite being a theoretical villain, he still wanted to be a good neighbor. "I, um, actually don't watch the news much. I find it triggering."

"Ah, got it. He's Caucasian. Around six feet tall. Thin build. Strong chin. That's about it, really, though. His hood and mask obscure everything else."

"Well," Jamie said. A response came to mind, and he debated whether or not he was being too clever. His arms extended and a wry smile came over his face a little too easily. Maybe learning to play a villain had turned the gesture into muscle memory. "That sounds like me." The words came out smooth, just enough of a joking lilt that they threaded the needle between bullshit and levity. It came naturally, almost uncannily so.

For a moment, nothing happened. Neither man blinked, and even Normal stayed quiet. The only noise came from squeaking brakes as a car pulled into the adjacent parking lot.

Then the detective burst out laughing. "I like you," he said, before reaching into his back pocket. Jamie's hand moved into position, a subtle gesture that only he could detect should he need to brain-stun. His fingers rose ever so slightly in preparation when a buzz in his back pocket caused both men to stand at attention.

"Sorry, just my reminder," Jamie said after pulling out his phone. The device's blinking screen gave him an idea. "My weekly support group. I, uh, need to get going."

"Oh, of course. Good for you," he said. "It takes a strong person to seek out help." Jamie's head bobbed at the compliment, and the detective finished reaching in his back pocket. He held up a business card. "Do me a favor and call if you see or hear anything that strikes you as suspicious. About him or the Throwing Star. We're no fan of vigilantes, extraordinary or not. You can't just run around in a suit beating up people. I don't care if they're good or bad. You know, if either of them just called us first and said, 'Hey, we've got these abilities,' you can bet we'd have found a job for them." Chesterton glanced at the cat scratch on his hand before letting out a short laugh. "I heard she tripped in the Metro station and let the Mind Robber get away," he said with a headshake. "I guess 'extraordinary' comes in many forms."

All forms. That skepticism, if not admirable, at least provided some cover. "Right," Jamie said, taking the card. "I'll keep an eye out."

"Even if you hear anything about weird crimes in Hartnell City. Their PD asked us about the Mind Robber. Guess they're seeing some strange activity too."

"Of course, Detective."

Jamie's exhale was nearly as loud as the slamming of the door. He'd never been that close to getting caught before.

Who could have possibly tipped the police? He'd wiped the memories of any OmegaCars driver that took him close by, and even then, he'd always walked the last few blocks, taking different routes each time. Could the Throwing Star have tracked him? Possibly, but she seemed more like the "punch in the teeth" than "call the cops" type.

Questions circled as Jamie heard the roar of the detective's car coming to life. Through the blinds, Jamie watched a dark blue sedan pull halfway across the parking lot before pausing for a handful of seconds and then finally rolling away. Chesterton was gone for now, but if he suspected anything, the best course of action would be for Jamie to act as any normal civilian would. In this case, it meant going exactly where the detective expected him to be.

Normal meowed a farewell as Jamie grabbed a jacket—not his black hoodie—and locked the door behind him.

It was almost time for the support group. Even if he didn't want to go.

4

THIS WAS NOT GOOD.

Zoe knew that. She hadn't showered since sprinting back to her apartment building, scaling up to the roof, changing back into normal clothes and crashing through the door. Even *she* wasn't delusional enough to count that as self-care. And she'd never recovered her FoodFast shirt.

So much for her five-star rating.

The cheap futon frame in her living room creaked as she shifted her weight, the thin pad not making things more comfortable for her hip and shoulder. She looked past the coffee table with three empty beer cans—two from last night and one that she figured she deserved after the Metro station fiasco—and over to her wall.

No photos of people she knew or pretty sunsets. No decorations other than a small poster of a kitten clinging to a branch next to the words HANG IN THERE. All around that print, though, hung everything she could dig up over the past two years about her identity. Scribbled notes about her blurry early memories. Anything about the mystery company on her apartment lease—and the one-year renewal letter that just arrived a few months back. Rumors of strange incidents in Hartnell City, possibly other people with extraordinary powers, including news clippings and notes about the Mind Robber, though she originally never had any ambitions to track him down.

And an image. One single image in pencil, drawn from memory, though her artistic abilities failed to capture the moment. When she closed her eyes, she *felt* it—the cold night temperature, the hard cement under her, stars littering the sky above and a harsh breeze from being on a rooftop. Her hands pressed flat against gravel and chipped cement, and the whir of ventilation units all around, followed by the rhythmic *thump-thump-thump* of boots. Then across the rooftop, a light from a door opening, and the silhouette of soldiers or armed guards or something marching out in formation.

Then nothing.

A wall of maddening details, puzzle pieces without a frame.

Pinned at the center of the wall was a rectangular name tag, the top part stating "Hello, my name is:" in blue printed letters and the name *Zoe Wong* written neatly under it. Pin holes scattered across the top border for every time she'd torn it all down in frustration before reassembling it the following morning.

That first day, after waking up in this very apartment lacking recollection of who she was or how she got there, the name tag was the first thing she saw. It sat on top of two sheets of paper and a single key on an otherwise empty key ring; the first sheet was a one-year apartment lease fully paid for by 2D Industries LLC, and the second page held only a small scribble:

You are stronger than you think. Push yourself.

The space itself wasn't exactly quiet. Every layer around and above her was paper-thin, reverberating noises from all over.

And from outside too, it was as if the city's car horns and shouts funneled straight into her brain, an unnaturally loud soundtrack turned all the way up. And the note, was that to be taken literally? Who even had written it?

That day, she'd paced in her apartment, mind waffling between staying in the space for further explanation or getting the hell out of there.

The former never came. The latter became the only option, especially after she found an envelope filled with a thousand dollars in cash stashed in a drawer. By then, she'd become consumed with Zoe Wong. Was *she* Zoe Wong? Or did she break into mystery Zoe's apartment? The mailbox gave no clues, and the apartment itself contained only bare essential toiletries and some bottles of water.

That night, she walked the streets of San Delgado, a quest without a goal, like she was meant for *something* more but didn't know what. The feeling gnawed at her, which made buying a cheap bottle of tequila seem quite sensible. Drinking it in the adjacent alley made even further sense, especially when a light rain began sprinkling down.

She'd sat, nothing but the stench of the city surfacing from the rain and the poison-like taste of the five-dollar bottle in her hand. An entire day of seeing things, listening to people, trying to understand the colors she later figured out to be thermal vision, and it all led nowhere. Frustration boiled up, pressurizing at the pointlessness of it all, and fueled by the buzz of half a bottle, she curled her hand into a fist and punched a dumpster.

She watched it lift several feet above the pavement to fly down the alley, moving faster than some of the cars passing behind her.

Her inebriated stumble made catching up with it a chore, but her eyes locked onto the dent in its side. As she approached, the note from the apartment echoed in her mind, now a mission statement more than anything else.

She wound up and punched again.

Again, the dumpster skidded away, the echoey thud of fist on hollow metal ringing through the air.

One thought dawned on her, the only thing that synced up with both her mind and body.

Fuck it, she decided in that moment. She was just going to *take* the name Zoe Wong until the truth proved otherwise or a better idea came along.

And the name stayed, just like the name tag at the center of her detective board. After the papers had dubbed her the Throwing Star—another name she hadn't chosen for herself—she'd pinned a crude folded-paper throwing star next to the name tag, and wondered if she should try rebranding as Shuriken, the Japanese word for throwing star. Even though she was pretty sure she was of Chinese heritage rather than Japanese. But whatever. It sounded cool, which took higher precedence than accuracy.

Her eyes trailed over to the lump of wrinkled black leather pieces lying on the floor, the silver zipper tracks reflecting overhead light. At some point, she'd have to get it dry-cleaned, but how could she possibly explain the odd construction of a leather bodysuit in six pieces—two arms, two legs, a torso and a cowl with a mask, each with zippers at odd angles that when fully fastened, apparently formed a rough starlike shape. It was never intended to seem cool or, as one of her early rescuees told the media, *like a throwing star flying across the alley* after she'd sprinted in with her extraordinary speed. It wasn't even meant for hero shenanigans; she'd chopped up pieces of torn motorcycle suits recovered from the dumpster behind the Cycle Pro a few blocks down. She wore the leather under her FoodFast polo simply because it just held up better than street clothes for rooftop jumping and sprinting, and the cowl kept her ears and nose warm.

But sometimes she'd hear screams and yells at night, before or after picking up her delivery, and she'd make a choice. She wanted to be *more*, and the potential ached deep in her bones. She'd choose to take off her FoodFast shirt and hide her delivery bag. Choose to run off and make a difference. Choose to finally fulfill that constant nagging desire without fucking up again.

Then her legend grew. And the name stuck. She supposed it was better than just "Zoe, the crime-fighting semi-loser and sometimes food delivery person."

Her phone pinged the familiar chime of an available Food-Fast gig, though she couldn't accept it, not with her shirt lost on some random rooftop between here and the bank.

A new thought arrived, the idea of suiting up and going out intentionally, without any FoodFast commitments. But the one time she tried living up to the Throwing Star image had ended with her tripping over her own feet in a Metro station. She never even got to say the cool tagline she'd practiced on her way to the bank.

Zoe stood up, her bare foot knocking over an open can at the base of the futon. "Oh, goddamn it," she said, scrambling to get paper towels. Mental note: as someone who probably enjoyed alcohol a little too much, solid flooring was preferable to carpeting. If she ever saved enough to move out of this mysteriously rent-free place, that'd be the first thing she looked for. She pressed down into the mess, which was inches from similar stains from a few weeks back, skunky odor wafting up. The paper towels flew into the plastic garbage bin by the sink, and while warm water ran over her hands, she looked at the kitchen window. As she stood silent, the lights in her place dimmed, though the power fluctuation didn't seem to affect surrounding buildings. She watched across the way, spying on a neighboring family eating pizza, a cluster of children from small to nearly adult, and a smiling but clearly tired man.

The lamps flickered back on, blinking off and on until her eyes adjusted to the illumination, and in the glass, a different face watched her.

Not any of the neighbors, who blissfully ignored her regardless of whether she was an extraordinary or a troubled woman with a drinking problem. But her own deep brown eyes in the reflection, the strands of tangled black hair, and the barely present face around it, lines etched all around from fatigue and worry and sheer lack of care.

Her phone chimed, not FoodFast, but HorrorDomain, the free movie app that only had free "classic" horror films in the public domain, blasting a notification for their pick of the week, *Lo-Bot: Samurai Cyborg*. She'd seen the first half of that 1970s sci-fi slasher flick before, and it sounded enticing enough to sit on a beer-stained carpet and finish the movie, but then a different chime rang out, a single bell while words flashed across the screen.

Reminder: San Delgado Memory Loss & Dementia Support Group

She'd lurked at that support group a few times, kept the time in her phone just in case. It didn't make it onto her detective board because *looking* for clues felt easier than listening to people talk about losing their memories. Was her condition a form of dementia? Did amnesia and extraordinary strength go hand in hand? It's not like she could show up and open up. The memory loss. The day drinking. The crime fighting/getting her anger out. None of it.

But maybe it was something. Just to go and listen.

Or maybe more than just listen.

It wasn't like her life was exactly working.

5

OUT THERE, PEOPLE CALLED Jamie the Mind Robber. But in here, all of that was stripped away. Jamie looked at the faces, the eyes.

A sense of calm washed over him, something he hadn't felt all day. He never talked at these things, but somehow just *sitting* there created a sense of ease. The other members of the group didn't judge. They didn't suspect. They simply brought empathy. But that always happened when he came. He'd justify and bargain and deny himself when the reminder appeared, but on the odd week he forced himself, it always wound up feeling right. Even if today was only because the police had come to his door.

And someday, he might even speak. Someday. For now, he listened.

"I'd like to welcome everyone to the San Delgado Memory Loss and Dementia Support Group. As always, we are sponsored by our friends at San Delgado General Hospital. Their guidance and medical support helps all of us. Whether you're a caregiver, family member, friend or someone who experiences symptoms, you're in good hands."

Same speech as always. And soon, others would begin sharing their stories, either brain exercises they'd done to maintain the memory sharpness or the horror spawned from the chasm where thoughts and feelings used to exist. Sometimes during those stories, Jamie got the urge to blurt out, "But what if the memories were bad?" He never did, of course, yet the urge always danced on the periphery.

Jamie sat, reminded himself to keep moving forward, control only what he could.

"So, a few ground rules. My name is Ian Bradley and I'm the moderator, but that doesn't mean that I'm the leader. I'm just directing the conversation and keeping things going. We have an open sharing forum for the first thirty minutes or however long you need, then we'll discuss specific topics—this week's is new research released on the latest in dementia prevention."

In the room, a mix of people nodded. Jamie wondered who they were, whether they came because they faced growing pockets of missing memories or because they worked with people who dealt with that kind of mental reset on a daily basis—the kind of reset he'd experienced two years ago.

But really, what happened to him was unlike anyone else here. Amnesia, sure it happened, but coupling it with extraordinary abilities probably wasn't in any textbook. Not for the senior citizens, some of whom sat with their adult children, and not the handful of people who showed up in hospital scrubs. And certainly not the Asian woman with slightly disheveled hair and deep bags under her eyes, seemingly decades of weariness on her despite probably being only in her late twenties. Jamie thought he'd seen her at a previous meeting, perhaps once or twice in passing, though he was pretty sure she'd never shared before.

She, like him, probably felt safer lurking. At least that's what her posture said, her slumped shoulders and downward gaze more appropriate for a child in trouble than a medical support group.

"I see some new faces today. Remember, some people are caregivers and some are suffering from this disease. Because of this mix, I'd ask you to refrain from using last names. This anonymity allows us to be honest. It's a safe space here."

A safe space. The mere idea tickled Jamie in a way, igniting feelings that he…well, most people would have compared them to some sort of idyllic childhood or precious moment. Those didn't exist for him. But it felt good. Around the dingy meeting hall of the San Delgado East Side YMCA, people opened themselves up, one by one. José, who was an Alzheimer's researcher and explained how he had to counsel doctors on working with patients. Billie, who had lost four years of her memory following a car crash and battled depression despite the support of her husband and teenage son. Chung, who broke down while trying to explain that he had to introduce himself to his father every time he visited.

"Anyone else?" Ian looked around the room. The only response came in the form of the occasional cough and squeaking of chairs. "Last chance before we move on to our topic of the week."

Across the room, the quiet woman flicked her eyes up. From Jamie's angle, he could see her glance at the moderator before they met gazes. Jamie tried to offer a welcoming smile, but she dropped the connection, blending back into the harshness of the room made only bleaker by the fluorescent lighting. Everyone sat silent when the lights suddenly flickered; it went black for a good second or two, and Jamie swore he saw a bright blue flash before the lights came back on.

"Last call for shares. Going once? Going twice? And—"

"I'd like to say something," the woman said. She shuffled in her chair, as if her coat would swallow her whole. "My name is Zoe. And I suffer from memory loss."

"Hi, Zoe," Ian said. "I'm sorry to hear that. Take as much time as you need."

"Well, I…" Her voice was dry, the sound barely escaping, though her sigh filled the room. "I'm sorry, I just don't talk about this. But I can't remember much of my childhood. I can't remember much of my life really."

"Zoe, I have to tell you that we are a support group, not a diagnostic clinic. Most of us are caregivers or friends or family. We are all sympathetic to your situation, but we can't offer medical advice. We are, though, here to listen."

Zoe's black hair swished back and forth as she nodded. "Right, right. It's cool. I'm not, like, looking for a cure. It's just…hard, you know. You feel like there's something behind the curtain, something there, something holding you back. My memory, it's like a black hole. It just sucks me in but it's too strong and you can't see anything. It's just there."

The description lingered in Jamie's mind, short-circuiting his thoughts. That wasn't how he'd describe his own memories; his felt the complete opposite. Not a black hole, but a supernova, exploding over the details and blinding out everything in existence.

Though Zoe was a stranger, something about her seemed so familiar it pulled on his curiosity. Jamie scanned his own memories to see if he could place her, but nothing came up. Yet, a certainty tugged at him, a *knowing* that they'd encountered each other before.

Despite a sea of heads in his view, he could tell her eyes stared ahead with a palpable intensity. The chair beneath him squeaked as he leaned forward to hear her better, as if the extra few inches could explain *why* she drew him into her orbit.

Was she from one of his bank robberies?

"Really, most of my memories start from about two years ago."

Two years ago?

Those few words turned curiosity into urgency.

It couldn't be a coincidence.

For nearly two years, Jamie had purposefully *not* sought out his other life. Every time the thought appeared, something ran interference, telling him to stay ahead of it, to keep going.

But he'd never been this close to it before. To even the remote possibility of it.

Zoe took in a breath and the group waited for her to gather herself. Jamie went down the rabbit hole of his own memories, but nothing placed her face. Instead, a rapid-fire punching of what-ifs hounded him, demanding an answer.

He'd vowed repeatedly to never use his abilities when he was off the clock. Being the Mind Robber, dealing with banks, that was work. Reading memories, that was a skilled task. Using it in real life would be a violation, make him a true villain rather than an act he put on.

Yet given the circumstances, the decision came with surprising ease.

Just this once.

"I live my life. I have a job, a home." Zoe hesitated, took in a sharp breath, paused to scratch the back of her head. "But I just wonder, is this it? Is this what I was meant to be? Shouldn't there be more? And it feels like all the answers are hidden behind this…" Creases formed across her face, mouth twisting into a frown. "This wall. And I don't know how to break it." After about thirty seconds, he locked in, and a flood of images transmitted from her brain to his. A different kind of guilt came to him, not the mystery one that arrived with his missing past, but the sense that he was violating the most personal of private spaces by doing this.

The images were neatly stacked, thumbnails in a filmstrip speeding by: a nearly empty studio apartment, a view from the roof, a hallway with even worse lighting than the meeting space.

"It's funny, because I listen to people when they're stressed or need help. I guess you could say I'm a therapist of sorts."

As Zoe began diving into her share, her emotions turned up and her guard went down. The pictures slowed, became brighter, sharper, bigger, more focused.

"Sometimes, I can help them."

She took in a breath, and a single image appeared, most likely the active memory she currently pictured in her mind's eye. An older man in a business suit stood in an alley, tufts of silver hair on the side, glasses slipping off the bridge of his dark brown nose.

Whoever this man was, it was clear that something was very wrong. His eyes were wide, his mouth was open, his hands were up. And his image, a weird outline kept obscuring him, like someone scribbled a highlighter of pulsating red, the intensity fading in and out.

"I help them through it. Which is part of the problem, isn't it? If you're the one everyone relies on, if you take on people's burdens, sometimes there's just not that much left of you."

Zoe's view whipped around back past the frightened man until centering on a blurry figure with a similarly fuzzy outline. It gradually sharpened into a bulky male silhouette.

Gloved hands. Fingers curled around...something. A handle of some sort. Zoe's memory camera pulled back, and the rest of the object came into focus.

A knife.

"Especially when you don't know who you are. Then you do stupid things. Like drinking before work."

Things snapped into real time, though her own movements felt like fast-forward. From her perspective, she whipped around. One dodge of the knife. Then another swipe and miss. A second mugger appeared, a similar stance and a similar weapon. They stepped forward and Zoe immediately darted to the left and leaped against the wall, faster than seemingly possible, legs compressing in before propelling her sideways. Then another jump. Then she was behind the duo. Emotions didn't normally transmit to Jamie, but a palpable thrill rippled in this memory.

In one move, Zoe slid between the two. *Thwack.* Her forearms hit the backs of their legs, buckling and staggering the muggers. *Crunch.* Zoe's fist flew up and slammed both men in the jaw, and she stood. *Whoosh*. Her leg whirled around with a round-house kick, boot connecting from one head to the next. Euphoria washed over her, so strong that it made Jamie cringe. "That sense of self I'm missing. Even when I'm helping people. No matter what I do, I just wonder if it's enough. If it's who I'm meant to be."

The muggers slumped down, the colors over them dissolving. Behind her, the old man rushed up and grabbed her by the shoulder. Zoe turned to find an ear-to-ear grin. "The Throwing Star," he said, "I can't believe it's you."

Jamie pulled out of her memories and returned to the YMCA, though he couldn't fight the pit in his gut. Zoe looked up and once again they locked eyes, but unlike before, she lingered on him.

"I think that's it," she finally said. "Thank you for listening to me. I feel..." For the first time since arriving, a small smile crept onto her face. "I feel a little better. It's nice knowing that people care."

But she wasn't just Zoe. Jamie sat silently, horrified at himself for breaking the sanctity of the group. As the moderator thanked her, the lights flickered again.

Some ten minutes later, Jamie stood in the break room struggling with the coffee machine. He considered probing the mind of the moderator for any inkling of how to use the damn thing, but opted against it—not just because he was talking about the latest in dementia-related research or due to the sanctity of the group, but poking away at needlessly complicated coffee makers took his mind off of Zoe.

Had he been a little slower today, things would have been completely different. She would have caught him, he may have tried to erase her mind in self-defense, and who knows what would have happened from there. Broken bones for him, a disabled brain for her, or something in between.

Instead, here they were, under crappy lighting with a coffee machine that was seemingly smarter than everyone in the building.

"Oh good," a female voice said with a laugh. "You're here."

Jamie turned to see Zoe blocking the exit.

His body tensed, alerts and warnings telling him that she could overpower him in a blink. Instead, there was only one route to go. Jamie rubbed his chin, the subtlest way he could think of to get his fingers in position to do their work. His mind reached out, invisible threads locking into her brain, though it needed a good thirty seconds or so. Sometimes more.

Especially under duress.

"I've been looking for somebody who knows how to work this stupid coffee maker." She laughed at her own admission, and then pointed at the giant black-and-brown technological behemoth on the counter. "Here are the packs—" she gestured to the box next to it "—but where do you put it? There are three slots."

Jamie's hand dropped, and he let out a sigh that prompted a curious look from her.

"I think this one." He pointed to the slot on the left. "But then I'm not sure what to do. I use a carafe for pour-over coffee. It tastes better. It's worth the wait."

"Mine is so much easier. Put a pod in, push a button, that's it," she said.

She tapped through the touch screen menu, going through the options for hot water and espresso and bold. As Jamie watched, curiosity crept in.

What *were* those powers of hers? And how did she get them? Did she remember anything?

Once again, Jamie's mind reached out, plugging in and connecting with hers. His hands stayed at his side—there wouldn't be any defensive surgery going on here, just reading—while she stared at the coffee machine, scratching the back of her head. A minute later Jamie was sifting through thoughts and memories like randomly sampling files on a laptop.

The strength, the speed, something happened a few years back, but she didn't recall what or how or why. She just knew that her body went far beyond normal human physicality. The fighting skills, those came from practicing to free "cardio kick-boxing for moms" videos on her phone. Which probably didn't make for technically sound martial arts but being stronger and faster clearly helped.

Beyond that, she couldn't remember.

Also, there wasn't a clue regarding how she did the cool hovering thing.

But the colors in her mind's eye, that gave another advantage: a type of thermal vision that helped her track down her foes at a distance, especially when combined with heightened hearing.

Like a bank robber escaping down the street.

"Yes!" she shouted. The machine whirred and churned, and out poured steaming hot coffee into the paper cup. She turned to high-five Jamie.

Smack. Her palm slapped his, and he stifled a grimace, his hand stinging as if it had smashed into the bumper of a moving car. A single thought entered his head as he noticed a blush come over her cheeks.

She could destroy me without even trying.

Her speed. Her strength. Her ability to track. She could hunt down the Mind Robber—him, Jamie—win the battle in a single move and probably with a brutal swiftness before his probing could even start.

He sighed again, this time with the realization that his only hope against her *ever* would be to erase her mind before she could strike first. It wasn't the police or some do-gooder at a bank, someone who could be swatted away with strategic use of his own powers. She was too fast, too powerful for that. She could freaking *fly* over him and drop him with a swift kick he'd never see coming. This woman, Zoe, who had needed compassion but also nearly crushed him earlier that afternoon, really was the biggest threat to his simple goal of retiring to the Caribbean with his cat.

6

SOMETHING TICKLED THE BACK of Zoe's head. She scratched at it, an involuntary gesture at first, but soon she realized her fingernails rubbed against scalp—right when she noticed Jamie looking at her with a strange unblinking gaze. Not quite staring, but something was definitely off.

She scanned him up and down despite her fatigue and hangover dulling everything. The longer she did it, the more his heat signature intensified. In that short span, his entire presence changed: shoulders tensed, lips pursed and body temperature rising.

His height—medium stature. His build—slight but not unhealthy. His face—beady, intense eyes, and a wide chin framed by pale skin and gaunt cheekbones.

It couldn't be.

This man spoke with a gentle British accent but those videos...

The Mind Robber's voice on the security footage from social media, she thought of the dozens of times she'd watched them, and there was always something slightly off about how he talked. Then she pictured him with a cheesy eye mask and a hood over his head.

Suddenly everything locked into place.

The scratching. It wasn't an itch or dandruff or an allergy. She *felt* him breaking in. Was he looking in there now, sifting through her memories? Trying to eradicate her mind for hunting him?

Questions swirled in Zoe's mind, though they all landed on one thought:

He could destroy me without even trying.

The coffee machine stopped its whirring and beeped to announce that the drink was ready. Neither Zoe nor Jamie moved. Instead, their eyes locked. She didn't want to look away. She *couldn't*, otherwise he might strike first.

Did he worry about the same thing?

They stepped back in unison. Her arms rose to a fighting posture. His hands went up, presumably to do his mind-robbing thing, but maybe just to look cool.

The lights flickered, as they'd done all night. It didn't distract Jamie; he stayed fully focused on her. She mirrored his intensity.

Should she move now? Use her speed to take him out, drag him to the San Delgado Police Department? Maybe she could do it without anyone noticing, without the police arresting her for being a vigilante.

But why hadn't he stunned her yet? What was he waiting for?

This time, the room went completely black for a good ten seconds. Zoe checked her feet and clenched fists to check it wasn't some Mind Robber trick; in her peripheral vision, a burst of bright blue blinded her right before the lights returned. She blinked hard, and the Mind Robber was still *right* there, the tension between them so thick that it practically smelled like burning.

"We don't have to do this," Jamie finally said after several more seconds of staring. His hands were still raised.

"I should take you in right now." Zoe began to move but stopped when Jamie's hands tensed up.

Of course. He *should* be afraid of her.

"Please don't. I don't *want* to do anything to you. I don't want to hurt anyone."

"That's nice of you to say. You hurt someone today. She's in the hospital because of you. What's stopping you—"

"*I know that.*" Jamie's expression broke in a way that Zoe wasn't expecting. "I know that. I don't want to hurt people."

A different kind of silence came between them. They remained still, but the fierce tension broke. Zoe watched as Jamie exhaled, his eyes falling, and though his hands were still up, his posture slumped. With that, her own muscles relaxed by a mere fraction. Something changed.

"You steal their money. That hurts people."

"From big corporate banks. They're covered by the FDIC. Come on," he said, arms finally dropping the Mind Robber pose to wave in exaggeration, "it's simple, like, law stuff. No one gets hurt from that."

A scream came from the second floor. Zoe held her ground. Jamie didn't react, either.

Maybe because he was the one who caused it.

Zoe inched forward, arms back in ready position.

"Whoa, whoa. Come on," he said. "Don't make me do something I don't wanna do." He took a step back, matching her pose.

"What's going on upstairs?"

"What?" He looked up at the popcorn-textured ceiling. "I don't know! Isn't that the Y's lounge area?"

Another scream. More yelling. And then the thump of footsteps. All from her enhanced hearing, something that others failed to detect.

"What did you do?"

"I didn't do anything!" Jamie bit down on his lip and glanced at the meeting room. Zoe's eyes traced his, and though her angle was off, a few heat signatures in the other room had looked their way. Their standoff was drawing attention.

She better do this quick if she needed to keep her anonymity.

"Okay, seriously. I don't know what you're talking about," he said. "Let's just calm down and talk this through, I'm honestly rethinking a *lot* of things right now and—"

A voice broke into their conflict, coming in from the other room and down the short hallway. "Fire!" he yelled. "Fire on the second floor!"

The burning smell. It hadn't been her imagination.

The lights flickered again, this time a quick strobe that seemed to put things in slow motion. Bright flashes of blue burst in and out all through her peripheral vision. When things stabilized, the odor got stronger—but this time, it came with a trail of smoke from the kitchen's electrical sockets.

Jamie dropped his arms.

If this was some sort of diabolical scheme, he wouldn't be showing so much concern right now.

Smoke detectors rang through the space. From above, a small mist came down on them, little bursts of water that choked to come out. Nothing that could put out a match, let alone a fire. Voices formed into a huddle, and Zoe tried to force the overwhelming volume down to something reasonable. A look past the short hall connecting the break room with the main space showed Ian ushering people out. She tried to focus, isolating voices past the panic and coughing to hear what was happening all around.

"This shitty place. I knew it was a death trap."

"That old couch, it's on fire!"

"The front entrance is blocked!"

"Did anyone call 911?"

She dashed into the meeting space, where people clustered

at the room's entrance. "Let me through, let me through," she said at full volume, instincts telling her to throw herself into the chaos. "What's going on?"

Ian came back, arms waving above his head. "It's no good. Six people got out before the entrance got blocked. A beam fell and caught fire. This place has to be decades behind code."

Zoe whirled around, only to find Jamie right behind her, eyes closed but face turned upward. "Eight people down here," he yelled over the commotion. "There's no one left upstairs."

"How do you know?"

"I don't sense anyone," he said, opening his eyes. "Do you see any thermal...thingies?"

Ian looked at both of them and blinked.

Another look upstairs showed that Jamie was right, and she didn't see heat signatures floating around up there, though a few barely visible ones stood on the other side of this hallway. So some people definitely made it out. Smoke began to plume in from the staircase off to the side, rolling in and spreading across the top of the room. One man sprinted to the break room before coming back. "Isn't there a goddamn emergency exit here?" Behind him, another man yelled incoherently, and next to him, a woman started to scream back at him.

A tap came down on Zoe's shoulder, and she turned. But once she realized it was Jamie, she pushed him away, restraining enough so he didn't get sent flying across the room. "I'm trying to help," he yelled over the alarms and voices. Above them, the sprinkler mist sputtered before slowing to a drip.

"I don't need your help."

"Everyone calm down. We can find a way out," Ian said. "There's a beam in the way. Maybe we can find a way to push it out."

"Use your strength," Jamie yelled. Zoe threw him a menacing glare, but she knew he was right.

The idea of getting burned didn't seem appealing, but dying

was certainly worse. "Let me through," she said, pushing through people before getting to the cramped hallway.

In the way sat a fractured beam, the splinter in the middle of it forming a *V.* Smoke and heat funneled in from a hole in the ceiling where the beam had collapsed, and beyond it, the small entry of the YMCA had functioning sprinklers on only half the lobby.

But—the Mind Robber was here. What if this was all a trick to trap her, eliminate her? He could be making her use her strength to free them, then stun her until the fire burned her alive.

At this point, what choice did she have *except* to trust him?

Jamie knew how to brain-stun people. But could he just get them to shut up and calm down?

It sure would have helped. Half the remaining people seemed like they went into logic overdrive, searching every corner for a magical way out. The other half coped by yelling, though the alarm sirens drowned them out. The yelling could have been at each other, at the city departments who let this building get so dilapidated, the manager for putting in highly flammable old furniture.

Zoe dashed back in and motioned Jamie to come forward. "I'm going to move that beam. It's on fire but I'll heal. You try anything and I'll throw it on you."

Jamie put his hands up. He knew they'd just about had a battle of extraordinary abilities, but really, this wasn't the time. How else could he make that clear? "Okay. Can I help?"

"No. Stay away from me. Far away. I don't trust you."

"We're in a burning building. I don't want to—" He shook his head, deciding not to go there. "Okay. Okay fine. We'll wait here. I'll try to keep people calm."

Zoe turned and opened the door, then hesitated. She looked at the crowd, including the panicking people and Ian trying to talk them down, then at Jamie. "Actually, one thing. Keep them in here. So they don't see me doing..." Her hands waved in a short gesture. "Doing my thing."

"Go. I got it."

Zoe disappeared beyond the door. One man tried to follow her, but Jamie grabbed him. "What are you doing?" he said, arms pushing beyond Jamie.

"You gotta trust her. She's going to get us out."

"How? How is one person going to get us out? What are we doing sitting in here?"

"She's not just one person."

The man began yelling at full volume, and though he stood shorter than Jamie, his presence became more threatening. "What the hell does that mean? Get out of my—"

His voice halted and his eyes looked blankly ahead. It was the lightest of brain-stuns, though not the best place for it. However, if Zoe could *fly*, she could surely carry one stunned man out of a burning building.

A scream erupted down the hall, loud enough to break past the noise of flames and alarms, followed by words clearly from Zoe: "Ow! God fucking damn it!" One look behind him showed Jamie that Ian and the others must have heard it; they all stared at him, wide-eyed, and perhaps Ian just realized that Zoe wasn't there. He stood and began approaching when Zoe burst through the door.

"It's clear. But you have to go *now*."

Ian nodded, then began ushering people out. There they went, three, four, five people, and no one seemed to notice the one brain-stunned man, probably because the chaos matched the oncoming smoke. Zoe squinted, looking distant—maybe thermally tracking them—and then turned to Jamie. "They're out."

Three people remained: Ian, the brain-stunned man, and then another man who had collapsed to his knees, face covered by his hands.

"He's panicking," Ian said, a calm group-leader tone still in his voice despite the chaos.

There was one way to get him to settle down.

"Go," Jamie said, "we can handle this." Zoe shot him a look, one eyebrow raised, but there wasn't time to discuss. "Go, now. Trust us."

"Alright," he said. He opened the door, yelping when he touched the doorknob. The bright orange of licking flames radiated into the space before he sprinted out, coat over the top of his head.

"He's safe," Zoe said. "I think. Hard to see heat signatures with all the flames. But pretty sure. What's your plan?"

"You carry him to safety." He pointed at the currently stunned man. "While you do that, I'll stun that guy over there. Then we run out together."

"Did you steal that guy's memories?"

"What? No, of course not. I stunned him. He was trying to chase you. I was protecting your secret."

Despite the thickening smoke and oppressive heat, Zoe shifted in her stance. Sweaty, dirty and caked in soot, somehow she looked more vibrant than the woman who shared earlier today.

"Thanks," she said. "I appreciate it." She tossed the man over her shoulder with frightening ease, as simple as when Jamie picked up Normal, and then she sprinted out at full speed, like a coiled-and-ready horse bursting out of the gate. By the time Jamie stunned the panicking man, Zoe had returned.

"Holy shit, you're fast."

"See? I would have caught you today if I wasn't hungover."

"Well, lucky for all these people, then. Let's finish this." He gestured to the stunned man, whom Zoe picked up. Jamie pulled his sleeve down over his palm and gripped the doorknob to toss the door open, only to reveal that another beam had collapsed. Rather than a hallway, a large wooden X blocked their way, and it was on fire.

7

ZOE BLAMED ALL OF this on daytime drinking. None of this would have happened if she'd avoided doing that.

"You know how you said we don't have much time?" Jamie turned to Zoe, his expression matching his aura. Weary, defeated, but mildly amused. "We're out of time. It's just fire. From top to bottom."

The man on her shoulder stirred, and she adjusted him enough to maintain her balance as she kicked the door. It tore off its hinges and flew down the hallway, colliding into the beams. Yet the wall of fire still blocked their path, just like what the Satanic magician did to his terrified audience in that one movie she saw a few weeks ago. But the hero in that, a wiry man with a curly brown mullet and an even thicker mustache, found a way out— not *through* the flames, but via a crack in the wall made bigger by a conveniently placed axe.

As she scanned for any way around, pain seared her palms, a reminder of the debris she'd just cleared minutes earlier. Bruises healed quickly, but burn scars were something new to deal with.

"Well," Jamie said. "You wanted to catch me. This was one way to do it."

"Hold on." Zoe searched the room, eyes darting quickly. *Think, think, think,* she told herself. If mullet-mustache guy in *The Magical Death Show* could find a way out, so could she. They were trapped, the path up the stairs blocked and the four walls around them solid. No windows, no emergency exit, just beams and concrete.

Concrete. Of course. The back wall.

Concrete wouldn't burn. But it could be knocked down. She could be mullet-mustache guy *and* the axe all in one.

Zoe set the man down on the floor. "Stay with him. I don't know how long this is going to take."

"How long what's gonna—"

Zoe didn't let him finish. She sprinted full speed and launched herself at the back wall. Her shoulder slammed into it, creating an oval dent and crack lines spidering farther out.

From behind, she heard Jamie say, "Holy shit."

Pain radiated from her shoulder, but she shook it off. One look around and she knew none of that mattered right now. She took a good dozen or so step backs, then rammed the wall again, then repeated it two more times until the divot became a deeper hole, the cracks giving away to falling chunks. She turned on her hip and started kicking the largest crack, dust flying in her face, mixing with the thickening smoke. "Come on," she yelled, throwing her foot over and over, then switching over to punches that tore apart her knuckles. Another punch and another punch and finally another, and suddenly her hand exploded through the other side of the wall, fingers touching the cool night air.

Almost there.

Zoe kicked at the perimeter around the hole, loosening and clearing as much debris as possible. Then she ran back from the wall, turned and launched into a full-speed sprint toward the damaged wall. A few feet before impact, Zoe angled her shoulder forward and leaped off her feet. She felt her body's impact with the concrete: first her shoulder, then her face, then her ribs and arms.

When she blinked, she was face-first on the ground, dust and grime covering her. More importantly, cool air and the sounds of sirens. From behind, a voice screamed out. "Zoe! I need your help!"

Jamie. And the stunned man.

Bloody handprints planted on the ground, and as Zoe pushed herself up, she coughed and spit, her body rejecting soot and debris. "Zoe! Come on!"

She craned to look back at the person-sized hole in the concrete, jagged rebar edges and crumbled pieces scattered around. Inside, Jamie dragged the stunned man, arms around his chest and pulling with each step.

Zoe stood up and stumbled forward, leg catching on the bottom of the punctured hole in the building wall. She hopped over debris, then waved Jamie away. Though she was sore—in some places, screaming with pain—carrying him out while injured was still easier than the whole "smashing through a wall" thing she somehow decided was a good idea. They cleared the broken threshold, and Zoe set the man down.

Jamie immediately collapsed next to him, coughing. "Well," he said in between coughs and spasms, "nice to meet you, Zoe."

Zoe pushed her fingers through her hair and knelt down beside the two men. She tried to laugh, but each breath felt heavy and thick.

"Hey." Jamie pulled himself up to his knees with a groan. "Promise I'm not trying to be a villain here, okay? But hear me out."

Fatigue and pain made it easy for Zoe to drop her natural skepticism. "What's that?"

"I should erase his memory." He tapped the stunned man on the shoulder. "Even though he was having a breakdown, he might remember something about you or me."

"Will it...will it hurt him?"

"No, he'll just have a gap. I'll leave it at the point when there are a few people in the meeting and they know there's a fire and that's it. Ian will probably tell him later he was having a panic attack. Between that and the smoke and the stress, he probably won't even notice." They met eyes, and one quick look of approval later led to Jamie doing some weird finger waving. The man didn't flinch, didn't convulse, didn't give any sort of reaction. He simply sat, and then a few moments later, Jamie looked back over and said, "That's it. It's done. Let's bring him up front so the EMTs can take care of him." Zoe scooped him up rescue-style with her arms but Jamie quickly waved it off. "No, we gotta make it look good. You're not the Throwing Star, remember?"

They shared a laugh, something that would have felt impossible an hour ago, then propped up the man between them, his arms each over a shoulder. A sharp observer would have noticed that she supported all of his weight as Jamie merely framed his other side, and that the man's feet floated a few inches above the ground. She carried the load at full speed until they emerged from the alley to flashing red lights and the loud water pumps of fire engines. "Hey!" Jamie yelled. "This man needs help!"

Ian saw them and flagged more EMTs to run their way.

"He's in shock," Jamie said through huffs. "He had a panic attack. And the smoke, or stress or whatever. He seems unresponsive right now, but I think he needs just a few minutes."

EMTs wheeled over a stretcher; latches clanged and clacked, and the air filled with medical speak as they checked him over. Though Jamie had gone a long way to earning some level of trust, Zoe still lingered just long enough to hear the EMTs pronounce the man's vitals as steady and stable.

The Mind Robber kept his word.

And suddenly, those moments of chasing him down seemed a little different.

★ ★ ★

As two firefighters passed by, one commented about how a blown transformer on its own shouldn't cause such a big fire, not at that speed. The other said it looked like the building's old wood structure probably didn't help, though its earthquake retrofit with concrete had kept the whole thing from toppling down.

Blown transformer. Did that explain the flashing blue and sudden blackouts? An hour had passed, and while the danger of the fire was mostly gone now, the burnt stench lingered in the air. Combined with the incoming bay fog and light rain overhead, the whole place became a stew of all the worst smells. Jamie adjusted on the bus stop bench he shared with Zoe as they watched the firefighters. Lights from police cars brought flashes of blue into the mix, though there looked to be a plainclothes officer helping out.

They hadn't really said much during that time, mostly commenting as the firefighters and EMTs did their job—"true heroes," Zoe called them—though they played up the adulation when Ian came by to thank them, before dropping back to tension just as quickly. Jamie didn't think Zoe was going to break him in half or turn him in, though she had just thrown herself through a concrete wall. So she was probably a little impulsive.

"What's it like?" Zoe suddenly asked.

"Huh?"

"Doing the…memory thing," she said. She tugged on the blanket provided by the EMTs, eyes still forward. "What's it like?"

"Well, it's um…it's kind of like watching a movie? You can fast-forward or rewind. Or pause." He waved his fingers around. "Fingers help, they kind of act like controls. Like, um, swiping to move around. And delete."

She finally looked at him, eyes wide but not combative like earlier. Instead, she leaned forward, the questions coming out at a much quicker clip. "Anything in their memory? Like even stuff from way back when?"

"As far as I can tell, as long as it's in there, like if their brain is still capable of recalling it, I can access it. Sometimes it looks a little hazy and then it focuses." Jamie broke eye contact, even though he could feel her gaze lingering. "But honestly, I try not to pry too much. You know, it's creepy to do that. I usually just cover my tracks and that's it."

"Even yourself?"

Jamie's muscles locked up. This had to be leading somewhere. While the fire and ensuing rescue had occupied their focus over the past few hours, there was no getting away from the original reason they were there. Or was it a trick? She had, after all, been chasing him. He weighed his options and realized that sitting next to someone with extraordinary speed and strength left very little margin for error. "Not myself," he said, breaking the silence. "It's like what you said about the wall. I'm like you. Who I was before two years ago, I'm not sure."

"Two years. That's gotta…" Zoe's voice trailed off, her brow suddenly furrowed before her eyes locked onto his with a sudden intensity. "Have you tried pushing past it?"

"A little. But I figure, what's the point? I am who I am now. You can only move forward from that. You go backward, you'll only find that it wasn't the way you imagined." He opted to *not* mention the strange underlying sense of guilt the past seemed to spark. "I try to look ahead." She remained still, the *putt-putt-putt* sound of the fire engine in the background. "You?"

"I've researched." She didn't blink; in fact, she didn't move, almost to the point that he wondered if he'd accidentally brain-stunned her. "*Something* has to explain it. You hear the rumors from Hartnell City? I—" She stood up and stared off, the connection broken. "Never mind. I should go."

"Can I ask you something first?"

"Sure." The smallest of smiles came to her lips.

"I get the strength and speed and stuff. But how does the whole hovering thing work?"

"Oh that—" her laughter filled the air around them "—I don't even know. It just does."

Simple as that. Zoe seemed to blow it off like floating in the air was the same as doing a cartwheel. Jamie couldn't do either.

"So what are you going to do now?" he asked, his breath puffing into the night sky. This was the logical question, one he'd hoped would have come up by now. It hadn't, so he figured it was on him. This was one variable that couldn't be left unchecked. Not after this morning. Not after evading her.

Not after saving people together.

He went on, "I mean, look, I'm pretty tired after tonight. So if you're going to turn me in, I think I'd like to skip the whole beating up part."

"No." A gust of wind kicked up strands of her smoke-matted her. "No, I'm not going to turn you in. I think you've earned a bit of good faith. It's too bad, 'cause I had the best catchphrase I was going to say when I caught you."

"Thanks. Maybe save that for another villain? Well, I guess we know if we wound up working as EMTs together, we'd be okay."

"Yeah." Zoe's head bobbed in a quick nod. "Guess you could call that teamwork."

She turned, the lights from beyond obscuring her expression, though he could see her mouth drop. "What you said about—" she started before cutting herself off and looking down. "I mean. Never mind. It's been a long day. I could use a shower."

"Right. I should get home to my cat. She's probably wondering where I disappeared to."

"You have a cat?"

"Yeah. Her name is Normal. She's...not that bright." Her persistent meows and awkward gait popped into his mind, prompting a laugh. "Definitely can't survive on her own."

"Huh. Well, people can surprise you every day. Look, I'll stay out of your way. You stay out of mine. Okay?"

The question lingered, a bit of a truce in the air.

"Yeah. Sounds good."

Zoe nodded again, and though he wanted to say something more, the right phrases refused to form. They stared at each other.

Maybe it didn't have to be this way. Maybe they didn't have to be at odds.

Maybe they could even help each other.

"You know—" he started, but as he did, Zoe gave a quick wave and turned. She walked off down the alley, looking left and right but not back, then sprinted off with her extraordinary speed.

The drizzle picked up, washing soot and debris off his clothes, out of his hair. And though he considered trying to catch up to her, for now he decided to leave it be. All around him, the power fluctuated again—the lights on the fire engine, the streetlights, the surrounding buildings.

They stabilized, and Jamie stood and looked straight at a flyer on a telephone pole.

The flyer was for some furniture clearance sale, nothing to bother with. But burned into it, as if someone had taken a pencil of electricity and charred the paper with it, was the word *STOP*. The edges of the lettering glowed, little flecks of ash blowing off in the wind.

Questions formed in Jamie's mind, pondering not just the word but how it got here, *why* it got here. It had to be deliberate, for him to see—with the rain and the madness of the evening, it had to be. But he would have noticed someone coming in with a cigarette lighter or something and burning the word in there.

Stop? Stop what? Stop the fire? Stop being the Mind Robber? Stop Zoe?

"You alright?" a voice called out. The tone was familiar and

Jamie looked up to catch sight of the detective from earlier. He immediately straightened up—Chesterton, that was his name. "Oh. We met earlier, didn't we? This was your support group you mentioned?"

Jamie told himself to relax. It was completely reasonable that a police officer, even a plainclothes detective, would help out with a downtown fire and not be tracking him from earlier.

"Yep. That was me. Oh," he said, trying to turn on an extra level of gracious vibes, "sorry again about my cat earlier."

"My fault. Never say hello to strange animals. Common sense. I heard you helped get some people out here?"

"I just did what anyone would in that situation."

"Well—" he smiled as he looked over at the open ambulance door "—the city is grateful. San Delgado could use more people like you."

Best to leave. "Thanks, Detective. I appreciate it."

"You're okay? You need anything?"

"Yeah, I'm good." He oriented himself using the towering and brightly lit TransNational Building as his guide, then set out to the nearest Metro station, just as he did nearly every single day. But this time, each step felt a little different, as if the world had suddenly shifted from a few hours ago, and it had nothing to do with the burning building or humming fire engines.

8

GETTING WOKEN UP BY Normal's frantic meows had happened once before. Jamie's first day, in fact. Well, his first day of *this* life. Back then, those initial moments had the meows coming through an open window, so rhythmic and purposeful that they shook him out of his stupor. Even after he'd taken several minutes to try to piece together his new life, the meowing *still* rolled, enough for Jamie to look out the window of his seemingly normal apartment, revealing a run-down complex somewhere tucked away from distant city towers. The courtyard, with its dying lawn and thin trees, offered a picture of suburban normalcy. The parking lot, the faded exterior paint, the garbage and recycling dumpsters, it all seemed cookie-cutter, though nothing activated specifics in his memory.

And then there was the source of the meowing: a gray cat with orange and peach patches lying in the courtyard sun. A crow landed next to it, trying to get a nearby piece of bread. It poked at the cat, the beak picking the feline's fuzzy side, small tufts of fur floating into the sunlight. The cat continued letting out helpless meows, and Jamie watched the scene repeat for about a minute before stepping outside and shooing the bird away, the cat too inept to save itself. "You're not normal, are you?" he said to it after it began following him.

The cat might have been his for all he knew, and for that reason, he'd let it go inside with him following his inspection of the courtyard. A sunny spot seemed to call to the creature, and it sniffed for a few seconds before rolling on its back, a soft purr finally replacing the frantic meows from before.

That day, Jamie searched all the cabinets and drawers, and the only things he turned up were two sheets of paper. The first was a one-year lease agreement signed out to 2D Industries. Weeks later, he'd call the number on there out of curiosity, only to have it go direct to a generic voice mail.

The other was a note with a short sentence written by hand. "You can read their memories."

It was such an odd statement. Was it literal? Was it a joke? Was it an incomplete statement? How did someone read memories?

What about his *own* memory? He'd tried to press into it, but trying to remember was like diving into an abyss, an impenetrable but blinding fog everywhere he turned. One single flash came through, surprising him twice—first that it existed and second with the content.

It appeared to be a hallway, some industrial complex or maybe an old hospital. Grim fluorescent lighting turned up the contrast, making hallway corners and doorways seem like creases in a drawing. A metal door sat in the middle of the hallway, and at the end of it lay…something just out of frame. Crumpled silhouettes on the floor in the far room.

Outside, car doors slammed and chattering voices approached, the sound of the swinging crackle of plastic bags and footsteps breaking him out of the mystery image. He peeked out the window at an older couple walking slowly across the courtyard.

Seeing that he had zero recall of who he was or how he got

there, trying to read someone else's memory might have been only the second strangest part of his day.

He squinted, staring, as if that was the path to jumping into someone's mind. Was there a gesture or magic word or something that was supposed to activate it?

And nothing.

The room filled with his sigh. He closed his eyes. Something invisible tugged on his hands; he raised them, and there was a subtle temperature shift underneath the skin when he extended his fingers and gave in.

Then images flew into his mind.

It wasn't anything groundbreaking, like learning someone's deep dark secret or the key to their soul. He saw through the eyes of a driver while a car lurched into a parking spot, handicap placard swaying. He heard the sounds of a man's grunt while pushing himself out of the passenger seat. He heard the *thunk* of the car's trunk slamming shut after that same man removed several plastic bags.

And he felt the warmth of two hands together.

All through the eyes of an old woman.

It was strange, this person who'd lived decades more than him, who probably spent much of her time living in memories, she managed to captivate him at a moment when he had *no* memories, and the simple gesture of holding hands with her husband defined the significance of the present rather than the past.

His eyes snapped open to find the cat staring up at him, unblinking. "I guess I'm not normal, either," he said, hand extended. Her ears perked up at the words, and she rested one paw on the palm of his hand, right above where a scar cut diagonally across the skin. "Or maybe you are? Normal?"

The cat replied with a meow, the same awkward staccato meow that he first heard.

The same meow that woke him up off the bed here, now.

He'd dozed off, open suitcase next to him. A week had passed

since the fire at the YMCA, something that the authorities
chalked up to an electrical fire that spiraled out of control given
the condition of the building. No one mentioned the Mind Robber or the Throwing Star, though apparently Zoe was still on
the job; news outlets were reporting she'd taken down another
mugger two days ago and also rescued someone from a wrecked
car that had hydroplaned during the recent storm.

Jamie, however, didn't want any of it. Not the fame, not the
media adoration, or the social media speculation. Not anymore.
Zoe seemed to be a perfect fit for whatever that life entailed.

But not him. He spent the afternoon considering all the vari-
ables: his abilities, the amount of cash he still had, Normal and her
care. Other than his phone bill and the bank account he used as an
intermediary for the cash he stole, there were few ties to this place.
No car, and very few records under his own name. Library records,
sure, but of all the places with an official identification, a library
card seemed the most benign. Even this apartment was signed to
some mystery corporation, absolving him of the responsibility.

Everything he needed was right here. That, and the extra mo-
tivation from the morning news: the injured woman from the
bank was going to speak. It spread quickly to every possible media
outlet. Even simply walking in the park for fresh air blasted it in
his face. Every passing TV in every restaurant, everyone's conversation along the way, even the tiny screens he saw in people's
hands while waiting in line for a coffee, they all focused on the
news that she'd regained consciousness. Journalists rushed to get
her first exclusive interview while police fought them off, asking
for everyone to back off so she could give an official statement.

The first victim of the Mind Robber who remembered the
encounter. Even though Jamie felt secure that she couldn't identify him, the sheer presence of the chatter and the focus bore
down on him, urging him to escape. He didn't need another
unpredictable element in his life.

And yet, something didn't quite allow him to just make the

move, to pack everything up, pick a destination and go. People like customs officers, ticket takers, security desks, all could be handled with a combination of timing and the right level of brain-stuns. Normal might get stressed, but her everyday state seemed to veer into jumpy and neurotic anyway. He hadn't quite reached his goal, but if he budgeted right, maybe he could still make the Caribbean work, a place where work records and IDs mattered less than simply showing up and being a good person, a hard worker, someone who just wanted a quiet night to read memoirs with a cat on his lap.

And that would erase all the nonsense created by the Mind Robber, turning it into a footnote in San Delgado's history, a thing for people to obsess over in online forums and social media.

So easy. Too easy. So why hadn't he done it? He'd stared at the suitcase all morning, going over option after option until he finally decided to sleep on it. One nap later, all he registered was Normal's growing hunger rather than a path forward.

"Alright, alright," he said to the meowing cat. She did the usual hunger dance, moving in figure eights between his feet as he opened the can and filled her little dish. Normal waited, eyes fixed on him until he reached into the fridge and got out the carton of coconut water. He was mixing several drops into her water dish when a knock came at the door.

Things had been quiet in the past week. But Jamie knew he couldn't be too cautious, and he approached the door with his guard up and a cap covering his hair and face. His shoulders tense, he peeked through the side of the window, expecting to see the detective from last week.

Instead, he laughed to himself. *Of course.*

Because Zoe stood at the door, afternoon sun behind her poking through gathering clouds.

"I can see your heat signature, Jamie. You might as well open it. I'm not here to beat you up. Or turn you in."

Jamie unhooked the top chain—a chain wouldn't stop her—

and he cracked the door. "Hey." From just the little sliver of space, the air felt thick, giving away an imminent rain.

"Hey. Can we talk?" she asked. Zoe stood stronger than the woman he'd seen at the support group. The lines under her eyes were gone, her posture was straighter and her hair was neater. Even her clothes gave off the vibe that she'd recently done laundry.

"I thought we were going to stay out of each other's way. I haven't done any robbing, mind or otherwise. But you've been busy."

"Oh. Yeah." Despite standing in the shade of trees from the apartment complex's courtyard, Zoe's cheeks burned a visible red. "Yeah, I've put the suit on a few times."

"A few times" seemed to be an understatement. Rolling blackouts hit the city almost every other day now with no official explanation, just a promise from San Delgado's utility provider that they'd get to the bottom of it soon. Problem was, criminals found blackouts to be a good time to loot stores.

That was, until the Throwing Star showed up.

"Well, you don't have to worry about me," Jamie replied. "I'm on indefinite hiatus."

"Good. That's good to hear."

"But remember that I didn't really steal from anyone. FDIC coverage and all that."

Zoe nodded, the sides of her mouth curled upward. From behind Jamie, Normal clawed at the rug, meowing to herself relentlessly. "You have a lot of books," she said, pointing at the stack of library returns he set near the front door. Normal seemed to take that as an invitation, and the chubby cat trotted over before circling in and out of Zoe's legs, which was already better than her reaction to Chesterton. Jamie made a note to stop Zoe if she tried to pet the cat, though if Zoe handled puncturing concrete with ease, a cat scratch probably meant nothing.

"Oh. Yeah, I like memoirs. Everyone has a story to tell. Library is filled with them." The small talk chewed at his anxieties, and maybe it was because she failed at social cues. Not that he was much better. "How did you find me?"

"Oh. That night after the fire, I tracked you when you went home."

"Tracked?"

"Yeah. I followed you," she said with a shrug. Nothing extraordinary about it.

"Are you just checking on me?" Jamie asked.

"No. Actually, I have a proposal for you."

"A proposal? This isn't one of those 'let's get married for tax or citizenship purposes' proposals, is it?"

"No," Zoe said with a smirk, and Jamie smiled back. It was natural, not awkward or forced or defensive. The very fact that such a moment could exist between them felt like a small miracle. "It's much more interesting than that. Can I come in?"

"It's fine. Normal likes you anyway."

Zoe knelt down, hand extended. "Hi, kitty. I'm not that bad. I protect San Delgado from criminals and—"

The room echoed Zoe's sneeze. And another. And another. Sudden tears began streaming down her cheeks, and the sneezes went rapid-fire. "Oh crap," she said between sniffles.

"You allergic?"

"I guess so." She stepped back outside, head in hands, and Jamie followed. "Ah. Alright, we're not talking there. Is there a good bar nearby?" she said through sniffles.

"I don't drink. I don't like feeling out of control."

"Okay, then. That's probably a good idea. Booze and me have not been pals lately. Coffee?"

This time, it was Jamie's turn to smirk. "I *love* coffee." He pointed past the courtyard toward the strip mall nearest to their neck of suburban South San Delgado. "There's a good spot a few blocks that way."

"Okay, then. Let's—" Zoe stopped abruptly, a full-fledged grin lifting her cheeks and brightening her eyes. "I got an idea. You curious about the hovering thing?"

9

GODDAMN RAIN.

Zoe looked up, the drops gaining momentum from a sprinkle to a downpour in a quick minute. Still in her clutches, Jamie seemed too stunned to notice. His eyes barely blinked beneath his windswept hair.

Zoe had instructed Jamie to trust her; they'd walked discreetly to an alley between buildings, his posture tight. He kept insisting he was fine, and right before they launched up, she realized that this wasn't about trusting her.

Jamie was nervous about trusting *anyone*.

But like she did on her FoodFast deliveries, Zoe stayed on the highest rooftops, jogging while hunched over to keep an eye out for maintenance workers or drunks. The darkening clouds and disappearing sun helped too, and they probably moved fast enough to be a mere blink for anyone up there.

To Jamie's credit, he held tight and didn't scream or flinch, not even when she jumped roof to roof. Her speed remained controlled, faster than human but not enough to require her suit and/or cause Jamie to barf. During work, she usually packed the food tight in a hefty backpack lined to keep the meals warm; Jamie was heavier, bulkier than that, though she kept a brisk pace, even when they stopped to figure out where the coffee shop was and how to get back to ground level in the most discreet fashion.

By the time raindrops started painting the sidewalk, he seemed to relax, and they walked into the café like old friends rather than rivals, her opening the door for him, making jokes about the wet rain, ordering at the counter together. Jamie even offered to buy her a pastry, which she gladly took him up on.

"Well," he said after they slid into a booth, water still dripping down the tips of his hair. The back of his hand wiped his forehead and they locked eyes.

No tickle at the base of her skull. He was holding up his end so far.

"Where do we begin?"

"I've been thinking," she said. "We worked well together. I think we've even earned a little trust?"

"When you save us from a burning building, that's a few points right there."

"When you protect secret identities, there's another few points." The coffee burned her lips with the first sip, one packet sugar and one packet creamer, just the way she liked it. Jamie went the other route, the deep black pool thick enough to be sludge. "Mmm," she said, "this place *is* good."

"People forget about us out here in the south suburbs. Since we're so far away from the city center. For a lot of reasons, most of them valid." He sipped from his mug, and groaned with satisfaction before letting the space drift into awkward silence.

Uncomfortable pauses were the worst. This was why Zoe didn't deal with others. "So? What do you think?"

"I think…" Jamie hesitated, Zoe clinging onto the passing

moments. Her pulse quickened, the answers so close that they seemed ready to emerge from the shadows if he only said yes. "Best coffee around. There's another branch in Oakmount—"

"Damn it, I'm serious. We work well together. We should do it again. A trade," she said. "I help you. You help me."

"A trade? Sorry, I'm a bit skeptical. You don't need me." He gestured to her, then around the room, which presumably meant the city. "You can *fly*."

"You can read minds—"

"Memories. It's a little different."

"Right. Whatever. Memories. Look, that's exactly what I mean. I can't *punch* my way through memories."

It seemed like Jamie needed a moment to fully grasp what Zoe said. Which wasn't much, and maybe more than she wanted to lead with. But still, his brow crinkled and his fingers tapped against the mug. Seconds ticked by until he took another sip and then locked eyes with her. "You can get away with anything. I don't understand why memories are so important. Why not just get a ton of money and hide forever. Live in security. Peace and quiet."

Zoe was hardly an expert on people, but even she could pick up on the hint of jealousy in his voice. "That's what you want, isn't it? Peace and quiet. Security." She held the half-empty mug to her lips, coffee no longer steaming out of it. "Robbing banks doesn't seem like peace and quiet. Why not, I don't know, rig the lottery? Or a casino?"

"I can't rig the lottery. That's predicting the future. And I can't read minds. Only memories. There's a difference. I've tried the casino bit. It doesn't quite work. You need to wait for the dealer to observe the cards and imprint it in memories. Then it takes a little bit to get that and make a decision. Creates a lot of awkward silences. It's like files saved on your computer. Not livestreaming."

"I don't have a computer. They're expensive and break."

"Okay, but you get the analogy, right? This is easier. And this part?" His arm twirled dramatically and his chin stuck out; if he'd been wearing an eye mask, he would have exactly matched the security footage floating online. "It's all for show. The more people who know *that*, the more scared they'll be. And the less trouble they'll make for me. I get in and I get out."

"Except when someone has a heart condition."

"Yeah." His face dropped, eyes staring at the table between them.

"Sorry," she said. "I shouldn't have said that. I know you feel bad about it."

"Are you being my therapist?"

"Better. Extraordinary therapist."

"Good. I need that. So we've established that I'm not a terrible person. I'm just trying to get by." He shook his head with a short laugh. "Alright, fine. How do we help each other? Besides therapy?"

"What I said at the support group, it's all true. I think— *think*—this whole Throwing Star thing comes from the not knowing part." Hours of staring at her detective board and some recent reevaluation of things made it easy to say that part. But that was merely the surface. "It eats at me," she finally admitted, perhaps more to herself than Jamie. "Who was I before this? Why do I feel this drive to be *more*? Don't you wonder where it all comes from? The abilities, the memory loss? What happened to us?"

"I told you before, I'm all about moving forward," he said. "Only bad things happen when you look back."

"You say that like it's a certainty."

"It's a hunch. Something in my gut tells me that."

"It's *all* I think about," she blurted out. Well, there wasn't any walking back that statement. "I've tried to piece it together, you should see the wall of my apartment. Pictures and notes and strings connecting them together, like I'm trying to be the world's greatest detective. But I'm not. I don't have the skills or resources. Who am I? What did I leave behind? I need to know that I'm *someone*. I don't even need to be extraordinary. I just need to know that I mattered. Though you know, I've never been to a therapist. Well, maybe I have. I just can't remember. But..." Her voice trailed off, and she took one long draw of coffee, emptying the mug. "You can get into minds. You can dig into memories. Maybe you can find something in mine to see who I am. Where I came from. I get these fragments. Me being chased or cornered, like on a rooftop or something. That has to be connected to everything."

Jamie's brow crinkled in sympathy. "I want to help you. But there are no guarantees. I'm not sure what I might find in there."

"There has to be *something*."

"But what if there's not? Can't you just be happy being...you? I mean, look at you. I'm sure kids will dress as you for Halloween. There's probably even bootleg merchandise of you floating around."

"It's nothing special. All it does is give me something to focus on. I need to know I'm more than a...a weapon. A weapon for justice, sure. But still. Just a weapon." They sat in silence, the rain tapping a furious rhythm against the window. Outside, the streetlight flickered, causing the shadows of passersby and cars to seemingly strobe as they came and went. Behind them, the din of cups on saucers, laughter and conversation sat on the periphery from their tiny corner of the café.

"So you help me," Zoe said. "You do your mind thing. You punch through this wall blocking all of my memories and find out who I really was. Really am. And I'll help you rob a bank."

Jamie's expression shifted. First a puzzled brow, then dropped jaw, then wide eyes, all before resetting to neutral. "Um... I think people will be able to see that it's you helping me."

"I have an idea for that. But I'm talking bigger than what you do. You're getting cash, right? But there's a limit on that. A limit on how much you can carry, how much you can get access to. You need a way to haul it all. To break through the vault doors. I can help you with that. You said it yourself, banks are insured. We won't be hurting anyone. You take that fortune and you set yourself up so that you never have to rob a bank again. Take that money, go live out your life. No more guilt. No more danger. Peace and quiet."

"Insured up to two-hundred-fifty grand per bank." Jamie leaned back, his gaze shifting past Zoe to the ugly wallpaper of stylized font and pictures of coffee beans. But she knew he was picturing something greater. "Peace and quiet. Maybe. Hopefully?" His wistful question dropped to reality, the lines on his face grounded in the now. "Without *him*, I could connect with people again. And maybe that's my best bet. A real life. I have a goal, you know. Me and Normal hiding away, somewhere on a tropical beach. With a lot of books and good coffee."

The lights flickered several times, prompting a murmur from the baristas and a handful of people in the café. At their table, the two of them stayed quiet.

"Tomorrow night?" he finally said.

Zoe was about to agree when the power cut out. The hum of the room—the music, the blow of the ventilation, the whirr of the espresso machines—all dropped, leaving only a room full of confused people. Seconds passed before everything returned. "Eight o'clock?"

"Yeah." Jamie nodded. "And you don't have to worry. Your secret's safe with me. Want to meet here? Should be quiet enough."

Such an easy pledge to make. Too easy, in fact, and the idea of a double cross floated through Zoe's mind. She considered secretly calling the police and having them lock away the Mind Robber forever. No more risks, no leaving herself vulnerable to the person who battled her physical strength with mental powers. But that also took away her only chance at having someone unearth the possibilities of her history. Stuck forever in a life of being the Throwing Star and nothing else.

Not good enough.

"My place."

Zoe considered her inner sanctum, her secret lair—which, really, was just a shitty apartment in the Lower Heights part of San Delgado. There weren't security measures or ways she could stop him if things went south. Her neighbors hardly spoke to her; they probably just knew her as the woman who stumbled home at odd hours, sometimes drunk and sometimes sweaty, and on occasion, both. If Jamie stunned her, or left her incapacitated indefinitely, probably no one would check on her until the odor of her soiling herself got too horrific to go on.

On the other hand, all of her notes and research were there. If this was going to be a deep dive, they needed all of that handy— her detective board, the folders and papers tucked away, the notebook of musings, all of it.

Jamie's brow rose, and he let out a low sound, the "uh…" of being caught speechless. "Are you sure that's a good idea?" he finally said after what seemed like far too long.

"Are you worried about a double cross?" She left out the part where she'd considered it too, the other way around. Maybe they *would* make good partners, after all, if they were equally suspicious of each other. But suspicions didn't amount to much in the big scheme of things, even with her true identity on the line. Because this life of fighting and rooftop sprinting and bad choices wasn't really a life. "You can trust me. Besides, why would I wait to double-cross you there? I know where you live. I could punch you out there."

"Fair point."

She asked a passing barista for a pen, and as she did, her ears picked up the familiar screams of someone in peril. About four blocks over.

She scribbled an address onto a spare coffee cup sleeve and

stood up. "I have to go." Adrenaline surged through her, the lure of danger and rescue locking her sensibilities into a tight focus, a coiled spring ready to explode. She offered a short farewell, then made a hasty exit and assessed the situation. Was there enough time to go get her suit? If not, maybe she'd just cover her face with her jacket.

Duty called.

No FoodFast shirt required.

Jamie watched Zoe dash out the door and run off despite the heavy rain. Her footsteps splashed in puddles until she ducked down an alley, and a second later the slightest of silhouettes flew upward, landing on a rooftop.

He leaned back in his seat, returning to the less extraordinary world of a coffee shop. As he did, something caught his eye. Not Zoe, she was long gone, not outside the window but *on* it. In the mix of rain and dirt on the glass, the word *HER* was smudged. The wind picked up, tossing the rain horizontally against the glass pane, and as the droplets danced off the window, they pecked away at the letters, gradually removing any sense of form to them.

He peered closer, reaching across the table until his face was almost against the glass. And from there, even as the letters became reduced to just another blemish on a storefront window, his nose picked up the faint smell of burning.

Jamie had told himself that he wasn't going to abuse his Mind Robber powers right now, that he was putting that all behind—especially given the deal with Zoe. But this was too strange. Was it some trick Zoe was playing on him? She did leave abruptly, and he had no way to know how sincere she was. It seemed possible that *acting* might have been one of her extraordinary abilities, as well.

Jamie's bottom lip stung as he bit down on it, pondering the possibilities. He decided to pop through the memories of the remaining patrons of the café, scrolling back through the recent past. Conversations, coffee, one trip to the bathroom (which he elected to cut off before it got too personal)—nothing seemed out of the ordinary until he got to the barista.

When the power had fluctuated, the woman behind the counter had been looking out the window. The lights flashed, the sound of machines died, and for a split second, she saw a glowing blue figure appear at the glass, like electricity in the form of a human. She startled, then muttered, "Whoa, weird lightning," and she went on with her day.

But Jamie was pretty certain a random lightning crackle wouldn't leave *HER* on the window.

And the message he saw last week burned into the flyer, *STOP*. That same smell.

STOP HER.

Was something telling him about Zoe? Could he trust her?

Nerves rattled through his body, a sudden edge to his thoughts as he considered the path before him. If he trusted Zoe and showed up, it might be a trap. Was that what he was supposed to stop?

Or maybe it was unrelated. There were, after all, a lot of *hers* in the city.

Zoe had dangled a carrot: freedom from this life. Regardless of what cryptic messages and blue-lightning guys appeared, that was the bottom line.

This was a transaction. Service for service. Mutually beneficial. With a worthwhile goal.

Running away forever sounded like a wonderful plan.

10

ZOE DECIDED TO CLEAN her apartment.

If someone snuck a look from outside, they'd have seen a blur of chores, including the occasional stubbed toe followed by "Shit! Goddamn it!" Her strength made it easy to do things like lift up a sofa with one hand while vacuuming with the other. She kicked a large crate of individual mac-and-cheese boxes, which she'd bought at the dollar store even though she tossed the cheese packets in favor of using similarly priced marinara jars, into the corner. Her hands swept over the worn edges of the coffee table, something she'd rescued out of the apartment building's hallway some months ago despite the bleach stain on one side (a little paint helped bring at least a sense of respectability).

This is what she had to do. For the hour prior, she'd stood in front of her detective board, searching once again for the connections that weren't there.

The lease. Printouts of every company she could find with the name 2D in it. LinkedIn profiles of people who'd worked for those companies. Rumors of people with abilities in other cities, from sightings in Hartnell City to rumors of so-called magicians dueling in New Turning. Social media tracking of those reports, printouts of internet forum discussions. All tied together by string, lines zigging and zagging back and forth.

And the name tag. It always came back to the name tag.

Twenty-one million results came up for the name Zoe Wong. She'd dismissed it early on after crossing off Zoe Wong the entrepreneur, Zoe Wong the Australian artist, Zoe Wong the food critic, and all the others who were clearly not her, clearly not the identity she'd assumed. The name tag stayed on the board, but the mystery *behind* the name built around it.

It culminated in a point of frustration, one that manifested itself in a tight fist. With a slight tremble in her hand, she actually considered how long it would take to jump out the window and hover over to the corner liquor store, buy and pound a bottle of the cheapest rum available, then make it back up and brush her teeth to hide the smell.

No, she told herself. This was about finding the truth, a truth that might connect all the puzzle pieces about abilities, about her history and who she was. Which made having a preemptive drink seem counterproductive.

Usually when she felt this pull, she loaded up another cheesy movie on HorrorDomain; since the robbery, she'd actually donned the suit a few times with the intention of being the Throwing Star of media creation, not just someone who improvised while delivering food. Enough shitheads did horrible things that it really only took minutes before she gave into jumps, sprints and a series of violent blows leaving bystanders either gawking or applauding or both. But right now that wasn't an option, nor was watching the second half of *Lo-Bot: Samurai Cyborg*, not with Jamie's imminent arrival. So she'd cleaned, and now as she took in her handiwork, she wondered if she should be a maid instead of delivering for FoodFast.

A knock interrupted her thoughts. She took one last look at her now-spotless home before opening the door.

"Hi," Jamie said. He was holding flowers. Not a bouquet, but a small potted plant with a few petals between green leaves.

"Oh," he said. His heat signature glowed with burning cheeks. "It's a peace offering. Good faith, you know? I mean, you're supposed to bring wine to a social gathering. But I don't drink so I didn't know what would be good. I considered ice cream. But that might melt. Um, then pie or a dessert, but I don't know what you like. So then I thought flowers but then flowers are like for a date and this—" he nodded, shifting his weight as he stood in the door's threshold "—clearly isn't a date. So then I figured a plant. Plants are good. You know? We could always use more of them."

He seemed nervous. And curious. Especially when she tracked his eyes to her detective board. Not once did she detect anything threatening.

"Come on in," she finally said. She pointed at the counter, the place where empty plastic bottles and cans sat merely an hour ago. "I could use a nice plant."

As he entered, Zoe loaded up, ready to release and explode. She awaited any clues indicating an invasion from the Mind Robber. With each further step he took, the tension escalated, even as he looked at her detective board and motioned to it. Monitoring him, preparing for any possibility of shit going wrong, stole her focus from his questions. Though she still nodded in generic response.

As far as she could tell, he was showing curiosity, especially when he looked at her futon, of all things. And a little fear. And some distress, or maybe caution. That was it. Nothing aggressive or malicious. All logic pointed to him *not* being such a good actor that he could completely suppress his emotions and intent.

"Hey look," he said with a laugh. He tapped a few printouts on the detective board. "That's me."

Maybe it wasn't *him* per se that caused her to tense. It might have had more to do with the fact that since she'd lived there, only one person had come in outside of her landlord. And that was to fix a leaking toilet.

"You have…a name tag?" He pointed at the center of the board.

"Yeah. It came with the place."

Zoe watched as Jamie examined the folded paper throwing star next to the name tag. "Did it come with this too?"

"No, I made that myself after the media came up with the name. But…" She paused, considering what she should say. This would be the first real test of the other hero name. "I thought maybe 'Shuriken' might be better. It's Japanese for throwing star."

Jamie's expression didn't change either way, which meant he wasn't listening or didn't think it was a cooler name. Or maybe he was too focused on the rest of the board. "Huh." Jamie let out a soft chuckle as he shook his head. "I didn't get a name tag."

"No name tag? How'd you get 'Jamie'?"

"I looked up lists of common-but-not-too-common names," he said, his brow crinkling. "Just picked what felt right to blend in."

"Did you get a lease?" Zoe asked.

"Yeah." His finger tapped against the yellow carbon-copied paper of her lease. "2D Industries."

So there *was* a connection. The very fact that they both dealt with the mystery company ignited her nerves, almost magnetically pulling her forward. This was a good first step. Better settle in. "Let's start with that. And see?" She threw her hands up. "I'm not double-crossing you. All good."

"Right. Right, right, me too," he said with a sigh. "Formal agreement to not double-cross?"

"Signed and co-signed."

"If you break me apart, then who will feed Normal?"

"Okay," Zoe said, a genuine laugh while trying to stand in a relaxed position. "I won't kill you."

"Thanks. The Throwing Star is a friend of felines."

"And a good host." She opened the cabinet above the kitchen sink and slid out a plastic cup with a fast-food logo. "Water?"

Jamie hadn't been this nervous using his powers since he first considered robbing a bank. On that day, he'd smiled despite the racing pulse hammering through his veins. The envelope in his hand crinkled, sending tension through his body as the pressure of the moment dialed up. He'd presented the package, holding it a few inches over the cubicle desk until he felt the sturdy grip of acceptance on the other side. His fingers let go, and the temp agency staffer, a very polite woman named Meredith, returned the smile and nodded.

"Thanks," she said, totally oblivious to the magnitude of the moment.

That day marked the third time he'd attempted to use a driver's license and birth certificate—both forged and purchased off the internet, of course—to join the roster of a staffing agency. The first time had wound up as an epic fail on his part, where nerves got in the way of remembering details and ultimately he'd brain-stunned the staffer, grabbed his things and got the hell out of there. The second time, it actually worked, and Jamie worked four gigs over eight months. Everything ran as planned, almost shockingly so as check after check arrived; he cashed them at a nearby service before bringing the paper bills to a local bank branch, slowly filling up his goal chart.

Then questions about his tax-exempt status came up.

He'd weighed opening up, of course. After all, it wasn't exactly his fault he couldn't remember anything. But too many what-ifs chased that idea—what if he had a criminal record? What if he'd get arrested for fraud? What if there was something weirder, more sinister behind it all?

No, he resolved not to take those chances. Instead, he took the option of "get the hell out," hopefully disappearing into obscurity following several days of skulking around the agency's office in various disguises to perform memory surgery on his so-called talent advisor.

All that effort just to get back to the start: another intake with a different agency, this time with a different set of fake documentation. Meredith removed the ID card and birth certificate from the envelope, and though she skimmed it over with a totally normal look, Jamie caught her eye double back before her expression froze. The grief almost made him wonder if it was worth the hassle. Low-paying physical labor offered much more accessible work and much less scrutiny.

Problem was, he'd *really* preferred something indoors and quiet.

"I'm going to make copies," she said. Jamie nodded, a pleasant "of course" accompanying it, until she stood and turned.

His shoulders crept up, with a tightness that turned the screw on all his thoughts and feelings. If she had suspicions, then he'd have to reset the process again, find a different agency, perhaps even rework the documents. Options began playing out in his head, though the current of anxiety made it difficult to concentrate. He tried to calm himself, setting his focus to the benign chatter still in earshot from the lobby area.

"Why do we do this? Every few months we're someplace new," a woman said, her voice laced with a gravel that betrayed a significant amount of smoking.

"Gotta pay the bills," the man sitting next to her said with a heavy sigh.

"You know what I'd do if I could? Like if I was invisible? I'd rob banks."

The man responded with a laugh, but his friend continued. "Seriously. I'd rob banks."

"You want cops chasing after you?"

"I said if I was invisible. Then I wouldn't have to temp anymore."

"Okay, but the whole 'stealing people's life savings' doesn't bug you?"

This time, it was the woman's turn to laugh. "Life savings?

You think anyone actually loses anything in a bank robbery? Government insurance covers that. Here," she said, grunting as she shuffled in her chair. "I just looked it up. Insured up to two-hundred fifty grand per account. And there's no way these arms are strong enough to lug out that much cash in one afternoon. Besides, it'd give the local news something to talk about for a few days."

The pair chuckled at each other, then continued onto a tangent about best bank heists from movies, but ideas had already starting setting up shop in Jamie's mind. Suddenly, it snapped into place. He wasn't invisible, but he could be invisible to memories. And he wouldn't be stealing from people, just from large faceless entities.

This made sense. It made too much sense.

Jamie realized he'd started to lean forward in his chair, and told himself to relax when Meredith returned with his paperwork. "Sorry about the delay, Mr. Sorenson," she said. By then, he'd gotten used to the last name that he'd picked mostly because it sounded good. "I just had to verify something. But it's good now, so we can dig into the details. First, were you thinking long term or short term?"

Robbing banks. With his powers.

It was so obvious. He just had to figure out how.

"Short term," he said.

After that day, he was the Mind Robber.

And now he was going to plunge into the Throwing Star's brain.

Jamie watched as Zoe sat down across from him, eyes closed. "Do you need to, like, rub my forehead or something?" she asked.

"Nah. I can do it from here." Which was mostly true. In a few bits of experimentation, he'd found that physical contact did lock things in better. But that would put him within striking distance of her, and part of Jamie still worried that Zoe would turn, grab him and toss him out the window. Truth was, he almost chickened out. But that would have pissed Zoe off even more, and the last thing he needed was the Throwing Star tearing into his apartment to exact vengeance over a missed therapy session.

"You think the extraordinaries in Hartnell City do stuff like this?" Zoe asked.

"You really believe those rumors?"

"Oh for sure. We can't be the only ones."

"I don't know if I find that idea comforting or frightening." Jamie adjusted and did a calming internal countdown from five. "Ready?"

Zoe sucked in a breath that drove up her posture, and her shoulders didn't drop until she spoke. "Ready."

"Okay, just...relax." Eyes closed, his fingers went up, not to remove any memories but to better lock into the connection.

"Can I talk during this?"

"Actually, I'm not sure. I've never played therapist during these things."

The first memories appeared, as if projected onto a screen in his mind's eye. It rolled chronologically, and Jamie's fingers twitched as he pulled them, first with her cleaning the apartment, then some rooftop dashing, then the YMCA, then the chase down to the Metro station. He maneuvered around, slowing down moments and exploring them, simply to get comfortable before reaching deep into the past.

"What do you see?"

Guess she *could* talk during this.

"Watching you beat the shit out of criminals is fun. As long as it's not me. Okay, I'm going to go back. When I find things, I'll ask you about them, see if you can place them. To kind of gauge your memory so I get the context of your life." Jamie pulled harder on the memories, and it triggered an audible grunt from Zoe. "You okay?"

"I'm fine. Keep going."

Images rifled by, a flip-book of random moments. Tapping

away at her phone. Walking up and down the hallway. Grocery shopping. Liquor stores. Some terrible and gory movies—
he really should give her book recommendations. And a lot of
running.

Discovering her ability to hover. Dumpster diving by a motorcycle shop to get pieces for her suit and watching videos on how
to stitch things together. Squeezing into it and zipping it up, but
almost always with a FoodFast polo shirt over it and bundles of
food on her back.

Except when she ditched the food and polo shirt to fight
crime. But Jamie marveled at her ability to come back to her
thermally sealed backpack and still make her delivery after
punching bad guys.

Jeez, he thought, she's good at her job.

He pulled further and further until a blank wall stopped him.
It wasn't black, and it wasn't white or even cloudy; instead, a
sense of *obstruction* occupied his mind. Scaling back a few moments, he got a still photo of this apartment. Except he moved
it back and forth, and no further memories came by, and Jamie
began to wonder if this was a memory glitch until he noticed
the clock in the corner ticking by.

These were her first awake memories. He explored more and
saw that she'd stood there in a stunned stupor, probably similar
to when he did a brain-stun, for a good hour or so.

"What is it?" she asked. "Something's up."

"It's nothing. It's just, I found the moment you awoke here.
You were conscious enough to process memory but didn't move
for over an hour."

"I remember that. Like feeling like I was gradually entering
my own body."

Jamie sifted through the memories some more until clear
movement showed in her mind's eye. She explored the space,
wandering from corner to corner, pausing to look at a mirror.

Then she noticed something, something on the small coffee table—the same coffee table in front of them right now.

A note.

And on it, a message.

Zoe must have heard him gasp. "What?"

"That note. Do you remember that note when you came to?"

"'You are stronger than you think. Push yourself.' Yeah. It was my first clue."

"I had one too. It told me I could read memories. Do you still have yours?"

Zoe went quiet, a thrum of her own feelings blurring into what Jamie could read. "I, um, tore it up. One night while drunk."

So that's why it wasn't on her board. "Okay, I'm going farther back. There's like this wall blocking it."

"What happens when you go past it?"

"I'm not sure."

"Try it."

"Are you sure?" Come to think of it, Jamie realized he had never attempted such a rapid leap in scope—when he learned his skills, everything was a very gradual, very controlled test rather than a "what the hell" jump forward. Who knew what going farther might do? It was the freaking *brain* involved, so could one more poke wreck her base instincts, things like breathing and heartbeats and stuff? Or would it send her into a seething rage, something that was all abilities and zero self-control? Or maybe it would shatter Zoe's existing persona? Uncertainty— or perhaps self-preservation—held him frozen. "I've never done this before—"

"Try it," she bit out. Her words came clear and strong, forceful even. "I'm not quitting now."

"Okay…" Jamie worked through the memories; nothing came, the same emptiness surrounding him, almost collapsing around him. He pulled and pulled, and though he couldn't quite explain why, he *felt* his memory tug moving through sludge. He pulled again, the mental intensity causing a layer of sweat to form across his forehead. Another and another, and another; he pulled for several minutes until finally an image flashed in front of him. His fingers fluttered in reverse, searching for the image mired in nothingness. And when he found it, he forced it to stay there, as if a single memory fought for its very existence.

"I see something. It's dark. I see stars." He held on, pieces of the image coming into focus. Details colored and filled in, shapeless blobs becoming sharp lines and real objects. "A roof... it looks like a rooftop. But not any of the ones in your other memories." Jamie bit down on his lip, a pounding in his head as he willed the image to steady. "It looks like...feels like...you're cornered. And across the way, there's a light. It came and went and now there's..."

"I know this. It's like the only thing I can grab but it comes and goes so quickly I can't make out any specifics."

Jamie knew he was navigating *her* memories but pushing through, finding these flashes of details, something instinctive poked through for *him*. His mind, his nerves, his suddenly twitching muscles all urged him to let go, turn away, disappear. The feeling trickled down into his connection, things blurring in and out of Zoe's memory, but he'd come this far. And besides, she'd probably hurt him if he let go at this point.

Jamie ignored the creeping fear and forced himself to hold on. "People are coming. I hear radio chatter. There's someone else with them."

The image became fully realized and the small apartment in Lower Heights filled with a scream. Jamie opened his eyes, but Zoe wasn't sitting in front of him anymore.

Instead, she levitated against the ceiling, hands to her head, a petrifying sound coming from her mouth and invading every corner of the living space.

11

THE ROOFTOP.

Zoe knew Jamie *saw* the rooftop, the one from her only sliver of memory. And suddenly she was there too, like his handiwork turned all the dials up on her mental viewing. A blend of confusion and fear and adrenaline flooded over her, so much that it screamed in her head. She heard cross-chatter, like voices barking orders and asking questions, louder and louder until it all became white noise.

And a scream. A scream to pierce right through it.

A new voice came into the mix, something different. Not the squawking tactical efficiency of the others, but this one repeating with desperation. "Zoe! Zoe!"

Were her eyes closed? No, they couldn't be. She *saw* this, yet her limbs froze, immobilized, and gradually she realized that the pressure on her skull came from her own hands. And the scream that filled the void, came from her own mouth.

"Zoe!"

That voice. It was Jamie.

Something tugged on her foot, and from pure reflex, her leg coiled back and kicked as hard as it could. Right when she did that, her eyes opened and she watched Jamie sail across the room, his back hitting the blank wall of her apartment with a dull *thunk*.

She dropped to the floor, bare feet feeling the carpet fibers. "Oh shit, you alright?" In two bounds, she'd leaped over the coffee table to him. His shoulders bounced with low coughs and gasps, and his hands searched before finally holding the back of his head.

"Okay," he managed between breaths, "I get it."

"What's that?"

"Don't ever cross you because you could really beat the shit out of me. You proved your point."

"It wasn't quite that."

"Next time you're in a floating screaming trance, I'll try to help you from a distance." He looked up as flecks of drywall and paint fell on his head. "Soft landing, huh?"

"Good thing this place is shitty. Seriously, are you hurt?"

Jamie flexed his fingers and moved his legs. "Everything hurts. But like an equal amount all over. So I think that's good?"

"Come on, let me help you up."

"I'd like to not move if that's okay." He shut his eyes and bit down on his lip as he shifted. "There was a memory. Beyond the void. A rooftop at night."

"With guards. Or soldiers or something."

"You recognize it?" he asked.

"Yeah. But just a flash. That little clip, that's always been there."

"But it's gotta be something. Maybe that's where they did this—" he gestured to her "—to you."

Zoe stood and marched over to her detective board. "A medical facility. Or a prison. Or something like that." She stared at the papers and printouts, names and details. "Nothing like that here." She spun back and looked at Jamie until he locked eyes with her.

"Maybe that's what 2D Industries actually is?"

"More than just leasing shitty apartments?" They both laughed, though Jamie squinted through the pain with each chuckle.

"You need to dig deeper," she finally said.

"Got any body armor?"

"Kinky." For the first time since Jamie arrived, they smiled at each other. It was brief, something that came and went faster than Jamie's flight across the room. But it was there, the smallest of warmth between adversaries.

"I can control it this time," Zoe said. "Promise."

"I, uh…" His voice trailed off. Zoe could feel the weight of skepticism in his eyes. "That, erm, really hurt. I would like to *not* experience that again."

"I can contain it."

Jamie's expression did *not* change, despite her assurances.

"Okay, look," she said. "We're trusting each other, right? So trust me."

Jamie's face turned from wary to a less-skeptical weary smile. "Right. Trust. Just please don't kick me again."

"Seriously," she said, her lip curled up in a grin. "I can hold it in."

Jamie grunted as he struggled to his feet. "I'm pretty sure your neighbors might be freaking out about the screaming and crashing." He propped himself against the wall, teeth visibly clenched. "I think I'd hurt less if you broke every bone in my body."

"Lemme help." Zoe put one arm around his back, then scooped him up by the knees. She levitated them up, floating across the space. As they did, Jamie's legs dangled, and though it seemed to hurt him to turn his neck, he looked down, and she could see a smirk come over his face. She set him down on the futon, moving as slowly and gently as she possibly could.

"So, your neighbors?"

"I've heard worse, actually." Zoe looked off, as if she stared past the stucco and pipes between apartments. "That's the thing about these abilities. You know you can do something about it."

"Do you?" Jamie asked, grabbing his ribs with the question.

"Sometimes. Sometimes I call family services. Sometimes I find other ways to—" she couldn't stop herself from smirking ever so slightly "—intervene. Those rolling blackouts can come in handy if they occur at the right time." Zoe picked up a chair, then plopped down onto it, hands gripping the sides of the seat. "Can we chat about being neighborly later? Come on, something's there and we have to find it. Once you got there, the memory turned from a vague feeling to that *thing*."

"Okay, okay. So much for small talk." Both Jamie and the futon groaned as he sat up. "Anything before or after? I was searching and that was all I found. Like everything around it was scrubbed and they missed that part."

This apartment, it was the first thing she remembered. And that note. She closed her eyes, willing things to go back farther, to bring that moment back.

The stars. The soldiers. The voices.

Bringing it back prompted a nausea in her gut but she forced herself to see and examine it. But nothing moved around the memory. There was no forward or backward, just the moment and what she could pull from it.

"Nothing. We need to go back."

Jamie looked her over, then brought his hands up, flexing them and pulling them. "It's all in the fingers," he said. "Okay. But any screaming or floating and I'm stopping. Got it?"

"Got it." She steadied herself in the chair, back straight and fingers digging into the wicker structure. She watched Jamie close his eyes and put his fingers up. The base of her skull tingled, and Zoe shut her eyes too.

Fortunately, the rest of the evening went by without Jamie sustaining further injuries. Instead, they knelt side by side on the floor, Jamie drinking cup after cup of coffee, both scribbling down furiously on Post-it notes and notebook sheets all of the details they could find.

It came in snapshots, little clips found among huge swatches of nothing. Six hours passed, including a pizza break—Zoe dashed off to get it, but Jamie paid, having recently robbed a bank and all—and yet nothing exactly matched up with the clues on her detective board. If anything, it just made it more of a mess.

"Well, so we know you had parents. And there were a few snapshots in high school but we don't know where."

"And a shitty car. Did you catch a plate on it?" Zoe asked.

"Nope. And I'm terrible with cars, so other than blue, I'm not much help. Other memories, there was snow. It couldn't have been here. But with memory wipes, tiny fragments always remain. It's pretty meaningless without context."

Zoe tapped the sheet at her feet, the rooftop sketch she'd pulled down from her detective board side by side with Jamie's own interpretation from tonight. "This one. There's gotta be something there. I *feel* it," Zoe said.

"You have psychic powers too?"

"No, I just hit people really hard," Zoe offered with a grin.

"And hover. That's kind of better than being psychic. I can't imagine how much money you save that way."

"There is that." Zoe tapped at her crude sketch again. "But no, call it a gut feeling. There's something else. One more try."

Jamie told himself to let go of all the muscles that suddenly tensed up.

"You're giving a look," Zoe said.

"No I'm not."

"Yes you are." Zoe pulled her shoulders up to her ears and looked down while her teeth formed a grimace. "Like this," she said through gritted teeth. "Too much coffee?"

"Not enough. Except—"

"Except what?"

"That memory," he finally admitted. Zoe's drawing wasn't much more than conjoined rectangles or glorified stick figures. "It was the hardest to get. We only got that flash. And even that seemed to be enough to cause you to freak out."

"There has to be more. Come on." She stood up and dashed to the closet. "We are *so* close." Her voice came muffled from the closet, the strange sounds of shuffling and clinking carrying through the space before she emerged holding...

Jamie blinked to make sure he saw it accurately.

A chain.

"Why do you have a chain?"

"Tie me up. Make sure I won't kick you."

"No, why do you have a chain? Chains belong in, like, car repair shops."

"Oh." Zoe stood there, a thoughtful glint coming to her eyes. "It's just, you know, extraordinary strength. Wanted to test it."

It took way longer than Jamie anticipated to wrap Zoe up in the chain. He'd mused that he didn't know if he could untie such a heavy thing, but she assured him she'd break it if absolutely necessary.

Jamie stood over her, the chain wrapping her like the metallic tortilla of an extraordinary burrito. "Chains are way heavier than I thought."

"We'll be fine. Safety first, you know?"

"Right. I may rob banks but I don't have health insurance, so I appreciate avoiding any trips to the hospital."

Links in the chain shifted, creating a symphony of squeaks and pings. Zoe let out a breath and closed her eyes. "Let's go."

Jamie closed his eyes too, his hands extended to lock in. Back he dove, past her conscious time as the Throwing Star, beyond the first few moments in this apartment. The memories they'd uncovered over the past few hours remained, fragments of Zoe's life. But the roof, the soldiers, it stayed elusive, a glint of clarity among a sea of distorted blurs. All he could grab was that one singular image even though he knew she was right.

Something lurked just past that.

"It's no good," Jamie said, his eyes snapping open. "I can't get a good lock. It's like trying to climb up mud."

"Would it help," Zoe asked, her head sticking out from the wrap of chains, "if you got closer? Like touched my forehead?"

A few days ago, Jamie would have assumed such a request was a trap, a way to sucker him in so she might get a good grip for knocking him out. Even with the chains. Now he offered a mix of concern and uncertainty. "I'm not sure if it will help."

"Try it. We're so close."

Jamie put his fingers on Zoe's forehead, but the physical contact didn't change things. Minutes passed, with Jamie trying variations of formations to connect. "Nothing."

Zoe's mouth twisted in frustration. "Can you at least scratch the back of my neck? It itches from all this."

The floor creaked as Jamie knelt down next to her, one hand sliding behind her neck. He'd intended to merely scratch an itch. But as his fingers connected with the base of her skull, a heat radiated off of them; he couldn't tell if that was from her or from him but it drew him in. His hand held the position, locked into the mystery force while the rest of him angled and contorted to lie down next to her. "Wait a minute," he said, now lying sideways, the lower arm still reaching under her neck while the other lightly placed on the wrapped chain for balance. "Stay still." He closed his eyes and found himself sucked right into the vision.

Everything projected with greater vibrancy. The colors shone brighter, the sounds lighter, even a feel of temperature rippled through him. And that moment of Zoe on the roof, he found it with greater ease. Pieces were still missing, but the further he dug, the more scraps appeared—an image, a sound. With each new memory, Zoe's own tension amplified, causing her to shift underneath the chains. Their struggle became unified, and Jamie fought alongside her to keep it together, to prevent her from exploding out of her confines and unleashing a banshee scream that might level the block or at least prompt the neighbors to call the cops.

The images told a story of some sort, and Jamie kept pushing until he could get to a definitive start point. She'd awoken in a room—a cell, all industrial with harsh fluorescent lighting. Groggy, a vague notion of *something* pulling at her, something telling her to run. And the evidence pointed to herself as the catalyst for the destruction around her.

She'd looked down at the floor. Bodies. There were bodies, though she felt shock at seeing them. Then she looked across the room, only to notice that the door had been knocked off its hinges. In fact, it looked like she'd punched it hard enough to knock it down the hall.

"I see it!" Zoe said, her voice bright and urgent. "I'm getting pieces. A room? And…bodies? Are those bodies? Are you seeing those too? Shit, this is just like *Psych Ward Takeover.*"

"I am. Hold steady. Concentrate."

Jamie dove back in. Voices, and then Zoe ran before the voices could catch her. A stairwell, then up to the roof.

"It's going too fast," Zoe said. "I'm missing it."

"Don't worry. Let me read it, you just stay in control."

Several minutes in the dark but then an image appeared. It lay buried, and as Jamie dug further, wiping off the layer after layer of mental fog and dust, Zoe's internal resistance grew. The chains rattled as her body began vibrating, and her teeth clenched, groans of effort filling the room. Heat came off of her, not just from the mental connection but a full-body fever that created a cocoon of warmth. "Keep going!" she yelled through gritted teeth, and he could feel the pushback—for every corner he wiped clean, new obfuscation generated, a battle against mental fog rolling in until he ripped it apart piece by piece.

The image snapped into focus and Zoe's voice roared through the apartment.

"Hold it," he yelled. "Just hang on!"

He kept the image steady, taking it in to absorb whatever details he might find. Nighttime. Rooftop. Eight soldiers in two rows of four. And a lone helmeted figure in official-looking armor came in from behind them, splitting the middle. Audio began fading in and out, and the memory itself blurred even as it continued.

"What's happening?" Zoe asked in the apartment. "I'm losing it."

"Focus. We're almost there."

Voices came through distorted, syllables slurring into each other, and a fuzzy blur moved across her vision. The image sharpened just enough, like staring through a frosted window, and Jamie could see the lead man approach and kneel down. He yelled something, though the helmet's visor muffled his voice even further, even beyond Zoe's weakening connection.

Yet instead of charging, the soldiers in the background remained. And the man leaned forward farther.

"Zoe," Jamie said, "I think this is really important. You gotta push yourself, we're close." Beneath him, she grunted, and things snapped back into focus, except something was different.

The helmeted man's left fist uncurled to reveal writing on the palm. He moved it directly into her view, and in the memory, she struggled to move as if she were...

As if she were stunned.

The only movement she was capable of was involuntary blinking, and her eyes stayed trained forward, on something scribbled on the man's pale skin. Everything blurred before Jamie could catch the details. Zoe's memory connection was loosening.

"Motherfucker," she yelled in the room. "This is *not* easy."

"Hang on, hang on, hang on," he told her before muttering under his breath, "Come on, come on, come on."

The memory returned, a clear and distinct image.

On that rooftop, she had stared at a palm. With a word written across it.

Telos.

Over a scar crossing diagonally across his palm.

A scar that *exactly* matched the one on Jamie's hand. The one he lied to Chesterton about. The one that had been there since day one.

The memory was so clear now, the connection so strong, that clear audio finally returned. "Okay, then." Muffled behind the mask, but Jamie caught enough to notice his British accent. The man spit in his palm and rubbed the word away. "She's ready," he said. Gravel crunched as he stood, both hands extended, fingers vaguely pointed her way. And then the memory went black.

In the apartment, Zoe's howl ramped up into a full body scream, and her vibrating body lifted off the floor despite being weighed down by metal chains. She screamed one more time as the connection severed and she fell to the carpet, unconscious.

That was him. That was him in the vision, and even though it wasn't the cool thing to do with someone you just kind of became friends with, Jamie let Zoe remain passed out for about twenty minutes or so. Other than regularly checking in to make sure she was still breathing, he'd spent that entire time switching between staring at the scar on his hand, pacing around Zoe's apartment, gawking at her detective board and pondering his own memories. When she finally began to stir underneath the chains, Jamie considered the options before him.

Option A: he could tell her. Sub-option to that: he could

leave her chained while he told her. Just in case she didn't take the news well.

Option B: he could leave that information out. Because it sure didn't look good for him to be leading the charge, then brain-stunning her *and* wiping her memory. Why would he leave her a word? A test of some kind, to see if memories carried over? That seemed to be the logical choice given that nothing benev-olent happened during that whole sequence. Chasing someone down with armed guards generally didn't fall under the category of "good buddy behavior."

Jamie didn't know, he didn't *want* to know, he *never* wanted to know, and the universe was forcing his hand into diving back. How deep, how far, he wasn't sure.

But now Jamie and Zoe were linked. And not just by the chain he started to unwrap.

"It was a word," Jamie finally said after it was clear that she was coming back around. He gradually freed her from the chains, and by the time they sat side by side on the futon, he'd made his choice.

"I can't pull any of it," she said. "I get the room. The rest of it is flashes. It's a rooftop. There are people in armor. A hallway leading to it. Little bits like that, but nothing stays long enough to grab details. Hey." She turned to him. "You can try going back in—"

"No." Jamie stood up. "There's no need." He paced over to the window, staring at the side of the neighboring building. If she didn't recall it, then at least she wouldn't know about the scar. At some point, he'd have to tell her. But he needed to understand the hows and whys of every second leading up to that rooftop before he revealed the truth. Even then, maybe he shouldn't.

"I can tell when you're lying, you know."

"What?"

"You're lying. Right now. People's brains stress when they

lie and it shows up in their heat signatures. Unless they're, like, really sociopathic."

Damn it.

"Which, hey, you're not. At least." Zoe offered a smile with her words, which only made Jamie feel even worse.

"I'm not lying," he said, despite knowing he was indeed lying. "Well, look. Yes, I *could* dive back in. But there's no point. You're clearly drained—I mean, you levitated off the floor while screaming. That's not good, you know?"

"Fair point."

"Besides, this word. Let's start with that. No more chains until we figure out what that means." *And no mention of a scar on a hand.*

"You think Telos…" Zoe pointed to the hodge-podge of papers and scribbles that made up her so-called detective board. "Telos, the rooftop, all of it… I mean, it has to tie into our abilities. And our missing memories. Right?"

Jamie pictured the memory again, the scar on the palm as clear as a photograph on a screen. His left hand closed, as if he could will it to go away.

"Has to."

But it didn't go away. It was still there, the knowledge that *he* was somehow involved. Maybe she'd be okay with it.

"I swear," Zoe said, a growl entering into her voice, "if I find any of the motherfuckers who took my memory, I am gonna punch them through, like, ten buildings."

Or maybe not.

Not yet, anyway. No, his plan was sound. That info would stay safely hidden until absolutely necessary.

"Zoe, I promise you. We've got something to go on. That word. It has to mean something. Why would someone leave such a clue?" Jamie asked, catching himself from saying "I."

From behind, he heard her grunt as she stood up. She walked over at a ginger pace, and he didn't need her reading abilities to know she was sore. "Not much of a view, huh?" she asked.

"No. Not until the neighbors put up Christmas lights I bet."

"Yeah." Zoe let out a small laugh. "The family across the way does a good job."

They stood in silence, the rev of passing cars and honking horns coming through the window. The mirror reflection brightened, and Jamie turned to see Zoe tapping at her phone. "Actually, you're right," she said. "We have something to go on."

Jamie's eyes adjusted to the brightness of the screen and he read the website's headline. Telos Foundation for a Better Life.

A foundation. In fact, some sort of mental health rehab center, the kind of place you paid five grand and yelled at pictures of your parents while standing in the woods. Things started to lock into place, and though the gap between that place and the rooftop incident remained wide, they finally had a direction. And a direction meant no need to revisit Zoe's memories. "I'll go tomorrow," Jamie said. "I mean, it's not like I have a job to get to."

"Let's both go." Zoe's response came with wide eyes, a nearly manic energy. "I think the city can live without the Throwing Star for one day." She moved to a counter drawer, pulled out a notepad and pen. "Telos. Let's dig up everything we can on it."

"Look at us, making plans, sharing pizza. Not killing each other." Jamie turned to the open pizza box on the coffee table and grabbed a limp piece, slapping it onto his paper plate, grease pooling beneath it. "Like partners."

"Yeah," Zoe said. "Partners."

Or close to partners, at least. A partnership would imply honesty with each other. But between the scar on Jamie's hand and the mysterious "Stop Her" message, at this moment the only person he could fully trust was himself.

12

JAMIE NEVER DID MEMORY lifts when off the job. In some cases, after he'd safely gotten a few blocks away from the bank he'd just robbed, he'd take a cab, go seven or eight blocks farther, then make sure the cab was safely parked when he removed the driver's memories of their trip—with payment in full left on the seat, of course. He may have been a criminal, but he wasn't a jerk.

Today, however, was different. He'd taken a cab out here, some fifteen miles north of the San Delgado limits, past the long row of docks and across the area's largest bridge—more expensive than getting a ride with OmegaCar, but those only took electronic pay and he wanted to leave zero trace behind. Tucked behind the office towers and the condos built into the sides of the nearby hillscape, a series of three connected buildings sat on the waterfront, the bay breeze swaying surrounding trees. He made the driver park there, then removed the memories of their trip and left cash before walking two blocks over to meet Zoe, who was already waiting for him.

All of that was according to the plan. Which he followed meticulously. So much so that he used the checklist app on his phone to make sure he didn't miss a step.

Zoe, on the other hand, appeared to have forgotten what they'd discussed last night.

"Are you, um, gonna change?" Jamie asked without trying to sound too accusatory.

"What?" Zoe replied. She blinked at him, and he managed a quick gesture at her outfit of track pants, a tank top and a stained dark blue cap with the words *Gone Fishin'* on it, which clearly contrasted his slacks and dress shirt. "You don't like my disguise?" she asked, pointing to the hat. "Found it on a roof, thought it'd be perfect."

After leaving Zoe's, Jamie spent last night reading anything and everything Telos. The facility seemed like an expensive therapy center: addiction, depression, anxiety, midlife crisis or postdivorce soul-searching; under the so-called Telos Principle, all of those things were driven by an underlying root cause they deemed the "catastrophic emotional self." They even had scholarship programs and tiered payments for people with severe issues and no support, and happy patients left all sorts of testimonials for them.

"Oh, it's...it's a cool hat," he said with a forceful nod. "I just thought we were, you know, going to pretend we were inquiring about a tour." That simplified things to the short-short version; in reality, Jamie had texted an entire phased approach after thinking about it during his ride home last night. It involved them pretending to be a couple on the brink of divorce, and they viewed Telos as a way to both heal their relationship and understand their own damage better, but they needed to tour the facility to determine if it was better to visit as individuals or as a couple. That then created a set of options where, if the opportunity presented itself, either could break off into an individual tour to explore, take notes, then examine potential

areas to exploit for further reconnaissance should it feel necessary. Zoe had replied with, *Okay see you there*, which Jamie took
as complete agreement.

But perhaps not.

"We really should look the part," he said, gesturing to himself. "Did you bring a change of clothes?"

"Wait, what tour? What are you talking about?"

"I…" Jamie bit down on his lower lip and he almost dove
into Zoe's mind to see if she remembered texting her reply. "I
sent a plan last night."

"Right. Meet here."

"But to, like, pretend to tour the place so we can assess the
situation. Find clues. Detective stuff to go with your detective
board. You know?"

Zoe's lips pursed as a gust of wind tossed her hair back. She
turned to face the facility, then she looked back at Jamie. "Is
that what that was? Sorry, I was brushing my teeth when you
texted and a bit tired, so I didn't really read it."

Deep breath. Deep, deep breaths. Jamie squashed the urge to
cringe, exhaling at the cognitive dissonance being played out
in real time here. He'd never worked with a partner before, and
maybe that had always been a good thing. "I'm…okay. I think
this can still work but—"

"I thought about it while waiting for you, though. I was just
gonna wing it."

The tour offered a reasonable way to get inside. It was much
better than Zoe's non-plan. "Look, I know we haven't been on
friendly terms for too long, but I just have to say it," Jamie said.
"Winging it is a *terrible* plan. You sure you don't want to take—"

"Nah." Zoe waved it off and looked skyward. "It'll be fine.
Find a way in," she said. "I'm gonna scout."

Find a way in. "Okay, well." Jamie pulled out his phone and
suppressed the urge to sigh. "Just stay in touch." He looked again
at the Okay see you there from late last night; in the midst of

absolutely poor plans for spycraft, there was at least the lovely absurdity that the Mind Robber and the Throwing Star were texting.

Zoe nodded, then crept into a shadowed spot between a building and a tree, she shot off and disappeared vertically, and a *thump* sound above him. He looked over at the Telos building up the small hill, its seemingly benign mix of polite modern architecture and occasional passing traffic feeling so ordinary. Though the facility sat on its own with its rear facing the water, a large fence surrounded the property. At the base of the hill lay a handful of small buildings, some occupied and some for lease, but nothing more than glorified mom-and-pop stores in a sleepy town primarily known for bed-and-breakfast stays and nearby hiking.

But beneath it all, perhaps there was *something* related to the extraordinary. He looked up to track Zoe leaping into a line of trees at the property's edge before heading in.

It was just them. And one of them bounced on rooftops.

Nothing nefarious stood out as the sliding doors opened up to tranquil indoor fountains, soft music and the soothing voice of a woman on a welcome video. He stood in the middle of the large foyer, pretending to take it in but in reality stretching out for a mental lock. A security guard approached, probably to ask him about his business. In his jacket pocket, Jamie flicked a finger, the lightest of brain stuns, something to disorient the man for a few minutes while he scanned around.

He walked up to the front desk, suddenly aware that outside of the stunned security guard, no one was coming or going. In fact, the only entrances or exits were the main doors and, across the lobby, an armored locked door held by an intimidating metal frame, all chrome shine and weighty thickness.

A man sat behind the counter typing away, something he kept doing even while looking up and nodding. Jamie started a short greeting before pausing midsentence. "I should take this," he said, picking up his phone and tapping the side button to make the screen glow. "Hello?" he said to no one in particular.

Walking a good seven or eight feet away, Jamie blended next to an overhanging plant, occasionally nodding or saying benign yesses and nos. All the while, his mind flicked through the memories of the receptionist for something, anything. The most recent images played out as standard office fare, paperwork and spreadsheets and phone calls. He dipped farther back, skimming over the weekend out at a hike and walking an adorable orange corgi. Beyond that, most of his work life involved that desk and the occasional escort of a new patient, though someone else almost always immediately scooped them up and whisked them off down the hall.

In that glimpse, it was clear that things lacked the grim quality of the scene in Zoe's fractured memory. This place could have been any health-care facility built in the past few years.

At least up front. He needed to get inside, a closer look. "Hi, my name is Gordon Wright," he said, using the alias he'd created last night, though the backstory came on the spot. Hopefully his improv skills passed the believability test. "I have a four o'clock appointment for a tour. We are trying to convince my sister to come. She's struggling with a messy divorce and a drinking problem." The words came out smooth but quiet and in his native accent, the complete opposite of the Mind Robber.

"Certainly. I'm sorry you're in that situation but I hope we can help. We have an excellent record of changing people's lives here—" The keyboard clacks stopped as the man frowned. "How do you spell your last name?"

"W-R-I-G-H-T."

"Hmm. I'm sorry, I don't see you booked. Our tours are confidential and coordinated to ensure patient privacy. I'm sure you can understand."

"Right, right. Well, the thing is I flew in from Los Mondas

just for this trip. Can I at least speak to a therapist or program coordinator?"

The man hesitated, looked at his screen and then back up at Jamie. "I think we can try to accommodate that. Let me see..." His fingers flew over the keyboard, clicking away as the screen flashed, illuminating his face in various colors. "A lot of our staff are tied up for the moment but maybe Dr. Waterfield is available." Another few button presses and he began speaking into his headset. "Hi, it's Archie from the front desk. I have someone here who scheduled a tour and we hit a snafu. Can you speak with him a moment? Okay. Okay. Great. Sorry about the short notice." He looked back up and nodded. "Dr. Waterfield will be right up. In the meantime, I need you to sign in."

Winging it, indeed.

He pulled out a tablet from a drawer, then handed it over. "And I'll need your phone."

"My phone?"

"We respect the privacy of our patients. To ensure that, we check in the phones of all visitors to ensure no recordings or photographs can be made. You must understand, many of our patients come from volatile situations and are in fragile states. That kind of intrusion can lead to undo stress."

"Right, right. Okay." Jamie pulled up his text messages and quickly tapped one to Zoe. Going in. Will be off-line for a bit.

"Thank you," the man said, taking his phone. He put it into the drawer, then locked it. "It'll be right here when you leave."

Jamie used a tablet to fill out—bullshit—a registration form, complete with selfie photo. A badge was printed out on a small counter console, and Jamie turned to see a pleasant woman, tanned face and close-cropped hair, in a white doctor's coat. "I'm sorry about the scheduling issues. I'm happy to show you around." The massive door opened with several clicks and beeps.

"Please," Jamie said, shaking her hand. "I'm very curious about this place."

★ ★ ★

Dr. Waterfield's sheer niceness unnerved Jamie. "We have patients from all over the country. Even international," she said. "We're only five years old but we're developing quite a reputation. I'm sorry I can't give you a proper tour. There are a lot of rules around that."

Jamie nodded, his eyes drawn down to the scar on his hand. It traveled from right below the forefinger all the way to the opposing wrist, an exact line in a clean diagonal. Was it the result of a cooking accident? A car crash? As he studied it, a low nausea started in his gut and he looked away, focused elsewhere to reset everything.

In the end, maybe it didn't matter. The whole life before this life stayed safely put aside *except* for being on the rooftop with Zoe that night. Why would he be leading those soldiers?

The best bet for that answer, for Zoe's past, for all of it, sat in the computer on the desk. From the reflection in Dr. Waterfield's glasses, the screen still appeared dim. He needed data and access, some way in front of the keyboard, then a path past whatever security protected the data. "Since I can't tour the facility, can you tell me about some of your patients? I get that there's patient confidentiality. But just keeping their anonymity, what kinds of people come here? How long they stayed, their successes, beyond what's on the website."

"Sure. I understand that this is a big life decision." She tapped a key in rapid fire and finally the screen came to life. She hit a few more keys, then poised her hands to type before striking Enter. The reflection changed again. "Let's see what I can tell you about."

"I appreciate it. My sister, it'll take a lot to convince her to come here. We'll need all of the reasons we can get."

"Of course. And we have coordinated with families to prepare for imminent arrivals. Our programs range from weekend intensive therapy to three-week facility stays, and those include some overnights out in our beautiful redwood forests. There's little that's better for the soul..." As she continued, her attention focused on the screen, enough that Jamie's subtle hand movements went unnoticed. She was halfway through insurance coverage details when her eyes grew wide and her expression went blank.

Jamie had done probably fifty or so brain-stuns by this point, enough that the process was old hat. But given the stakes here, the strange normalness of the facility and its security, he didn't take anything for granted. One hand waved in front of Dr. Waterfield's face, then another. With nary a blink in reaction, he ran to the keyboard before it could time out.

She was in. Thus, he was in.

Every brain-stun was a little different. And usually he didn't stay on scene to gauge how long the victims stayed stunned. For the purposes of digging up confidential patient info, those metrics would have helped.

The clock showed a quarter past four, and an internal deadline of ten minutes seemed like a safe bet. Simply stunning her again was feasible if necessary, but given that he'd never stunned anyone multiple times, best not to start experimenting now. Instead, he wheeled her static body several feet over, the chair squeaking with each inch, and he hunched over the keyboard.

She was in a patient database. A list of names sorted by check-in time. There were other fields: a line for conditions, discharge date, current status.

And next to all of that, some of the patients had photos.

Think, think, think. He'd woken up in the apartment nearly, what was it...twenty-two months ago.

He used that as a starting point, then started sorting beyond that time range. The little wheel on the mouse clicked as he scrolled, pictures flying by of different faces.

And there it was, about two and a half years prior.

The hair was different, it was nearly shaved off. The eyes

weren't focused; in fact, they looked tired, defeated. But he knew that face, the wide chin, thin mouth, and deep eyes.

He saw that face every morning. And he tried not to think about it.

He *was* here. But how did that lead to him joining a commando group that hunted down an unleashed extraordinary patient?

Urges pulled at Jamie to shut it down, leave it behind, leave Zoe's crusade and run off. But the guilt gnawed at him, always the guilt slowing things down until no other thoughts entered. Maybe guilt was an additional ability of his.

Forget the guilt, he told himself, mentally pushing the rooftop away. Instead, he imagined a tropical beach, the peace and quiet attainable only when stability deemed the Mind Robber unnecessary. Once he helped Zoe, then he'd get his money and he could disappear to a warm, sunny place where that rooftop, that moment, really didn't matter.

He double-clicked the profile and forced himself to read the name, a tremble rippling through his fingers.

Frazer Troughton.

He wasn't sure what he expected, like if a thousand light bulbs were to activate in his memory. But they didn't. Nothing budged, not even random memory snapshots like what he'd unearthed for Zoe.

He counted down, and he told himself it was fine.

He scanned through the profile fields and saw nothing surprising, but at least it was specific. A birthday, an address. And a strange status: *Sent to Reconditioning Facility.*

Could that be the place from Zoe's memory? At this point, she might have been either soaring among the rooftops or off the wagon at the closest liquor store. He clicked open a web browser but the immediate page was a reminder that only the Telos internal network was available for patient safety purposes.

With no external web and no phone, digging deeper into the mystery reconditioning facility would have to wait.

A quick time check showed six minutes had passed. The clock was ticking, and a glance back showed Dr. Waterfield remained stunned, though he didn't know for how long. He was about to scroll through other profiles when he noticed a tab labeled Intake Comments.

A quick click revealed a thumbnail image of himself, apparently seated at a desk not unlike this one, a small triangle icon indicating it was a playable video.

Leave the past behind. That's what he told himself. Even seeing his old name and other tidbits from his old life, it conjured zero emotion. He was fine being Jamie, he didn't have a big gap to fill, no burning desire like Zoe fought.

But maybe there'd be a piece of the truth there. The truth that mattered, anyway. Jamie's finger rested on the mouse button, the cursor lingering over the play icon. Questions and doubts dug in, preventing him from moving, even the tiny twitch of a finger needed to click a button.

13

ZOE OPTED TO WATCH a movie.

At first, it was because twenty minutes passed and her sur-
veillance proved to be dull. Seriously, how did people do stake-
outs for hours on end? She opened HorrorDomain and loaded
a movie with a werewolf, whose foam head barely stayed on,
fighting zombies who were just people in ratty clothes and green
makeup. She kept it going, half watching while moving from
place to place, as her amplified hearing caught snapshots of employee and patient conversations from balconies and open windows and courtyards. All benign. Someone's kid had a hockey
game soon. Someone's spouse forgot dinner last night. Someone complained about his car having a rattling sound. A group
of patients discussed what it really meant to make amends, and
that held her interest for a few seconds until the werewolf found
herself in a graveyard against an army of zombies.

Even though people walked the grounds in everyday clothes,
they all wore lanyards—patients at this facility, she assumed. She

vaulted to the Telos building rooftop, occasionally stopping at a ventilation unit and pretending to mess with the access panel on it in case anyone caught a glimpse of her and wondered why she was there.

It wasn't until she got to the very back of the structure that she noticed a separate entrance, fenced off from the rest of the seemingly friendly and professional facility. It led to a small driveway that descended into what appeared to be an underground level. A white van, unmarked other than several numbers on the side and a license plate, sat idling by.

Next to it stood two security guards.

Their vests, the position of a radio on their shoulders, the curved edge of the helmet brim and holsters with pistols hanging on shoulders, all seemed a bit much for a therapeutic retreat.

She paused the movie.

Adrenaline pumped, a momentum pushing so hard that she needed to steady herself. Zoe crept down the side of the building, hovering while grabbing ledges and vents for balance. She remained a good fifteen or twenty feet above them, then wedged herself into a corner, as covered in shadows as possible. She zeroed in with her hearing, trying to pick up anything from the guards or their walkie-talkies. One leaned against the truck until the sound of a heavy gate rumbled, then the squeaking of wheels.

Zoe hunched over, hands clinging against the corner of the building's facade, nails digging so hard that the brick started to crumble under the pressure.

Her ears picked up some unintelligible mumbling. If she'd been closer, she might have been able to put a face to the sound. Instead, it got masked by the opening of the van's back doors. More walkie-talkie chatter cut through, and while describing drive times came one repeated word. A name? A code word? She wasn't sure.

Reconditioning.

Her pocket buzzed, and she hung on with one hand while checking her phone. Going in, the text read. Will be off-line for a bit.

Jamie was in but couldn't help her right now. She considered breaking into this place, kicking down doors and punching out security until she found a firm answer. But given the dashes of violence from her memory, the decision for stealth won out.

And Jamie said winging it wasn't a good plan.

Zoe waited. One guard got in the passenger side while the other circled the perimeter before climbing into the back. The doors slammed shut and the van roared to life. Zoe weighed her options and how much time she had to choose.

Fuck it. At least this was going somewhere.

She leaped off the ledge, then hovered down over the vehicle's roof. She touched down with the slightest of impact, hopefully a noise no bigger than a bump in the road, then lay flat on the roof. She pulled her phone out to send a message to Jamie.

This might take a while.

The last time Zoe had hung on top of a moving vehicle was nearly a year ago. Back then, she'd merely been exploring the range of her abilities, but no one had heard of the Throwing Star yet—not even her.

That night began like most of her nights. She'd finished with her FoodFast deliveries and was rewarding herself the only way she knew how: with two plastic bottles of the cheapest possible vodka in her arms. She fumbled in her back pocket for the twenty-dollar bill she knew she'd put there earlier.

"Go ahead of me." She sighed as she motioned the pair of men behind her to the counter. She'd almost given up her search, but was trying one last chance through all her pockets when she realized one of the men was staring at her.

The other had a gun pointed at the cashier.

"You," the armed man said to the cashier, whose arms were held straight up. "Empty the register. Fast. No tricks."

The words triggered a realization in her: even though she only watched horror movies, she *still* knew that the thug's words were as cliché as it got. That triggered a laugh, first stifled, then a snort too loud to ignore, prompting all three men to turn her way.

"Something funny?" the triggerman said. "You, keep filling the bag. And you, you wanna say something?"

Maybe it was her lack of a past. Or the urge to do more than just be a FoodFast delivery person—a good one, for sure, but still just a delivery person.

Or maybe it was just funny.

"Sorry. It's just what you said. It's super cheesy. Couldn't you at least, you know, be original?"

The gunman's eyes widened. His partner, though, started snickering, which prompted a daggered look from the man with the firearm.

"She's kind of right, bro," the other man said.

"Shut up—"

"I just mean—"

"SHUT UP—"

In that split second, Zoe recognized that the two men took their focus off the robbery and instead turned to each other.

They were distracted.

Zoe made a single firm decision to change her life. She sprung forward faster than anyone in the small shop had likely seen a human move before. The gun dropped to the floor and Zoe spun on her heel, her arm extending into the now-disarmed gunman. He flew into a display of six-packs, the whole thing collapsing on him. He lay prone, breathing, but only a low groan coming from him.

"Oh fuck!" yelled his partner, and he dashed out the door.

Behind the counter, the cashier hammered the alarm button. Zoe turned, her eyes tracking the heat signature as it sprinted away, growing smaller and smaller. It stopped, then the outline knelt down—hesitating or hiding or possibly something else. Whatever the reason, he froze.

Meaning if Zoe really, really wanted to go after him, she could.

She turned, focus cycling between the cashier and the knocked-out robber and the one halfway to escape. If she let him go, would he do it again? If he was capable of this kind of violent crime, what else would he do?

Her instincts told her to get her shit, go home, forget all this. But a scream and a yell came from the street, amplified by her heightened hearing.

She had a choice here. Even though it fought against her instinct to take the easy way out, she still had to make a choice.

"Keep an eye on him," Zoe said to the cashier, pointing at the incapacitated man before running out the door.

At that time of night, the streets saw little activity, the sidewalks even less. Zoe's heightened hearing picked up panicked footsteps across the street. She dashed, suddenly feeling vibrant and alive in a way that had seemed impossible before, and looked to both sides.

A heat signature showed up across the street.

Then footsteps, followed by the slam of a car door.

The alley.

Zoe took three giant steps forward, then a hard turn as she propelled herself down the garbage-scented alleyway. Headlights popped on; though blinded, she still tracked the man's heat signature. The engine revved, and Zoe grabbed a garbage bin, its bottom scraping against the pavement as she lifted it with one hand and hurled it at the car like a pitcher tossing the worst-smelling baseball of all time. The bin crashed on the windshield, cracking it and splattering filled plastic bags around. The car lurched forward with a tire squeal; Zoe jumped up, and out of instinct her hands went palm down, a strange magnetic bounce pushing against them.

And suddenly she was hovering. Not for long, just a flash, but enough for her to notice that the usual rise and fall of physics weren't applying. She let go, and landed knee-first on top of the shitty sedan. The front edge of its decade-old sunroof was propped open a sliver, enough for a handhold, but as the driver punched it and turned hard, momentum nearly tossed Zoe off. The instinct that told her to put palms out to hover fired again, prompting her to do a similar gesture to balance herself from flying off the car roof.

They sped down one block, then two, then three, all the while Zoe's hearing picking up an endless spew of cursing over the engine's *chugga-chugga*. She looked ahead at an otherwise empty street, not even headlights bearing down on the opposite side. Her mind clicked, figuring out all sorts of dangerous—but cool—possibilities, and the opening was clear.

Metal and plastic ground and bent as she twisted at the sunroof until it sheared off in her hands. She reached down for the man, who fortunately—unfortunately, really—forgot to buckle his seat belt. Holding him by the scruff of his jacket, she leaped off, kicking the car as she did to barrel it onto its side. It rolled, crunching glass and metal and plastic with each rotation, and the geriatric engine mercifully pumped its last breath.

Her feet landed together and she held the man up against the gated front of an electronics shop, his trembling mouth a mix of spittle and lost syllables. "Stop stealing shit," she yelled, and when he didn't respond, she did it again at twice the volume. "Stop. Stealing. Shit. Okay?"

He barely got a response out when she slugged him across the chin, her control of the punch a tad bit looser than she would have liked. But still. No permanent damage, and she got the point across.

That first night, the sheer thrill of taking on the bad guys—

no, *punching* the bad guys—had been her gateway into becoming San Delgado's hero. And if not hero, then at least headline-making vigilante, when time allowed.

Until recently, that was. This hero biz was starting to get into her blood.

And while this trip on the van rooftop wasn't quite as eventful yet, something was about to unfold. Because straight down a deserted two-lane road was a row of chain-link fences and guard stations, and beyond it sat an industrial mess of lights, concrete and steam.

14

FOUR MINUTES LEFT. ALTHOUGH, Jamie had made the estimate with some degree of safety built in, so probably five or six minutes to go. But he couldn't push it much further than that, especially because Dr. Waterfield's phone had already rung twice.

Still, the video taunted him. He *told* himself that the past didn't matter, and he certainly believed it.

But that was before a possible answer stared him in the face. Zoe sought this out. He never did. Except neither of them had ever had a chance to actually know more.

That was the catch, wasn't it?

He could still watch it, maybe even get a clue about how he'd wound up on the roof with Zoe. And the past *still* didn't have to matter. Those two ideas could coexist. If it was too damn devastating for him, there was always the whole memory removal thing. He was, after all, the Mind Robber.

The thumbnail loaded to a full-screen image, a static camera that framed his face just off-center. His features showed the inverse of today: close-cropped buzz cut instead of a longer fop and a thick stubble instead of clean-shaven. The eyes too. They carried a different feeling from what he saw these days. Heavy. Unfocused. A little lower, the thin crooked line between lips seemed unfamiliar, and lower still, the slouched shoulders told their own story.

"Tell us why you're here," a voice said off camera.

"I'm here, well…" Still an English accent. "I mean, why else do people get help? You know? I've made my money. My products have come to market, been bought by bigger companies, turned into commodities. That's not a reason to come to rehab. No, you fuck up your life enough, the lives of people around you. I drank too much. But that was only a symptom. And it's either they say stop or you say stop."

"That's why you're here? You said stop?"

Video Jamie looked down and bit on his bottom lip. Five or six seconds passed, the only noise the hiss from the microphone.

"No. He did. And when I didn't listen, he left."

"We hear that a lot. Choosing to get help can be an essential step in reuniting couples after alcohol fractures their relation-ship—"

"There's no reuniting." In the video, Jamie's mouth and brow finally matched the look in his eyes. "Francisco's gone. When he makes a decision like that, it's final. I get it. He gave me enough chances. I mean, if someone wrecked what I wrecked, I don't know if I'd give them a second chance. Or a fifth chance or whatever."

"You blame yourself?"

"Well, someone was too hungover to make it to the adop-tion interview. I'll give you one guess who that was. Look, I'm a bullshitter at heart. It's how I got everything. I can't code, I can't debug, I can't do any of that. But I can convince anyone that anything is a great idea. Even myself."

"I see."

"If I ever need a reminder, I have this." On the screen, Jamie held up a bandaged hand. "My last bender. Fell through a glass coffee table. When your husband leaves you and you slice up your hand, that's kind of like rock bottom, isn't it?"

In the office, Jamie matched the on-screen pose, hand held up. Except there was no bandage in the present, just a scar that cut deeper than he'd thought.

"Well, Frazer, we want to help. We have one of the highest success rates in the country. Our methodology is holistic—mind, body and spirit. Past, present and future. Your pain isn't about the drinking or what you call 'bullshitting' or work. It's what those do for you. But the thing is, once you identify that, heal it, get your mind and body and heart healthy, you'd be surprised at how strong you can be. Maybe your husband will like that version of you. More importantly, maybe you'll like that version of you."

"Maybe."

"So, what are your goals?"

"Me? At this point, I'd like to just disappear. Not bother anyone. Not make a fuss. Just—" on-screen Jamie shook his head and took in a long draw of air "—be."

"We'll do our best. Oh, and I'm required to tell you that we do offer a unique new treatment protocol for the most extreme circumstances. It's experimental and completely voluntary. Sometimes people need something more, and that's what this is. Honestly, it is privately funded and proprietary, so even I don't know the specifics. But if you're interested, I will let Dr. Kaftan know."

Kaftan.

From behind Jamie, Dr. Waterfield groaned, and rather than sitting motionless, her hands moved to her stomach. The phone rang again, and that seemed to trigger little bits of consciousness, prompting her to go from blank stupor to gradual awakening. Jamie closed the video, then skimmed through the files, jumping ahead months.

Thumbnails of faces came and went, names that meant nothing, the same categorizations over and over: discharged, completed and variations on that, but only a handful mentioned reconditioning. Jamie clicked on a random one, a woman named Susan. He scanned the information as fast as he could, but everything here seemed to match expectations with a rehab facility: her sister held an intervention. She put grad school on hold. She had talked through sexual abuse from a neighbor at age thirteen, which she'd previously hidden from her family. She got physically healthy. She understood the how and why of everything, who she hurt and the impact of her choices. And she left. The column for Current Status noted a courtesy check-in with a thank-you note sent from her three months ago, and that she was happy and sober and finishing her graduate degree.

No indication that she'd gained extraordinary abilities.

Dr. Waterfield grumbled again, except now she started to blink.

Jamie closed the profile, then skimmed the list again, a last gasp for any further information.

Then he saw it.

The face was hers. The hair, the eyes, everything was exactly the same.

Even the name. The name was exactly what he expected: Zoe Wong.

Zoe's her real name.

This was everything Zoe sought. This was her path to whatever sense of peace she needed, and for him too. Except his came in the form of a lot of money and a plane ticket elsewhere.

"Where...what?"

Jamie turned on his heel. Dr. Waterfield stared at him—or really, more through him. Jamie remembered the way he'd felt after he lifted his own memory, the strange sense of floating back into his own body, aware but not really.

A knock rapped against the door. "Dr. Waterfield?"

"Where am...who are..."

"Dr. Waterfield? Your patient is waiting."

He double-clicked the profile and it exploded on-screen.

"Dr. Waterfield?"

The doorknob turned.

Dr. Waterfield groaned again.

Jamie let the screen be and scurried into the corner as the door swung open. "Hey, you all—" The words stopped midsentence. Jamie put his hands down from the brain-stun.

Dr. Waterfield had turned her attention to the newcomer, though her focus still floated. More voices came from the hallway and Dr. Waterfield's phone rang again. Jamie put one shoulder under the newcomer's arm and yanked, though his legs stayed put, leaving Jamie to awkwardly bend him at the waist. He stepped behind, pushing his legs like an exoskeleton until he had enough clearance to shut the door. His fingers flew up, ready to do their surgery; he dove into Dr. Waterfield's mind and plucked out the last ten minutes or so, everything between greeting Jamie and the moment he sat down. Between that and the brain-stun, he figured she'd felt like she'd spun around too fast—or she just woke up from a bender. Probably somewhere in between.

Jamie dashed back to the computer to learn Zoe's past, but it was frozen behind stock images of tranquil scenes: a bluebird on a branch, an ocean at sunset, the earth from space. Jamie punched the enter key, and a log-in came up, the images still cycling behind them.

But he needed a password.

Jamie dove back into Dr. Waterfield's memories, but she hadn't looked at the keys when typing in her password. The audio fragments of her mind didn't help; logging in had been autopilot for her. "Damn it," Jamie said before looking around the room and typing anything that might have been an appropriate password until the log-in box turned red.

You have exceeded the maximum number of log-in attempts. Please contact the Help Desk to unlock your system.

Shit.

A name would have to be good enough. He told himself that, but it didn't feel good enough, just like knowing he'd been on the rooftop didn't feel good enough without the *why*.

The desk chair squeaked as Jamie shuffled Dr. Waterfield out of her doctor coat. He put it on himself, the too-tight shoulders draping over him like a spandex, though he wasn't feeling particularly costume-worthy at the moment. He adjusted it at the lapels, making sure it sat the least awkward way possible before finally leaving.

As Jamie closed the door behind him, Dr. Waterfield's phone rang one more time. He ignored it and hustled to the elevator, arms crossed to hide her badge. All around, staff passed by, coming and going to different doors, different hallways. He scanned around him, pinpointing all the possible areas of cross traffic and security cameras.

He needed the fastest, safest route out of there.

15

SUNSETS WERE PRETTY FROM the top of a moving vehicle.

The sky had turned to a blend of oranges and purples by the time they pulled into...wherever it was they were. Somewhere a good hour or so outside of San Delgado, somewhere where cell phone signals were nonexistent.

Of course, that might have had more to do with Zoe using the world's cheapest provider rather than any sort of secret jamming tech. She'd stayed on her back the entire time, fingers wrapped around the roof racks for stability, her body only shifting with braking or turning. She wasn't sure if anyone even noticed that, hey, a woman clung onto the top of that van. With her hair under a hat and an effort to stay as flat as possible in her "all black but not Throwing Star" garb, she may have just looked like a piece of rumpled debris at a glance.

By the time they'd escaped city limits, traffic lessened with every passing mile, an eight-lane highway whittling gradually to a two-lane road. Zoe had no memory of ever doing a scout program, but she knew enough about sunrises and sunsets to know that they'd headed mostly east.

And that there was pretty much nothing else around.

The van paused at the gate, and Zoe heard low-key identification chatter before it pushed forward. A quick look ahead showed a parking lot with a mix of everyday passenger vehicles and unmarked vans similar to the one she rode on. Air slapped against Zoe's cheeks when she leaped off, and jagged ridges of bark dug into her palms as she clung to a tree and watched the van roll out of view.

Shadows had already begun descending around her, and she surveyed the scene. One main entrance was at the front, probably with all sorts of badge-protected doors and live security. A few floors up, the heat signatures of two people came through on a balcony, though their casual posture suggested it was simply people taking a break.

The building itself looked like a combination of an old refinery and an abandoned hospital. A tower stood, surrounded by stacks blowing out steam, and in front of that lay smaller structures, all with scattered lights creating an industrial constellation in front of her.

What was this place? And why would a rehab facility be associated with it? Zoe checked her phone again, and though she didn't get any signal, she at least was able to take some photos.

The van pulled into a small loading dock almost directly beneath her. Its occupants stepped out, one with the gait of calm professionalism and the other with glances of nervousness. They opened the back double doors, and a few *click* noises later, a gurney rolled out.

On it, a prone man, gray straps crossing the olive hue of his barrel chest. A breathing mask covered his face and an IV was embedded into his right arm, a bag of fluid attached to a hook next to him. The duo rolled the gurney, one person in the front and one person in the back, only to stop and punch in an intercom. "Retrieval team two-three-three with a live specimen for Project E."

Specimen?

Was she once a specimen too?

"Understood. Someone will be down to bring the specimen in."

The van's duo engaged in small talk, oblivious to her presence. Sports, local restaurants, the sort of typical discussion coworkers had—except this was over the body of some prone individual, at some remote facility that had layers of security measures to protect it.

Through the building, faint heat signatures started to track—a single person leading, flanked by two others on each side. The leader walked with a steady cadence, a coolness so strong it felt like a beacon through the concrete and metal.

At the balcony, the duo appeared to be finishing up—the *thunk-thunk* of a trash lid opening combined with the scuffing of a shoe sole putting out a cigarette.

The front entrance or the balcony? One had all sorts of people coming and going, possibly armed and at least on alert. The other was two people finishing a break.

Path of least resistance.

Tree branches shook as Zoe propelled herself off them and over a second layer of barbed wire fencing to catch the left side of the main tower, a structure that seemed to have six or seven floors. Her hands found holds, rigid and angular: vents, pipes, awnings, shingles, helping her scamper up and around the balcony with spiderlike ease. She was up above the small landing when her foot slipped and a chunk of loose concrete kicked free, landing in between the two men.

These guys weren't guards. Scientists, maybe, or technicians or something. Regardless, as Zoe dropped, she told herself to *not* hurt them too bad. If only she had Jamie here to stun them, remove their memories. Instead, one roundhouse kick clipped the first in the jaw, while the second withstood an open palm to the nose. Both collapsed, the second man's nose bleeding enough to create a small pool next to the extinguished cigarette. She grabbed the ID badges from both of them, then buzzed herself in.

Messier than she would have liked. But sometimes a blunt instrument got the job done.

Harsh fluorescent lighting filled the space, and the hallways were devoid of any corporate niceties. No artwork hung on the walls, just signs identifying wings and doors, along with the occasional screen cycling through reminders to lock up desks when leaving for the night and security schedules. She wandered, her thermal vision and heightened hearing allowing her to stay out of the way, though *where* she headed remained undecided. She went with the logic of the higher the floor, the more important it was, and within the walls she'd found that her distant heat sensing had much better range than peeking in from the outside, probably due to the layers of insulation, piping and concrete keeping out the elements.

On her way up the final flight of stairs, a color caught her eye. She blinked, thinking it was a flicker of something else, maybe even dust in her eye from the industrial air. But as her boots echoed down the cavern of the stairwell, it grew in intensity step by step.

A deep, burning red. Like someone had painted the color of blood in her eye. By the time she exited the stairwell, it might as well have been a spotlight. She marched silently, using that image as her compass, and every ten feet or so, the lights flickered—not the buzzing of dying fluorescent bulbs, but a systematic on and off with rapid frequency, as if someone had hacked into the wiring and set it to switch at rapid intervals.

The halls eventually funneled into a longer hallway, doors on either side. And at the end, another door, but one with a blacked

out window and what looked like extra security. Through the
end door, the red heat signature intensified.

Only one way to go.

She stepped carefully, marveling how this hallway mirrored
what she'd seen in *Psych Ward Takeover*: the faded paint, the clip-
boards hanging on the walls, the occasional cart of deactivated
medical devices. That movie ended with a guy wrapped in gauze
terrorizing a pretty blonde night-shift nurse in a too-short skirt.

This would be different. Zoe's tensed body and extraordinary
strength would make sure of that.

The door buzzed as it accepted her badge, letting her into a
new space—a brightly lit small hallway, the only thing of note
being the heavy door at the end and the digital clock above it,
large blue digits tinting the color of the space.

No other doors. No guards. But one glance showed something much more important.

It had *clues*. The view synced into her recovered memories.
Sliced and fragmented, but still a mirror image to what she'd
seen, from the layout to the lighting. Those existed as fragments
in her mind, but being in this space cranked her recall, pieces
falling into place. *What* this place was, she didn't know, but it
was important. It was involved.

She pushed the images aside, past and present melding into
one before she turned to the oversize hunk of metal at the end
of the hall.

The door was smooth and completely flat outside of pock-
marks worn by time and usage. No knob offered entry. Instead,
a small black panel with a tiny blue light sat adjacent to the door.

And a security camera above.

Zoe considered punching it out, but the element of surprise
was probably gone by now. Or maybe no one noticed. She was,
after all, still standing there.

A quiet-but-harsh buzz played when she tried the first badge.
But the second one received a simple beep, and three deep *thunk*

noises came from the door, followed by a click and a motor sound. A hydraulic released and the door swung inward.

She stepped in, a light from ahead causing her eyes to adjust to the contrast between bright and dim. Farther in, lamps glowed—not the cheap fluorescents of the hallways, but bright and warm, making it easy to take in the array of panels and buttons and screens. Above the controls and monitors sat a large window separating this observation room from what looked like a lab space. Beeps and boops fired off at regular rhythms, and the volume of instrumentation overwhelmed her hearing. Trails of wires and cables snaked into the space beyond the window, traversing from above into hanging tendrils that ultimately terminated into a capsule that glowed red.

No. That wasn't it.

Zoe blinked her eyes and squinted, turning down the volume of her thermal sensing. It withered, turning translucent. There was a man inside the capsule.

The capsule wasn't glowing red. That was the man's heat signature, seemingly a product of all the tubes and wires tied into his body.

16

JAMIE DECIDED AGAINST ANY further brain-stuns, and instead, he walked holding up a random document grabbed from Dr. Waterfield's desk, all in an effort to keep people from asking him anything. One man shot him a strange look and he debated whether or not to remove any trace of himself from the man's memory. Speed won out and he moved swiftly to the elevator.

The button lit with a glowing blue and Jamie waited for the whirring gears and pulleys to announce the elevator's imminent arrival. It chimed and the doors slid open, revealing an empty space.

He stepped in, halfway to the goal of exiting this place. It rumbled and hummed, bringing him lower while he pondered what to tell Zoe. Her name, her real name, but then what? The fact that they were both patients here? The seemingly normal facade? The fact that he was the one responsible for her missing memories?

His own discovered history?

He pushed that question aside, but it kept fighting back. Images from the interview, Frazer's voice—*his* own voice—all crashed into his mind, as if hitting the damn play button on the video unleashed a torrent of thoughts and feelings without the memories to sort them into proper context.

The elevator continued to rumble, and he told himself to at least freak out about his identity later. Surely Frazer would agree to that, given the circumstances.

His hands clasped, thumb instinctively rubbing the scar on the other palm. This place—that was the appropriate mystery to ponder at the moment. And nothing explained the "Stop Her" message—who was *she*? It *might* be Zoe still. It made sense, given that she was handed a name and something of an identity right away, like whoever it was behind this knew that she'd be punching and flying. Or maybe it was a metaphor, like how people used feminine pronouns for boats.

Maybe.

The elevator chimed again with three floors to go. Jamie sunk into the corner, eyes planted firmly on the floor and arms folded across his chest. He didn't look up when a woman walked in, though she seemed to hesitate for a moment. From the corner of his eye, he picked up small details about her: she stood nearly as tall as him and also wore a white lab coat, which contrasted with the rich brown fingers sticking out of the sleeves. Her lab coat rested half-open over a purple dress and black shoes, but she had no photo badge or other identification.

It didn't require psychic powers to know that she looked him over, more so than his other encounters—in fact, even more than Dr. Waterfield did during the start of their interview. She shifted her balance, her posture leaning in like a shadow draping over him, and though she stayed quiet, he swore he heard her inhale sharply.

The elevator chimed to announce their arrival on the ground floor. Jamie broke past the woman, who remained standing, and though the exit was to the right, he turned left toward the bathroom signs.

The door locked behind him, thankfully a single private stall. A tremor rippled through his hands as he fought his way out of the coat. The hinged lid of a waste bin swayed back and forth after he pushed the coat all the way to the bottom. Outside, voices came and went, along with the buzz of the PA and the sound of footsteps.

Jamie waited until no further sounds floated through the door. Just to be safe, he reached out with his mind, feeling for the presence of anyone else. When he'd done this before, it was to confirm he'd accounted for all the people in a bank.

Today was about a clean exit.

With no other minds popping up on his radar, Jamie turned the door handle, the locking mechanism clicking as it released. He swung the door open and turned to the exit.

He stopped immediately. The woman from the elevator was standing in the middle of the hallway.

In the middle of his path.

Her unblinking eyes locked on his, stealing his breath. "Excuse me," he said, "I've just finished a tour and I'm going to talk to my family."

The woman nodded and stepped aside, an arm extended toward the front lobby. "I hope you found everything you were looking for," she said, a hint of a South Asian accent to her words. She smiled, though they never broke eye contact, as if *she* was trying to probe him. Jamie centered himself, a quick sanity check to make sure he didn't feel the tingling at the base of his skull associated with a mind invasion.

"Thanks," he said, forcing out a smile.

"Let me walk you to the lobby."

"Oh no, that's fine. I remember the way."

"I insist."

"Um...all right." Jamie began a swift walk, telling himself to be casual but quick. She kept pace, and he strategically positioned his fingers to attempt to pry into her mind.

But nothing worked. It may as well have been a psychic brick wall. The realization caused him to stop and look at her out of pure instinct.

Nothing seemed out of the ordinary with this woman. She was dressed professionally, shoulder-length black hair with a slight wave, and she wore a light amount of makeup, perfectly expected for a fortysomething woman at a health-care facility. There was no magnetic helmet or magic pendant or anything else obvious that would prevent him from locking on.

Yet, this marked the first time he *hadn't* been able to break into a mind.

The realization caused him to step away from her, something that didn't change the woman's neutral look. "Something the matter?"

"No," he said after a second. "No, I was just wondering how we might be able to afford a place like this for my sister."

"Ah. Well, we offer a few different payment plans. Your sister may qualify for a scholarship. Our priority is the health and stability of our patients."

"Right, right. I should go, I have to call my family." This time, Jamie walked straight to the door, his pace far quicker than a casual stride, but he didn't care. He jammed his hand against the panel to open the main lobby access door, its heavy secured weight and tight hydraulics making a mere second feel like hours before it began to swing open.

"Let us know if you have any questions, Mr. Wright," the woman called.

Jamie shuffled silently through the checkout procedure at the reception area. The fact that she knew his alias, the fact that she watched him sign forms and get his phone back, all of it propelled him to take each step a little faster on his way out.

Twenty minutes later, Jamie sat in the backseat of his Omega-Cars pickup, wondering if probing the driver's mind would cause them to veer off the highway. He'd stayed quiet the entire time, lost in thought from the moment he opened the app to hail a ride to this moment, sitting in commuter traffic. The only time he broke out of it was for the odd sight of a helicopter leaving the back area of the Telos grounds, and when he realized that Zoe had sent a text about following a lead that included a selfie from apparently on top of a van traveling down a two-lane highway. A quick probe into the mind of the driver showed that he wasn't on the Telos payroll, though he did give his sick cat regular IV treatments. Jamie made a mental note to leave him a bigger tip.

That should have been enough to make him relax. Except as he sunk into the backseat's weathered upholstery, something caught his eye among the suburban mix of sandwich shops, coffee chains and big-box stores.

A white van. Unmarked. With two unfriendly-looking people glancing in his direction, their exact focus hidden by sunglasses.

He couldn't be too paranoid, could he? Jamie considered the possibility as they idled six or seven cars behind a red light. "Ah, this goddamn light," the driver said. "This one always backs up. You'd think they'd sync it up with the crosswalks."

The light turned, and cars shuffled along, someone in front slow to move forward. "Come on, come on, stay green," the driver said as it turned to yellow. "I'm gonna punch it."

"That's fine." A quick glance at the van showed them obeying the traffic laws and slowing to the line.

The light changed to red just as their car crossed the line. It jerked forward as the accelerator roared, putt-putt-putting the decade-old sedan across the intersection. From behind, tires squealed. Jamie turned, hands perched up.

Instead of waiting at the crosswalk, the van broke the red light and surged toward them.

"Oh shit," Jamie said as they safely crossed the intersection, the freeway on-ramp now just ahead.

"Sorry, sorry. I know, I should be more patient. This light just irritates me."

Jamie nodded, but his eyes widened, watching as the van's engine revved up to catch them. Now it was directly behind, and Jamie could see the driver and passenger talking to each other, and the passenger putting a phone to his ear. They rolled onto the highway, speeding up to keep pace with the other cars zooming past them.

"God, I probably just got a ticket, huh? They have cameras on those lights."

The van kept up, staying right behind them as they changed over into the carpool lane. "You know, this lane doesn't help much at this time. Even though we're going against traffic back into the city. We're still gonna hit a slowdown at the eighty-two interchange."

Jamie reached out with his mind, fingers poised on the back headrest. He *felt* the minds in the van, but something wouldn't let him lock on.

For now, he hoped it stemmed from separate moving vehicles and *not* whatever tactics the woman employed in Telos.

"Damn," the driver said again. "See, it's just rush hour. I swear, this place gets worse every year. It's all of the tech jobs coming here. I never thought I'd say there are too many jobs, but there are too many jobs."

The brakes squeaked and red lights flashed in front of them as their car slowed to a halt. Behind them, the van did the same, and Jamie closed his eyes, trying again to find a path into the mind of either the passenger or the driver.

And then he was there. Watching them load into the van. Seeing a photo on their tablet.

His photo. From when he registered at the lobby.

The mystery woman barking orders then saying something about how she was taking a helicopter to "the facility." Even finding Dr. Waterfield in an unexplainable stupor.

Jamie pulled out of the man's memory and looked forward. The sea of brake lights let up, and they moved onward, going several minutes at thirty miles per hour before slowing down again. Another car changed lanes, getting between them and the van, though the height of the van made its passengers still visible.

"Are there any alternative routes?" Jamie asked.

"Like side streets?"

"Yeah."

"To get into the city?" the driver replied. "Sorry, man, all you've got is this highway. The traffic map says it's another forty-two minutes."

Jamie pulled out his phone. Still no messages from Zoe, though now that he knew the people from Telos were tailing him, who knew what they'd put on his phone while it was there. He typed out a quick message to Zoe. I have to ditch this phone. You should change yours too. Something is definitely up. Find me.

He tapped the send button, and the icon showed a green check mark before returning to his home screen.

From behind, the passenger held up a tablet and turned to the driver. Jamie couldn't read lips, but he bet they were talking about how his phone just sent a text to Zoe.

They stopped again, and Jamie reached out into the van driver's mind, holding his spot. "Hey, do me a favor," he said to his own driver. "Let me know when you see the other cars starting to go."

"Huh?"

"Like when traffic is about to go. Just let me know."

"Okay. Sure. What's up?"

"It's, um, a timing experiment."

It might have been a mere sixty seconds, and it might have been ten minutes, Jamie wasn't sure. His entire resolve was required to stay in the driver's mind, watching as new memories of traffic and idle chatter formulated and set in his mind.

"Looks like we're rolling."

Now. Jamie took in a breath, then poked, hitting the van's driver with the hardest brain-stun he'd ever attempted. Using such force drained Jamie, sucking the air from his lungs and giving him a dizzy spell in the backseat of his OmegaCars ride upon opening his eyes.

Jamie forced himself to focus and watched as the driver spasmed forward. Even beyond the van's windshield, he could see the driver convulse, at least until the man lurched forward and vomited into his own lap. The OmegaCars ride began to pull away, then the car behind them, but the Telos van only set forward at a gentle roll, most likely from the driver's sudden inability to control the breaks. Horns started to blare and the van began a gradual crawl, veering partially into the shoulder. Jamie tried to lock on to the passenger, but even the attempt to reach out felt like every muscle in his body was too weak to form even the lightest fist.

Then they were out of range.

The van remained still, now trapped by the whirlwind of cars around it. It grew smaller and smaller until they veered away from it. Jamie shut down his phone, then rolled down the window. "I need some air," he said.

"No prob. Hey, it's up to sixty. Maybe luck is on our side after all."

"I'll take it," Jamie said, wiping the sweat off his brow. The breeze clipped the top of his hand as it lingered just outside the half-open window. He counted to five, then released the phone.

The driver didn't notice. Instead he chattered about how well traffic was flowing.

17

WAS THAT...A BODY?

The lights behind Zoe dimmed, then flickered again before restoring, but that didn't change the scene in front of her. Inside the capsule, the body—corpse?—tiny plumes of smoke blended into a bright red heat signature, the faint smell of burning giving her a different type of nausea than hangovers. She leaned forward despite the odor, inching toward the mess of wires and electrodes and sensors attached to the man. A central metal tube enclosed his body from the knees up to the collarbone, though his limbs remained exposed.

Burn scars covered his face, a patchwork of scar tissue and raw wounds that went down his neck, shoulders, and Zoe guessed everywhere else. A few wisps of short black hair remained at the top of his head, and sunken cheeks slightly huffed with each intubated breath.

"What the hell are you?" she asked, more for herself than him.

But his left pinky finger twitched in response.

Zoe gasped, frozen in her footsteps.

It might have been electrically stimulated, she told herself. Who knew how much voltage pumped through all those wires? She knew muscles reacted to bursts of electricity, like puppeting a cadaver limb with the right setup—that's how they did it in that movie about the mad mortuary worker who reanimated dead criminals. Though that might not be the best guide for scientific accuracy.

Then the man opened his eyes.

Not for too long. A few seconds, enough for them to angle toward her.

Moments later, an alarm rang out. Zoe's enhanced hearing picked up the sound of footsteps, in unison enough that she knew there were multiples, but she couldn't filter it down to a clear number.

A look around the space showed no windows, no doors.

Her phone still lacked signal, and no word from Jamie, either. Did they figure out he was at Telos? Or did its respectable front keep things calm and collected?

The only certain thing was that she needed to find Jamie and see what he'd discovered—and if she wasn't making one big adrenaline-driven mistake by being here in the first place.

That meant the only way out was through.

The footsteps got closer and louder. Now voices entered the mix, and through the walls, she started to pick up faint heat signatures. They arrived first as a blob before splitting into individuals, though they formed back into two lines that hid their numbers.

Zoe blinked. Had she seen this space before? Something about it seemed familiar yet different, and though she'd spent hours agonizing over the memories that Jamie unearthed, this whole thing put it all into some context. She dashed out of the room with the glass capsule into the observation room up front, facing the only way in and out.

One set of doors opened and closed in the distance. Her muscles tensed for a fight and she felt herself lifting onto the balls of her feet, body amped as if it *needed* to burn off the sudden surge that lit her body. This wasn't like her usual moonlit delivery runs across rooftops, and it was far from her beer-impaired chase of the Mind Robber.

The voices approached closer and closer, and Zoe found her legs pumping like a prizefighter warming up in the ring. Her hands went into battle position—was she levitating? She *was*. An inch off the ground, but still, the energy and emotion pushed her into a greater high than any cheap vodka.

The way out was clear. And she'd punch her way there if she had to.

Their voices came through clearly. "Behind this door. On three. One."

But she should be smart about this. Standing in one spot front and center made her an easy target, no matter how ready she was.

"Two."

She threw herself against the wall adjacent to the door hinges, arms propped up to brace herself from its swing.

"Three."

The door's electronic lock beeped and its hydraulics began to swing the heavy metal slab open. A hard *thud* sound pushed the door further. Zoe propped it with her hands, and it seemed like no one even noticed. Instead, she watched as each sentry's heat signature walked in lockstep, six total, two rows of three each. They moved forward, then a voice yelled, "Secure Project E. Four up, two back."

The guards lined up against the glass capsule and called clear.

The lights in the outer room flickered, just as they had minutes earlier. This time, it bathed Zoe in a strobe light, while the instrument panels by the capsule surged. Zoe sidestepped away from the door and now had a clear view of everyone—including the encapsulated man.

His body spasmed, fingers vibrating at a rapid frequency and heels kicking at the table beneath, and the lights in his immediate space intensified even more than when she'd approached it. The flickering around her stopped, leaving it only pitch-black. She squinted, questioning what she saw.

Was he opening his mouth?

A voice boomed, half shriek and half language, cutting through as if it were a death howl issuing a command.

She couldn't quite decipher it, but if she had to guess, the word was "Now."

Heads turned in confusion, and Zoe examined their positions, identifying the best order to pick them all off. The lights strobed. She steadied her back leg to launch her assault on the team when she noticed that the man had turned his head. He locked eyes with her.

It lasted for a split second. There may not have even been a message involved. But in that moment, Zoe turned in the other direction and sprinted down the hallway at a pace that none of the guards could match, so fast that it tore her pants at the knees. She punched through door after door, and suddenly the layout of the space came back to her. She *knew* when to turn left, when to turn right, when to make it to the stairwell, so much that when she heard another set of footsteps coming by, she opened the door to the stairs as wide as possible, letting the gradual hydraulics close it slowly for the appearance of escape.

When four more sentries followed her false trail, she took two steps back and rammed her shoulder as hard as she could into a thinner metal door, one that didn't guard experimental human projects or advanced glass capsules that did whatever, but a simple break room with a refrigerator, table and a newspaper on the counter.

And a window.

Zoe took a metal chair by two hands and rammed it through

the glass, then cleared out the edges. She peered out. Six stories up? Whatever.

It was fine. This would be fine. This is why she could hover.
Winging it.

She took four steps back when a voice called out.

"Zoe. Zoe Wong."

In the hallway stood a lone figure, a single woman in a lab
coat. "Welcome back, Zoe. You've been busy."

Zoe walked to the woman, someone who looked too put together with her heels and coiffed hair and pleasant smile. She
took cautious step after cautious step until they were only a few
feet apart.

"I'm sure you're wondering what's going on here. Let's go
have a talk. I think you'll—"

Before the woman could finish the sentence, Zoe punched
her across the mouth. She flew back into the wall, letting out
an "oof." Zoe nearly leaped over with an urge to give her adversary one *more* hit. Just to make sure.

Except the woman didn't even drop, instead giving her jaw
a quick rub and steadying herself. She stood, her feet stable and
her stare focused, as though it had been a mere nuisance rather
than a full-bodied smash from the Throwing Star.

That wasn't good.

Violent urges could wait.

The woman started to speak. She didn't get a complete word
out when Zoe charged full speed toward the broken window
and jumped.

18

AS FAR AS JAMIE could tell, no one else followed their car. He got dropped off right within the city limits at the Metro station right alongside Dock 4, then promptly removed the driver's memory of their whole interaction. He tuned the car's stereo to the new age Zen station; hopefully the driver would figure he pulled over from fatigue and was having a forgetful moment.

With each push forward, his senses reached out, scanning for signs of being followed. It wasn't an exact system; identification this way was mostly guesswork, suspect at best, but at least he *felt* better doing it, all the way through the Metro station and onto the first train. To be safe, he overshot his stop by two exits before boarding another train and returning, all while doing his share of spy-film trickery with waiting at the door, getting off, then getting back on.

If anyone tailed him, at least Jamie did his best to make it difficult.

After all of that, some two hours had passed since the highway. He half expected Zoe to already be at his place, maybe lingering on his building's roof or up the tallest tree lining the parking lot. But there was no trace of her, and as he put his key in the apartment lock, Normal mewed and pawed at the door. That was a good sign; if anyone was waiting to ambush him, Normal would have hidden rather than ask for dinner.

Jamie stepped in and turned on the lights. In return, Normal greeted him by walking back and forth between his legs, her gray tail wrapping around his ankles. "I know, I know. You must be hungry."

The cat replied in staccato mews, and they only intensified when he pulled out a can of cat food. As he did, the power fluctuated, spooking Normal and putting Jamie on high alert. Yet nothing came from it, not guards crashing through windows or writing mysteriously turning up on mirrors or counters. He peeled open Normal's dinner then considered his options.

But there were no options. With no phone and no means of contacting Zoe, waiting *was* the only option. *How* he waited was another story. The coffee mug in his hand trembled while his laptop connected to his neighbor's Wi-Fi, everything he'd seen at Telos piping back through his memory.

He could try to figure out who that mystery doctor was. Or dig up more about Telos. Or even see if more information about Zoe was available somewhere.

But no, his mind remained fixated on the video he'd seen. Who was Frazer Troughton and how did he wind up hurting the people around him? How did he go from there to erasing Zoe's memory?

As the computer screen came to life, he settled in and forced himself to push aside urges to run off, and instead the most unexpected epiphany arrived.

Frazer was the key to that rooftop.

Jamie's fingers trembled as he punched in the name, one character at a time. His pounding heart pressed against his chest, as if it might just shatter the bone and muscle holding it in place. He didn't have a big detective board like Zoe. He didn't agonize over it like Zoe. And yet, now he had the opportunity Zoe craved.

She'd seriously punch him if he didn't take it.

Jamie hit Enter.

The screen went black as it began the loading process, digital ones and zeroes reaching into the past to inform him who he was.

He figured it'd be a few results. Probably the odd mention in a local newspaper, maybe an old bit of social media. What he got, though, were dozens of results, articles and posts made by Frazer Troughton bloviating on the future of technology and other such bullshit. In some cases, the byline identified him as a thought leader and an innovator; in others, it called him cofounder of CyberController Limited.

But for the volume of results, none seemed more than that of an industry blowhard. He hadn't been a celebrity or person of cultural significance. Instead, he was a guy who made some software and because of that, he wrote in some industry blogs. And that was it. Some two dozen articles skimmed, all of which espoused seemingly important ideas about secure and transparent decentralized database technology, all filled with the same repeated buzzwords. None of it meant anything to him, Jamie, and there were no mentions of any personal life, not even if he liked sports or films or anything along those lines. His social media accounts still existed, untouched in several years but with the same breadcrumbs of faux innovator speak and very little personality.

He clicked through, eventually piecing together a timeline that showed that he'd been in tech for about ten years before a larger company bought out his company. Then he seemingly dropped off the planet. Only one forum post peeled back a layer of truth.

That guy? I heard through the industry grapevine that he got bored and started drinking after the buyout, then his husband/boyfriend/whatever left him. He's probably hiding on some island now.

Six or seven pages in, one small paragraph mentioned an official death notice.

He was a mouthy person who made something that got bought out by someone else, then disappeared with an addiction problem. Then he died, officially.

And now he robbed banks. With, ironically, the goal of hiding on some island.

Jamie leaned back in his chair, and he realized that the brilliant purples of dusk had now shifted into the deep and dark blues of night. His fingers itched to move, wanting to tell *someone* the whole story, the how and why it all happened.

But he couldn't. He had an identity to protect, a truth to safeguard from everyone else.

Suddenly, the single lamp in the living room flickered, then went out, only the laptop's battery-powered screen providing illumination. Outside, the rest of the world fared much better. From upstairs, he could hear a neighbor's TV, the hurried voice of a sports announcer doing play-by-play coming through the thin ceiling. Out the window, the building's exterior lamps still operated, sending in the harsh yellow-orange glow of wholesale lighting.

It was as if the power grid singled out his specific apartment.

Given the past two years, coincidences stopped being coincidences.

From behind, the light from the laptop dimmed, then intensified, a brilliant blue bathing the nooks and crannies of the apartment. Jamie turned to see if the computer displayed the blue error screen, only to find a person standing in front of it.

A person made up entirely of blue electricity.

The figure lurched forward, a living neon silhouette with brilliant tiny flecks sparking off it and burning out to orange-yellow before disappearing in tiny trails of smoke. Details gradually came into view as Jamie's eyes adjusted: distinctly masculine eyes and nose and cheekbones, all blurred out in crackling electricity, like a digital photo with the filter sliders turned all the way up.

And a mouth. A mouth that moved, and when it did, a voice escaped. Not a voice in the truest sense, audible soundwaves powered by air and vocal cords, but a distorted screech that somehow formed words.

"Stop her."

The figure approached, limbs moving with a smooth, almost unreal detachment, like its image was simply cut and pasted into this world.

"Who?" Jamie asked. "Who is *she*? Give me a name, show me something? Is it Zoe? Why do you want me to stop her?"

Its feet stepped forward, despite floating inches above the ground. It approached in slow motion, a neon puppet caught in ethereal molasses, and as it inched forward, it raised one hand, a finger tapping its own forehead and causing sparks to shoot off upon contact.

Then it pointed at Jamie.

Several seconds passed before the message crystalized. Jamie set his fingers out, reaching to see what secrets lurked.

The connection offered an unusual clarity, and instead of sneaking into the photo gallery of someone else's mind, this felt more like a live feed. But rather than being filled with the brilliant radiant blue of the figure in front of him, he only had a static point of view that made little sense. Hardware of some kind, buttons and displays, some wires poking out of panels, all of it in perfect re-creation but zero context. And silence, other than the rhythmic hum of various machines. The visuals sharpened, brightened, came more alive, and in doing so, the background light seemed to dim. The field of vision moved, ever so slightly and a voice—no, a thought—came through with piercing clarity.

There.

Jamie snapped back into his own mind and body, only to see the figure begin to flicker, blue light flashing throughout his apartment. Its mouth opened, and as its body began to wither from existence, a final distorted voice arrived, but any message got buried under the sheer density of scratching distorted noise.

A moment later, the lights returned. The refrigerator began humming again, the ceiling fan whirred back to life, the microwave beeped. All of the ambient noises that provided the soundtrack of modern living returned to their regular rhythm, providing a hypnotic comfort for those that found silence too eerie.

But the peace only lasted for ten or fifteen seconds. From outside, footsteps pounded before a loud *bang* caused the door to visibly vibrate. "Jamie! Open the door!"

19

ZOE HAD BARELY MADE it there.

She ran all the time for work, dashing across rooftops and jumping over alleys, using her momentum to propel forward. She'd chased down muggers and thieves as well, tracking them via heat signatures, then sprinting at extraordinary speeds to cut even the most considerable leads down.

The past two hours, though, had been different. After leaping out the window, she'd hovered down, only to encounter a mass of guards with weapons trained on her. Her hearing picked up orders through their headsets—they were specifically told *not* to kill her.

Incapacitate her, fine. Injure her, fine.

But kill her? That was a definite no-no.

Still Zoe preferred to avoid getting shot in any capacity. And trusting those guards to *not* murder her, well, she felt a wee bit skeptical. Zoe gripped the frame of a parked motorcycle and held it in front of her as she crouch-walked behind it. Bullets bounced off it, ricocheting off nearby cars and walls. From her thermal view, a group of five rushed in, all running at maximum adrenaline.

These guys were trained. Whatever happened to the "do not kill" order, she wasn't sure, because discharges peppered the dark evening parking lot. She made it behind a car and waited until the sentries recalibrated to her position. That single breath was all the time she needed; she flew above them, hurling the motorcycle as hard as she could. It smashed into the concrete, tearing into another car while splintering off metal and plastic in a spray of debris.

In the commotion, she sprinted and jumped over the barbed wire fence, then began moving through fields and off road, a sheer blanket of black encroaching as she made it farther and farther away from the facility's lights. The empty stretches of dirt and weeds gave way to a wooded area, enough cover to obscure any potential tracking. Her legs pounded with each frantic step, her direction somewhat aimless except *away*, until she came across a one-lane road and a car pulling out of a driveway.

There weren't many options here.

The car screeched to a halt as she dashed in front of it, both hands up. Skid burns wafted into the air, the odor of rubber filling the country road, and the vehicle's sudden stop wasn't enough. The bumper tapped into her knees; most people would have been knocked down, but Zoe pushed back a step, then adjusted.

"Oh my God," the man yelled through the windshield. "Are you okay?"

"I need your car." Zoe marched over and met him face-to-face, his eyes wide and mouth open. She craned her neck to see any signs of pursuit—*something* was there, but from where and how many, she wasn't sure.

"Wait, are you okay? Slow down."

"No," she said. Her hands gripped the bottom of the front driver-side tire, the rubber still warm. She lifted, as easily as someone might lift a carton of milk. The man gasped loud enough to be heard through the closed car door. "I. Need. Your. Car. Step aside."

The man nodded as the car collapsed down. As Zoe grabbed the door handle, he let out a tiny question. "Are you the Throwing Star?"

It was a reasonable question given her body type and what she'd just done. But answering put her anonymity at risk. Zoe bit down on her lip, considering the possibilities, then went with the easiest answer: ignore. "I really need your car. Get out. *Now.*" She didn't need Jamie's powers to understand the fear the guy felt, but he could go to counseling about this later. Zoe *had* to move. Her arm curled back to do *something*—she hadn't quite figured that part out yet—when the man's mouth shifted. It lasted a fraction of a second, though its very existence was a problem.

He knew something bad was going down.

In the distance, her enhanced hearing picked up rumbles, vibrations, shouts and walkie-talkie squawks. An indeterminate number, an imprecise distance, but they were coming—and Zoe didn't have time to play the hero. At a core level, the whole extraordinary vigilante thing was about scratching some sort of emotional itch. She knew that, despite having never gone to therapy (at least that she knew of). But generally being *good* to people sat right with her, or at least not doing harm.

This would be harm. Or at least expensive. But making it to another day so she could help more people, that was doing good, right?

Yeah. She went with that for now.

The man's eyes grew wide, his expression changing in almost slow motion as she formed a fist and pulled her arm back. Faster-than-normal healing, tougher skin and muscles, all that was normal for her by now. But she still wasn't sure what might come out of this.

The quiet of the night broke as a loud *clang* cut through, the sound repeating in softer and softer echoes—only to be absorbed by the whip of helicopter blades. Zoe turned to catch the thinnest of lights shining down between tree leaves. She pulled her hand out of the mangled hole in the car door, and looked the man in the eye.

"Get out."

His shaking hands took several seconds to undo the seat belt and open the door; he exited the car, more of a stumble-and-fall on the way out, a move that left him on his knees, dirt clouds rising around him.

The noise crept closer. She needed to get onto the main highway. Now.

Her leg swung into the still-idling car and as she settled in, his uneasy voice cut through the air. "You saved my sister. Two weeks ago."

Two weeks ago—Zoe actually had those memories except they existed as a jumbled mess, a blur of nighttime running and colliding fists. Countless people thanked her, hugged her, shook her hand, yet those interactions registered as ephemeral, disappearing as quickly as they came. She changed people's lives, and the only thing that remained came in the form of a rush of heat signatures and the satisfaction that came with punching someone.

Maybe she needed more support group time. Extraordinaries Anonymous. That would have been perfect.

"I thought you helped people," the man finally said.

"Yeah..." was the only thing Zoe could utter. She wanted to say something reassuring, to let this man know that this was a one-off means of survival. Something profound. Or at least witty, like the crap Jamie said in the videos of him robbing banks. Instead, Zoe's gaping mouth and dry throat failed to come to the rescue. "I—"

From afar, voices shouted.

"I need to go. Sorry." That would have to do, though she wanted to leave on something a little more reassuring. She was, after all, totally stealing his car. "I'm sure your insurance will cover this."

The engine revved, and in the rearview, the man stood, his phone now recording. Zoe considered stopping, sprinting out and grabbing the phone just to make sure these shenanigans didn't turn into a viral video. But the helicopter's searchlight loomed in her rearview. She jammed the accelerator, putting everything behind her. A minute later her pocket buzzed, showing that signal had finally returned.

I have to ditch this phone. You should change yours too. Something is definitely up. Find me.

Better to be safe. Zoe took the phone and shoved it through the gaping hole in the door. For a moment, she felt the wind whipping through her bloody knuckles before she let the device go.

An hour passed with Zoe on the road, only taking one wrong interchange before she had to loop around, but in the end it wasn't a total loss. At least that might have shaken anyone on her tail.

Without her phone, though, figuring out where Jamie actually lived had been a chore in itself. Fortunately, her FoodFast training gave her a strong sense of direction and the ability to note landmarks along the way.

The door flew open seconds after she banged on it. "Zo—" he started before she pushed him out of the way and slammed the door shut behind her.

Her pulse screamed, not just from the running but the constant looking over her shoulder. But now, in the confines of thin apartment walls and honest company, things finally started to relax. She turned to Jamie, who'd stayed by the door, as if waiting for permission. "I got your message," she finally said.

"You look...rough."

Zoe noticed Jamie gawking at her pant legs, which had nearly been torn off at the knees, chewed threads dangling loose. "Oh. I'm all right. If I sprint too fast in regular clothes, they tear. Especially if I catch a corner or branch or something. That's why I need the suit."

"You've been busy?" Jamie walked up to her, kneeling to match her hunched-over position. He looked at her, his mouth hanging open as if all different words jammed up on their way out.

"Yeah. I got shot at. The usual, you know?" The words came out with as much of a casual tone as she could force into it. "Shot at" usually meant a guy pulling out a handgun—and her knocking it out of his hand before a single bullet left.

This was quite different. But she didn't want Jamie to see that. "And I saw...this guy, like all burned and stuff, but hooked up to wires in a glass capsule. But then I got chased, so I jumped out of a tower and threw a motorcycle at guards." She made it through all that, and yet being in Jamie's apartment slowed her down, as cat allergies started burning her eyes. "Oh, and I stole a car."

"Okay," Jamie said slowly. "Let's rewind a little. You want a coffee? And an antihistamine?" He pulled out two mugs from his cabinet. "I saw a lot too. Didn't get shot at. Chased, though." He laughed and shook his head. "Winging it."

"Nice!" Zoe held out a hand, waiting for a high five that came about five seconds later than it should have. "Look at us. We came out unscathed."

"I don't know about that. I vote for a plan next time." Serious creases framed Jamie's eyes; apparently, he didn't appreciate the visceral thrill of escape. "There's a lot you need to know." Her coffee remained mostly untouched for the next ten minutes other than for downing the allergy pill, and was now probably cold as Jamie spilled the details: the weird woman in purple who may have been the same woman she punched, the database of seemingly legit rehab patients, the questions about an experimental new treatment.

Jamie's true past.

And a glowing man who appeared and disappeared.

But he'd started with the name Zoe Wong—the rest of it didn't even need to exist. All that time with the detective board, piecing together seemingly unrelated clues and searching for fragments of her own memory, it had all been there on the name tag the whole time. And she'd never even bothered to dig deeper. It felt too easy.

"It's all connected somehow. Telos is definitely more than rehab. I wonder if they have something similar out in Hartnell City." Jamie stood and started pacing back and forth, long fingers pointing and poking at the air to push his thoughts forward. "That place you went, I'm sure it's listed as something else. The thing—the man."

How common a name was Zoe Wong? She'd searched before, but that was years ago, and now that she *knew*, it changed everything. Where to start? Social media? Facial recognition?

"And me. I mean, I sounded like a terrible person. And I was clearly a patient. But still, armed guards?"

Searching online was a start, but where? Records for Zoe Wong could be from anywhere. She could have lived across the country. Parents? Friends? Would her name and photo on social media help old acquaintances just *find* her? She had little experience with any of the social media sites, what with trying to keep a low profile and everything, but there were plenty of stories about miracle reunifications through them.

"And that woman was creepy as shit. How did she block me?"

And it wouldn't be just about who Zoe Wong was. But *what* she was. So she could finally answer that nagging question that always lingered in the back of her mind, that sheer drive of wanting something more. What did she miss out on? What path got derailed from gaining the ability to hover and catch petty street criminals?

"And then ten cows appeared and murdered everyone in sight."

"Right, right." Maybe she could start with a list of every Zoe Wong she could find but whittle it down to her age range and—

"You're not listening."

"Of course I am. The clinic and the blue guy."

"And the murderous cows."

"Wait, what?"

Jamie shot her a look, an arched eyebrow that proved his point.

"Okay, your name was…" Zoe bit down on her lip, trying to pull back that one fairly important detail. But it wasn't there. If Jamie had dived into her memories, he would have only found blurry images and muffled audio, things eclipsed by her own name and pondering what might have been. "Okay, you're right. Maybe I'm overthinking it right now."

"Yeah, let's just slow down. Take a break. I mean, I don't sense anyone out there. Do you?"

Jamie was right. With her thermal vision and extraordinary hearing, no threats emerged on her personal radar. Just neighbors doing neighbor stuff. "A break sounds good," Zoe said, and suddenly her mind rushed with a different type of spark. Months and months of isolation and obsession—and inebriation—all culminated in this moment, something that seemed impossible a short time ago and now seemed so necessary. "I got an idea." She reached into her back pocket for her phone before realizing that it was lying on some two-lane country road miles away. "Can we use your laptop? I wanna show you something."

Jamie cringed as yet another head got severed. He peeked over at Zoe, whose cheeks seemed to be permanently up in a grin. "Oh!" she yelled, as Lo-Bot, the titular cyborg samurai of

Lo-Bot: Samurai Cyborg, decapitated three demonic ninjas in a single swipe on his small laptop screen. "I can't believe I waited to finish this. This is so freaking good," she said, stuffing bits of microwave popcorn into her mouth. Jamie tried not to mind the fact that she didn't wipe the grease on napkins before planting her hands on the futon cushion.

He tried—seriously—to match her enthusiasm for this low-budget 1970s Japanese horror movie, complete with poor American overdubs. But all he could do was sit back befuddled, though as Zoe oohed and aahed at sloppy choreography and blood that seemed far too liquidy to pass for real, he found himself smiling.

Really smiling.

Not at the movie, because it was terrible. But because they sat on his little futon, Normal on his lap, screen propped up on the coffee table with a stack of his library books. And not as the Throwing Star and the Mind Robber, but as Jamie and Zoe.

"Dude," she said as Lo-Bot and his canine sidekick walked off into the forest while credits rolled.

"What?"

"You've got this weird look on your face. Oh no," she said, "was this too gory for you? There are less gross ones that—"

"No, no, it's fine," Jamie said with a quiet laugh. "I'm just..." he hesitated, searching for the right way to express his epiphany "...not used to having company over."

"Hey, we should have like a weekly movie night! There are so many on HorrorDomain. I mean, we can still rob a bank and everything. But also movie night. Because really, you gotta see some of these."

"Maybe. They have movies at the library too, you know. Ones with slightly bigger budgets." Another laugh came, this one loud enough to cause Normal to readjust on his lap. "You're a good friend, Zoe Wong. You should know that. And a pretty badass hero."

Zoe's movie-spawned grin softened, the angles becoming

less sharp as it exchanged sheer enthusiasm for something a little more vulnerable. And her eyes, the excitement dimmed, becoming a glint of something deeper. She shook out of it, head
bobbing with an aw-shucks demeanor, then she punched him
in the shoulder.

It was probably supposed to be a joking tap, except it really,
really hurt. Jamie grimaced through the pain, knowing she
meant well.

"Whoops. Sorry 'bout that. So," Zoe said, snapping back to
her usual cadence, "this movie got me thinking. Like, really
thinking. I know this whole thing started off kind of by accident. The hero stuff." As Zoe spoke, Normal poked her head
up and looked diagonally into the corner of the room. She
shook her head, collar jingling, then pounced off of Jamie's lap,
her back claws pushing out enough to dig into the fabric of his
pants. "And I know I haven't been a textbook hero by far, but
something about it feels right. Being *her* feels right. I mean, Zoe
Wong is going to exist but just like Lo-Bot embraces himself
once he meets his dog, I think I really am the Throwing—"

Jamie felt a sting in his neck, then a second in his back. It
wasn't pain that dropped him to the floor as much as a total collapse of his muscles. A bang sound clapped through the space and
he saw Zoe drop to the floor after five or six darts flew into her,
limp arms failing to brace her. Jamie's face slammed to the thin
carpet, and from his view, all he saw were Normal's two eyes
glowing from under the coffee table before the world faded out.

20

THERE WEREN'T MANY TIMES when Jamie would have rather had Zoe's power. Maybe the hovering bit, but the speed and the power? Those were all tools, but tools still operated as steps in a process, a means to an end. On the other hand, lifting memories and brain-stunning, that was a cheat, a direct line to the finish.

This was the exception to the rule. For starters, Jamie was bound to a chair, so tightly his hands throbbed from the lack of circulation, and that certainly didn't help with his ability to attempt any mental invasions. A simple application of extraordinary strength could break the chains and ropes tying him up, probably even the metal folding chair, as well.

Then there was the issue of the person in front of him: the woman from the facility. Sitting face-to-face with her now, Jamie studied her in ways that weren't possible back at Telos. Being tied up helped in that regard.

But she wasn't just anyone. Her mind shielded itself from him.

He couldn't even sense it, eyes closed or open. And if she was the same woman Zoe encountered, she took a punch in ways no normal human should be able to withstand.

With her neat hair and purple dress, she may as well have been sitting for a job interview. Everything about her look projected professionalism. And calm. Calm exuded from her entire body, from her neutral expression to her relaxed posture.

She was calm probably because she knew she was invulnerable to Jamie.

Which was the second reason having Zoe's powers would have been nice here.

"Welcome back. Jamie now, right? Or Frazer? Or Bill? Have they all been the same?" Her head tilted, her left eyebrow rising. "No, I don't think so. This version of you seems a little—" she sucked in a breath and pursed her lips "—quirkier than before."

Jamie pondered his options. Getting out of the chair—bound hands made that impossible. Appealing to the mystery woman's sense of compassion? That seemed *less* likely than escaping.

Threaten her?

Maybe that was the only route. On the off chance that *her* presentation was just that, and she didn't realize her immunity to his abilities.

"I think you don't know who you're dealing with here," Jamie said, switching to the false bravado and bad accent of the Mind Robber. "The police couldn't catch me. The Throwing Star couldn't catch me. Bank security couldn't stop me. I am—"

The woman's heavy sigh interrupted his train of thought, stealing the rhythm of his speech. He coughed, not because any phlegm caught in his throat, but to buy him a few seconds to catch himself, reset.

Okay. Take two.

"I am San Delgado's most wanted criminal, the city's most feared foe, the one person that—"

"Really?" The woman sighed again. "I mean, I know you

don't remember who I am but this whole song and dance seems a bit pointless, right? We saw you. We tracked you. We found you, and now you're tied up. Do you really think a speech is going to scare me?" She leaned forward, her arms crossed. "Especially since you can't..." She raised a single finger, then tapped it against her forehead. "You know."

That cleared that part up.

"And you really have to drop that accent. It's really bad." That sigh again. "You know how some British actors just can't do American accents? You're one of those. So let's drop everything. The defenses, the accents, the threats. Okay, you really want to try your powers on me. Let's do this, just to get it out of the way. Prove a point."

The woman stood, walking with a strut that exuded confidence. Or maybe it was a scare tactic. Jamie considered that—after all, Zoe's tale might have been an exaggeration, or Zoe might have missed her punch and been too proud to admit it. That seemed like a Zoe thing to do.

But then the woman gripped the chains wrapped around his waist and flicked them off like the metal links were wet paper. They flew through the air, smashing into the concrete wall of the dimly lit space hard enough to leave a harsh indent.

As Jamie watched dust and debris trickle from the gash in the wall, the woman walked behind him and tore the ropes off his hand. "Come on, stand up." She nudged the chair with her foot, then did it again, scooting him several inches, the metal legs scraping against the floor. "You're the Mind Robber. Your hands are free. Dive into my mind."

For every bank robbery, Jamie planned possible scenarios, ways things might go sideways and how to counteract them. A stray guard, an overzealous customer, a terrified employee. Even considering the unpredictable still lent a certain level of predictability. And he'd been able to pull it all off under duress. This, however, froze him.

"You're nervous. Would a cup of coffee help?" She opened the door and looked at him, suddenly a barista taking an order. "No cream, no sugar, just black, right?"

He replied with silence and she stepped out, the door closing behind her. Except, did the lock latch? He wasn't sure, but as he reviewed the memory, the lights started to flicker.

On the floor, the thinnest blue line started glowing a trail. It started faint, so much so that Jamie wasn't even sure if he saw it or if his eyes were merely adjusting. It grew in thickness and brightness until pooling in the center of the room, erupting into the blue figure that had appeared in his living room. The eyeless figure turned to him, a distorted scream bouncing off the four walls before fading away. Everything went back to black before returning to normal lighting, the mystery woman staring straight at him, now with a white paper cup in hand. "Did you see that?" Jamie asked. "What was that?"

The woman appeared to hesitate for a beat, her focus drifting around the room. She snapped back, as if the interlude never occurred, and instead held up the coffee. "Your favorite. I apologize that it's from a pod. I know you prefer the pour-over method. We're a bit limited here," she said, gesturing at the dingy confines of the space.

The smell hit him strong enough to signify its authenticity. Could it be poisoned? That seemed possible, but to what purpose when they held every clear advantage?

Jamie closed his eyes and wondered why he ever agreed to help Zoe, why he ever decided to be an extraordinary bank robber. Life would have been so much simpler and less threatening if he'd found a less publicity-fueled way to make money. He would probably be sitting with Normal, a steaming mug of coffee in one hand and a good book in the other.

But no. He had to try an American accent and rob banks and help out emotionally damaged extraordinaries.

From that perspective, he kind of deserved to be here.

"Okay, then. Maybe later." She set the coffee on her chair. "Break into my mind. Put me into a stupor. Or, if you want—" her laugh came through with a snort "—attack me." She paced the room, giving Jamie time to get to his feet, circulation returning to his extremities. "We're kind of short on time, so if you could finish this demonstration, that'd be great."

"I…" Freezing like this, being unable to conjure words for a performance, that never happened, not even at his first bank robbery. Granted, he'd prepared for that moment, rehearsed it until it became muscle memory like an actor practices his lines. This was a little different. "I… Fuck."

The woman started to laugh, not one of those evil villain displays, but a genuine circumstance-induced chuckle. "We really don't have time for this. Are you going to rob my mind or what?"

A hint of amusement came with her intense glare, goading him on. Jamie's hands went up, mind reaching out to lock on to something, anything, sheer concentration causing sweat to form along his scalp.

And nothing. It wasn't just stress or anxiety that limited his ability with this woman. She was simply invulnerable to his abilities.

"Okay. You proved your point. What do you want?" Jamie asked in his normal voice, falling back into the chair. "Do you want money for the Telos treatment?"

"No, you paid that years ago. Before Frazer died." She tapped the TV on the wall and its screen came to life. On it was a static image of Zoe. "My name is Sasha Kaftan. And it's nice to officially meet you. Now tell me, out of all the things you've been able to recall, do you remember ever hearing about Project Electron?"

"Is that…like a rock band or something?"

"Project Electron was the brainchild of Dr. Waris Kaftan. My husband. He had the most extraordinary mind. His research on electricity in the human body was groundbreaking. Cutting-edge. Did you know the human brain fires off hundreds of billions of electrical signals for the basic things we do, to eat and sleep and breathe and think? Electricity is what makes the human nervous system go. Now what fuels the human body, that's calories. The food you eat, that becomes energy, allowing the body to fire off all those electrical signals. Food is the bridge between resource and output. Project Electron bridges that gap."

Sasha's speech came off as half sales pitch, half educational seminar.

"Well…" Jamie said, searching for words. "That's cool?"

"It is *more* than 'cool.' Project Electron could completely change the world. Electricity. Generated by renewable resources. Being converted into energy used by the human body. A way to remove the need for food. Think of all of the wars, the economic oppression, the pure suffering simply created by lack of food. The industrial complex that devastates our planet's delicate balance for mass production of food. Remove *all* of that. What could the human race accomplish? How might the earth recover? That is the scope of Project Electron."

"Sounds great. Where do I donate?"

"Waris came close to achieving this. He created a successful electrical-biological system, something that connected to the human body. Now the amount of electricity the body could take. That—" her defenses broke, her eyes softening "—that is where Waris ran into a…problem. At low volume, the project worked. But anything greater than a snack, the equivalent of a granola bar, an apple, it shocked the system. Waris was determined to find a way to make it work. To tweak the equations. He was so close. And then…"

This time, Sasha's guard really dropped. Her eyes got glassy, her shoulders drooped, she stood silent for what felt like minutes.

"The man in the capsule," Jamie said, finally putting it all together.

"Yes. Waris. That capsule keeps him alive. We are tweaking the genetic code," she said. "We are using electricity to activate new parts of the human brain. You. Zoe. The others who've been experimented on."

Others? So the rumors about Hartnell City must have been true. Were they in this facility too?

She went on. "But we need to find a way to *heal* Waris. So he can become whole again, and finish Project Electron. I used myself as the trial run on all serum variations until four years ago. Until my body couldn't be pushed any further. But then we found Zoe. Each time Zoe's memory was reset, we evolved the serum formula. With every revision of Zoe, she becomes stronger. Last time, she even got thermal vision. Her brain is activating more, her body becoming capable of more. Everyone else's body burns out, but hers, she shows us that it's possible for a body to safely bond with the regenerative properties of our serum. We just need full cohesion between the brain and the body. Only then can we give it to Waris. We are *so close*, but we need to reset Zoe one more time. That's where you come in."

Jamie looked back at the screen, at the image of Zoe tied to the chair, the same way he was. Her matted hair fell in front of her face as her head fell forward, unconscious or at least very groggy.

"You're not resetting me?"

"No. Your evolution into memory powers are a valuable tool. We don't want to mess with that. We need two things to bring Waris back—the city's electrical grid and Zoe. Well, three things, really. Because you need to do what you've done before. You need to wipe her mind again."

Again? Jamie was starting to piece together the picture here, that previous versions of himself had used his abilities for them. "What? No!" Even though he never wanted to really *hurt* the Throwing Star, removing some of her memories wouldn't have seemed like the worst thing in the world. But not now, not after everything. Zoe's whole *goal* was to discover who she was meant to be; he couldn't take that away from her.

"We've reset her powers. Letting her keep her memories while we await the next serum's results puts us all at risk. Unless you think holding someone with anger issues and extraordinary strength and speed contained here is a good idea. I certainly don't. And I'm not putting my staff at risk. No, we reset her and let her organically activate her abilities. Something about being out in the world triggers the evolution in unique ways. It's the best way to test them."

"Why are you even telling me your whole plan? That's really *villain* of you."

Sasha shook her head with a very nonmaniacal frown. "Villain. That's funny. Now, I'm not just telling you my plan. Our plan. I understand you've become friends with Zoe. Hurting your friend is hard. But consider what you're doing it for. Eliminating hunger. Changing the way the entire planet handles resources. Literally saving the world. You would be doing that by wiping Zoe's memory. There's no way she'd cooperate with the experiment if she knew what already happened. Look, Zoe is not really your friend."

"I think I'm the better judge of that."

"Not the real Zoe. The original Zoe. That person is long gone. You interacted with a fragment of her, a controlled experiment, for a few weeks? How does that make you a friend? You think about that for a minute." Sasha got up before he could respond and stormed out the door, her gait completely different from her departure to grab coffee. A minute later, she appeared on the screen's security feed, now with a cart behind her. She pressed a button on the cart, and suddenly the device on it lit up with a blinding blue, a light so intense it caused trails across the screen. With clinical precision, she pulled out a tube connected to the device and attached a needle to it.

"Oh shit," Jamie said under his breath.

Sasha looked directly at the camera and nodded, then jabbed the needle into Zoe's arm. Ten, maybe fifteen seconds elapsed before Zoe's body seized up, causing the blue light to fluctuate. Her neck was thrown back, her shoulders tensed and bounced and fell and repeated. The cycle continued, throwing Zoe's body into an ongoing cycle of seizing and relaxing. Sasha threw another look, a message in itself to Jamie, before exiting the cell.

Outside, several doors slammed before Sasha came back in. "Her body is resetting. Now it's time for her mind. Look, I'm not sure what it is about you two. The last time we reset her, she escaped to the roof. We caught you talking to her, but we weren't sure why. That's why your mind was erased. You volunteered to do it, as an apology for stepping out of line, and we reset you in your apartment. We gave you the illusion of freedom to let your ability evolve organically out there, safely away from any other experiments at the facility. Never expected the whole Mind Robber thing to happen, though."

"You left those notes? You set me up? Why would you do that?"

"For this exact moment. I've been watching you this whole time. Who do you think sent the police your way after the last bank robbery?"

That evening, before the support group, when that detective showed up at his doorstep for no particular reason. Sasha did that?

"I'll tell you why," she said, as though she read his thoughts. His eyebrows arched up and he glanced at her. "See, I can read memories. Like you. But I can't pluck them out. I'm not as powerful as you. You have read-write access. I am read-only." She gave a short laugh to herself, and Jamie told himself to laugh too even though her joke wasn't funny. "I did that to keep you in line. We need you, your powers. We can't be having you get caught or killed.

"Now that you're here, you know the truth—that we own

you. And you can't disobey. There's only one thing you can do and you *know* it. Help us change the world. Help us save humanity. Bring Waris back. You need to wipe her mind. And I'll check her, make sure you didn't leave anything about her identity."

Sasha's truth sank in. There was no way out of this room *or* this situation. His teeth ground while his mind raced for something different, something new. The walls were concrete. She had extraordinary strength. Every single angle tilted in her favor. The only difference was that Sasha *needed* something from him.

The only measure of control in this situation, the fact that he alone would be performing the surgery.

But maybe that was enough of an advantage. "You know, there's never a one hundred percent memory wipe," he said, the words coming deliberately while an idea formed behind it. "There's always a fraction left of scattered memories." The statement caused Sasha's head to tilt. "Scan me. You'll know I'm not lying. I just want to make sure you know this so you don't hunt me down if you see random fragments in her mind."

"I understand," she said, standing up and gesturing at the door. "It's time."

Jamie watched as Zoe's body shook and raged, driven by unconscious turmoil inside her body. There was only one way to help her, to help both of them.

"You want to be a hero to the world," Jamie said. "Alright. Then I'll be the villain."

21

THEY WERE THE MOST lovely dreams.

Not just hovering, but *flying*. Endless propulsion upward, forward, zooming down, and when Zoe *did* hover, the most effortless of hovers, a giant tiger-bird floated up to greet her. It nudged her with its cat nose while feathered wings beat at a soothing rhythm, then it looked up.

Of course it looked up. Because falling oh so gently from the sky were tacos. All sorts of tacos: crisp corn-shelled tacos with ground beef, soft tortillas with fried fish, tiny street tacos with carne asada. They floated down, slow enough to take a bite out of passing tacos, and she looked at the tiger-bird; it looked back and they hovered somewhere above the clouds, eating tacos together.

But when she looked down, she realized that her feet were now stone. Not just feet, but all the way up to her knees. Zoe ate more and more tacos, and every time she looked down, the farther the stone inched up. She should stop—she wanted to

stop—but she couldn't, as if her arms moved on autopilot, grabbing and shoving tacos into her mouth until her fingers stiffened
and everything up to her neck was solid rock.

Then she started to fall, her powers gone. Frozen, arms outstretched, weight of her now-stone body caused her to circle
continuously while she dropped, the tiger-birds laughing at her,
tacos pelting her in the face all the while. Her shoulder slammed
into the ground, splintering the stone shell and opening up a
torrent of blood and the sharpest lightning strike of pain. Zoe's
eyes flew open, and rather than being surrounded by tacos, she
found herself in a dingy room, fluorescent lighting overhead
showcasing the sharp contrasting tones of, well, everything.

She blinked as details came into focus, or at least she thought
so. Maybe. There weren't that many details to grasp for this drab
space: walls, a door, some cracks in the floor and a whole lot
of olive green, or at least that's how it appeared given the harsh
lighting. Except for when the lamp flickered, a brief flash of
blue coming through as Zoe's visual focus returned.

Then it went again, everything becoming blurry as the pain
in her shoulder hit her conscious mind. In fact, it hurt so much
that it rippled up and down her body, causing her head to sting
and her legs to ache. She craned her neck and saw a bandage,
a small dot of red oozing into the middle of the white gauze.

Arms. They were tied up. She wiggled her fingers, all while
telling herself to pull details of what transpired. She'd rushed
back to San Delgado after leaving a facility.

A facility with grim walls and ugly lighting. Just like this one.
Shit.

And then she'd sprinted to Jamie's apartment. They were talking. No, not just talking. They were finishing *Lo-Bot: Samurai Cyborg*. Goddamn it, they actually finished it and right now
she couldn't remember the way it ended. Jamie's cat was there,
though, and then something happened. Noises, lights went out.
Shouting. And hitting the floor.

"Jamie?" She tried to yell, but her strength wouldn't let her. It came out a meek call, sounding more like scolding someone who held up the table's order at a restaurant rather than a desperate cry following a crisis.

But it wasn't just her voice that lacked strength. Her fingers flexed behind her but when she tightened her arms, they failed to snap the ropes that bound them. Her legs too, they should have been able to somehow get out of whatever was binding her, maybe even propel her up into a hover.

Instead, only pain registered. Her shoulder for sure, but it went beyond that. Everywhere else joined, from burning in her veins to pounding in her temples. Clearly she'd picked the wrong time to try to be responsible.

This all seemed familiar, and for a moment, Zoe wondered if another memory might be surfacing, a true memory. Her eyes squeezed shut, her mind urging something to come into the light. It did—except it wasn't her memory. No trick from a prior escape or secret visit arrived to rescue her, and instead she remembered a similar scene in a 1980s slasher flick called *High School Basement Massacre*. Spoiler: the chained-up teenager died in a gruesomely fake way. Not the preferred ending for her own story. "Come on," she muttered to herself, the chair's legs scraping and bouncing against the floor. Then the doorknob turned.

The door pushed open, squeaky hinges preventing any sort of stealthy rescue. But it didn't matter because unlike *High School Basement Massacre*, a friendly face appeared.

"Jamie!" she said, a surge of adrenaline bringing things into focus. At least for a moment. The reality of whatever they'd stuck in her clawed and grabbed her back toward reality. Her mind and body remained a step out of sync, both like a car engine that simply refused to turn. "Jamie," she said again, her voice softer, not because of relaxing or wanting to keep her voice down, but from barely being able to function.

Why wasn't he responding? Her words seemed to bounce off

him; he didn't look at her, and instead he paced the room, back and forth, mumbling to himself. His words lacked the projection necessary to be audible, and...

Where was his heat signature?

No strength.

No thermal vision.

No detection of any kind.

This wasn't good.

And a thick fog over her consciousness. It came and went, spiking and crashing, bringing her thoughts and muscles into alignment for seconds before everything felt like a muddy mess. Even her eyes blurred.

The fluorescent lights of the room buzzed as they flickered. In the corner of the room, she swore she saw a flash of blue again. What did Jamie say about the blue before? It *meant* something, something important, but the moments leading to her capture blurred out the most. "Jamie, quit pacing around. My powers are gone. We gotta get out of here."

Jamie kept talking to himself, a rhythm to his words even though Zoe couldn't hear the specifics but their singsong nature reminded her of almost a children's nursery rhyme.

"Zoe Wong," he finally said, turning to face her. "That is who you are. Not who you *think* you are—the Throwing Star." He gave a quick laugh, and even though he spoke in his native British accent, his words carried the pacing of his Mind Robber speeches. "Does your arm hurt? Is it sore? You'll find that it's more than a little pain. You see, your days of going out to fight crime are over. It must have been fun, playing vigilante out there. Thinking you could do something special, the whole city working together to cheer you on. Well, this is the thing, we were all having a laugh at you when we got the sense that you were trying to do something a little more. A little too much. But then one more impossible thing happened, more impossible than the chance you'd meet me."

He rushed in close, noses practically touching. So close that she could see the sweat on his brow, and though his words and tone communicated venom, his eyes showed something different.

Fear.

"You got caught."

"Jamie, whatever game you're playing, you can act like a maniac later. We need to get out of here."

His brow creased and his eyes gave away a sense of vulnerability or hesitation or something that wasn't this act he'd been putting on. He stood back up. "They expect to see you all over the city," he yelled, his voice louder than she ever recalled hearing, continuing as if he didn't even hear her. "In the Banking District. At McCrimmon Square. On top of the TransNational Building. At Dock 19. They all look for you. The woman walking her child to the grocery store. The couple meeting for the first time downtown. The man braving the cold bay wind with a long scarf. They look outside at ten, eleven o'clock, midnight, hoping to see you. Hoping that you'll be out there trying to make a difference. 'I'll wait every night for just one glimpse, one second of something extraordinary' they tell themselves. But no more."

This wasn't the Jamie who'd researched Telos over pizza with her. Or helped rescue people out of a burning building with her. Something was different. Did they do something to him?

"Jamie! It's me. Help me." Her elbows pounded against the chair. "Help me. Please."

His arms flew up forming a *V* over his head. He held the moment, perhaps for too long. If he was going for theatrics, this went from brilliant-but-scary performance to overindulgent, like the moments when she'd either decide to go all in on watching a movie or turning it off. The only difference was that this moment existed in her reality. If the context weren't so terrifying, she would have burst out laughing.

"I am the Mind Robber."

He spun on his heel, one arm outstretched, finger pointed directly at her.

"This is my victory over you. You have lost."

All of it was a lie. Was it? He couldn't have. He couldn't have been that good of an actor, could he? And yet, seeing him do his stupid Mind Robber schtick hit her harder than stumbling over her feet in the Metro station. Her stomach sank, her shoulders slumped, and the burning in her wrists from her struggle withered as everything melted into the chair.

Even steps clicked across the floor as he approached her, and the back of her neck began to tingle. "Jamie, don't do this. We're friends. Don't—"

"I win. And you will never," his voice came out in a low growl, "remember that my name is Jamie."

A sweeping dizziness enveloped Zoe before everything went dark.

22

JAMIE LOOKED OVER HIS shoulder again, scanning around the wharf. Not the tourist part on the north side of the wharf, but the quarter-mile stretch tagged for redevelopment. Shuttered windows lined the old factories, piles of garbage went unchecked in alleys, and the stink of algae permeated through the air. And yet, he'd gone there night after night, starting as soon as Kaftan released him.

Just in case.

Night six was here, and it looked pretty much the same as the five nights prior. Traffic didn't change, it was too late in the evening. People didn't pass through, evening watering holes and clubs lived on the other side. Even the weather, which occasionally got temperamental in San Delgado, remained remarkably consistent on all six days, cool enough for a coat but dry enough to go without an umbrella despite the constant bay mist tickling his face.

He waited an hour every time, leaning with his back against

the pier's fencing. On occasion, footsteps or voices would precede the appearance of a silhouette. But he knew right away that they weren't the reason why he came.

He knew immediately that none of the people were Zoe.

One time, he dove into someone's mind, simply to assess if that person posed a threat. Late-night hangouts in the industrial end of San Delgado's wharf weren't exactly safe, but a quick flip through the passing man's memories showed that his pursed frown and tense stance had more to do with a recent romantic breakup than any intent to mug Jamie.

The first night, he figured that she wouldn't be here. He knew Kaftan's team had released her at some point so she could "organically activate her abilities." A little bit of detective work combined with some memory-diving around Telos confirmed that theory; that, along with knowing that Kaftan *needed* Zoe's next iteration to fulfil her plan of reviving her husband, it all pointed to Zoe being let out...somewhere. Maybe in San Delgado, but maybe in a neighboring city. Maybe Hartnell City, to see how she'd collide with the other rumored extraordinaries. Maybe even Janloon, with new rumors of extraordinary-powered gangsters getting into bloody turf wars there. But digging any deeper would have required going online, and at this point, any sort of digital trail was out of the question. Everything required safe distances and a pad of paper, not just because of Sasha's potential digital tracking, but also the fact that a viral video of Zoe stealing a car on a rural road had gone viral. That hadn't endeared extraordinaries to the general public—or the police.

Discretion across all fronts, though the goal was the same: find Zoe.

She could be anywhere, really. She could be dead. They might have lied.

Or she just needed time to piece things together.

That's what he was counting on. How long it'd take her, he

wasn't sure. But he came here every night at ten o'clock, thermos of hot coffee to go along with his hope that she'd make it.

Five minutes left. Each night he waited from ten to eleven, a full hour. Zoe would be fine if she made it. At least, he assumed so, given that Sasha's current serum was a variation of the previous injection that gave Zoe abilities in the first place. Remove, reset, restart—that seemed to be the plan.

Jamie figured it would take her mere hours to figure out her powers. But how long would it take for her to piece together the clues he'd left behind? The cold air nipped at his cheeks, and he tightened the long scarf to keep the warmth in around his neck. He'd originally included that detail so she could spot him from a distance, but it proved to be quite functional right now.

Jamie's phone beeped to tell him that eleven o'clock had come and gone. Day six down. Twenty-four more to go, for a total of thirty, or one month. One month of hoping Zoe would put it all together. And then he could put *her* back together, as much as he could.

If not, there was plan B: pack up Normal and hide somewhere in the Caribbean. Anything to get out of San Delgado, away from Kaftan and whoever might be watching him. His goal chart wasn't totally filled out, but he preferred safety over hitting his projected retirement needs. That would have been plan A, that *should* have been plan A. But even with all of his instincts telling him to run like hell, the least he owed Zoe was a chance to become herself again.

Time to go. She wasn't coming.

A cool breeze kicked up, picking up mist from the adjacent bay. Jamie closed his eyes, letting it wash over him as he considered another possibility.

Maybe she did figure it out and simply chose not to come.

It seemed unlikely, given Zoe's instinctive pursuit of truth. But even though everything that he'd said and done was a form of best-case scenario for their circumstances, he'd wondered if things could have gone differently. Instead, he'd jumped right into it without even consulting her. That was a form of betrayal in itself, leaving him with an underlying fear that he'd given up on his only friend.

Well, not only friend, but only human friend. Normal still counted.

Jamie adjusted the backpack weighing down his shoulders, scanned the scene behind him one more time and started his usual walk down the pier.

23

SHE WAS NOT JUST Zoe Wong. She was the Throwing Star. She knew that now.

It took some legwork to get there.

When she awoke a few weeks ago, her eyes focused on a name tag in her dingy apartment. Senses started activating, taking in sounds and smells, along with the realization that she stood in the middle of an empty room, light casting in from its single window overlooking the Oakmount port, San Delgado's cityscape visible across the bay. Dirty carpet, a sleeping bag and a crisp name tag sitting in the middle of the room, the name "Zoe Wong" scribbled across it in felt-tip marker. Next to it, a smartphone that got full service without any need to activate an account.

At the time, she wasn't sure if that was her or someone else. Maybe whoever owned the place, the landlord or current renter or whomever. But the weird note next to it, the one that said "See how strong you are," that stuck in her mind more than the name.

That wasn't what you'd normally tell people. Even if you

were, like, a professional arm wrestler or something. It really didn't make for an appropriate welcome note from a landlord. So that was weird.

Plus, there were the memories.

They didn't make sense. They seemed scattered, random, as if someone took a few dozen screenshots out of a movie and placed them out of order. Most of them involved this man, a slight man with floppy brown hair and a British accent. But what he said made no sense. Was he a boyfriend, a boss? Why did half the memories take place in some ugly warehouse room? And the other memories she had, they were the opposite of that—visceral, kinetic, still images of being at great heights or punching someone in an alley. Brief, but tangible, and always fleeting, like they were on their way over a cliff but if she thought hard enough about it, she could throw out a hand and rescue them.

The questions remained over the weeks, but at least now she'd partially found stuff to furnish the place. Her notebook rested on a coffee table with one cracked leg. In the corner, a fan helped circulate the air in the room, despite kind of smelling like wet dog. In the other corner a plastic penguin greeted her whenever she came home. And in the center, a lawn chair recovered from her building's lobby that she'd managed to scrub clean enough to use without leaving dirt smudges on her pants each time.

Zoe sat down, her eyes closed and hands against her temples. She *must* have been the Throwing Star. Her memories showed it. Searching online brought up stories of things she *knew* she could do. The speed, the strength. Articles didn't mention her thermal vision, but maybe she'd just never told anyone about that before; either way, it was really cool. And after reading about the whole hovering thing, she decided to try it out two nights ago and go figure, she could hover, and it was *awesome*.

But where did someone even get a suit like that? Did she have a partner of some kind who furnished her with supplies? And why did she carjack that guy—and why did she let him record it?

Zoe shut her eyes, teeth grinding into her top lip as she attempted to *will* more memories out of herself. They had to mean something, this random collection. Most of them surrounded that mystery man, a seemingly nonsensical conversation they had in that grimy room, but others showed her flashes of her powers. There was one, though, just one that didn't make any sense at all.

It was a wall of some kind. A wall with the strangest decor, but focusing on it, getting it to stay still enough with the details, that proved to be the hard part.

She'd take one more shot at this. She slid out of the relaxed pose of the folding chair, her bare knees scraping on the rough carpet floor until she was kneeling. Her eyes closed again, her entire body tensed and she urged the memory to come to life, from the pale lighting to the haphazard elements pasted on the wall. *It had to mean something,* she kept telling herself, some place or some code or some clue to who she was, what she was meant to be.

The thoughts swirled around, and though her hands were balled into fists, a strange urge took over. As if by autopilot, her left hand raised, a single finger pointed out, and she tapped the air, nerves at the back of her neck tingly and alive.

And suddenly the memory appeared in her mind's eye, as clearly as if she were looking at the decorated wall in that moment.

Her finger held, a strange tension wrapped around it, and when she angled her finger one way, she noticed something strange about the memory: the cheap analog clock on the wall began ticking forward. Angled the other way, and the second-hand backed up. Held still, and the image held still.

Zoe snapped back into the present, eyes flying open and sweat dripping down her cheeks. Her breath heavy and her body so tight it might snap the floorboards in half, she stared straight ahead until a sense of composure returned, focusing on the blank wall in front of her.

Her eyes shut again, a canvas of black to view images. With

a few minutes of practice, jumping back into the memory became as easy as turning a page in a book. Her hand extended, she held the image of the wall and saw it clear.

It wasn't a wall. It was a corkboard.

And they weren't decorations. They were a web of documents and photos pinned to the wall, all tied together point-to-point by string. But diving back into the image, examining it, *staring* at it in her mind, the details didn't make sense—buildings and people and printouts, and the image wasn't close enough for her to read the details, leaving the whole thing as random as—

As random as her memories.

If she could do this with one of her memories, maybe she could with others?

It took about two hours for Zoe to sort through all her memories, or at least she felt certain she'd covered them all. Next to her sat a pad of paper, one of those free bits of stationery that Realtors leave in the lobby of buildings. On top of that lay a pen, a clickity-click pen with the logo of a local plumber, which she'd found wedged into the back of an otherwise empty drawer in her apartment. Thirty-two memories, it seemed. Thirty-two very specific memories, some nothing more than a half-second flash and some as long as two or three words. Nineteen of them were from a conversation between her and the mystery man, and the rest seemed to showcase her powers: a kick here, a punch there, sprinting along a rooftop in the rain.

But the words, the man's words. What could they possibly be describing?

1. *As the*
2. *You fight crime*
3. *At dock 19*
4. *My name is Jamie*
5. *Working together*

6. *I'll*

7. *10 o'clock*

8. *I'll*

9. *Throwing Star*

10. *Got caught*

11. *We were*

12. *Meet me*

13. *With*

14. *You are*

15. *When we*

16. *Wait every night*

17. *At*

18. *Zoe Wong*

19. *A long scarf*

It read like a book with pages torn out. Pieces of the story were missing, huge gaps connecting the dots between these various words and phrases. Jamie—Jamie was the man. That had to be it. And there was confirmation that she was the Throwing Star. But the rest of it? It sounded like some incident happened, maybe at that Dock 19. She lived in Oakmount, across the bridge and about twenty miles from there. Dock 19. If she got out to the library tomorrow, she could research any incidents that might have involved Dock 19.

She stared at the list, wondering if any words and punctuation had been lifted out of it. They remained puzzle pieces without any edges or corners, no final image for reference and scope. There may have been a handful of words between them or they may have all been one bit each from each chapter in her life.

Her eyes closed, trying to will some logic out of it all. But logic didn't arrive.

Something better did.

The memory of the corkboard. The individual disparate pieces, all connected together by string.

What if the words weren't clues to a bigger message?

What if they *were* the message?

Zoe moved at accelerated speed, tearing individual sheets from the notepad, and transcribing each statement onto its own piece of paper. She spread them out in a large arch in front of her, and though her body moved at extraordinary speeds, her mind failed to keep pace. Moving the pieces back and forth, here and there, swapping them, inverting them, trying to make sense of them, the bigger picture eluded her.

She knelt down, staring at the words, holding each sheet up to her face, as if proximity would create the connective tissue from one word to the next.

Except maybe being close wasn't the trick.

Zoe vaulted up then threw her palms out, hovering in her apartment, loose strands of her hair brushing against the popcorn ceiling. From there, she could see all the phrases as equals, and her mind locked in, the logic beginning to take form.

She landed with a thud, probably frightening whoever lived below her. On her knees, she swapped pieces of paper, moving them into slots until some form of coherent message appeared. Fifteen minutes later, something finally made sense, not just as words but with everything else that remained in her mind.

You are Zoe Wong. You fight crime as the Throwing Star. My name is Jamie. We were working together when we got caught. Meet me at Dock 19 at 10 o'clock. I'll wait every night with a long scarf.

The small of her back ached from being hunched over for so long, a pain that resonated differently than what she felt after her clumsy experiments to test her powers or trying to live up to the legacy of the Throwing Star. She stood, arms stretched overhead, mind filled with possibilities at the untangled mystery before her.

24

THE CLOCK KEPT TICKING on Zoe, and with each passing evening—twenty, in fact—Jamie wondered, well, he wondered about many things. Were his clues too vague? Would she even be able to recover them? Had Dr. Kaftan moved her all the way to the other side of the continent?

Even if they reunited, then what? He knew what would be next for him—a plane ticket with Normal in tow. But would Zoe try to take down Kaftan? Or would she disappear in her own way?

He supposed it didn't matter. He owed Zoe the chance to become herself again. Anything else was up to her. Jamie sighed, his breath curling into a little fog visible in the cool night. From afar, something clattered; a quick look down the wharf showed no signs of people, not even a silhouette in the distance.

Perhaps just a cat in the alley. Hopefully a cat somewhat more capable at survival than Normal. Jamie smirked to himself at the thought, and memories surfaced naturally—no digging around or pulling up or freezing, no hand gestures. This was simpler, the mere come and go of warm memory, of that first day and Normal's courtyard ineptness at handling a bird. Jamie let himself sink into the memory, unable to fight the smile coming over his face.

"What are you grinning at?"

That voice.

Jamie spun around, eyes and every other sense on high alert. No one at the abandoned factory to his left. And no on at the empty adult school on his right. Nothing behind him, nothing straight ahead, nowhere for the voice to come from—

Nowhere but up.

Of course.

A three-story office building across the street, a place that probably didn't look so unfriendly during the daytime. There, at the very top, he saw the silhouette of a woman standing at attention. He waved before he thought better of it, and as he checked his surroundings again for anyone or anything that might have caught the gesture, she leaped off the rooftop, hands extended and palms flat. She descended to the ground at a soft speed, landing with barely a clack of her shoes.

Jamie jogged forward, one foot landing ungracefully in a puddle as he went to meet her. The backpack on his shoulders bounced up and down with each step, and the now-soaked bottom of his left pant leg sprayed dribbles with each movement. It didn't matter, though. She was here. She made it. Jamie wasn't much of a hugger, though maybe he simply didn't have the opportunity due to the whole avoiding people thing. In any case, this felt like an arms-wide-open moment. "Zoe!" That came out louder than it probably should have, and his legs nearly tangled between themselves as he dashed across the street without looking both ways.

Except she didn't return the gesture. Both of her hands went up in a defensive posture, though not quite as crisp as he'd seen before. Her body probably retained some of the muscle memory from all those Throwing Star hours prior to the erasure, though he guessed that whatever specific training and experience she had must have reset too. Jamie stopped several feet from the curb. "You made it." He tugged at the wool around his neck, "Did the scarf help? It seemed kind of silly but I thought *something* visual might help."

An oncoming rumble made Jamie suddenly realize that if a car came zipping by, he'd be a goner. He took two steps forward, only for Zoe to dash backward at a frighteningly instant speed, her fists still ready.

"Wait, wait, wait. I'm just trying to not get killed by that," he said, thumbing at the truck rolling by them. "You're here. It actually worked."

"Who are you?"

"My name is Jamie and I'm—"

"Yeah, yeah, I got that. But *who* are you?"

Jamie's hands shot up, palms out. Zoe's eyes were wide but focused and she inched toward him before angling off to the side. He tried to meet her gaze but she refused to look at him. "You've rediscovered your abilities," he said, searching for something to break through with her. "This is good."

"You're in my memory," she said with a sneer. "Why?"

"Okay. Okay, look, let me fill you in. I laid clues in there for you with the hopes that you'd put them together. Where did they stash you this time?"

"Answer the question. Who are you?"

"My name is Jamie," he repeated, "and I'm your *friend*." Urgency pushed the words out at an accelerated clip. Though he didn't have Zoe's emotional detection, tension clearly escalated in her. "I'm like you. Not *exactly* like you but I have abilities. Yours are physical. Mine are mental. Look, I—"

Before he got the words out, Zoe grabbed him by the collar and launched upward. Air stung Jamie's cheeks, the already cold

night breeze suddenly a hundred times more intense for a sprinkle of seconds. Jamie's stomach dropped as they hit the peak of
ascent and landed on the rooftop of the adult trade school. Zoe's
boots crunched into gravel and Jamie gasped for any oxygen
that might restore everything that was just knocked out of him.

"There," Zoe said. "Out of sight. So, *Jamie*, you left all those
clues for me. How do I know it's not a trap? Why don't I just
throw you into the bay from here? What's in the bag? A weapon?
Poison? Something to block my abilities?"

"No. No, no, it's not that at all." Jesus, becoming friends
with Zoe had been hard enough the *first* time. He had to break
through her suspicion *again*? "Look, let me just show you—"

"Slowly. Back away."

"Zoe. Listen to my voice. Think about the memories. Can't
you tell I'm being honest?" He locked eyes with her; there had
to be *some* connection there. "And a little, you know, terrified?"

"If we're friends, why did you tie me up?"

"Tie you—no, that wasn't me. But they sent me in to, um…"
Probably *not* the best thing to lead with. "Look. It's complicated.
Can I *please* show you what's in this bag?"

Zoe didn't respond. Her whole body remained a coiled trap,
and if he said the wrong thing, it would trigger, which probably would lead to him flying off this building.

"I'm gonna open this bag really slowly." Jamie undid the straps
across the backpack's top flap. Weeks ago, the very same backpack lay strapped to his shoulders, piles of cash bouncing around
inside while he'd run as fast as he could from the Throwing Star.

And now, he reached in for something of much higher value.

"Is that…" Zoe leaned forward, her posture suddenly halfway to relaxed. "Is that a binder?"

"It is." The now-empty backpack landed at Jamie's feet and
he held the binder out with both hands. "Okay, there's this scientist named Kaftan who's experimenting with people. Giving
them powers and observing them. It's a long story. Kaftan just

reset your memories a little while back. This binder, I know it's not the same as having your memories. And there's only so far I could go back. But as far as Zoe Wong, the Throwing Star, this is everything I could figure out about who you were. From what you told me, what we did together, what we researched."

Though the binder was filled to capacity with sheets and sheets of paper, Zoe lifted it out of his hand as if it were a single sheet from a newspaper. "Why didn't they reset you?"

"My guess is that Kaftan thinks I'm cornered. That I'm not a threat. And they didn't foresee my whole Mind Robber fiasco last time around, so it was easier to keep tabs on me this way." Jamie thought of all his research, all his plans—the saved money, the possible beach locations, maybe even temping again if he had to.

He supposed Kaftan was right.

"This," she said, holding it close and opening it up, "looks like a lot."

"Yeah. Well, when you don't have a day job, you find time to do stuff like this." Jamie chuckled to himself, breath rolling into the night. "You could say I'm pretty good with memory."

Zoe's face twisted, lips pursed and eyes shut. A convulsion whipped through her body and she handed the binder back to Jamie.

"Whoa, whoa, whoa. What is it?" he asked. "What did they do to you?"

"I don't…" Zoe said before her nose twitched again. "I don't," she tried again before exploding out a sneeze, one that echoed across the night.

Jamie looked at Zoe, then the binder, then back again. "Oh shit."

"What did you lace that with?" Zoe said between coughs, tears streaming down her cheeks.

"Nothing. It's nothing. It's cat hair. Normal must have rubbed on the binder. I left it on the coffee table, sometimes she lies down on random flat surfaces and—"

"Your cat is named Normal?"

"Yeah. And you're allergic to her. Sorry about that."

Zoe nodded, wiping her nose. Jamie tried not to look at the unsightly drip that dangled seemingly without Zoe's notice. "I, um..." He patted his pockets, then opened up the front backpack pouch for his usual stash of emergency napkins taken from coffee shops. "Here. They're a little rough on the nose but they get the job done."

"Thanks." Zoe took the napkin, leaving Jamie to wonder if extraordinary nose blowing cleared out sinuses more effectively than for regular humans. "Hey," she said. "You wrote all this from memory?"

"Yeah, why do..."

Jamie stopped midsentence. He didn't need an answer. The way Zoe held her hand up, index finger out, told him everything he needed to know.

"Holy shit, Zoe. You can..."

"Yeah," she said with a grin. "I can."

Was that her next evolution? Kaftan had mentioned something about needing the serum to work on both a physical and mental level. What was the word Kaftan used? Revision? Perhaps this *revision* represented the next step, the final goal in the process. Possibilities exploded, but they hung counterbalanced with his own urges to safely pack up Normal and run. One look at Zoe, though, showed that her grin pushed even wider, her eyes glowing with excitement. Except for one quick glance at the scarf around his neck, her focus locked in, confidence practically dripping off of her.

It couldn't hurt to try, could it? He just needed one thing.

"Okay." His head began to bob up and down in a rhythm of

nods. "Okay, then. If we're gonna do this, I just have one request. Can we go somewhere with coffee?"

"Sure. By the way," she said, "the scarf kind of works for the
Mind Robber. Looks cooler than a hood."

25

JAMIE HAD LIED TO HER.

That night, when he first helped Zoe break through the wall of blankness protecting her memories, he'd seen something and he'd lied to her about it. Now she knew.

And yet, she wasn't mad about it.

Back then, he didn't have the proper context for it. And maybe he still didn't, other than the fact that at some point during his employment under Telos, he grew a conscience and then was reset himself. But when he—the version of Jamie currently sitting with her—discovered that memory fragment, he felt immediate guilt. She knew this, the guilt so powerful in his memory that it colored her reading of that moment.

It was a lie. But done for a purpose. And the anguish he felt over that decision ate at him enough that she opted not to bring it up. Instead, she chose to gloss over that moment for now.

So much else was there.

Not everything. But thumbing through all of Jamie's memories told Zoe enough.

Enough about who the Throwing Star was.

Enough about who Zoe was. Some things seemed to be universal about her, even down to the free movie app she still used on her phone.

Enough about who the Mind Robber was.

Enough about Jamie's cat. Actually a bit too much. He really spoiled that cat.

And enough about Telos, Kaftan, Project Electron. At least she didn't make Jamie regurgitate Kaftan's whole speech trying to justify experimenting on desperate people to save the world in a really, really roundabout way. And who wanted to *eat* electricity anyway? That sounded terrible. Even if it was in the form of electric tacos.

The worst part was apparently she'd done some really, really cool stuff. Breaking into Kaftan's facility, taking out guards, jumping out a high window while being shot at. But the only thing she'd seen was herself *telling* the story, no cool first-person experience of it all. But the secondhand tale would have to be enough to boost her confidence.

Zoe Wong was a total badass. She liked that.

"Are you, um, done?" Jamie asked. They'd settled into the all-night café where they had been not that long ago, only a few miles from Jamie's house. Seriously, Jamie drank a lot of coffee. For a moment, Zoe stopped thinking about the bigger picture and wondered just how Jamie wasn't jittery all the time given his level of coffee consumption.

"I think so. I might need to fill in the blanks later."

"Do you... I mean..." He paused, then glanced around with a worried grimace. She tracked his eyes, matching his scans of the place. It was late—past midnight—and other than one person on her laptop, earbuds in, only a pair of employees lingered behind the counter. "You're good with everything you saw?"

The rooftop. He had to be dancing around the whole rooftop topic. But that wasn't a conversation for now; plenty of questions still needed answers, but they could wait till later. "Yeah. What's next?"

"You know what I can do now," Jamie said. "Have you ever tried anything like that?"

"No. I mean, I just figured out this whole memory viewing thing this morning. So it's been a bit of a crash course." A grin took over, Zoe's mind alive with possibilities. "Hey, you can teach me. I mean, maybe we'll even unlock new possibilities for you. Think about it."

Jamie took a sip from his mug, holding it at his face. His look gave away the fact that this wasn't exactly lighting a spark of enthusiasm. In fact, it seemed quite the opposite; everything about him appeared frozen. Zoe glanced around to make sure the world still moved around them, in case she'd developed the ability to pause time over the past few minutes.

Given everything that had happened, it wouldn't totally be out of the question.

Zoe's elbows landed on the table, her left index finger pointed at Jamie.

"Whoa, hey, what are you doing?" Jamie asked with a sudden jerk.

"Heh. Got your attention. Come on, let's get *excited*," Zoe said with a light smack of the table. "It's you and me. Back together. We broke into Telos, you know? You got in their computer system. I rode on top of a truck. I threw a freakin' motorcycle at armed guards."

"That has yet to be confirmed. You may have been exaggerating. I don't know. But," Jamie said, draining his mug of coffee, "I wouldn't put it past you. Trying to impress me."

"I've tested my abilities. I'm pretty sure I pulled it off. Full stop."

"Okay, then. Mark me impressed."

"Right? See? We make an awesome team." Sleep would be impossible tonight after discovering all this. Every night opened up to new possibilities. Zoe wondered why the old her chose a FoodFast job and occasionally drinking too much. That version and her current self didn't seem to diverge too much other than developing memory powers. So what was different? What nudged the needle this time?

The question paused her momentum, freezing her until she caught Jamie staring at her.

That simple, huh?

"I'm slightly terrified of your sudden confidence," he said. "That's new."

"Come on." Jamie winced at her near giddiness, so much that she told herself to rein it in a little bit. "Look, Kaftan and her team, they may have already figured out that we reconnected. They could be spying on us right now. First strike, you know?" She was *glowing*. She couldn't help it. This was *way* better than discovering her powers on her own. This was knowing that beating the shit out of any adversary, that being able to launch out of sight and hover out of reach, she could go bolder and better than she even imagined.

Who wouldn't be happy about that?

Jamie, apparently. He shook his head and his voice kept low. "No one's here. I've been monitoring the café. Everyone here is legit."

"You know what I mean. Maybe not *here* here—" her arms swooped around "—but around. Watching. How else do you think they tracked us down before? But if we go in now, boom, element of surprise."

"I'm sure they are watching. Kaftan wants your abilities to evolve. But that doesn't even matter." Jamie's head shook again, this time accompanied by a frown. "No, no, no. My coded message for you wasn't about trying any sort of frontal assault on Kaftan. It was restoring who you are. So you didn't wonder. That's all I wanted to do. Normal and I are going to go somewhere. I keep thinking about the Caribbean. Have you ever tried coffee beans imported from there? The real stuff? It sounds like a dream. Working in a little café. Quiet. Reading a lot of books. That was my plan B if we didn't reconnect. And now it can be plan A."

The wistful glint in his eyes betrayed that he probably visualized reading books around his allergy-bomb of a cat while sipping strong coffee on the beach right now.

She supposed that sounded appealing to some. But not her.

"Zoe. You are my friend. I don't..." His mouth formed a thin line while he paused. "I don't make friends easily. So it was important that I bring you back. But now that I have, I can say goodbye."

"You can't give me all of this and then take off. Jamie, listen. Isn't Kaftan going to hurt more people?"

"We don't know that."

"Yes we do. She needs the power grid to do whatever she needs to do. You take that out, lots of bad things happen. Look at all the crimes that happened during the rolling blackouts. That was, I dunno, half of the dudes I beat up. Think of the people in this city, all at risk. Like..." A flash of one of Jamie's co-opted memories came to Zoe, perfect for this type of convincing. "Like that nice old couple who live across the courtyard from you. They're the people who'd be vulnerable during a blackout. And for how long? An hour is bad. More than that..." The true consequences all seemed theoretical at this point,

"No, look. You're the hero, not me." He pointed at her, his look way too serious and solemn for this moment. "I wasn't even that good of a villain. True villains are, like, sociopaths who don't care. I don't know what the word is for 'extremely pragmatic bank robber,' but that's me. That *was* me. And that's not me anymore. Now? I'm just..." He looked up, straight up, and blew a sigh into the air. "I'm just done with it all."

"You're scared," she said after a pause. "You're scared of her?"

"Given the fact that I can't fly or throw motorcycles at people, yes. I am *terrified* of her."

"You're selling yourself short." Zoe spoke with brightness in her tone, like a life coach more than someone trying to coax a partner into highly illegal but morally justified crimes. "You broke into Telos—"

"Because you bribed me."

"Because you *cared*. See, here's the thing. Yeah, I can read memories now, but it's easier than that. You don't risk everything you did because you don't care. There are better, safer ways. You wanted to help. And look at *how* you broke into Telos, that's like some real spy movie shit right there."

"I thought you watched horror movies."

"They have some pretty bad '70s spy movies too. Come on, we go in, we take her down and we finally figure out who I really am."

"You're mistaken. I think…" Harsh lines creased across Jamie's forehead, visible even through the brown hair that drooped over his eyes when he looked down. "I think you're an optimist. Maybe that's who Zoe Wong really is."

"You could be all that too. We can do this."

Jamie lifted the cup of coffee, his lips stuck on the rim for several seconds. Which meant he was either thinking or stalling, because she'd seen him empty the mug a few minutes prior. He lowered it back to the table with a *clink*, his eyes still drawn low.

"Okay, look," Zoe said. "Let's assume you get out, go to the Caribbean or wherever. Kaftan would still be out there. She'd *still* be experimenting on people, people who never asked for this sort of thing. Think for a minute, really think about those people.

"Those people went to Telos for help. With addiction or depression or other stuff that was eating away at their lives. And Kaftan, she took that good faith and completely betrayed it.

Used it for her own gain. She took advantage of people in need. People like Zoe. The old Zoe.

"People like Frazer."

That pulled Jamie's gaze up to meet hers.

"The ends *don't* justify the means. That's what real villains think. We're better than that. We can stop Project Electron. Maybe it goes beyond us. Hartnell City, the rumors elsewhere. We can help people like them. We can help people like us. We do this, Kaftan stops hurting people and you get to live without guilt." *Guilt.* That single word fired off a cycle of colors in Jamie's heat signature, from the burning in his cheeks to the rapid increase in his heart rate.

She'd hit a nerve.

"I mean, that's what's driving you, isn't it? Guilt?" she continued. "Guilt about Francisco brought you to Telos in the first place." She selectively omitted his clear guilt over lying about the rooftop. "And now it's all you feel. That's why you only rob big banks that are insured. It alleviates the guilt. That woman who got injured, I saw how it weighs on you. Let's absolve you of this. I'm pretty sure taking out the mastermind behind countless genetic experiments and shady deaths balances the karmic scale."

His fingers rapped against the table, a rapid-fire beat left to right and right to left, eventually leading to a heavy sigh.

"Besides, we pull this off and I'll still help you rob a bank. No more Kaftan, you save San Delgado, *and* you get all the money you need to hang out on a beach with nothing but coffee and cats. Forever."

He looked up, meeting her gaze. "Seriously?"

Now she had him. "A deal's a deal." She threw her right hand out and waited. His eyes darted in different directions, first at her open hand, then the coffee mug that needed a refill, then the exit, then the barista cleaning the counter who seemed far too spry for this time of night.

"What the hell," he said in a soft voice, and their hands clasped together for one good shake.

"Besides," Zoe smirked, "they're insured by the government." She sighed. "I just wish I remembered how I made my suit."

"Ah," Jamie said, his energy perking up. "Well, I don't have sewing patterns or anything. But I do have the next best thing."

Zoe's eyebrow ticked up into a firm arch.

"You wanna give your powers a test?"

26

A GOOD NIGHT'S REST didn't come easy after the late-night coffee shop talk. Zoe told him that he'd drank too much coffee, but Jamie knew better. What-ifs swirled through his head, gathering momentum until he'd stared straight at the dark ceiling over his bed for most of the night. Normal must have picked up on that. She circled between his legs on the bed, meowing and kneading and plopping down, only to repeat the whole thing every ten minutes.

Zoe, on the other hand, had zero issues falling asleep. For a solid eight hours, her snores filled the front room, as if someone had simply flipped a switch and knocked her out on the futon, though it might have been the antihistamines. However she managed it, she seemed rested and refreshed.

Now, they waited together on a rooftop, Jamie biting down on his lip in tentative measure, fatigue and anxiety tearing at him from both sides, the only reprieve coming from redoing his calming counting every few minutes. Next to him, though,

Zoe's internal motor already seemed to be running at top speed, waiting for a green light to let loose. They watched together, staring at the window four across and two down.

The light turned on.

"There," Zoe said. "Let's get my suit."

"Whoa, whoa, whoa. Let's *not* get your suit just yet. Remember, this is a test of your powers. So, close your eyes. Can you sense him?"

"I sense a lot of people in that building. They kind of look like ghosts."

"Okay, good, but focus. You'll get a lot of cross-chatter if you let them all in. Lock in on just one person if you can."

Jamie waited, thumb nervously rubbing against the warm side of his coffee thermos. Jumping in this far, this fast suddenly seemed like a bad idea. What if Zoe came with other powers that she didn't understand yet, that she couldn't contain? Was there more Kaftan waited on? "Just…take it slow," he said, as if that gentle reminder would keep things in check.

A strange sound came from Zoe, and he checked himself to make sure he heard it correctly.

Was she…laughing?

"I'm okay," she said, words tangled in the chuckles. "I'm okay. It's just, this is so weird."

"Not that different from yesterday."

"Yeah, but that was like the demo version. This is the real thing."

"Focus, Zoe. We shouldn't be doing this for too long. We're too exposed to be fully protected from Kaftan's people."

"Right, right. Okay." Zoe held up her fingers, the little twitches indicative that she was sorting through her target's memories.

"Remember, you don't have to find anything specifically with him looking at the suit or touching it. It could be in the background or—"

"He's got it in his closet."

So much for that.

"Are you sure?" Jamie asked. "It's not just, like, a leather jacket or—"

"No, he's looking at it right now. It's his most recent memory. He's telling a...friend, I think, about it. He's filming it on his phone." Zoe stood up, eyes open. "Motherfucker. He's posting this on social media." Her knuckles cracked as she flexed her fingers outward. "That's my suit, you asshole." Her voice came out somewhere between a statement and a yell, and Jamie's hands waved with a shushing sound.

"Don't give us away," he said, probably quieter than was necessary given they camped out on a rooftop.

"Sorry. It's just that, you know, that guy has my suit." She turned to him, a gust of wind blowing hair in her face. "How did you even find this guy?"

"Well, I had some free time waiting for you to figure out the clues. So I did some scouting."

Zoe grinned. "Look at you, taking the initiative. See, you *are* a badass." Her fist landed on his shoulder, and though the punch was playful camaraderie, it still hurt way more than it should have. Jamie winced and reminded himself to give her a pass. Either she didn't recall the last time she'd punched him jokingly or she failed to contain herself.

She was, after all, pretty excited right now.

"So what does 'scouting' mean?" Eyes closed, her fingers stretched outward again, multitasking her newfound powers with the mundane task of listening to the person next to her.

"I went back to Telos a few times. Followed some of the staff around, dove into their minds to see what they knew."

"Yeah?" Zoe was in full pump-up mode now, bouncing on the balls of her feet and swinging a few punches into the air.

"Most of the staff seemed to have no clue what's really going on. But I found one guy guarding the back. He led to something much juicier. And that guy led to a meeting of a few of them. After that, it was just investigating." He laughed, which drew her attention. "I used a detective board."

"Shut up. How come I didn't see it?"

"Well, Normal kept clawing the strings I used between pieces, so I had to put it in the closet. But this guy, he asked specifically for the suit as a keepsake. Not the best guy around, that's for sure."

"Does he deserve an ass-kicking? Because I can oblige."

Zoe probably figured the more gung ho she was, the more it'd rub off on Jamie. But that wasn't the case, and in fact, it felt like it pumped *more* of his internal brakes. "Okay, remember what I said about your newfound confidence? Let's try to rein it in a little. Besides, you're here to practice. Try to brain-stun him." Jamie fought the urge to cringe, thinking at how long it took in his early days to master brain-stunning. "We're not winging it this time."

Zoe grimaced, alternating between staring at him and across the street long enough that several cars passed by on the road below. Finally, she gave in with a grunted affirmative. "Right, right. Forgot about strategy." She blew out a breath and pointed her finger back across the street.

"Just like we practiced."

"Can you hit people from this distance?" she asked.

"It's tricky but I can do it if he's by the window. Structures complicate things a little bit."

"Great, so how do we get him by the window?"

That was a good question. They hadn't really thought that part through, Jamie focusing too much on the actual mechanics of teaching brain-stuns and not enough on the logistics of the actual event. "Okay, let's see—"

"Hey! Fuckface! Give me back my suit!" Zoe yelled, though Jamie didn't know if that involved extraordinary vocal cords or if she was just really, really pissed. "What's the guy's name?" she asked at a normal volume.

"Richard," Jamie said, regretting the decision instantly.

"You! Richard! That's my suit!"

While Zoe continued berating the neighboring building—and drawing the unwanted attention of *other* residents, causing random lights to flash on and windows to open—Jamie reached out with his mind, tracing his path. He saw the man's movement; first a stop, then a turn, then another stop, then finally a step toward the window. "It's working. Get ready."

Zoe and Jamie crouched in unison, shoved up against the building's concrete ledge. Zoe had her fingers outstretched inches over the ledge while Jamie pulled out binoculars to get a better look.

The window slid open and the man's closely shaved head poked out.

"Now," he said. "Now, now, now."

The man looked down at first, probably thinking the voice came from a heckler on the sidewalk. Then he looked left, then right, then his head snapped back, as if an invisible fist punched him.

Okay, so that didn't happen when Jamie executed his brain-stuns. "I think you hit him too hard," he said, watching as the man stumbled out of view. Zoe stood up and perched on the edge, and as she did, Richard fell forward, his momentum throwing him halfway through the open window. "Oh shit, he's gonna—"

"I see it," Zoe said, scooping Jamie up before he could protest. She leaped. They zoomed across the divide, Zoe's lack of aim getting them too far up; she braced their impact with one outstretched hand, then they dropped straight down, slowing only when they got close. Still holding on to Jamie, she took one boot and shoved the man by the shoulder back into his apartment.

"Get inside," she said, and Jamie clambered over the ledge, not bothering to check if anyone saw them.

Zoe landed looking no worse for wear. Richard, though, lay facedown, his arms and legs spread in awkward-but-not-broken directions.

"Might want to go easier the next time you do this," Jamie said.

She didn't respond, and instead marched straight over to the closet by the entry door. She opened the closet, then gave the door a good yank to tear it off its hinges and threw it on the floor, hard enough to earn a giant crack in the middle of the wood. "*My* suit," she said, picking up the folded stack of leather pieces. "Hey. While we're here, we should investigate. See if he has access to anything Kaftan's been up to."

"I'll dive into his memories, you search around the place," he said.

"Good call," she said. Shortly after, the sound of drawers opening and closing came from the bedroom.

Jamie didn't bother to check if she was making a mess and instead focused on the man's memories. He flipped through the different images, skipping past mundane stuff like Richard's previous job as a plumber or the bag of groceries that remained unpacked on the counter (he took a minute to double-check and indeed, some ground beef and eggs sat in the bag, and he briefly considered putting them away so they didn't go bad, at least until he imagined Zoe's reaction to that); digging further, he saw that the man bought a dozen lottery tickets tonight, and slightly further back, perhaps an hour or two, he'd loaded a large sum of cash into a backpack.

That bit felt familiar.

But where did he get the cash?

Even further back, the man was at the facility, not the dingy lab part but a place that looked like a clean conference room. Kaftan was there, but Richard must not have been paying attention because her voice came in and out. Only bits and pieces landed, "for your service" and "coming to completion" and "severance package." She handed paperwork for the people to sign, sheets that looked like a nondisclosure agreement, and handed them each stacks of cash.

Jamie pulled back to the present, teeth digging into his top lip. Kaftan was getting rid of her security protocol. But why? Why give them severance packages and NDAs?

Why—

Because something must have convinced her that Zoe's latest serum was working.

"Zoe!" he yelled as he stood up. "We've got a—"

The sight of a trashed apartment stole his words. Every drawer and cabinet lay open, clothes and mail spilled all over the floor, forks and spoons lay sprinkled across the kitchen linoleum. The mess tickled at Jamie's nerves, pulling at him to scramble onto the floor and begin restoring everything back to its proper place. He took in a breath and counted to five, and as he did that, Zoe walked out of the bathroom—Jamie didn't want to know what she possibly could have done there.

She patted him on the shoulder as she passed. "What? This guy stole my suit. Besides," she said, holding up a key card with Richard's photo, "look what I found."

"Right." Better make that a ten count. "We should get going. I think Kaftan is happy with your serum."

"What makes you say that?" she said, grabbing a bottle of vodka and pouring it all over the unconscious man's head and shoulders. "See, *he* did this to himself. Proof is in the empty bottle."

"Okay. Fair enough. Look, I dove into his memories. Kaftan paid off her security team today and made them sign NDAs. I think whatever it is she was looking for out of you, she's satisfied." Everything started to line up, puzzle pieces tumbling together and locking into place when Jamie considered the bigger, more frightening picture. "She said she needed two things to bring back Waris. You. And the city's electrical grid. I knew she'd be monitoring your powers, but...oh shit."

Zoe took a swig of the last few drops remaining in the vodka bottle then set it on the floor next to the man's hand. "What do you mean, 'oh shit'?"

"They gave you a phone this time. I thought it was just a logistical thing or something, but they must have used it to track you. You have mind powers now. I think that's what she wanted to confirm. Waris needs his mind and body to be stable. You already showed the physical strength, the mind powers must be the part that affects the brain, that keeps it stable during this process. Shit," he said, "they must know we're here. And if she's close to activating Project Electron..."

Zoe's eyes snapped to attention, locking into his. "Jamie. This is it. We gotta go stop her. If she takes the city's grid, it'll be chaos for who knows how long. Let's go right now."

"What?" There was that enthusiasm again, but sprinting to the front gate seemed like the easiest way to get killed. "I'm not sure if an impromptu attack is our best way to stop Kaftan."

"You have a better plan?"

"Okay, let's think this through. If we just show up there, she's bound to be waiting for us. Her or whatever security detail they have left. It doesn't matter how strong we are, they'll be prepared. They'll be watching for us." A facility. In the middle of nowhere. With just two people approaching it, and the element of surprise seemingly evaporated. That wasn't going to work. Jamie's mind raced, considering all the ways to turn their disadvantage into an advantage.

"But what if it's more than us?" he finally said.

"And who would that be? We're not exactly social people—"

"We don't have to be," Jamie said. He pulled out his phone to check the time. Nearly seven in the evening. They'd need to move quick. "I've got someone in mind."

Zoe pumped her fist and immediately followed it with a full-body seizure that caused her limbs to stiffen and back to arch. She fell on the floor next to the puddle of spilled vodka, motionless for several seconds before she picked herself back up.

"What the hell was that?" Jamie asked.

She blinked several times, then looked at him, staring in a way that made him fear she'd lost her memory again. "Jamie," she said, tension in her voice giving him chills, "I don't see your heat signature."

27

WHAT THAT HELL WAS THAT?

Zoe had felt many different emotions in the several weeks since awakening in her Oakmount apartment. Confusion for sure; anger, excitement, joy at discovering her abilities. Pain, mostly on an emotional level when she considered all the ways she couldn't sort out who she was.

But this was the first time for this, whatever this was. Her pulse quickened, her breath shortened and her eyes darted.

Oh shit, was this *fear*?

Jamie's heat signature was gone. She moved to the apartment window, her legs stuck in mud and her body burning from the inside, like someone poured acid directly into her veins. Looking out, she couldn't pick up any heat signatures there, either. She whirled around and closed her eyes, but only darkness greeted her, none of the ghost silhouettes she'd seen with active minds. She stormed past Jamie and went straight to the unconscious man on the floor, reaching to pick him up.

One hand should have worked. But she definitely needed two. And even then, she barely managed to roll him over.

"Oh fuck. My powers. I can't…" She jumped in the air, only getting about a foot off the ground, and definitely not hovering. "I can't feel it. It's not there. Like someone turned off a switch."

"Okay. Okay, okay. Look, sit down for a minute."

"We can't stay here," Zoe said. She reached over to the counter and grabbed the standing grocery bag.

"Wait, what are you—oh no, not the eggs," Jamie said as she dumped the bag's contents all over the floor.

Zoe went back to her suit, which had stayed out of the path of destruction on the coffee table. She shoved it into the grocery bag, the layered girth of folded leather causing the paper bag to reach capacity. "You said it yourself. They're probably tracking us. Come on."

"You just had a seizure," Jamie said, his words slow and deliberate. "Or something. I don't think getting a move on is a good idea right now."

"We're also breaking and entering and making a big fucking mess of someone on Kaftan's payroll."

"We? I didn't dump the groceries on the floor."

Zoe ignored Jamie's neat-freak comment and knelt down, frisking the still-unconscious man. "Keys. Got 'em. Come on," Zoe said, pushing Jamie out the door. He crossed the threshold first, then she did, followed by her closing and locking the door behind her. She gave the handle a solid tug to make sure the latch completely locked.

And it snapped right off.

Jamie came up next to her and the two stared at the broken mechanism, the sheared handle still in her hand. "Did you," he said with a slight pause, "did you mean to do that?"

"No." The doorknob dropped to the floor with a *thump*.

"Okay. This is good. Maybe your powers are slowly coming back."

Zoe held her palm out, pushing it around the air. Her fingers wiggled and her arm stretched; though it took several seconds, *there* it was.

A slight pressure. A little bit of invisible thickness. A sense of something tangible though not quite there.

"I think they are," she said. One look at Jamie and the slightest of heat signatures returned. She blinked several times, just to make sure it wasn't her eyes adjusting to the bright hallway lighting. "Slowly. But I think so. Come on, let's steal this guy's car."

"Zoe. That's good news," Jamie said, "but also can we not just go on a crime spree?"

"Hey, you're the bank robber. You can't complain about this." They marched in unison to the elevator, but then he motioned to the stairwell, which seemed to be a better choice for avoiding people. By the time they got underground, opening the door to the parking garage felt simple, as easy as a simple finger poke, and she welcomed the stale humid air beneath the building. Key ring in hand, she tapped the key fob repeatedly until they heard a horn beep. "There," she said, and they made their way over to a very practical light blue hybrid car, as plain and drab as a vehicle could be except for a vinyl sticker on the back windshield that said Keep San Delgado Green.

Jamie glanced at her. "You look stunned."

"This isn't what I'd expected."

"Gun-toting mercs can care about the environment too. Lemme drive," Jamie said.

"You don't trust me?"

"It's not that." Jamie shook his head, hand held open. "Do you ever remember driving?"

"Well, no, not really. But that doesn't mean I never got a license. Hey, maybe they have DMV records in Kaftan's facility. Damn it, we should have checked for that at Telos."

"Right. If we don't die tonight, we'll look for your DMV records. But for now, Kaftan's people are probably tracking us."

Zoe held up her phone. "You think I should toss this?"

"No," Jamie said after a moment. "No, let's not tip our hand. We should head out. And let's at least *try* to drive safe."

Zoe's sigh cut through the grime of the underground air and she dropped the keys in his palm. "Fine. I should rest up my powers anyway. By the way," she said, opening her door. Did the Throwing Star need a seat belt? Better to be safe at this point. "You never said which friend you were going to call."

"Yeah. About that." Jamie stretched out his arm and looked over his shoulder as the car went into reverse. "I don't know if you'd call him a friend."

28

SOMEHOW, THEY MADE IT HERE, a rest stop in the middle of redwood trees some ten miles north of San Delgado.

Well, technically about twenty feet *above* the rest stop. On a thick tree branch of a redwood tree, lukewarm cup of coffee warming Jamie's hands. The altitude's wind bit at his cheeks, causing his long scarf to whip out behind him. The scarf was wrapped around his hood, which made zero sense from a costume design standpoint but Zoe insisted he add it when they'd stopped to grab his Mind Robber getup.

"I don't detect any heat signatures out there." She pointed straight out, then gestured at the trees around them. "He's either late or trying to bore us to death."

Jamie had called Detective Chesterton on a burner phone with a very distinct message: "This is the Mind Robber. The Throwing Star and I have uncovered a major crime and have joined forces to stop it. We need your help. The fate of the city

---

is in your hands. Come alone, Moore Forest, third rest stop after the exit, eight o' clock."

"Maybe it's the location?" Zoe asked. "I think half of horror movies wind up with murder in the woods. It's not quite 'meet me at the dog park at noon.' You know? Or maybe he thinks it's a prank call? I mean, 'the fate of the city is in your hands' is pretty…" Zoe's voice trailed off and she avoided his look. "Melodramatic."

He lowered the stupid eye mask, sweat and grime having made the underside a hot and sticky mess. It hung around his neck, sitting on the wool scarf, and Jamie realized that the thing he missed least about being the Mind Robber had to be the ridiculous outfit. "Well, let's give him some more time. He's—" From the distance, two headlights showed up, first as pinpricks of white in the darkness, then twisting and turning until they hit a patch of trees, creating a strobing effect along the way. They watched in silence as the car slowed to a halt, brakes squeaking and leaves crunching underneath the weight of wheels.

"Well?" Zoe asked. The door opened and out stepped a figure, a distinctly male silhouette. Sturdy build, dark skin, bald head. He *looked* like a cop, despite his plainclothes appearance.

"I think that's him. Why else would anyone come?" he said. She knelt down, keeping her balance way easier than Jamie did in the tree. Her fingers extended and Jamie forgot to keep his voice down. "Whoa, whoa, whoa. What are you doing?"

"I'm checking his memory."

"Did we not just realize that mental stuff drains your powers?"

"Okay, matter of practicality," Zoe said, holding her pose. "One, we need to make sure it's him. Two, if we're going to do something as dumb as break into Kaftan's laboratory again, I may need this. I should practice it in a safe circumstance. Three, I'll take a look and see if it's a trap. You know?" She craned her neck, angling in different views. "I'm not seeing any other heat signatures out there."

Wind whipped in Jamie's face and tossed his scarf. He steadied himself and considered the options in front of them. "He might have someone listening. Or maybe he's about to radio in for reinforcements."

"Do you really think they'd be a problem for us?" Zoe's voice was bright, as if her confidence went hand in hand with how she felt about her powers. "I mean, it's us, right? If we needed to zip out, we could do it."

"Okay, look. First time he came to my place, I ran through all the possibilities of what to do. If I brain-stunned him or wiped his mind, the PD would *still* know he came. See, that's the thing, you have to learn that it's not just about the functional part of dealing with someone's memory, you have to consider all the logistical implications. We can't just wing it. We need a plan."

"Did you forget I could basically *fly* us out of there?"

"Zoe, let's be realistic. You're having problems with that. Even if you're feeling good right now—"

"Even if—"

"Hey!" the man yelled. "I can hear you two arguing. Might as well come out before I record it and give it to the evidence people."

Mystery solved.

Zoe's elbow poked into Jamie's side. She probably meant it as a friendly tap—now seemed like a really inopportune time to turn on him—but her extra strength knocked Jamie off-balance and almost off the branch. She reached over to steady him, and as their hands interlocked pine needles shook off and fluttered their way down.

"Come on out," Chesterton continued. "I'm here to talk. See?" In the distance, his hands went up. "Let's chat. I'm alone."

"Alright," Zoe said. Jamie glanced upward to see her straightening up, the final cowl zipped into her Throwing Star outfit. "I'm good to go. You?"

He matched the move, sliding his eye mask back onto his face, and was fairly certain that he didn't look anywhere near as cool as her in doing so. "Yeah. Let's go try to do something good." Zoe wrapped an arm around his chest and propelled them forward, the acceleration causing Jamie's hood to blow off his head. They punched into the dark night before she extended a palm to slow their descent. Except halfway down, her powers sputtered, like a jet pack's engine suddenly misfiring. Jamie held on to Zoe tightly and they bobbed their way down before hitting the earth slow enough for her to do it with a teeny bit of grace—but hard enough for the shock to rattle his body.

Zoe let go and Jamie realized that he must have appeared completely undignified being carried around like a child's doll. Chesterton eyed them both. Jamie tugged his hood back over his head and glanced back at Zoe, who was all tough grimace and steely eyes.

No matter how hard he tried, he was pretty sure he still failed to look badass. Must be easier when you were the one who could fly.

"Flight path's a little off, huh?" Chesterton said. They stood silently, the detective eyeing them over before pulling out his phone and taking a photo. "I was wondering, how do you do that? I figured maybe you're manipulating magnetic fields or something like that."

From the corner of his eye, he saw Zoe shrug. So much for keeping in character.

"So, the Mind Robber," he finally said, pointing at Jamie, "and the Throwing Star." His finger angled over Zoe's way. "Which one of you is the hero and which is the villain right now?"

Jamie waited. This *seemed* like Zoe's cue, given she was the one who flew them in and he was the one who got carried like a child. But reality showed that she still hadn't figured out the public-facing side of her abilities, especially when she rarely interacted with people as herself.

This was a moment for the Mind Robber.

"There are no heroes," he began, in his best American accent to match previous footage. "There are no villains. We have come together, not as adversaries, but partners. To join forces against a much greater foe, one that threatens every single living being in San Delgado."

His eyes remained locked on Chesterton's, though he knew, he just *knew* that if he looked back at Zoe, she'd be choking back a laugh at his performance. "Sometimes there is a situation far more risky than you've ever imagined. And the only way to defeat it is to work with your mortal enemy."

Mortal enemy. That was a bit much, wasn't it? But too late now. "What I mean," he continued, "is that—"

"Alright, alright. I get it." Chesterton shook his head. "So he's the mouthpiece and you're the muscle. But that still doesn't explain why you two extraordinaries are working together."

Was he *not* listening at all?

"Okay. I'll go over it again. I—"

"It's simple," said Zoe. "We have abilities. Whatever gave us these gifts took our memories. Who we were before this, our families, our friends. We don't know. But they came from the same source. A scientist named Sasha Kaftan. And she's going to do something really, really stupid soon."

Jamie considered interrupting because that point hung on a bit of a technicality. They did know *some* details, and he'd seen the whole Frazer intake video and everything. But that information probably would have just confused things.

"Okay. Your message implied people were in danger," he said, once again pointing at Jamie. "Who's getting hurt? And why?"

"That kind of comes in multiple stages," Jamie said, holding his accent. "When your experiments give subjects extraordinary abilities, there's bound to be some misses."

Zoe jumped in without missing a beat. "And we're not talking about Hartnell City. It's all here. When you're doing all that shit because you want to do some mega experiment that shuts down the city's power grid, that's gonna lead to a whole bunch of other issues."

Judgment came in the form of darting eyes, though Chesterton's scowl didn't seem to be one of sincere concern for the city and the victims of genetic experimentation. It looked more like a "What the hell are they on about?" complete with raised eyebrows.

"And how did you discover this?"

The side of Jamie's mouth lifted into a smirk. "She has a detective board."

"Had."

"What?"

"*Had* a detective board. I don't have one in Oakmount."

"Right. Okay, *had* a detective board. And—" A hearty, full-bodied sneeze came out of Zoe, one so loud that even Chesterton stepped back. They all paused, taking turns looking at each other, Chesterton at Zoe, Jamie at Zoe, and Zoe blinking at an uncontrollable pace, teeth biting into her bottom lip. Her head shook and another sneeze came out.

"Wow. Seriously?" Zoe said, wiping her eyes. "Was Normal sleeping on my cowl when we went to your place?"

"Did you leave it on the floor?"

"Yeah, but just for a *minute.*"

"Don't leave stuff on the floor. She'll make a bed out of anything." Jamie realized he'd let his accent slip during their spat, and all of those little bumbles collided into something that completely vaporized their momentum. Instead, he stood there dumbfounded while Zoe started wiping her allergy-induced tears from the underside of her cowl. Chesterton pulled out a notepad. His fingers flipped the sheets over the spiral binding, somehow able to see in the dimmest of light.

"Normal," the detective muttered.

Oh shit.

This time, it should have been Jamie's turn to punch Zoe in the shoulder. She certainly deserved it, sneezing or no sneezing. But he didn't dare, partially out of fear of her reaction and partially because now seemed like a very bad time to fracture their tenuous unit.

"A cat named Normal scratched me," he said. "So that tip was right."

"Well," Jamie said, flipping his American accent back on, "see, that's the thing about that tip, it was actually Kaftan trying to push my buttons and—"

"Okay. Jamie Sorenson. I remember you. You can take the mask off. It looks like a kid's Halloween costume. The scarf doesn't work, either." Zoe angled her head, glaring at that comment. "And you, you should probably take yours off too if you want to stop sneezing."

Was this trust? Or an admission of guilt? How did you ask to pause a meeting with police in order to discuss strategy? "I don't know about that—" Jamie started until looking over at Zoe. Her cowl was already off, and even in the dim light, her puffy eyes were bloodshot and sniffles still took over her nose.

"Jamie, he knows everything. There's no need to keep this up. We might as well not look stupid."

Jamie blew a sigh into the night, the puff of air illuminated by the bright headlights of the still-idling car. "Fine, fine," he said, taking off the mask. It *did* feel better as cool air touched the skin of his face, but an overwhelming sense of vulnerability took over.

There was nothing left after this.

Jamie shoved his mask in his pocket. But he kept the scarf on for the windchill factor.

"Hey, any chance you got any nasal spray?" Zoe asked.

"I don't think so. But you might be in luck," Chesterton said. He held up his phone and took photos before walking back to the open driver's side door. He said something, though it was inaudible to Jamie's ears.

"Can you hear what he's saying?" Jamie asked.

"Kind of. The car engine's muffling it. Maybe he's calling in backup?"

"Alright, you two." Chesterton walked back over. "I've got good news. There's no cats where we're going. You might even be able to find someone who has nasal spray."

Jamie and Zoe locked eyes, both equally uncertain about what to say.

"Um," Zoe said through sniffles, "where's that?"

"Jail." The detective reached behind him and pulled out two sets of handcuffs. "You, for armed robbery. And you, for vigilantism and public endangerment. You're both under arrest."

29

ZOE NEEDED TO GET a message to Jamie. A *secret* message.

Sitting in the back of the detective's car didn't force them to stay silent, but what they said, how they said it…being in the back of a detective's car *did* limit those possibilities. If they were being strategic about the whole thing. Though Chesterton hadn't exactly told them to be quiet or anything like that. After his big proclamation, both she and Jamie stood there like idiots. Zoe couldn't say for sure what Jamie was thinking, but she'd weighed the pros and cons of smacking the detective, picking up Jamie and getting the hell out of there.

Did Jamie consider the same thing, only with his abilities? He hadn't moved his hands into position, but maybe his arsenal contained more subtle tricks for mental thievery. She kept waiting for him to make his move, and when he put his hands out for handcuffs as commanded, she figured that was the setup, especially when Chesterton got in close to slap the handcuffs on.

A simple flick of a finger and mental surgery, the whole thing would be done.

Except he didn't act. He stood there, his face unreadable, just staring forward. Zoe tried to break into his head to see what went on in there, if anything. But if some switch in her head turned on the ability to read thoughts, she hadn't found it, and instead, his immediate memories didn't exactly help. Worse, that little dive-in seemed to sap her own abilities, so even if she just wanted to explode out of there, that option vanished. Temporarily, but enough to back them into a corner for the moment.

While she pondered what to do, the detective came around. A few clicks later and suddenly *she* was in handcuffs. Without her strength, all she could do was push her forearms against the cuffs, which merely cut off her circulation, and maybe frayed some of the stitching on her suit.

Instead, she followed Jamie to the car, his only words being a simple "Just go with it."

Now they sat in close proximity, though they probably still had thirty minutes or so to wind through the mountain roads north of San Delgado and into the police station. Thirty minutes to come up with a plan, though really, probably more like twenty-two or twenty-three minutes, because once they crossed the Gateway Bridge, things would be fairly locked in.

That meant that Zoe needed to have a real conversation with Jamie. Not frivolous discussions about how the view was nice—which it was, given that the clouds parted for a twinkling skyline and lit-up TransNational Building—and not any pleasantries about how the car was remarkably clean—which, again, it was, so kudos to Chesterton for that. But something along the lines of "How do we get out of here, head to Kaftan's facility and somehow convince the police to come with us?"

In other words, Serious Business, with capital letters.

But Jamie continued to sit silently, like nothing mattered.

He stared forward, and if he was panicking, he definitely failed to show it.

"So," Zoe finally said, "tonight really is not the best night to arrest us. Not with Kaftan out in full mad-scientist mode. If you just drive out to this place in the middle of nowhere, we can show you what we're talking about. It's like ten miles north of Terese."

"Think about it. Why would we lie about this?" Jamie asked, in his normal voice. The silence finally broken, Zoe shot a glare at him that should have hit harder than her full-speed punch. But he kept his track, his stare still forward. "A lot of people might get hurt tonight. We're trying to help them. But to do that, we need your help. In fact, we need all of your help. Go there and bring backup with you."

Chesterton seemed focused on the road as the car took a curve. They made it to the base of the hill, the shift from downhill to flat surface testing the quality of the car's shocks. Pretty good, in fact. He finally responded, "How do I know you're telling the truth? Kind of hard to say for someone who has mental abilities."

"I'm asking you to trust me. Trust us." Jamie imbued his plea with sincerity. Zoe didn't need to be a mind reader or a Mind Robber to detect that. It was *sincere* sincerity, not just for leverage or justification, though maybe he'd lost that level of credibility simply being who he was. The Mind Robber didn't exactly have the best public standing.

"And your accent," Chesterton said. "I always thought your voice sounded off. I thought you were Canadian."

"I know, right?" Zoe let out with a snort before she thought better of it. This time, Jamie finally broke his focus and shot her a glare. "Come on, Jamie. It's not a good accent."

"What I still can't figure out is why you two would work together. Weren't you just chasing him a few weeks back?"

"That probably tells you something about what we're dealing with here," she said. "It's big and it's shitty and we both care enough about people to drop the bullshit, call a truce and work together. See, that's the thing I found out about Jamie. If you look at how he does his whole thing, it's all set up to protect everyone involved. He's using his abilities just to earn a living. His goal isn't to hurt anyone. That's just an act."

"What about the woman at the bank?"

Jamie spoke up, his voice dry. "That was an accident. I couldn't have known she had a health condition."

"So you can't protect everyone in that line of work. Maybe you didn't think it through. In addition to the whole 'robbing people' thing."

"Banks are insured," Zoe interjected before Jamie could say anything.

"Look. Point taken," Jamie finally said after a minute of si- lence. "You told me weeks ago that you didn't understand why the Mind Robber and Throwing Star didn't just work with the police, play by the rules. But that's very black-and-white, isn't it? You have bureaucracy. You have departments and proce- dures. And let's face it, some people are there just to do the job. And some aren't exactly the best people." Chesterton's shoulders tensed, and even from Zoe's angled view behind the passenger seat, she saw his jaw tighten. It came and went, and if she'd been a little better at the whole socializing thing, maybe she'd get a read on if he was offended, mad or just had bad leftovers for lunch. Jamie seemed to notice too, pausing for a moment be- fore resuming his speech. "But here's the bigger problem. Sasha Kaftan has not played by the rules. She has a remote facility. She's doing secret experiments, she lures victims in a way that can be covered up, she's thought this through. If we played by the rules, we wouldn't have discovered all this. We would have never dug deep, and quickly. You have to know when to bend rules, as long as you're making the right choice."

They continued rolling in silence, hitting the small downtown at the base of the hills. The car idled at a stoplight, waiting for a young, probably slightly drunk couple to cross at the crosswalk.

"Nice speech," Zoe said under her breath. She still hadn't been able to figure out Jamie's angle. Other than dropping the whole act and basically pleading in a really nice way. But now they had no leverage, no mystery. He'd basically given away everything to Chesterton. Which didn't seem like the best way to recruit someone who'd just slapped on the handcuffs twenty minutes ago.

The light changed and they continued, through the short pier area and up into another set of winding hills that led to the Gateway Bridge, its lit massive beams starting to creep into view beyond the hills. The car rumbled forward, the only noise coming from the occasional police band radio chatter. If the detective was considering Jamie's speech, he certainly didn't show much for it.

Several minutes passed without a word, all leading to the bridge's entry ramp. On the other side sat the dense population and constant noise of San Delgado. If they were going to launch a getaway, now would be the time. Zoe closed her eyes and focused, and she could *feel* her strength restoring to peak performance. If she wanted to, she could snap the handcuffs, kick out the door and fly out, Jamie in tow. Though she sat, anxiety crept over her, causing her to fidget in her seat. Next to her, she saw Jamie mumbling to himself, but zeroing in with her extended hearing, it was nothing more than counting and breathing.

He was freaking out. But trying to stay calm too.

She really needed to talk with him.

The car hit the bridge, dots of light from the tall beams and the tourist walkway flashing at them as they drove by. Zoe angled her neck to look at the cityscape. Parts of it looked as expected, the mix of twinkling and moving lights from buildings and cars. But other parts looked strangely black, entire square patches of dark, like someone cropped out pieces of San Delgado. Zoe was about to nudge Jamie about this when Chesterton said something.

Except it wasn't to them. "Dispatch, this is six-eight-six-nine. I've got a situation here."

Rather than listen in on the conversation, this provided the audio cover to finally get through to Jamie. She nudged him with her elbow, and when he finally turned, she whispered. "Why aren't we breaking out of here? Now's our chance. Look at the city. Blackouts."

"Because," Jamie said, "one cop isn't going to get Kaftan's attention. She might just take him out on her own. We need as many there as possible. We need to expose this."

"Well, we're not exposing anything sitting in the back of this car. And definitely not in jail."

"Just trust me. Okay? I have a plan."

Jamie had a *plan*? "Whoa, whoa, whoa. Why didn't you tell me your idea before? I thought we were partners."

"Hold on. I'm not going rogue on you." He nodded to Chesterton, who seemed to be too involved in some sort of argument over the radio to notice their discussions via harsh whispering. His voice dropped even lower. "Because it just came to me. And I can't really talk about it in present company."

As if on cue, Chesterton scoffed loudly, then replaced the handset, probably rougher than it needed to be. "You two suddenly got chatty."

"Yeah," Zoe said. "We're plotting our escape."

That was enough to get a laugh out of the car, first Chesterton and then Jamie caught on. Zoe laughed too, one of those uncomfortable chuckles caught on the momentum of others. But that didn't really change anything, and a minute later, they passed the Gateway's toll station and began the final descent into San Delgado.

If Jamie really had a plan, the countdown to its effectiveness accelerated to the end. The car rolled off of the bridge and onto the adjoining road, a few winding streets that hugged the edge of the water before they splintered off into piers on the left and waterfront mansions on the right. They drove straight ahead, diving into the heart of San Delgado, leaving the sleepy hills behind them on the other side of the bridge.

Zoe nudged Jamie again but remained silent. He looked at her, then raised his eyebrows and nodded, whatever that meant. She nodded in return, which offered more of an acknowledgment that they shared some exchange of gestures than actual plan.

At this point, there was nowhere to go but down. They passed first into the small stretch of suburbia within San Delgado, where homes sat sandwiched side by side, the architectural equivalent of cans in a cabinet. Then it was through the heart of the city, tall angled hills lined with cafés and restaurants, to the huge structures with high-density housing where Zoe used to live. Sidewalks and streets came to life, filled with evening dog walkers, bad first dates, rowdy friends and impatient children tugging at sleeves—little details that always seemed to dissolve into the background until the moment Zoe got stuck in the back of a police car. Stretches passed in silence, until they hit the downtown area, storefronts and bright signs creating a perimeter to the large block that hosted both city hall and the main police station. The car rolled up to a barricade that needed a code and voice identification for entry, which then led down to a much sturdier iron gate. Chesterton repeated the same process, and the answer came in the form of a buzzing sound and the gradual movement of the gate.

It finished sliding aside and Chesterton pulled the car forward, the bottom scraping as it hit the acute downward slope. Police cars lined the sides, along with the random passing officer, both uniformed and detectives. But as they turned the corner in the lot, Zoe picked up the audible chatter of people. Not just the usual random discussions people had in a public place, but words that stood out.

The Throwing Star.

The Mind Robber.

Those people, police officers, were talking about them. But it wasn't just police, spotlights and cameras gave away the fact that somehow the media had caught wind of this and forced their way into the underground garage. "Goddamn it," Chesterton said as they rolled toward the front. "Sorry about the commotion. I asked for someone to meet us. I didn't expect a parade."

"You're the one who likes audiences," Zoe said to Jamie.

"Not really. It's only an act. With a script." Jamie tensed up so visibly that Zoe sensed it without even looking at him. "What are they here to do?"

"A few officers are going to escort you in. The rest?" The car lurched to a halt as he let out a sigh. "It's not easy being extraordinary, is it?"

30

EVERYTHING OUTSIDE OF THE car windows was glowing, not because of anything from Kaftan and Project Electron, but about a dozen individual bright lights that blinded Jamie. Silhouettes broke in front of them, rushing back and forth, and suddenly the light split into individual pieces, the shapes cutting between them. Even with the car windows up, the yelling became audible and Jamie didn't need Zoe's extraordinary earing to decipher what was being shouted.

"How did you catch the Mind Robber?"

"Is the Throwing Star under arrest for the incident caught on video weeks back?"

"Are they working together?"

"Do tonight's blackouts have anything to do with San Delgado's extraordinaries?"

Chesterton turned to the backseat. "So much for privacy."

"Alright, alright, everyone give space," someone shouted

from…somewhere. Several black uniforms got in front of the car windows, gradually pushing a path back.

The driver's door opened and Chesterton yelled back. "Who let them come in?"

"That's not good," Zoe muttered. Which was kind of funny, considering she could probably flick her pinky finger at each of them and even the burliest, strongest police officer would fly across the parking lot.

The driver's side door swung open farther, complete with Chesterton cursing under his breath. "Looks like you caught the big fish," a voice said as the awaiting officers broke formation and split into each side.

"Fishes," another voice said. "Who has the latest bets on how tough they are?"

"Yeah, that's not fair, Chesterton. You had all the fun yourself. Did you put them to the test?" the first voice said.

The detective stepped out and voices immediately surrounded him. The door slammed shut behind him and Chesterton's words immediately got muffled by the composite and metal and glass of the car body.

Finally, a moment to show her he actually had a plan. "Okay, look. Here's the deal," Jamie said, turning to Zoe. "We get in, we tell *everyone* about Kaftan, we tell them this is related to the blackouts and we need them to go with us tonight. We make a scene, get the media's attention and make so much of a stink that they *have* to check it out. And bring *everyone* to the facility."

Zoe's mouth opened, but not in a jaw-dropping kind of way. Instead, she squinted at him, then fumbled for words. "That's your plan?"

"Well…yeah. I mean, we're at the police station. We need them to come with us. It's not going to work if we just run out and go to the place on our own."

"Yeah, but…that whole time you were quiet. *That's* what you were doing the whole time?"

"No, I was trying to probe Chesterton. To see if we could trust him." Jamie glanced out the window at the detective, who stood in a stern pose complete with arms crossed. "Problem is I couldn't go too deep."

"Jamie, if there's a time to go deep, it's now."

"Not when he's driving. One wrong move and he'd veer off the bridge. Safety first. Besides," Jamie said, craning his neck to get a better look around them, "I think we can trust him."

"Well, he arrested us. So I'd say otherwise."

"No, look. It's a good test. He could have been doing this because he wanted the attention or something like that. Or maybe he's even working for Kaftan. But he's not. He's by the book. He's boring. Almost like he's trying to *not* get a promotion or be noticed. Those other cops talking about taking bets and stuff? That disgusts him. He's not in this to be known in the history books as the person who caught the Mind Robber and the Throwing Star." Jamie glanced up to find the police discussion still in full form, everyone nodding and talking over each other. "There's something more, but I couldn't quite figure it out. Something different about him."

"Okay. Fine. He's not corrupt or looking for attention. I'm still not seeing the whole plan. What if they don't listen to us? What if they lock us up?"

"Then we break out," Jamie said. "Cause a scene. And get the media to follow us. Two different paths. Same goal."

"Jamie," Zoe said. Her head started to bob up and down, teeth biting down on her top lip. She looked at him, focused with what seemed like steely resolve. "This is a *terrible* plan."

The statement stung, not really with hurt, but more of the truth. She was right: the goal of getting everyone there was probably correct, but the method of "tell everyone and hope they listen" was, well...

It was a terrible plan.

At the same time, given everything they'd been through, a terrible plan seemed fitting.

Maybe it wasn't better than winging it.

Laughter overtook Jamie, starting with his breath and working his way to his eyes and shoulders until it was a full body chuckle, the sheer absurdity of it all sinking in. What were they doing? Locked up in the back of a police car, scheming to somehow lead an army of cops and media to a top-secret test facility in order to stop a mad scientist with extraordinary abilities and some guy made out of electricity?

"Is that your villain cackle or are you just losing your shit?"

Deep breaths. And a countdown. Jamie re-centered himself, then blinked several times to focus. "A little bit of both," he said.

"Uh-oh," Zoe said. "I think they heard you."

"Hey. Mind Robber." First a shout came through the closed door, the echo loud enough to be audible, then a tap on the window with a nightstick. "You think this is funny?"

Jamie looked up, tears still crawling down his cheeks, and with handcuffs on, he couldn't do anything about them, even though he tried to wipe them with his shoulder. "We'll be fine. We make a good team."

"Right. Remember I can still punch my way out of this."

"I thought your powers were fluctuating."

"Even still. I can take them."

"No punching. That's not going to help right now. Those are cops, remember? Not mercs hired by Kaftan. Just follow my lead," Jamie said. "I'm good at these speeches."

"Yes and no on that," Zoe said. "You're better than me. And yet we're still in here."

The voices outside intensified before the familiar *click-thump* of the door's handle broke through the space. "Here we go," Jamie said with a nod. "Just follow my lead. We'll convince them. We have to. Remember—"

The door flew open, and before Jamie could finish his sentence, two hands grabbed him and yanked him out of the car. His eye mask dangled around his neck by its elastic strings as they jerked him forward, and suddenly any speeches or even opening lines went blank on him. Something jabbed him in the gut, stealing any breath before he could open his mouth. Instead, he tried to keep moving while they carried him, one officer each grabbing an arm, and dragged him toward a door. He craned his neck to look at Zoe, but he didn't even manage to make eye contact before a buzzing sound cut into the air and he was pulled through a door.

Behind him, the door buzzed again, and the sound of locks and latches snapped into his ears. Somewhere back in the parking lot, Zoe sat by herself.

"So," a new officer said, "we've finally got the Mind Robber."

Zoe was right.

This *was* a terrible plan.

31

WHY DID ZOE LISTEN to Jamie?

As she sat in the police interrogation room, hands and feet chained to the table, all she could think about was the last thing she said to him: *This is a terrible plan.*

Because it was. Look at where it got them, Jamie locked away somewhere and her pinned down to a table. Physically being pinned down by chains didn't bother her too much. Even though her powers fluctuated, she could at least *feel* when they were and weren't working. She wasn't at her strongest right now, but probably enough to snap out of the chains.

But not fast or strong enough to outmaneuver four trained police officers with their guns on her. Even if she was at her peak, they still had the advantage.

They'd been silent since escorting her in, the few things she'd said getting a response of stony silence. Guess they were ordered not to say anything to her.

Finally, the door opened and in strode Chesterton. Someone who hopefully *would* talk to her.

"Zoe Wong," he said, tossing some papers on the small desk. Was that her profile? She nearly asked to look at them, in case they offered a hint to her actual past. He scooted the chair out before sitting down in front of her, his key ring jingling with his movement. "The Throwing Star. San Delgado's hero. You know, my neighbor's kid made a costume like you? Duct tape and trash bags. People think you're cool. And you do good work. I mean, I'm not a fan of vigilantes, but street criminals are terrified of you. In a way, you've been an effective deterrent. But I'm guessing you didn't think about the bigger picture. Because in some ways, you've made things worse."

"Worse?" Zoe finally got some conversation here and it came loaded with insults? She knew she should have suppressed her eye roll, but it came too naturally. Part of her wondered if the Zoe Wong of old, the pre–Throwing Star, pre–Telos Zoe Wong would have reacted the same way. Somehow, it felt ingrained, like it was part of her very core. "How does it get worse if more criminals are off the street?"

"Bigger picture, remember? You attract a lot of attention. And criminals talk. Most know someone somehow that's been taken out by you. So they're terrified. But that doesn't mean they're going to stop doing what they're doing. It just means they're going to do their best to avoid you." His tough-guy front shifted; his shoulders relaxed and his expression followed suit.

Guess he felt bad for her.

"They listen in on the police band, they have friends and rivals and all that stuff. Twenty years ago, when I first started, they didn't have the means to communicate quickly. But now you have hashtag ThrowingStar and people reporting where they see you. So you take out one criminal, but that means all the other guys go to work on the other side of town. They know you're busy. You can't be everywhere at once. And guess who gets stretched thin by that?"

"Oh," Zoe said. "I, uh, didn't think that would happen."

"There's a system in place. It's not perfect. I know there are problems. I want to change them. I wish it was better. But it got the job done as best as it could. What frustrates me is that you didn't have to take things into your own hands. You could have worked with us, figured out the best way to use your abilities with us. Team up. But you didn't. And now no one knows what to do with you."

One of the guards snorted, and Chesterton turned, shooting a dirty look that quieted the room.

"Maybe I just promise to go home and watch a movie and that's that? Have you ever used HorrorDomain? It's free."

"Well, there's the little matter of all those laws you broke."

Zoe nodded, but then started to tune out as Chesterton continued. It wasn't so much that his words were boring or senseless, but more that her damn cat allergies came back. An itch tickled the tip of her nose, and the back of her neck, probably where Normal's hair collected into her cowl. The itch had been coming and going for minutes now.

"Hey, I got a stupid request," Zoe said, interrupting him. "I have the worst itch at the back of my neck. It just comes and goes. And, oh, there it is again. Can you please scratch it?"

The detective's brow crinkled, and if only he had mental powers, he could see that she was being really, really, really sincere—this damn itch would *not* go away. But proof of it remained intangible to the detective at the table and the officers standing guard. The best she could do was add in another "Please?" He looked back and forth at the other police in the room; they nodded at him in turn, which ultimately led to him standing up, walking around the table and scratching the back of her neck.

"Yeah, that's it. Oh, jeez. I swear, my allergies. Never team up with someone who has a cat." Zoe blew out a satisfied huff, and Chesterton went over to talk in private to the officers. She would have tuned up her hearing, focusing in on their whispered discussion but the itch came back and it just would not go away. She tilted her head back, rolling her head left and right and back again to try and get it to stop.

Which it did. Completely vanished. Zoe relaxed and her eyes wandered to the red LED numbers on the wall, which ticked from 9:40 to 9:41. As it did, the itch started again.

Jesus Christ. It was persistent, as if...

As if it wanted her attention.

Could Jamie be trying to break into her mind?

Zoe sat straight up, thoughts suddenly whirring through her mind. *Jamie, can you read this?* she thought with intent. But he couldn't do that, right? He said to her that reading memories was different from reading minds, which was why he couldn't ever try to win big at a casino card table. It needed the mind to process and record things. *Files saved on your computer,* he'd said. *Not live streaming.*

Alright, if that was Jamie, then he was trying to communicate with her. Or he might have given up and just wanted to be a jerk to her. But probably the former.

So what could she say and retain to verify this? A simple test? While not giving herself away to the officers in the room?

Zoe played the process back out in her head, from what little experience she had with it. The images presented themselves as a glorified movie, with the ability to replay and freeze. Thoughts weren't part of it, it was simply audio/video captured by the brain. So any messages left for Jamie had to be extremely clear.

He'd left messages chopped up into pieces, a code to be taken apart and put back together. This would require similar stealth. Except there were people in the room with Zoe.

"Boy, I really felt those itches. It was like they were trying to...um...tell me something."

Okay. Not the smoothest. But at least the justice patrol on

the other side of the room cared only enough to give her a short glance.

The itch returned. Unlike before, this came and went in a blink, like a ping of notification on a phone.

Maybe that's what it was. Now to experiment. "So…two scratches would be a big yes. And one would be a no." Chesterton shot another look her way. "By no, I mean like not enough. This shit itches. Got it?"

A minute passed on the clock, though it felt like way more, everything moving in slow motion without any powers to cause it. Perhaps she'd imagined it all; Jamie could be locked away, incapacitated, knocked out, even dead.

Ping.

An itch, long enough to be noticed, but short enough to not be irritating.

Then ten seconds later. *Ping.*

He'd heard. Or saw, or however you put it. They were in business. Still stuck on the chair, Zoe's excitement caught her practically bursting out of the handcuffs holding her down. She told herself to settle down, think this through. They could communicate in simple yes/no language. And their goal was to come back together.

That meant she needed to see him. Not his true self, that wouldn't be possible. But if his heat signature stood out, if the emotion captured enough intensity, that could do it.

"I think I got it. Tell me when you're ready."

This time, the detective's focus remained steady in response. "Ready for what?" he asked.

Above them, light bulbs flickered, though the camera in the corner maintained its solid red dot the entire time. They fell into darkness for several seconds before snapping back on.

"Did you have something to do with that?" Chesterton asked.

Zoe remained quiet, attention only on any impending sensations at the back of her neck.

WE COULD BE HEROES

Two pings came in rapid succession.

Jamie was listening. And she needed some way to find him.

"I, uh…" *Thinking* was supposed to be Jamie's part of their partnership. She ran around and punched people. This type of cleverness was hard enough *without* being watched. "So I don't think I've ever really explained the way I sense heat signatures. Thing is with my powers, everyone assumes I'm all about speed and strength, but the heat signatures let me see people through walls and stuff. Like, the more you're burning up, the better. Usually happens when you feel an emotion. If you're super sad or pissed or whatever. Your body flushes and your heart rate goes up. And maybe wave. That would stand out."

"Okay, now I'm really confused," Chesterton said. "You're talking about…body temperature?"

There. Two pings, a binary acknowledgment to say yes, he got it.

So, he'd feel something strong, something to make himself stand out from the crowd. And she'd have to use her thermal detection to find him. Problem was, all of their experiments since leaving Richard's place showed that anything mental left her drained.

Zoe looked at the clock. Nine forty-five now. Maybe a few minutes for them both to prepare. "Nine fifty looks like a good time to feel a lot of things."

This time, every officer looked at the clock. Then back at her. Zoe offered a smile, though she had no idea how her forced grins played off to outside observers. She really needed more friends than just lapsed bank robbers. "So what do you guys think of the name 'Shuriken'? You know, Japanese for throwing star? Is that an issue because I'm not Japanese? At least, I'm pretty sure I'm not Japanese…" They leaned forward in unison, squinting. "Sorry, guys, I'm just really awkward in social situations. I'll shut up now."

Chesterton huffed, then turned his attention to the papers

on the desk. Zoe looked away from the bemused guards and instead watched the clock; its digits flipped minute by minute until a clear five and a clear zero burned red on the LED clock. Her concentration dialed in and the chatter, the footsteps from above, the sounds of doors opening and closing, all of it drifted into the background. At first, the other officers in the police station showed up, their blips all variations of the same shade of red. Zoe's body tensed as she tried to push further, farther. The colors amplified, gradually melting into brighter, tangible colors. The effort caused sweat to form on her forehead, something that caught the attention of Chesterton. "You feeling alright?"

She looked around, unsure if they'd taken Jamie above or below her or if he was close. Each direction proved fruitless, only a cluster of semitransparent outlines. But there, to the left and down, the tiniest flicker of color cut through that.

And it was waving.

Zoe took a deep breath, then sank into herself, her mind urging every bit of strength to pull from her muscles into something more ethereal. She locked into the color, marking it in her mind. But it faded, the toll of the past few minutes being too much.

Overhead, the lights flickered again, this time coming to a blackout that lasted a good five or ten seconds before returning.

"I don't like this. Something's up. Keep an eye on her." The door swung open and closed as the detective stepped out.

One less person to deal with.

The guard who snorted earlier turned, his voice quiet but direct. "No one knows what to do with you. Well, we've all seen videos of you. I'm pretty sure I could take you in a fight."

"Ha. No way," another officer said. "She'll knock you out in two seconds."

So these guys were idiots. But it bought her some time. Zoe shut herself off from the heat signatures, closing her eyes and keeping a regular rhythm of steadying inhales and exhales, trying to find that tidy balance between being able to sense Jamie and being powered enough to kick the shit out of anyone who stood in her way.

Without permanently hurting them, of course. She was in enough trouble as it was.

"She doesn't look too tough up close?" Snort Guy asked. "Maybe we should update the office pool? Pretty sure I could take her down."

Okay, maybe hurting them a *little* bit. Because it sure seemed like they deserved it. "I think I got it," she said loudly at the guards. "The itch. I think I found it. It just needs to stay there. And keep feeling that way."

Did that even make sense? Her attempts at coding any communication to Jamie probably came off as gibberish, and maybe it would have been simpler to say "Jamie, stay put but keep feeling extreme emotions."

Whatever the case, two more pings tingled the back of her neck. And as her strength returned, Zoe considered how exactly she would do this, what with armed guards at the door, an entire building she was unfamiliar with and fluctuating powers that drained whenever she used her compass. Plus apparently a department-wide betting pool on fighting someone just like her.

But the lights went out again, and the instant things blacked out, Zoe told herself to go. She may not have had a much better cover than that.

Fists tight, her forearms pulled and the handcuffs snapped.

Guess those cops were about to find out how tough she really was.

32

THE LIGHTS WERE OUT for a good four or five seconds. But the locks on the security door still appeared to be fully engaged; Jamie turned the handle but it refused to budge. Probably a combination of mechanical and electronic locks. San Delgado Police Department may have been somewhere lower on the extreme security scale than the most secure prison in the state, but they smartly seemed to have a plan for the Mind Robber if and when they caught him.

Three security cameras hung in the room, one directly above the door and two on opposite corners. When the power fluctuated, their red lights remained, probably a battery to keep power going even if their monitoring systems in some room somewhere may have rebooted.

No windows existed in the room, not even a small pane in the door. Chances were the PD didn't know the extent of Jamie's powers, that the ability to sense minds had nothing to do with visual connection, though that helped.

He simply closed his eyes and reached out and there they were. Presences pinged like on a radar, not the thermal outlines that Zoe saw, but more of a weight, a sense of existing within a three-dimensional space. Heat, smell, pitch of voice—it was like those types of senses, except this was internal. Everyone had a signature, some unique identifier that formed ghostlike appearances in his mind's eye.

Normally, that kind of stuff didn't matter. Jamie never planned to visit the witnesses of his robberies again, nor did he care what the OmegaCar drivers did in their off time.

This time, though, it mattered. His senses reached out, seeking the one person in the building he should recognize. But where was she?

Where was *he*, for that matter? Upstairs, downstairs? Underground? They'd walked him so quickly through corridors and up and down stairs that it wasn't clear where he'd ended up. Maybe just tucked into a corner? Maybe three feet on the other side of the wall was a sidewalk and a lawn and low-maintenance bushes perfect for a governmental building.

Or, if they'd really prepared for the Mind Robber, he could be in as protected a corner as possible.

Jamie kept seeking, left and right, above and below. Part of the issue was proximity, a certain radius of effectivity existed, and if Zoe was outside it, he wouldn't be able to connect.

But perhaps the path to Zoe wasn't her. He scaled back, reaching out again for a different signature.

Chesterton.

The detective had been straight upstairs; since getting dumped in this space, Jamie had kept a rough track of his movements. Now checking back in, the detective was on the move to... somewhere. A quick search found that he'd walked from his office (he'd assumed) down the hall. Several seconds later, he took an elevator, and then farther down the hall, followed by a right turn. A hesitation, then several more feet, and suddenly Chesterton stood in front of another familiar presence.

There she was.

"Sorry about this," he muttered as he put his hands in front of him, fingers extended. Would the cameras catch that? Would they be able to piece together what this was all about? Anyone who reviewed security footage of the Mind Robber's work would have recognized the pose—a little more function and less flash, but still the same sentiment.

And yet, the room replied with silence. No one broke down the door, no gas filled the room, no spikes emerged from the floor. If they watched him, something like this fell into the "expected" category. Whether or not they had an expert on containing mental abilities, though, remained to be seen.

The mind connection clicked and out flowed Zoe's immediate memories.

There she stood—no, sat. Four guns pointed at her. And Chesterton talking. A lot. "They listen in on the police band, they have friends and rivals and all that stuff..."

Jamie gave her credit for staying still during that whole lecture. He jumped out, counted to five and jumped back in. Other people's minds pinged to him like a radar. Hopefully his presence did the same thing for her.

"So...two scratches would be a big yes. And one would be a no. By no, I mean like not enough. This shit itches. Got it?"

Yes, she'd heard him. Or felt him, or whatever you wanted to call it.

Also, Zoe was clearly awful at improvising words under pressure.

"If you're super sad or pissed or whatever. Your body flushes and your heart rate goes up. And maybe wave. That would stand out."

A strong emotion. Something to stand out from the people working in a police station. They'd likely be calm. Or angry.

Or focused. Or frustrated or excited. What could Jamie think about that might be different from that?

He started waving his hands in the air, pondering the best way to feel terrible about himself.

No. Not himself. Jamie was a protective shell, a recent episode, a shield anytime something from further back poked through and rang for attention. He turned his thoughts, not to any moment in Jamie's life, but to the snippet of Frazer that floated around, first in a video clip and then in his head. He'd tried to push it away, to snuff it out and treat it as just a *thing* that he'd viewed.

But the truth was more than that. Before all this, he'd been a villain. A selfish liar, an unreliable partner, a person so devoid of caring that he put up false fronts only to implode. The weight of that reality sank in, the fact that those few minutes revealed choices of a lifetime that he couldn't comprehend. The same body, the same brain, and yet how could he choose to do those things to Francisco? Jamie felt bad if he even fed Normal late or ran out of coconut water, and what Frazer had done was orders of magnitude worse.

Frazer was worse than the Mind Robber. In fact, the only good thing Frazer might have done was ask for help from Telos.

The thoughts that simmered since seeing that clip pressurized, but rather than push back, Jamie let all the defenses down. And soon, he didn't have to try to create an emotion to signal Zoe. The regret, the guilt, all of it was there, finally a part of him.

But he needed the feeling to linger, to act as his beacon. That snippet showed the worst of Frazer, but what was the worst of Jamie? The answer to that raced to the front of his mind. It wasn't robbing banks. It wasn't even the woman who fell during his last robbery; that was terrifying and haunting but still more an unfortunate overlap of circumstances than anything else.

No, there was one thing that even now, after the opportunity to come clean several times, even with multiple revisions of Zoe, that he'd simply not done. All out of cowardice.

Tell her the truth about the rooftop, about her recapture at Telos.

The lights fluctuated again, the intervals becoming more sporadic and longer, leaving Jamie in darkness except for the red lights staring down at him. He tapped in one more time. "The itch. I think I found it. It just needs to stay there," she'd said, right after the guards joked about taking bets to fight her. He refocused and counted, as he always did, both to re-center himself and also to sense time passing before the power came back on. And when it finally did, he reached back out, trying to reconnect with Zoe, waving all the while despite a developing cramp in his shoulder.

But something strange happened. Zoe wasn't there.

And neither were the guards. Suddenly, he only sensed one mind, and it was barely conscious, a beacon of light blinking in an ocean of blank space.

Zoe, though, was elsewhere. But *where*, exactly? He scanned around, searching for the unique signature of her mind. At first he tried to find her, though soon he realized he'd gotten it all inverted: all he had to do was follow the trail of emptiness in the police department, the rooms and hallways where maybe one person remained conscious.

So much for talking their way out of this.

Jamie moved quicker, skipping around, and then there she was—darting fast, her own signature fading, but not the way it did when someone lost consciousness (presumably from Zoe punching them). That was more like a flashlight going out, but Zoe's exertion made her signal fuzzy, almost blending into the background, like a radio broadcast coming in and out of static.

He skipped ahead to a cluster of minds probably about ten feet in front of her. He locked onto the first opportunity, but that went dark before pulling any memories. He jumped to the next one, finding the headspace and sinking in, except that one snapped shut, sending him out. He bounced again, diving into one more but that one knocked out even before he established a mental lock.

One last person remained in the group, and Jamie grabbed a memory the moment it processed. It was a quick flash, an instant before the whole thing went dark, and it was Zoe following through on a punch as an officer tried to contain her. She stood, shoulders heaving from heavy breaths, as if she was taking a moment to recharge.

Then she looked up, her eyes switching from weary to focused, and she leaped forward. The memory cut off.

Jamie's eyes flew open, jumping back into the present, not because of anything he saw but because of something he heard. It wasn't totally distinct, but it was clear and it was *loud*—he didn't need any sort of heightened hearing to figure it out.

Thump.

Crash.

Clang.

Jamie pressed his ear against the metal door, and that managed to get a little clarity, though a sudden loud *pop* caught his attention. That was followed by several sharp slams and a final dull *thunk*, and then quiet.

Eyes shut, he reached out again. And though he couldn't see anything, every other sense told him that the electricity flickered again.

The noises came closer. Jamie tried to filter them out, and instead focus only on sensing minds. He came upon a group of active beacons, like candles lit in a circle. But one by one, they went out, each mind starting to physically fall before going out.

Well, they *did* say there was a precinct pool. Guess they knew now.

The door rattled, accompanied with a loud *bang*. In fact, all of the muffled bumps and smashes from before were gone. In their place were voices, metallic slams, and two loud pops—one of which was followed by an audible scream and a female voice yelling, "Motherfucker."

Two echoey *clang*s of metal rattled the space. Several seconds of quiet, and panic flooded Jamie, reaching out to locate her.

But he didn't need to. He'd overshot, searching down the hallway. A sudden smack of the door, a violent rattle and the emergence of a fist-sized indent in the cell's door told him otherwise.

"Jamie?" Zoe yelled.

"Right here! You okay?"

"Yeah. We gotta move. Step back." *Clang. Clang. Clang.* Zoe's punches worked through the door until it finally flew off its hinges, sailing into the middle of the cell.

In the doorway stood Zoe Wong, hair matted and sweat dripping down her face. Jamie gasped as he realized her right elbow and bicep were exposed—it wasn't just a tear in her suit, but a wound with blood seeping out. He squinted, and as Zoe leaned against the doorframe, seemingly to collect herself, her blood apparently clotted in real time. Fresh, oozing blood became still, and though it remained liquid on the surface, beneath it formed a texture, a scab building at an accelerated rate.

"Zoe, did you mangle a cop?"

"What? No, of course not. Knocked some out, though."

"What the hell happened there?"

The gash on her arm warranted a mere glance from her. "Huh? Oh yeah, I got shot."

"Shot?"

"Yeah. It's fine." She scooped him up without asking, then adjusted him with a shrug. "Sorry if it's a bumpy ride. My powers are still going in and out a bit."

"I hope you didn't take them *all* out. We need them to follow us, remember? The media too."

"Well, I think I got their attention. Come on," Zoe said. "Let's go make a scene."

33

ZOE RAN AT HALF SPEED.

Which was still better than normal humans, and perhaps the exact percentage of her speed was off, but whatever. Even though she'd laid off the mental abilities and let herself restore for a minute before she took off with Jamie, things were awry.

She was injured.

Carrying Jamie seemed as easy as ever, but with a bullet wound in her shoulder, her legs refused to crank at the pace that they should have.

"We need a car," she yelled. Just like in Kaftan's facility, she tossed a chair through an upper-story window. And just like then, she jumped out, except this time she had Jamie slung over her shoulder. They hovered for several seconds, the solid push-back of air against her palms coming and going into something far less tangible than it should have, causing them to bob up and down in the air. She recovered and they floated long enough for her to see that the several blocks ahead of them seemed to have gone dark.

Whatever Kaftan was doing, the city was feeling it.

"You okay?" Jamie said as spotlights struck them, turning on one by one until their collective intensity shone bright enough to blur out the heat signatures of the people below.

"Yeah. Fine." But right when she made that claim, her powers gave out again, dropping them straight down.

One story passed, then another before her palms felt connected enough to slow their fall. "You hold on to me, I need both hands." Jamie did as instructed, wrapping his arms around her shoulders and locking his fingers. "I don't know how much juice I've got left. So hang on."

Zoe sucked in a deep breath and scanned the horizon. Buildings, streets, cars, all of it the usual bustle of San Delgado's downtown. But over to the left, there was a small patch of park with a toddler-sized play structure and some lawn. It'd have to do.

"There."

"There what—oh, oh shiiiiiii…"

Jamie's voice trailed off, or got knocked out by the wind. Either way, Zoe felt his grip tighten when she pushed them forward with all she had left in her extraordinary tank. They throttled through the air, first accelerating as her abilities propelled them, then decelerating when they refused to work anymore.

"Hang on," she yelled. Her left hand pulled at Jamie, rotating him over and she cocooned him with her body, impact with the ten-by-ten patch of lawn and a neon-colored play structure imminent.

Right when they hit, she spun and turned her back to take the brunt of the impact. Plastic shards and metal bolts flung through the air, bouncing off nearby mulch and stucco.

"I'm okay," Jamie managed with a weak voice.

This was worse than flying through concrete and rebar back at the YMCA. That night, she'd stepped into fire and gripped white-hot metal, all *before* hurling herself through a wall, and yet she'd basically recovered in a matter of hours, and everything *felt* better moment by moment.

But now, things were getting worse. The gunshot was increasingly sore. The ability to take a hit, to move with speed, to fly, all of it was degrading. Whether her journey through the police station had just worn her down, she wasn't sure—all that surging and draining and back again probably wasn't healthy. The problem now was that her power didn't seem to want to restore all the way. Stress, the wound or *something* else syphoned it.

Zoe tried to stand up; her legs didn't agree and she collapsed on one knee before gripping the side of the play structure's remains. Above them a helicopter soared into view, the *whip-whip-whip* of its blades overwhelming every other sound, and its bright lights eclipsing the fact that power seemed to be out on the block.

"You wanted to make a scene?" Jamie said. "I think we got everyone's attention."

Zoe arched up, though an unusual sensation overtook her arm. Pain. Pain, and the bleeding started up again. "Okay, then. Let's lead them to Kaftan. We'll need a car."

"A car." Jamie looked around as police sirens came into earshot. Alongside them, traffic whizzed by at its normal rate, people hardly giving a second glance to the two extraordinary people who just fell from the sky and destroyed a children's play area. "There." He pointed.

No, he wasn't just pointing. He was brain-stunning.

"You're kidding."

Jamie supported her, his shoulder under hers. "It's the only car that's parked. Come on, let's get them out."

Them, as in plural. Two people, to be exact, a cook and a server, a woman and a man both standing in a stupor.

Because he'd picked a food truck, its side displaying big letters painted over anthropomorphic potatoes. Effie's Stop Tot & Roll: Your San Delgado Motor Spudway.

They were going to take a goddamn food truck out to Kaftan's.

As they brought the stunned employees out, the smells of the truck hit her nose—like school cafeteria food, though given their proximity to downtown, probably the expensive artisanal version—igniting a new memory: picking up an order from a different food truck, this one with the simple name Tater Truck in big block letters and a receipt with "M. Peng" printed on it, then putting it in her big red FoodFast backpack before vaulting up to a rooftop and sprinting.

That wasn't an image put together by inferring from Jamie's notes. That was real. A very new, very real memory from before her most recent reset.

"Zoe!" Jamie yelled. He pointed at the wave of police lights heading their way. "We need to go *now!*"

"Right, right." Memories could be recovered later. They had more pressing things. Zoe grabbed a towel hanging off of the deep-fryer's rack and tied it around the oozing wound on her arm. "This time, I'll drive."

34

FOR A BANK ROBBER—a *former* bank robber, technically—Jamie lacked experience in running from the police. He'd certainly walked fast when police cars zoomed toward a bank, probably some ten minutes after he'd exited and the brain-stunned victims started to come to. Head down, legs moving at a good clip to be expeditious without giving off obvious bank robber vibes, all while police sirens whizzed by in the opposite direction. That fell more under the category of stealthy evasion than panic-induced escape.

Though Jamie supposed their current situation didn't totally align with that. They weren't running, after all, except in a metaphorical way. Instead, they were driving a food truck as fast as was safely possible. Zoe sat behind the wheel, though it soon became clear that she hadn't taken any driving lessons since her reawakening. But given the helicopter above them and the flashing lights behind them, Jamie had to be at peak Mind Robber, reaching ahead of them to catch any signs of potential barricades or police roadblocks.

"Lucky we grabbed something with a full tank. We've still got at least thirty minutes to go," Jamie said. Zoe grunted in acknowledgment, and he returned to looking at the path ahead. Fortunately, he'd figured out where Kaftan's facility was during Zoe's weeks of recovering her identity, so other than the last few miles or so, this would all be a smooth ride with only a handful of highway interchanges. And given the late hour, traffic was minimal.

At least, the traffic in front of them. Behind them, the barrage of law enforcement kept their distance. In fact, it appeared that they'd locked into a steady gap, never pulling too close and never dropping too far back.

Which seemed strange. "Zoe," he said.

"Yeah?"

"Don't you think it's odd that they're not, I don't know, landing a helicopter in front of us to block us in?"

Zoe's face scrunched, then held its twisted expression. Guess she hadn't thought about that. "Yeah. That is weird."

"Slow down. Just a little bit." Jamie unbuckled his seat belt and dashed to the back of the food truck. As he passed the deep fryer he grabbed a handful of the tater tots that sat in a basket and popped a couple in his mouth. He peered out the small pane that doubled as the back window and watched as the fleet adjusted to match their speed. "Now speed up. Way up."

The truck lurched forward, knocking him off-balance. He steadied himself, toppling a paper bag filled with napkins while doing so. Another look showed the same thing—most cars kept pace, and the ones that didn't soon accelerated harshly enough to get back in line.

"I think they're not trying to stop us. They're tracking us."

"Does that mean we can all take a break?"

"Just try to drive as steady as possible. I'll double-check."

Jamie reached out with his mind, farther than he'd ever tried before. But the relatively consistent nature of the distance between him and Chesterton made it surprisingly easy. It only took seconds to lock in, and from there, Jamie skimmed through recent memories, treading lightly to prevent any accidental brain-stuns. Most of it focused on the road ahead and the details on the dashboard, but Jamie did find one instance where back-and-forth communication broke through the pursuit.

"Requesting tire spikes at exit 119 on Highway 21 eastbound."

"Negative," Chesterton had said. "I repeat, negative on the road spikes. I don't want to slow them down or take them in yet. There's something they said they wanted to show me and I'm pretty sure they're heading toward that site right now. It sounds like it's related to the blackouts. Request that everyone else just concentrate on keeping people safe with the blackouts taking over the city. Please."

Jamie pulled back out, returning to the clanging back of the food truck. "You know how I told you that Chesterton seemed like one of the good ones?"

"Yeah. You were wrong?"

"I was right. For once. And it sounds like Project Electron is gearing up. He said the blackouts are getting worse." Jamie worked his way back to the front and settled back into the passenger seat. He held up a tater tot for Zoe. "They're garlic flavor," he said as she shot him a raised eyebrow and a nod. "He's letting us go to the facility. He wants to see what we're leading him to."

Zoe took the tot and popped it into her mouth. She chewed quickly, a thoughtful look on her face. "You know, that doesn't mean he's one of the good ones. It just means he's thinking ahead."

They passed a small strip mall on the left, the last real bit of direct civilization on their path. Overhead, helicopter lights maintained a steady drape over them, and behind, the flashing red and blues of police cars provided a constant reminder that this probably wasn't going to end well. "Oh. Well, that's a good point," he said, slipping out of his seat belt to reach the ice chest behind Zoe. "We've got a clear path. Let's get there quick." His fingers sank into the slippery ice cubes, searching for something smooth and metallic. "Want a soda before the final show?"

35

ZOE WAITED UNTIL HER powers returned.

The feeling was instinctive, like knowing whether you were hungry or full, cold or hot. "Okay," she said. "I'm ready." They'd arrived about five minutes ahead of the police and media caravan thanks to a winding dirt path that slowed the convoy down. Parked about a quarter mile away, Zoe and Jamie ran at normal speed over weeds and brush, dirt and rocks, all into the cover of trees. Jamie was the one to suggest stopping farther out to not tip the facility guards off, but it didn't appear Chesterton or the rest of the police agreed, even though the helicopter had peeled off a few miles back. As Zoe felt her powers coming back, so did her heightened sense of hearing. "They're close," she said, "I think I'm good."

"You sure? This would probably be a bad time for it to give out halfway up a tree."

"The alternative is to face the entire police force after I punched out a bunch of them. Though to be fair, *they* shot me." Zoe looked up and gauged the height. "Some distance would be good."

"Right," Jamie said. "Up and at 'em."

Zoe put one arm around Jamie, took a deep breath and hoped she'd judged this correctly.

They launched upward, the wind tickling her cheeks, until she put a palm out to keep them in the air and assess a soft landing point. Her foot tucked in the joint of a thick branch; between a few hours ago and this, she was getting pretty good at this whole "leaping up trees" thing. Maybe if she survived this, she'd offer people rides for a hundred bucks a pop. Seemed like a better use of her skills than returning to FoodFast.

One by one, the police rolled in, first Chesterton's unmarked sedan, then six squad cars, then just as many TV vans. Dust swirled in slow-forming clouds along the dirt road, and Chesterton's car lurched its way to the front gate. Behind the bars, silhouettes moved and the detective stepped out. Voices came from above the din of all the vehicles, but only bits and pieces passed their way, even with her hearing.

"Sounds like Chesterton's confused," she said. They continued watching as the detective talked through the gate, then pointed back at the cars behind him. "Can you see what they just talked about?"

Jamie nodded, then squinted, his hands in front of him. Zoe kept watching the scene unfold in front of them, though the drain on her powers remained palpable. Her palm flexed, searching for that invisible grip that propelled her, but only a faint brush arrived against her skin.

"I'm not sure what his agenda is," Jamie said, "but he's not throwing us under the bus."

"Yeah?"

"He might be buying us time. Or buying himself time. Or just letting things play out. He hasn't mentioned either of us. He told them that the city is experiencing a drain on the power grid and the city's engineers believe it has something to do with this facility." He looked over and offered a grin. "No mention of vigilantes or bank robbers. So it's good bullshit."

"That still doesn't tell us how to stop any of this."

"Well, look at the activity out front. We know that a bunch of Kaftan's hired goons were cut loose. But the guards are piling up in the main courtyard." He pointed, and Zoe followed his line of sight. Even without thermal detection, she saw he was right. "We should go now. Element of surprise. While they're looking the other way."

Zoe pumped her legs some more. The strength was there, but not quite the way she'd prefer it for invading a facility with armed guards. A few more minutes would have helped. But the balcony she'd soared into weeks ago sat ripe for the taking, if they could just make it there.

"Okay," she said. "Grab on."

"How are we going to do this?" he asked as he took her by the shoulder. "Are you gonna—"

Zoe didn't give him a chance to finish the question. Her fluctuating powers left too much to chance, and the ability to hover, assess and pick a route didn't exist here. Finesse wouldn't work, even if no eyes tracked them across the night sky. Instead, she threw them as high into the air as possible, some extra forty or fifty feet on top of the good twenty above the ground they'd started from. Even before they'd hit the apex of the leap, Zoe's fingers dug into the ether and pushed as hard as she could. They throttled forward, cutting through the air at a speed similar to her top sprinting pace, and as they flew toward the facility's upper level, Zoe cringed at Jamie's sudden terrified yell right in her ear.

Technically, they were headed toward the open balcony from her last visit. But without fine-tuning, their flight lacked accuracy. They aimed for a general direction where five feet one way would lead to an empty crevice between air-conditioning units, five feet another way would smash them straight into a wall, and just right might crash-land them onto a balcony.

Zoe just had to hope that she hadn't drained all her strength yet.

With Jamie clutching on tightly, Zoe waited until they were close to the wall—thirty, maybe forty feet? Who knew at this speed?—then threw her hands out, pulsating the ether to slow them, then she pointed them downward, a slow descent that let her fine-tune their direction until they hovered just above the balcony.

A simple drop.

"I've got a bad feeling about—" Jamie started, when Zoe's powers—or sudden lack of them—interrupted. They went from smooth descent to a sudden fall—straight down, at least. Her hands pumped vertically, palms out, and right before they hit the balcony, her powers kicked in and she managed to keep them floating several inches above the concrete floor.

"After you," Zoe said, letting Jamie down.

"Let's never do that again." Jamie moved to the front of the balcony, peering over the edge toward the facility's entry gates. "Check this out."

Zoe followed suit, but grasped on to the edge, shoulders rising and falling as she took in restorative breaths. In the distance, a group of police bunched together to form a rough line, and behind them stood an arc of media lights and cameras and reporters. "Look at all that media. I'm guessing those guys blew Chesterton's cover. There's no way they haven't mentioned us."

Popping sounds interrupted their discussion, and they both ducked, expecting gunfire from either the facility guards or the police or both. But this came with a specific rhythm, the pops hitting regular beats and a quick peek showed that tall lamps all around the structure were exploding one by one.

Something was happening with Project Electron.

Jamie stood up, lines etched into his face in concentration.

"No one knows anything about what just happened. They think it might be the region's power grid." The light and shadows hit him at an angle that made his Mind Robber hands and fingers look really badass. Though she knew better—he'd still lose in a fight. But hopefully he was getting some valid info. "Maybe they're right. I'm diving deeper. Those guys aren't standard security guards. They're like hired ex-military. One is from Russia. Wow. Kaftan did her research when it comes to tough guys. And I think—oh shit."

"Oh shit good or oh shit bad?"

"I'm not sure." He whirled around, then nodded behind him. "Kaftan's out there now. I jumped from person to person down there to scout it out but there's one mind I can't break into." He pointed at the door. "Element of surprise, right?"

"Have we figured out what we're going to do inside yet?" Zoe asked, gauging her strength before assessing the door. She took a step back, then formed a fist and was just about to launch at it when Jamie waved her to stop.

"You mean a plan?" From his back pocket, he took out the security badge they'd lifted from Richard earlier in the night. Waving it over the little black reader next to the doorknob produced a chime and the sound of a door latch. "We're terrible at plans, remember? Let's wing it."

36

IF THE TELOS FACILITY projected a facade of normalcy over something much more sinister, this place was the exact opposite. It was creepy, with only red emergency lights providing minimal illumination.

"This place didn't look like a horror movie last time," Jamie said, moving slowly down the hallway and trying to *not* trip over his feet. "It was more like a factory that needed an interior decorator."

"Funny, those are some of the few true memories I have." Zoe stopped, hands on knees and shoulders slumped. She took in a heavy breath, but waved away his hand when he offered. "From those snippets you left me. Definitely not horror-movie creepy like this. And I say that as someone who *likes* horror movies."

"Are you okay?"

"I'm fine."

"No, you're not. This power drain, it's been getting worse the longer the night's gone on. And I'm not talking about the city."

He gestured all around them, and she raised an eyebrow at him, a conversation built on shorthand to argue what he realized and what she refused to admit, regardless of how weary she looked. He punctuated his end of the exchange with a wrinkled brow and a bemused smile, all tied together with a calm, quiet voice. "It's taking longer for you to recover. Let's take a break," he said.

"A break's no good if they find us."

"*You're* no good if you're shot *and* have no powers," he said, keeping his tone even. "So, let's take a break. Mind Robber's orders." With eyes shut, Jamie took a quick assessment of the area. No minds appeared in the immediate region, at least for now.

While Zoe's stoicism came off as commendable, the lack of powers added to his worry. Having the Throwing Star by his side wouldn't do much good if she lacked strength or speed half the time, all in unpredictable bursts.

Of course, he couldn't *say* that. "There's no one close. Take a break." He scanned the room again, this time with eyes open, not for threats but for a conversation topic that might ease the tension, help reset things. "By the way, how *do* you know what's horror-movie creepy? Didn't I just tell you about that?"

"I know because horror movies are the best." Zoe shrugged, the leather of her Throwing Star suit crinkling with the gesture. "Some stuff must be universal even with a reset. Like your accent, right? And for me, horror movies. And the basics. I mean, I can read, write, drive—"

"—I don't know about that driving part. That was a rough ride."

"Hey, we got here, right?"

"Yeah, that's one way to put it. If we find your DMV records, I'm gonna put a bet on the number of speeding tickets."

A genuine smile crept onto Zoe's face, with squinted eyes and visible teeth. She pulled her sweat-matted hair back, grimacing at the movement with her injured arm. "I'll take that."

"What?"

"I'll take that bet. About speeding tickets. You said Zoe Wong's my real name. Now that we know that, it probably won't be that hard to figure out how many speeding tickets I earned. Maybe all that info is here. You know, we can dig up the Project Electron stuff to send to the press, but also my DMV record." Her eyes dropped to the floor, a rare pensive look coming over her face. "How many times do you think they reset me?"

Even if he knew that information, such a question came with so many *other* questions that no good answer existed. "Kaftan didn't say," Jamie said after several seconds.

Without a retort lined up, Zoe stood and fidgeted with her makeshift bandages. Her eyes looked everywhere *but* at Jamie, and when he stepped toward her, she turned.

Under most circumstances, he wouldn't dare approach her this way. She'd slug the shit out of him. This time, though, felt different. He could, in theory, dive into her mind, see what memories flew through there.

In that moment, though, Jamie opted to give her space. For once, he didn't need to fully understand something to embrace the moment. He did the usual five-second countdown, though this wasn't to re-center himself. He already knew what he was going to say. The countdown was to let *her* process it all first.

"Okay, I got it," Jamie finally said, holding out his right hand. "We get out of this alive and *not* under arrest, you help me rob a bank *and* I help you hack the DMV. If someone's gonna have records of every revision of you, it's gotta be the DMV."

The dim lighting fluctuated, darkness flashing around them, along with a sudden flash of blue. The red lights returned. And fortunately, no guards popped up around them. Or chainsaw-wielding serial killers, if this had been one of Zoe's horror movies.

Zoe gripped his hand in return. "Deal," she said, her smile turning into a full laugh. Her fingers felt loose at first, but seconds later they squeezed and grasped, an unnatural strength putting too much pressure on his knuckles.

"Zoe..."

"Yeah, I feel it." In the dim light, harsh shadows formed across Zoe's unmasked cheekbones, and the zipper teeth that formed the Throwing Star shape across her suit looked even more pronounced, like someone turned the contrast all the way up on their world. "The heat signatures are back. I'll scout." Through the tear in her suit, the towel tied around the gunshot wound oozed blood, the original light-colored cloth now nearly soaked through. Jamie watched her eyes, an intensity focusing them as her head gradually tilted from left to right. "I think it's only guards. Based on their outlines and stance. Scientists don't walk like that." She straightened up, taking a sudden look all around them, even up and down at the various levels before her face scrunched. "This place is nearly empty. If they were testing on anyone else, they're gone now."

Hartnell City. New Turning. Janloon. And other cities with rumors. Jamie wondered if test subjects got shipped out to those places when they were no longer deemed useful.

"Now, let's see..." Zoe said. Her finger went up, and Jamie recognized the gesture.

She was trying to brain-stun.

"Remember, it's a matter of finesse."

Zoe shook her head, frowning at the lack of result. "I'm not practiced enough. Or strong enough. Not sure at this point."

"How far away?"

"Other side of this hallway. Probably ten, fifteen meters that way." She pointed, this time strictly for direction.

Jamie closed his eyes and began sensing for minds; the thick matrix of concrete and metal dulled his range but there he was, the faintest outline of white floating in his mind's eye. A quick turn of the finger locked him in, bringing the presence from a cloud to a silhouette and recent memories flashed before Jamie's eyes. Most of the images offered little of note, nothing but patrolling hallways. However, one distinct memory involved an alert barked through his headset warning that the Mind Robber and Throwing Star were in the building, with orders on how to deal with them.

Jamie's heavy sigh blew into the stale air, and he started laughing to himself. His eyes shot up to the ceiling, his head in a constant shake.

"What is it?"

"They're gonna kill us," he said with a chuckle. "Oh crap, they're gonna kill us. His orders were *'terminate on sight.'* I take it all back about trying to do something good. We should have run off to the Caribbean. We could be sitting on a beach. I bet Normal would like the fresh coconuts."

"Can you brain-stun him? Before he gets close to us?"

"Sure. While I'm at it—" Jamie's fingers went back up "—I'll remove that memory of him receiving the order to kill us." The merc's mind synced up with his and Jamie flipped through the details like they were folders in a file cabinet, and one quick flick wiped it away.

Or at least it should have.

The memory remained, blurring out before snapping back into focus.

"Shit."

"Good news has never started with *shit.*"

He tried again. And several more times, but the memory refused to budge. Another flick *should* have brain-stunned the merc, but that failed to take too, and now the mind floated back and forth, signs of an agitated and pacing and very awake human being.

"I think it's the walls. My range is limited with this concrete. It must be dulling my abilities too. Well," he said, turning to Zoe, "if they didn't know we were inside before, they definitely know now. Do you see Waris?"

Lines of concentration etched across her face as she crouched down and slowly panned her head. She took in a sharp gasp, then squinted. "There. That's him."

"Okay. Let's get to him before he gets to us. Or blows up the city."

The sound of boots clacking against concrete echoed in the tight hallway, and despite the lack of light, Zoe's walk picked up in both pace and confidence. Jamie watched, and though she was several meters in front of him by now, he was pretty sure that her arm wasn't bleeding anymore.

37

A HAND-SIZED HOLE STARED back at Zoe.

Seconds before, smooth dull concrete sat there, but then she formed a fist and thrust it with controlled strength and fury, puncturing the wall and sending cracks outward from the industrial wound.

"Jesus." Jamie turned, his eyes wide. "What—are you, I mean—"

"Sorry," Zoe said, shaking dust and debris off her hand. "I was just testing things."

"Testing how hard concrete is?"

"Sort of. I was worried my powers were going out." She gestured around them. "There aren't as many heat signatures as there were five minutes ago. It's like they're vanishing from the map. But," she said, "it's not that. Some are up front with Kaftan dealing with the shit up there. Some are patrolling all over the grounds. I don't think they realize how far in we are. And we've got two in front of Electron's door." Eyes closed, she knelt close to the ground, not to sense anything further but to assess her own state.

"Save your strength," Jamie said, his voice in full concerned-parent mode.

"I'll be fine. It's just two guards. Besides, you can just brain-stun them."

In silence, she watched him, hands and face nearly all the way up against the wall closest to their eventual target. A minute passed, possibly two—which was good for her own restoring powers.

Based on Jamie's expression when he turned around, they were going to need them.

"I can't." His knuckles tapped on the wall. "Something about this. Maybe its thickness or...something. I'm not sure. I can sense them but nothing happens when I try to stun them. I can't even dive in. I just know they're there." He pulled the security card out from his back pocket and gestured at the metal door a few feet farther down the hall. "I think it's a hallway past here. Should I?"

Zoe considered the alternatives, but at this stage, no other bright ideas existed. The only way to Project Electron was through that door. "One second. I think this may be the one time when we do actually need a plan."

"Three," Jamie said.

Zoe nodded and leaped into the air.

"Two."

As she hit the ceiling, her palms went out, keeping her hovering. She threw her legs back, bracing up against the corner wall and pressing her as flat against the overhead concrete as possible.

"One." Jamie swiped the badge against the card reader. A beep filled the space, followed by the clicking and whirring of locking mechanisms systematically undoing themselves. The door slid open, and though Zoe felt her strength starting to pull away from her, she fought for more. Sweat beaded across her forehead and her pulse began to race as her grip on the ether caused her hands to tremble.

"What was that?" one voice said.

"Check thermal."

Thermal detection? Zoe wondered if the technology-based stuff was any better than what she naturally saw. Jamie would be obvious, with a person-shaped marker standing straight up. Would they detect her? She supposed it depended on if they were looking up.

"One target. Hey," the voice yelled, "this is a restricted area. All personnel should have cleared out hours ago."

Jamie glanced up at Zoe. He tapped the side of his head and mouthed "no," along with several shakes. From above, she saw him angle around the sliding door, probably debating whether to reveal himself for a clear shot at brain-stunning or to remain hidden in the corner.

"Jamie," she whispered. They met eyes, his containing clear panic. Which made sense, given the "terminate on sight" orders. "Stay there."

The footsteps came closer, and as they did, Zoe's arms and legs were in a full shake, struggling to keep the tactical advantage above. The guard was almost there. Almost, so close that his shadow broke the threshold of the doorway.

And first, the barrel of a gun poked through. Jamie flattened himself into the corner as much as possible, though his hands stayed up, ready to brain-stun. Could he lock on from there or did he need a clear line of sight?

The barrel began to turn Jamie's direction. Of course, the thermal detection. They knew he was there, hiding didn't do anything. She kicked the wall behind her with enough force to chip away debris. It scattered below her, confusing the guard at first, and that gave her enough advantage to fall straight down on top of him.

But without all of her strength. She gripped on to the large man's shoulders, and he swung back and forth, trying to shake her off. The guard's rifle went off, and she saw Jamie go down. He was either hit or using sheer survival instincts. One swift blow to the guard's hand knocked the rifle loose. From her peripheral vision, she saw the other guard begin charging.

Zoe locked her arms behind the man's and kicked out his knees. "Stun him," she yelled.

Jamie rose up, his hands out and eyes squinting. The guard struggled and she tried to pull him back, her diminished strength still greater than his normal human strength. Not by much, but enough to hold him steady for Jamie.

A second later, he went limp.

Zoe let him go, and the guard dropped like an empty puppet. But right when the guard's face smacked concrete, a flash came from the hallway and she was spun around by the impact of a bullet to her shoulder.

"Zoe," Jamie yelled, enough to get the charging guard's attention. Zoe fell backward and slammed into the wall, pain starting to kick in from the bullet wound on the opposite shoulder of the one from earlier.

One point for the San Delgado PD, one for these guys. She supposed that was karmic balance of some sort.

The man stepped past the doorframe, and as he did, Jamie used the fallen guard's rifle like a bat, swinging away. It didn't do much damage, but it created enough confusion to give Zoe an opening. She charged with her remaining strength, lowering her entire shoulder, bullet wound and all, then launched with what speed she had left into the middle of the guard's back.

The guard flew past Jamie and smacked into the concrete wall, causing a dent that was not quite as large as Zoe's test smash earlier. Jamie stepped over him and his extended fingers jabbed into the space above the man's face. The man convulsed for a second, then went limp on the ground.

"Zoe," Jamie said after finally looking up. "You're a mess."

"I'm fine."

The grimace on his face said more than any actual reply. "No, you're hurt." Jamie grabbed the walkie-talkies and their small single-ear headsets off both guards and handed one to Zoe.

"I'm *fine*. Let's go end this before more of these assholes try to murder us." She marched down the hallway to Project Electron. Pain coursed through her upper body. Her legs felt like they were bogged down in cement. At the door, mechanisms whirred, releasing locks one by one, and as each piece welcomed them in, the other side of the door suddenly felt like much more than a goal.

It was the portal to her entire life.

Zoe remembered.

This room, the man in the tube. She closed her eyes and saw the exact same thing in her memory, but a lifetime ago, when she was herself but a previous revision.

And yet something about this room, this space, this being with the fiery red glow, it suddenly came back to her, a switch flipping in her mind. The memory played with perfect detail: the way he'd looked at her, locked eyes and then let out the most horrifying *inhuman* sound ever to come out of a human body.

"This is him," Jamie said. "Waris Kaftan. Biophysicist. This is everything." He pulled out his phone and started snapping photos. "Damn, no signal. If I can get these photos to the police, we're good. We're in the clear."

"Jamie." Her voice was soft, almost a confession wrapped in a single word that *something* was happening. "Jamie, I remember. I remember how I was in this room before. With *him*, with all these devices. Wait," she said, surveying the room. "That wasn't here last time."

She pointed at a most unusual bit of technology that gave off a blinding glow, a brilliant blue like someone set the most perfect sky on fire. Jamie looked at it and inhaled sharply. "What is it?" Zoe asked. But she didn't need him to answer; several seconds was all it took to revive the memory from the interrogation chamber that she'd viewed in his mind.

"That must be what's causing all the power fluctuations. And it has to be tied to the blue person." Jamie gave it a close-up inspection before following the massive cables jutting out of its bottom port all the way to Waris. "Oh."

"What?"

"That machine. It's connected to him." He disappeared on the other side of the capsule as he gave it a closer look. "At the base of his neck. Jeez. How do you even do this?"

More rhetorical questions came from Jamie, but Zoe stopped listening. Instead, she took cautious steps forward, approaching the mystery cube. Half of it appeared like any sort of fancy lab equipment, buttons and displays and blinking lights. But on the right side, the half with cables sticking out of it, its blinding light also produced a low hum that may have only been audible to her ears. She put her hand up and inched closer to it, drawn as if by magnetic force or invisible pulley or just sheer curiosity.

And suddenly, the memories were there.

Not just of being in the room. All of it. Waking up in the apartment. Punching the dumpster. Thwarting her first robbery. All her choices. The memories were hers, not lifted from Jamie.

They made her whole. And she needed more.

Layers of her life arrived, her previous revisions turning on like light switches suddenly activating throughout a dark building. In one revision, the speed and the strength were there, but without the urge to fight crime. In another, weed rather than booze was her drug of choice. In another, she somehow *knew* that she could take flight, instinctively jumping out the window of the same old apartment on a whim.

But only one time did she put it all together to become the Throwing Star.

Zoe stopped and opened her eyes, putting the massive awakening on pause. One little detail forced a smirk—how about that? In each revision, she'd tried to watch *Lo-Bot: Cyborg Samurai*, and each time, she turned it off halfway through, at the exact same spot. Five times, in fact, always when Lo-Bot is confronted by his former police partner about losing his humanity with a solo quest for vengeance. Every time, she'd rolled her eyes and turned her attention to something else.

Except for that night with Jamie. And the movie turned out to be pretty good after all.

What else lay underneath? Her fingers reached forward, index finger out—not to rob anyone's memories but to get hers back.

"What the hell was that? This whole thing just…surged or something." Jamie's face popped up and scanned back and forth until landing on Zoe. "Did you touch that?"

"Jamie, this thing. My memories. It's like a goddamn switch in my head." It was as if the device, the energy radiating from it, somehow healed the gaps in her mind, reconnecting the neural pathways that held all of the data of experience. Jamie had it wrong; he hadn't lifted or deleted people's memories, he'd simply unplugged the connection, like a cell phone that suddenly couldn't get service. Her eyes closed again and the flow of information short-circuited her coordination, dropping her to her knees, arms hugging herself. She forced her eyes open, breaking past the onslaught of memories, to see Jamie kneeling in front of her. "All right here. I remember," she said. "Who I was before the Throwing Star. How many more lives are hidden?" She looked at the source of the brilliant blue glow. "How many more until I recover the truth? I've got at least five revisions back."

"Wait. Don't touch it again," Jamie said. "We don't know what that's doing to you. Touch it again and you might fry your brain."

"Or I could get everything back. All the way to the end. The original Zoe Wong."

"Zoe. You can't. Not now. Look." Jamie nodded to Waris, still contained within the Electron chamber. A rumble had started, shaking the floor panels and the devices around them. "Zoe, this is not the time for experiments. I need to figure out how to shut this all down. I need to get into his—" Jamie pointed at Waris "—mind. And I need you to guard us while I do that. If this thing knocks you out and guards find us, then that'll be it. Game over for us."

Mere inches stood between her and a potentially whole mind. All those questions, the months staring at the detective board. It seemed so simple.

"Please," Jamie said. She met his pleading eyes, lines forming on his brow. "For the city. If we don't stop this, the whole grid goes down for who knows how long."

The entire city without power. Once people lost any sense of control, they were likely to panic. Security systems down, traffic run amok. Zero communication, zero emergency services. Food, water, gas, all of it gone.

They were there to try to do some good. It just took a second for Zoe to remember that.

"Right." She nodded. "Better get to work."

"Thank you," Jamie said. He disappeared to the other side of the capsule, though his voice continued. "I'm not sure what to make of this mess underneath here. Is he responsive?"

The whole capsule seemed to pulsate with energy, its glowing buttons and indicators going at a consistent rhythm. Zoe leaned over, nearly on top of it now, when Waris opened his eyes and looked at her.

The facility lights dimmed and rose and back again, fighting to stay activated until they finally gave out, leaving only the flashing lights and displays of devices connected to Waris. Blue flashes whirled around the room, leaving traces of sparks that flickered into the dark. They zapped around the space, zigging and zagging until being pulled together, a shimmering pool made of electricity.

From the pool rose the figure of a man.

The figure stood, blue sparks raining off him.

"Jamie," Zoe whispered. The figure stared at her; no eyes, no face, just the shape of a head but she *knew* its focus landed on her.

"I can't get through," Jamie said, his hands up and pointed at the blue man. "It wants something but I can't get through. I can't—"

Before Jamie could finish his sentence, Zoe put her hand up, fingers out. A bolt of electricity flew out from the figure, connecting with her before everything went dark.

38

PITCH BLACK ENVELOPED THE ROOM. With the darkness came silence except for a quiet wheezing from Waris. Not even a backup generator hummed, which made Jamie question how well designed this place actually was.

Either that, or how much the blue thing wanted to do... whatever it did.

Then the silence broke—a quick *thump* followed by a louder *clang* which created an echo in the space. The whirs and rumbles of machine start-up cycles played a chorus of mechanical noises, soon followed by various beeps. Overhead, the lights flickered, breaking through the darkness to finally achieve full illumination.

Zoe was on the floor.

"Oh shit. Not now, not now, not now." His knees stung as Jamie landed next to her, and though he'd read up on general first aid since the bank incident, nothing quite applied to the situation of a woman with extraordinary abilities touching a mystery being made completely of electricity. He gently nudged her shoulders, trying to stir something without snapping her too quickly awake. She was, after all, capable of throwing him across the room if she startled back to consciousness.

How much time had passed? Was Kaftan still outside? The guards still appeared to be knocked out, but that could mean anything about the current state of things. "Come on, Zoe. Wake up, wake up, wake up," he said, being a little more forceful on her shoulders now.

Above him, a red light started to swirl around the room. This was different from the emergency lighting that illuminated the pathways along the floor.

This looked like an alert.

"Zoe!" he yelled. "It's a goddamn alarm! Wake up!"

"Hey," she said, her eyes gradually opening. "What's with the shouting?"

Relief washed over him, though panic quickly shoved it out of the way. "Look," he said, pointing at the alarm signal above, "they're on to us."

"Who are you?" Her eyes stared blankly upward. "Who am I? Where are we?"

No. Not again.

Chills rippled throughout Jamie's body and his chest tightened, panic ramping up into something far worse. He forced himself to do a countdown and exhale on each beat.

One, then breathe in and out.

Two, then breathe in and out.

Three, then—

Suddenly, Zoe burst out laughing. "You totally fell for it, didn't you," she said, sitting up.

Damn it.

His shoulders and posture collapsed, and though he wanted to yell at her for doing that, or about their dire circumstances, or for making contact with the blue *thing*, his instinct pulled him another direction.

He threw his arms around her and hugged his friend.

But when he pulled back, glistening patches of fresh blood transferred to his Mind Robber hoodie, matching the gunshot wounds on either side of her body. They both looked at the stains, though Zoe simply waved them away. "It's fine. I can feel my powers coming back. The healing will come back with it."

"Doesn't it hurt?"

"Oh yeah, it fucking hurts. But we've got bigger things to deal with." She stood up, then pulled him along with enough ease to prove that her powers did indeed return. "Waris."

"Yeah. We have to stop him."

"No. I know everything. We don't need to stop him." Her eyes were clear and soft lines of compassion framed her face. "We have to *help* him."

"So let me get this straight," Jamie said. His fingers danced in front of him, though rather than brain-stunning or diving into a mind, it was simply a physical gesture to help him process the massive info dump Zoe just gave him in a rapid-fire speech. "The blue thing is Waris. He can project his consciousness into electricity. He's been trying to warn us the whole time about Kaftan. And he's trapped in Project Electron and wants to die. But Kaftan thinks that your latest serum is working so she's trying to execute her plan *tonight*."

"Yeah. And they put in a fail-safe by mixing the reverse serum into it and…" Zoe's face scrunched up as she bit into her lip. "Okay, he said 'it triggers when your integrated powers demonstrate both sustained usage and…' Oh, shit, I dunno. It was technical. But whatever, that's why I'm losing my powers."

"Jeez." Jamie shook his head. Who knew that all they had to do was talk to a being made out of electricity to fill in all the gaps? "Anything else?"

"Yeah, he's kind of funny when he connects to you telepathically. Seems like a nice guy."

He *did* seem like a nice guy. And a *noble* guy. At least from the secondhand memories Jamie absorbed from Zoe, a shorthand version of images and audio direct from Waris. Including one fateful night, about fifteen years ago, when newlyweds Waris and Sasha sat out on a dusty plain in northwestern Kenya, watching the landscape catch fire from an electrical storm, burning crops withering away the hopes of a drought-riddled populace. They'd come as volunteers to provide humanitarian aid in the form of medical treatments and equipment repair, yet without sustainable food, their efforts wouldn't have a long-term impact. As they pondered the chaos in front of them, Waris turned to Sasha and said, "Everything here is beautiful. And brutal. Everything lost to that brutality. If only nature's brutality could make crops instead of destroying them."

But it was Sasha who said, "Maybe there's something to that."

Project Electron. Its birth was now a part of Jamie's memories, but the experience belonged solely to her. He'd received the abridged version.

"Well, tell him next time he tries to talk to us that the blue thing is scary, especially when it screams."

"I don't think he wants there to be a next time." Zoe's eyes fell to the floor, and of all the reactions to extreme situations he'd seen her in—panic, rage, triumph, fear and all the other big ones—he couldn't recall the look on her face *right now*. Her brow crinkled, her eyes were soft, and her lips formed a thin line. Whatever Waris had told her had tilted the axis of her world. "She was right, you know. This whole project was to do the right thing. And maybe someone will take the foundation of it and complete it. But not him. Right now, he's in this limbo state. Not alive. Not dead. Just there. With this power to travel through electricity that he doesn't understand." Her black hair swished back and forth as she shook her head, her gaze intensifying. "What he does understand, though, is how to shut this off."

They stood amid the blinking panel lights and hum of machines, their natural frequencies counting off units of time in their own way. Zoe straightened up and nodded. "We need to shut off the life support to his physical body. And then we go to the Electron core in the basement and shut that off. That'll make it all go away." Her gaze pulled away from him and lingered on the glowing cube. "Even that."

That being the thing that seemingly restored layers of Zoe's previous lives.

Her past or the city's future.

The burden of such a choice unfairly fell on her bullet-wounded shoulders, no matter how strong her extraordinary abilities made them. "Hey," Jamie said, a hand on her shoulder. "We can still find out who you are. Just not this way."

Zoe blinked, eyes darting between the remaining puffs of smoke where the Electron being stood, Waris's physical mutilated body and the device that could grant her everything she wanted. "I just...it's right there. Who I really am."

It struck Jamie, perhaps the way his brain-stuns struck others, that Zoe completely missed the irony in that statement. That the woman about to dash off through a labyrinth of military-trained mercenaries and one pissed-off extraordinary mad scientist to prevent the city from descending into chaos, that she of all people couldn't see who she was.

As if her actions didn't speak louder than words. Or memory.

"Who you really are is this. Zoe Wong. Standing right in front of me." Jamie laughed the smallest laugh, one of disbelief at how obvious it all was, how difficult they made it. "If you touched that, if you filled in all those blanks, would that change a single thing about what you're about to do? To save the city? To save Waris's soul? Maybe even Kaftan's? The good you've done this city, the good you've done for me, that says way more than whatever burdens your parents drilled into your head, whatever you did or didn't do growing up. However many speeding tickets you got."

Zoe's serious look cracked into a wry smile.

"I know who you really are. You are my friend. You have made me a better person. And someday, I hope to repay you. Somehow."

Jamie's heart pounded, not in the way that happened when he started stunning people to rob banks. And not the way it felt when he realized Kaftan had captured him, or even when Zoe had taken him for his first flight. This was different, the littlest flutter of something that took far too long to recognize.

Hope.

"Damn," she said, her voice dry. "You *are* good at those Mind Robber speeches."

"Well." Jamie matched her wry smirk. "I meant it literally. Because we're still going to rob a bank together, right?"

"Of course. But first," she turned to Waris's capsule, "he deserves peace."

39

IN THEORY, IT SHOULD have been easy. She had extraordinary strength, after all, so tearing cables—even big heavy cables braided with metal lace—out of their sockets should have been simple. Especially since Waris had shown her which ones specifically to do: first, the massive cable with a metallic braid connecting Project Electron to the glowing thingy she'd touched earlier. Then two cords that dropped from the ceiling and plugged into the control panel, each about an inch in diameter and in green outer sleeves. Then one about twice that size, except this one bolted to the bottom of Electron with a metal plate. And a final, simple connection, one that ultimately connected to the base of Waris's skull.

And yet, she'd got only three of the five cables unplugged, in the order specified by Waris, each with a spectacular flurry of sparks. Each of them came secured by multiple bolts and reinforcements, and it took Zoe's abilities to yank them out quickly and cleanly.

The only problem now stemmed from her strength. Or lack thereof.

"How much time do you think you need?" Jamie asked.

Air became a battle in itself, Zoe panting much harder than she should have been. Pain resumed from each of her gunshot wounds, though thankfully her body retained enough of its healing abilities to keep the bleeding to an annoying trickle. The answer to Jamie's question, though, remained tricky. "I'm not sure," she finally said.

"Maybe there's an easier way to do this. A little bit of finesse." Jamie knelt down to the fourth cable, one that traversed along the floor to the base of the capsule. "I think," he said, his fingers exploring around and above and below the connection, "I think this is just a cover plate. The connection must be under it. Maybe you don't need your full strength to rip the cable out. Help me get this cover off. It might just pop out."

Zoe filled her lungs, hoping that the simple act of bringing oxygen into her body might restore some of her abilities. She flexed her fingers before kneeling down to see what Jamie was talking about. A metal casing, the kind of thing she could crush as simply as an aluminum can. But as her fingers gripped it, an electronic squawk popped through her headset. She looked at Jamie, who was pressing a finger against the small speaker resting on his ear.

"Domino and Fives, you've missed your hourly check-in. What's your status?"

That voice. It was Kaftan.

Fear laced Jamie's tone. "Oh shit." He must have recognized it too.

That fear also spiked Zoe's adrenaline, enough for her to rip the metallic cover off the fourth cable, leaving only its radius of connecting bolts in place. "Here we go," she told herself, and she pulled on it with as much strength as she could muster.

Which wasn't enough.

"Damn it," she said through gritted teeth. "Come on." Again. And again. Each time, the impact of her force felt less and less, until her muscles actually ached and the wounds resumed bleeding.

"Stop," Jamie said in a gentle voice.

The headset came to life again. "Domino, report your position. We have suspected intruders."

"What do we do?" Zoe asked.

Jamie ran his fingers over the cable, then shot a look over at Waris before eyeing up the massive door at the edge of Project Electron's observation area. "You keep working on this. I'll go to the core."

"What? Jamie, they have guns. You can't brain-stun a bullet."

"What's that?" He pointed to the bloodstained bandage on her arm. "And that?" Then a similarly soaked spot on her opposite shoulder.

"That's nothing. My abilities will restore, they'll heal."

"Right. So you need to get this cable out. I'll figure out the other part."

"No, no, no. Damn it, if I can take two bullets, I can take a third. There's a set of doors here to protect you. You stay here. I'll go there."

"Zoe, this is not up for debate," Jamie said.

"You're right," she said with an exasperated sigh.

He knelt back down and returned to the exposed cable, which made him conveniently out of sight when she held her finger up and locked in, just the way Jamie had shown her. It seemed like weeks ago, but only hours had passed since the rooftop training in an attempt to recover her suit. Except unlike with Richard earlier, she used the slightest of taps, barely noticeable.

"Look, this is what you need to pull off—"

The words stopped abruptly, then she dashed over to see the results of her handiwork. He didn't collapse, though he seemed more immobilized than anything else. Unlike other brain-stuns, his eyes tracked her.

Guess she perfected the light touch.

"Blink if you can hear me," she said.

He blinked multiple times, eyes tracking her as she walked over and grabbed the walkie-talkie off his belt clip. "Looks like they're on channel four. Set ours to, say, nine? It'll just be us. So here's what's gonna happen. You're gonna get your feeling back and you're gonna find a way to take out those cables. And I'm gonna leave here and break every door mechanism I find on the way. That'll buy you time until I shut off the core and come back for you. Got it?" She finished switching the channel and placed it back on his belt clip, then adjusted the small head-set hanging off his left ear. "And our policeman friend. You've got all the evidence you need here. Make sure those photos get through. That'll clear both of us."

Jamie's eyes widened, his blinking intensifying. His ajar mouth opened farther as if someone turned an inner crank on his jaw muscles. An incomprehensible gurgling noise struggled out, probably his way of saying her name under this level of paralysis.

It didn't matter. Not this time. "We got this," she said. And though she couldn't see herself, the warmth that radiated from her smile went deep into her chest. One more nod and then a thumbs-up, and then it was time to leave. The door to the lab opened, welcoming her into the front observation area. On the other side, she waited until the door slid shut and used what extraordinary strength she had left to smash into the door's ID reader, then set out to do it again and again on the path to the basement.

The path that Waris showed her in her mind.

40

CLANG.

The noise rattled again, and Jamie dared to look at the thick door, indentations growing larger and larger. Next to it, the window showed Sasha Kaftan, still in her business suit, looking calm and professional.

Except for her repeated punches at the massive security door. About fifteen minutes had passed since Zoe left the room, six or seven since he'd managed to move freely again. And right before his arms and legs regained motion, he'd heard the first clang, not at the immediate door outside but somewhere farther out. Broken locks weren't going to stop Sasha.

Zoe's hearing ability wasn't part of his arsenal of tricks. So the massive *thump* must have been pretty darn loud to get all the way through to the Project Electron room. He had glanced down at Waris, who remained static. No blue figure materialized to help him out, and instead, he'd willed himself back into movement as the noises got louder and more frequent, eventu-

ally leading to Sasha breaking through the hallway leading to
the main entrance.

And now she was here, at the massive metal slab of door that
protected Project Electron from the observation space.

The reception icon on Jamie's phone showed a big white X,
and the text screen teased him with the endless rotating circle
next to the slate of photos that should have theoretically flown
through digital space to Chesterton. Mercs with weapons, an
animated burnt corpse in a tube, a person made of freakin' electricity talking with Zoe, that all should have delivered enough
to convince the police *something* in the place was worth investigating, hopefully to spark backup into storming the place.

Getting a phone signal in here sure would have helped.

Clang.

Anything would have helped at this point.

Jamie glanced back at Waris and the massive tangle of cables
connecting the Electron casket to power and monitoring systems and other devices. Only one remained, but the skin on
his fingers wore down raw as he tried to get the last cable out.
As if she read his mind, Kaftan's voice projected from beyond
the door. "Open the door, Jamie. I know what you're trying to
do. Pull those cables without managing the discharge and you'll
bring this whole place down on us."

That might be true. It might be a completely empty threat.
Jamie turned to Waris, whose eyes suddenly opened. "Three
cables isn't good enough here. A little help?"

Clang. Clang. Clang.

"Okay," Jamie said, on the off chance that Waris somehow
heard. "Here's what I'm going to do. In the interest of time. I
can't get this fourth one. So I'm just gonna pull the fifth one.
Out of order, I know. Sorry if it hurts. Right now, because your
well-meaning wife is trying to use her abilities to stop me. So
either point me to a toolbox with some screwdrivers or another
method, or perhaps both. Alright?"

The words failed to generate any reaction from Waris, but the thrum of fist-hitting-metal increased, both in frequency and intensity. "Jamie?" Zoe's voice squawked out of the headset.

"Zoe! Where the hell have you been?"

"Losing guards. There aren't too many of them, but I took a few out. You should have seen it, I ripped this huge machine out of the wall and totally used it as a barricade. Told you it would come back. Hey, when we meet up, you can watch it in my memories."

"You tore a machine out of the wall?"

"Yeah, came out pretty clean. Except there's this pipe of green goo leaking now, but whatever, Kaftan's mercs can do janitorial work. I'm almost at the basement."

Another *clang* rattled the room, interrupting the conversation. "Not good, Zoe. Not good at all."

"What?"

"Before you ask how it's going. Not good. I still can't get the bolts out of the fourth cable. I might just pull the fifth one. Or start smashing things." The constant barrage from Kaftan didn't help his shaking hands; his nerves probably hadn't been this frayed since the first time he'd attempted to rob a bank and failed to keep his face hidden from security cameras. "But I'm pretty sure *me* smashing things isn't as effective as *you* smashing things."

Another *clang* erupted, but it was soon followed with the squeaking and scraping of twisting metal. From behind, the corner of the door had been torn off, and a circular puncture emerged in the metal slab's center.

Things had moved past *not good*.

"Waris?" Jamie said, intensity ratcheted up in his voice. "Any time now."

A screwdriver. He was going to fail because of a goddamn screwdriver. On the other side of the room, the puncture in the door grew with progressive kicks—an impressive feat given that Sasha still had her heeled shoes on.

Then the kicks stopped. A shuffling noise faded away, followed by...nothing.

Jamie counted to five, then turned to Waris. "Okay, maybe we've got a little—"

Before he could finish, the damaged door flew off its top hinge, the mangled sheet now hanging by a twisted bolt on the bottom hinge. Behind that stood Kaftan, shoulder down and breath heaving, her face wearing the most intimidating look anyone in a business suit ever pulled off.

"Zoe?" Jamie said quietly into the headset mic, "we've got a bigger problem."

"What's that?"

"Well, I need a screwdriver to take off the cable. Flat-head. If you got it."

"Can you try, like, your fingernail or something?"

"Also, Kaftan just broke down the door."

"Oh fuck." Zoe's response captured everything, so much so that despite the situation, Jamie laughed.

"Yeah. I—"

"I'll turn around. I'll be right there."

"No, wait. How far away are you from the basement?" Jamie asked.

"The stairs are down a corridor."

Jamie's eyes widened as Kaftan stood up straight. She looked herself over, dusting off the debris on her shoulders from apparently doing a hockey body check into the metal door, then smoothed the front of her blouse. "Go now."

"Jamie, you listen—"

"No, seriously. Get to the reactor in the basement. I'll figure something out." He adjusted the headset on his ear and smirked to himself. "I'll figure something out" probably wound up being the last sentence said by a lot of people in difficult scenarios.

"Waris," he said as Kaftan began walking toward him, deliberate step after deliberate step, "if you got a last jolt in you, I could really use it now."

The last thing Jamie remembered was being tossed into the wall. From the human-shaped crack in the concrete, he guessed that he hit it pretty hard.

Fingers and toes flexed, confirming that they still had movement. Same thing with his neck, though turning from side to side proved to be against the laws of physics at this point. Ahead of him, Sasha Kaftan stood over Project Electron's console.

"Hey," Jamie managed in a weak voice. Scanning the floor by Kaftan's feet showed that the headset had flown off his ear and landed about five feet away from him, though the main walkie-talkie unit remained clipped to his belt loop. "Sasha."

She turned and glared at him, though he supposed the good thing was that she couldn't—or perhaps *wouldn't*—shoot lasers out of her eyes. "You were trying to murder my husband."

"I think you're misunderstanding the situation." Jamie tried to stand up but his back muscles seized, making his legs flailing extensions of his core. "This is a mercy."

"Mercy?" The word came out with a sharpness that may as well have been an energy weapon; its mere expression caused Jamie to wince. "Project Electron was Waris's dream. It will eliminate hunger. The only way to finish Project Electron is to revive him. And now I can finally do it. The latest evolution of the serum works. It's the one. We've been waiting for Zoe to finally get your powers. This," she said, holding up a small vial, "shows that she has regenerative physical *and* mental abilities. Waris will finally be able to heal body *and* mind, and sustain it."

"Sasha." Jamie's muscles burned as he managed to twist himself into a semicrouched position. "You realize that he's projecting himself as a being made out of pure electricity?"

"Of course I knew that. That preserves his mind. But it can't be sustained. Not until now." Her shoes clacked on the concrete as she walked over to him. "Getting up is silly. I'll just toss you back over. It's not my intention to hurt you unless I have to."

"Project Electron requires the entire city's power grid to infuse a serum in Waris. You said so yourself," Jamie said. "If you do that, you'll be basically dropping an EMP into San Delgado." Kaftan arched an eyebrow at him, but then turned away and started walking back to the console.

"We understand the sacrifice," she said without hesitation. "One city versus eliminating world hunger. Are you really picking one city over the entire planet? Your scope of things is so small. Project Electron will change the world. It will level the playing field for humanity. Imagine it. It just needs Waris. It needs his mind."

"Waris." Jamie's voice came with a mix of intensity and desperation, but also the tenderness of truth. "He doesn't want that."

The steps stopped. "Don't you dare lie to me about Waris." A cold edge carried Sasha's voice.

"I'm not." Jamie leaned further into gentle pleading, a quiet resignation in his tone. "I swear I'm not. He's come to us, both me and Zoe, these split-second visits in the form of electricity. But when we got here, we connected with him.

"Sasha, he wants to die. That's what he wants. He wants peace."

Fury returned to her eyes, an intensity that eclipsed her physical acts of violence. She stormed over to Jamie with one hand out. Her fingers grabbed his forehead, thumb and pinkie pressed against the temples. From that single grip, she raised him off the ground, as easy as a normal adult picking up a carton of milk.

"You do not get to speak about Waris. *Ever.*"

"Sasha," Jamie managed to get out. He reached out with his mind, seeking any possible way to get through to her, but it remained inaccessible, invisible to him. "'Everything here is beautiful.' That's what he said."

Kaftan's grip loosened, a hesitation replacing her momentum. Despite that, Jamie's breath slowed, everything becoming heavier. Waris, on the other hand, was starting to wake. If not physically, then mentally, his mind appearing as a ghost silhouette when Jamie shut his eyes.

"You figured out how to get in my head."

"No," Jamie said. "I swear. I can't dive into your mind. It's the opposite. Waris showed us everything."

"How dare you talk about my husband. One more word and I cave in your skull."

A single word. That was quite the risk. But given how pleading seemed to be Jamie's only remaining option, he gambled on using his remaining breath. "Please," he said, the pressure creating a deafening pain in his head. "Give me a chance to prove it. That night out on the plains. Watching lightning. When you got the idea. This isn't the way to achieve that. He never wanted anyone to get hurt. 'How many more people have to suffer?' Right? That's what he asked. That's what he wants now. Let me prove it."

Kaftan's fingers opened, and Jamie dropped to the floor. Pain echoed up and down his legs, then into his spine and shoulders. "Prove what?"

"Waris hears us. I can connect with him. I'll be the conduit. Zoe did it. You can talk to him directly. Then read my memories for his response. It's, um, a little clunky. But it gets the job done."

Kaftan loomed over him, a different kind of intensity to her glare.

"You're a good person. Waris knows this. He wants to tell you that there's another way."

She stepped back, hair falling in her face, and squinted, lingering for several seconds without a single blink. "You're not lying," she said quietly.

"He just needs to be fully conscious. His mind is there, but his body has to support it. Can you," Jamie bit his bottom lip, considering the right way to ask, "can you turn him on?"

Harsh cheekbones and a frozen stare framed Kaftan's face, remaining static for a good minute or so until they softened. A crack, a flash of something more *human*, then she paced around the capsule, her gaze focused on her husband's burned face. She knelt down and one by one, locked each of the cables Zoe had disconnected back into place.

Was she playing him? It didn't seem necessary, given her physical domination. Rather than try randomly mashing buttons on the console or pulling more cables, Jamie opted for patience. Patience, and a little good faith that Sasha loved her husband more than Project Electron.

As each cable clicked back in, icons and lights blinked on the main control display. Sasha walked over to it and moved some digital levers on the touch screen. "I'm going to awaken him," she said, a shakiness to her words that didn't exist before. More lights flashed, and Waris's measured, automated breathing took on an irregular pace.

His eyes flew open.

"Waris," Kaftan said kneeling down next to him. "I'm here. Can you hear me?" Her hand rose, and though Jamie braced himself for *something*, she motioned a quick wave for him to join her. "This is Jamie. I know you've met. He says you can communicate with him. I can read Jamie's memories. Anything you say to him will come to me. Do you understand?"

Beneath the burned tissue, muscles moved enough to pull Waris's mouth into the slightest of smiles, and Jamie noticed a softness in his eyes that stated exactly what he thought of his wife.

"Alright. I just need to know. Do you want me to finish the project? Or..." Through their brief encounters, Kaftan's demeanor projected a menacing, threatening air. Maybe that happened when belief of purpose intertwined with absolute commitment and deep love. But that delicate balance was suddenly undercut, leaving only uncertainty on her face. "Or do you want to let go?"

Waris's eyes turned to Jamie, and they were clear. The rest of his body may have been burned and scarred, but his eyes held the brightest of whites and the deepest amber hue. He looked at Jamie, and Jamie gave in, letting his own thoughts create the connection between the two.

Waris spoke. It was a message for his wife, for only his wife. Jamie bridged them, and because of that, he tried not to listen, to simply let himself be the conduit between two life partners. And when it was done, the connection evaporated, leaving Jamie only in the moment.

Waris no longer looked at him.

Kaftan stood up.

And finally, for the first time, he could see the presence of her mind when he closed his eyes. It was faint, a translucent fuzziness capturing her presence, but there it stood, plain as day. Perhaps understanding Waris's thoughts had finally managed to lower whatever shielded her mind.

Jamie considered his options. He could try diving in, stunning, wiping her mind or *something* to deliver the upper hand. But instead, he opted to wait, putting all his hope that she could move past her global ambitions to let individual humanity win out.

She didn't budge for several minutes. Jamie considered stepping past her to get the headset and check in with Zoe, but given the tension in the room and Kaftan's overwhelming strength, waiting seemed like the smarter play. Finally, she walked over, not to the main console, but the small laptop connected into it. Her fingers flew over the keys, the tapping creating a constant percussion as she went through screen after screen, message after message. Several more minutes passed, and finally Kaftan closed all the screens and turned back to Waris.

Once again, she knelt down beside him. "It's done," she said.

Jamie braced himself in anticipation of whatever "done" meant.

"I've uploaded the designs and initial data to a public server. Project Electron is now open source. Someone will finish this dream. But it won't be us." Any pretense of stoic resolve disappeared as Kaftan pressed a series of buttons near the capsule's edge. A sharp hiss cut through the quiet, then the protective glass covering Waris's head retracted. Kaftan reached in to cradle her husband's face. "It won't be us. It won't be us, and I'm so sorry about that." She leaned over and whispered in his ear, the briefest of sentiments before she tugged at each cable identified by Zoe.

Five pops later, each accompanied by bursts of sparks, and then the monitors around the capsule went dark. All except for one, that was: a simple EKG meter that let its steady rhythm turn erratic before leading to a flat line and an unending high-pitched tone.

Kaftan sat on the floor. Her eyes didn't move from the capsule.

Jamie got to his feet and grabbed the headset lying on the floor. "Zoe?" he said quietly.

"Jamie! What the hell's going on?"

"We did it. Waris is gone."

"Holy shit. How'd you pull it off?"

Kaftan still hadn't budged. Jamie wondered if she even listened to the noise coming out of the tiny speaker in his hand. "I'll tell you later. Can you cut the power?"

"Yeah. I mean, I have to hover to reach it, but I think I have the strength to do it."

"Okay. Do it and get out. I'll check back in in a few."

Seconds later, the lights dropped, wrapping them in darkness. A single pin of light appeared, so tiny that Jamie wasn't sure if it actually existed. But then others joined it, dots filling out a sketch of brilliant blue light against a canvas of darkness, all pulling into form in the silhouette of a man.

In his electric form, Waris walked over to his wife, a final surge seemingly to burn off the remaining power in the capsule. He extended a single finger, which she extended to match. Sparks flew off of him, leaving traces of singes and burns on her white lab coat, and Jamie watched as their fingers connected. Her mouth formed soundless words, and Jamie swore that he saw the blue figure nod in return.

Then Waris disappeared, electricity seemingly folding into itself before being pulled down to the floor, a snake of brightness drawing back to a sparking exposed cable along the wall.

The room lit up with a low red glow as the emergency lighting returned. Through the low light, a few fading sparks burned out and tufts of smoke dissipated where the blue figure had stood.

From his back pocket, Jamie's phone buzzed. He pulled it out only to see that not only did he now have full signal coverage, the photos had been transmitted to Chesterton, and even warranted a reply. Got the photos, it read, we're coming in. Looks like the entire facility's power is out.

"Power is out?" he asked aloud.

That question finally snapped Kaftan back into the moment. "How can power be out?" she asked. "That doesn't make any sense." From the observation room, smoke began to rise out of one of the stacks of hardware before it spit a miniature firework. The pyrotechnics ate up the hardware's display, shattering the glass and replacing it with small flames.

The headset came to life with Zoe's voice. "Jamie? You there? 'Cause something bad is happening."

41

MAYBE AN EARLIER VERSION of Zoe had a degree in engineering.

That would have helped, given the massive wall of technology looking like it was about to hit catastrophic levels.

"Define *bad*." Jamie's voice came in over the headset, and Zoe figured there was no science background bubbling under the surface of her memories. Everything in front of her looked like a mass of metal and wire and blinking lights and a few big hand-sized switches. If she had some sort of formal technical education, there probably would have been some sort of instinctive understanding of what sat in front of her, a "this goes to that goes to the other thing" logic that might have given a sense of why shit didn't work.

Instead, it simply looked like a bunch of *stuff.* "Well," she said, brushing the hair out of her face despite the pain coming back in her arm. "This thing doesn't want to shut down."

"That's impossible. I just saw Waris disappear."

"Well, I think the right part shut down for Project Electron. Because I saw one part go dark when I threw the switch. But then lights started blinking and— Oh, oh shit."

"Zoe!"

What she meant by "oh shit" was the fact that steam suddenly shot out of a pipe that tracked all around the basement walls, ending in the side of the hunk of metal in front of her. But she wasn't going to explain that to Jamie. "Stuff is breaking."

The headset went quiet, which meant either Kaftan had exacted vengeance or Jamie was struggling to form a response. More things started beeping around her, except this time sparks flew from above, and not the kind that meant a blue figure made of electricity would show up for some nice heart-to-heart conversation. Something somewhere popped, causing a piece of metal debris to shoot by her head, and some distance away, she heard a rumble loud enough that she also felt it.

"Motherfucker," Zoe said to herself. "Jamie," she said into the mic, back at normal volume but urgency tinting her words. "I'm just gonna start pushing buttons if I don't get any advice."

This time, the entire room shook, perhaps the entire building above her. She couldn't tell for sure, and though she had no memories of any specific earthquakes—at least not yet—she was betting on the overall experience being really close to this.

"Okay, seriously. There's like…" she did a quick count "… nine buttons here, four switches, and three really big switches. I'm just going to—" More flames erupted, this one from the console. "Make that eight buttons. So that's one decision out of my hands."

"Zoe, things are getting worse up here." Jamie's voice hit somewhere between panicked and yelling. "Something blew up in the Project Electron room. And I hear things breaking everywhere—"

"Get out of there! Like now!"

"Right, I think that's the—"

A loud crashing sound came through the headset, or at least that's what it sounded like until the communication cut off. Ahead of her, blinking lights continued to tease Zoe, each pulse a reminder that she had no clue what she was doing. "Jamie?"

"Okay. It's okay. We're safe."

"What happened?"

"The whole building's coming down. Kaftan carried me out. You know, she seems way stronger than you."

"Wait, did you say Kaftan?" Did some debris fall on her head? There was no way Jamie just said that he was working with Kaftan. "Sasha Kaftan? The woman who ordered us to be shot on sight?"

"Zoe," a voice said through the headset. But not Jamie's.

It was *Kaftan*.

"If you hurt—"

"Jamie's fine. No time to explain. I'm the electrical engineer who designed the power system. The system in front of you is the conversion chamber for Project Electron. It takes in electricity from the power grid and splits it into two parts. One part powers all of the hardware necessary for the Electron system. The other part acts as a containment field that feeds the electricity into a conversion system. It holds the energy and converts it into matter that can be digested by the Project Electron user."

Zoe really, really, really wanted to interrupt this lecture but decided she probably shouldn't.

"There's an overflow discharge process that normally dissipates to ground. However, the system is overheating. Looks like a coolant leak, which means it has hindered the discharge process. It's overloading the system instead of finding a path to ground."

Coolant leak? Zoe pictured the pipe of green goo jutting out of the wall after she tore the equipment off of it. Zoe kept that part to herself, given that they were in a freaking basement with ground all around her. But she had to say something.

"So what does that mean?"

"It means, the grid isn't getting back its power until you do this. It'll all stay here, building up until everything in the facility overloads, resulting in the reactor exploding. The coolant is highly flammable and if a flame catches a trail to it, this place sees extreme structural damage. And the city stays off-line."

"Wait, how is coolant flammable? That makes no sense."

Kaftan's scoff was audible over the headset. "Do you really want me to explain ethylene glycol right now?"

"Well," Zoe said after a pause. Steam shot out of overhead piping, singeing her hair. "The whole thing seems like a really bad design."

Jamie's voice popped out of the headset. "Zoe, you need to listen to her right now. Things are falling apart."

"Right, right." Hopefully Kaftan's mind powers didn't include the ability to detect eye rolls. "Did I say that out loud? What I meant to say was, 'How the hell do I shut this off before it kills all of us?'"

"First, you need to divert power to the facility's backup generator. That gets the doors and locks going again. And the main elevator. There's a large yellow knob. It should be currently pointing up. Push it in and rotate it to the left. Then throw the reset switch above it."

Zoe scanned the scene in front of her and confirmed to herself again that none of her previous revisions could have possibly been trained in anything technical. She barely understood the directions from Kaftan. "Okay, big circular yellow knob. Pushing it in." It sank in, with more resistance than expected. A sudden warmth covered her left shoulder, along with the sharp pain of a reactivating wound. "And turning." It landed with a heavy click, and though the space still rumbled with activity, several mechanical pieces locked into place within the reactor.

At least it sounded that way. Which was probably better than nothing happening.

Her fingers gripped the switch above the yellow knob. Wouldn't it have been easier if someone just labeled this *Reset*? She threw it down, and as soon as she let go, it sprung back up to default. More *bangs* and *thunks* rattled the space, then a separate set of lights showed up on the left side of the room.

"Done," Zoe said.

"That's it," Jamie said. "Doors are opening again. We're on the move." Over the speaker, other voices shouted, though it wasn't clear if they came from police or Kaftan's guards or something else.

"Zoe." Kaftan was back on the line. "The last step. Get down the next hall to the containment unit. You have to throttle the remaining power in the containment unit to discharge. From the amount of buildup, a sphere of energy will discharge. The room is built to absorb some of that and it should slow it down some. So you'll need to run as soon as you throw the switch. You'll have about five seconds to get out of the room. Then a minute, maybe two before it breaks that and vaporizes everything in its path, probably within a fifty-foot radius."

"So you're saying I'm fucked," Zoe asked, scanning the room for the door through the thick air.

"Run fast. And hope no exposed coolant lines are within the vaporization radius."

"'Run fast.' This would have been easier if you hadn't put power-blocking anti-serum in me. Thanks for that." Layers of grime caked onto her face where sweat and dust met as she moved across the reactor room to the small hallway. The sliding door thankfully actually worked, sending her to a smaller hallway. Her eyes adjusted to the near pitch-blackness of the space, the only light from a slit at the bottom of the door at the end.

Zoe wasn't sure if anyone heard her; the channel remained open, allowing a clamor of noise to come through, a blend of voices of all kinds and volumes—including someone, probably

Kaftan, saying, "If you want to do this, fine, but we really should take it outside before this place collapses."

That didn't provide much encouragement.

"They're on the move," Jamie said through the headset, his words hurried. A loud boom rippled through the space, only to be followed seconds later by an even louder one. Dust fell from the ceiling, and whatever was happening wasn't good. "Kaftan has surrendered. She's in custody. I'm on my way to you. Random stuff is on fire everywhere, so be careful."

"That's stupid. Get out now. I'm serious, don't make me stun you again," Zoe said as she reached the end door. It began to slide open, but stopped after only six inches or so. Her fingers gripped the metal door and she pulled despite the screaming pain from her gunshot wounds.

"No, we're in this together."

"Idiotic self-sacrifice is more my thing than yours. Get out now." One more hard tug bent the door enough for her to get through, revealing a grate bridge leading to the blue glow brighter than any electrical projection by Waris. She shielded her eyes from the light, allowing the finer details to come through—including what appeared to be a small control panel next to it.

A control panel across a bridge. This would be easy. She paused, squinting at the display on it—some sort of meter appeared to be filling up and right now it was a sunburst yellow color.

Yellow. Yellow was good. Yellow didn't indicate danger.

Two steps after that thought, another boom rattled the space. Above her, bits and pieces of concrete fell, starting off as a drizzle of dust before becoming an avalanche of pieces and chunks. When the dust cleared, a half-blocked path stared back at her, the opening from the bent metal door now not quite big enough to fit her, despite her small frame.

Now the lack of math skills *really* seemed like an issue. She gauged her powers and knelt down, willing them to restore just a bit faster so she could throw one massive punch at the door, just enough to increase the opening's size for her to escape. It flowed through her blood and lit up her muscles, flipping a switch telling her that she was ready to go when another massive sound rattled the space and the floor dropped out from under her.

Zoe had blacked out, but it had to be only for a few seconds. This was the logical conclusion because when she opened her eyes, pieces of the bridge were still being torn off of their main struts and landing in front of her. And Jamie's voice pressed through the headset, in its most affectionate and annoying way. "Zoe! Zoe! Come on."

Zoe found herself on her back, several pieces of sheared metal on top of her. She sucked in air, assessing how much of her strength she retained. *Good enough*, she thought before realizing the headset managed to stay on. If she made it out of this, she'd totally leave a good review regarding its sturdiness. "I'm here."

"Entire rooms in the facility are collapsing. You have to hurry. We're coming for you but you need to hurry."

From her spot on the floor, the display was out of view. But its screen illuminated the space around it, and instead of not-that-bad sunburst yellow, it now burned with a red glow.

That wasn't good.

"Jamie," she said, trying for once to project calm in her voice, "turn around and get the hell out. If I see you coming, I will use all my strength to throw you out of this place myself. You understand? I don't need your death on my mind."

"But—"

"Seriously. Shut up. Turn around." Metal clanged and scraped as she pushed the pieces off her, one heavy chunk at a time. The last piece refused to budge even though it was only about half the size of the others. Zoe's muscles burned, an unnatural feeling of completely natural organic processes that indicated her strength needed to return.

She looked again at the display, hoping maybe it had reverted back to yellow from red. It was still red. But now it was blinking.

No one in the world could help her now.

"Okay. You win. Zoe, this place is falling apart." Jamie's voice turned hurried but quiet. "Please move fast."

"Yeah. I'm on it." Her breath steadied itself, coming and going with a calm rhythm despite bits and pieces of concrete and metal dropping all around her. Zoe took in one more deep breath and shoved the remaining piece of metal over her. Something warm flooded her elbow, and a quick look showed that the gunshot wound had started bleeding again. But at least none of that falling metal had punctured her in the gut or her legs. She jumped up, palms out to hover at switch level but nothing took hold, air slipping between her fingers. "Jamie?"

"We're almost out," he shouted, the sound of debris crashing accompanying his voice.

"Keep moving." The blinking red remained, a beacon of the single simple goal she needed to get to if her body would just work with her. Throbbing continued out of her shoulder, a pulsing beat that reminded her for the moment, she was mortal.

She needed to wait.

"You're safe?" she asked.

"We are. Did you do it?"

Where was that tangible push, that invisible pressure that always propelled her up? The unseen force that kicked against her grip, the same way copies of the strongest magnets in the world would do everything to break apart—where was it?

But Zoe knew, she *knew* the answer to that question. Because for all the times she fought against serum after serum, memory erasure after memory erasure, every time she clawed back, she did it through sheer force of will. And this time, she needed more than that. She needed biology and Kaftan's serum to play nice with her stubbornness, and it wasn't happening.

"Not yet." She swallowed hard, looking at the distance between her and the control panel. Around her hummed machinery, the guts of the containment unit. "I need some time to charge up." She dusted herself off and marched forward until she stood directly underneath the control panel, probably a good ten feet. Her hand touched the wall, looking for a physical grip in place of the ether that let her hover in the wind; it singed a layer of skin off her fingers, the sheer heat from the pressurizing energy getting to be too much.

"How much time?"

There was nowhere to go but up. And up would take time.

"A few minutes." She took a deep breath and considered the path in front of her. "Hey, can I tell you a story?"

"Sure." That single word sounded like it took all of Jamie's energy to get out.

"I remember. I remember some of my revisions after touching the glowy thingy. And before I was the Throwing Star, they were testing my powers. I was actually cooperating with them. But to do that, I had to stay at the facility. Seemed like a good deal at first. You know, I'd do these training exercises and then return to my room. Watch all the movies I wanted. When you think about it, my family must have been pretty fucked up for me to go to Telos and agree to all that, right?

"Problem was, I got restless. I felt like I was meant for *more*, you know? And they didn't like that. They planned on resetting me again. I mean, they didn't tell me this, but see, there was this guy. British guy named Bill. Guess we'd become friends while we were there, and since he worked on the experiments, he had insider information. And he warned me. He said that if they found out, they'd make him wipe his *own* mind, but he didn't care. It was important that I knew.

"So they tied me down and injected me to reset everything, but I was prepared and I broke out. I tried to, anyway. The serum slowed me down and everything was fading. Made it to the rooftop. And poor Bill, they forced him to lead the team of guards to get me. But he did this really great thing. He said, 'I don't know if you're awake in there or completely lost. I'm still working on it and you're *different*, and they might get rid of me before I get good at it anyway. But if you're in there, I'm gonna leave you with one thing to remember.' And he showed me a clue he'd written. On his hand."

Zoe knew Jamie couldn't see her, and she probably remained far out of reach for them to connect minds and memories. But she hoped what she felt came through in her voice.

"You see? They keep setting us against each other. And we keep deciding that we're better off as friends." She laughed, because at this point, what else was there to do? "Even when I do wind up starting coolant leaks."

"The machine you tore out from the wall."

"Just my luck, right?"

"Zoe." A tremble carried his voice across the radio. "I knew that was me on the rooftop. I just didn't understand how—"

"Oh, don't worry about it. I know you were trying to protect me. What's that thing Chesterton told you? I read it in your memory the other night." Zoe bit into her lip before forming a smile that no one could see. "I think it was 'Extraordinary comes in many forms.'"

Steam escaped from the pipeline above, creating a thick humidity that mixed with the flying dust to form a thick muck on everything. The dim emergency lighting made it hard to see what was breaking and what was already broken, though when she stood up, a surge rippled through her body.

"I thought about that. It stuck with me as soon as I saw it in your memories. Because it's us. Extraordinary comes in many forms. Not just you, not just me. But us."

"Zoe, you're worrying me."

"Together," she said, stumbling forward, "we're extraordinary." Blood clung to the black leather of the Throwing Star suit as she wiped off the trail from the gunshot. Underneath, it smeared across her exposed skin, but no more came out. "I just wish my family knew that. My real family. The ones that did *something* to push me to visit Telos."

Zoe bent her knees, tensed and ready to launch upward. Her arms extended, palms down.

She was ready.

"We'll find them. And tell them. We'll make a plan," Jamie said.

She shot all the way to the top of the room, and as she descended, her hands flared out, bringing her to a gentle float until she held her position directly in front of the control panel and its row of screens and lights. She looked back at the blocked path out, going back to her calculation about what needed to be cleared and how fast.

It was simple. She needed to bend that metal door wide enough to break through. Five seconds, Kaftan said. Just five seconds.

Well, maybe she'd be wrong. Maybe it was, like, thirty seconds. Kaftan was a bit of an asshole, and assholes tended to be wrong most of the time anyway.

"You and your plans, Jamie. Remember, we make terrible plans."

Her fingers gripped the switch next to the electronic display.

"Hey, I never told you the catchphrase I was practicing. For when I caught you."

It flipped with a *thunk*, all the lights and remaining displays fading away one by one. Zoe waited, watching as each shut system fell into dark silence from right to left.

"Remember how I was considering the name Shuriken?" No reply came over the headset, just a static pop. "So when I caught you, I was gonna say, 'You thought you could escape but you Shuri-can't.' Get it?"

The emergency red lighting dimmed, disappearing into darkness. "Zoe, that's terrible," Jamie said, his voice dry.

All around her, sounds whirred down to nothing, leaving only silence even to her extraordinary hearing.

"No, Jamie. It's cool."

That was it. Power would cycle back to the city.

Five seconds.

She pushed back and vaulted, angling herself toward the blockade exit. Her body throttled forward, but halfway down to the path, she lost her grip, air becoming simply air, and she fell into the pit with all of the force of a regular human. Her shoulder slammed into the floor, momentum carrying her into a roll, but her mind stayed active, aware, telling her to push forward.

Four seconds.

The delayed feel of impact kicked in, a shockwave tearing at her legs and arms as she tried to stand up. She ran, or tried to, but her knees buckled and she fell flat on her face.

Three seconds.

Her body refused to agree when she tried standing. Legs gave out, failing to work in sync or even support weight. Belly down, she clawed against the debris, pulling herself forward and then upward. A sharp jab followed by warmth radiated from her shoulder, and it took an actual glance down to realize that the gunshot had started bleeding again.

Two seconds.

There was only one thing left to do. She checked the headset against her ear and adjusted the mic. This was important for Jamie to hear. "I'm sorry we didn't get to rob a bank together," she said.

One second.

"Wait, what? Zoe? Zoe?"

She craned her neck to look at the reactor. But rather than seeing destruction-in-process hardware, she saw a bright blue mass of living electricity emerging from the ground. The frame of hulking machinery began crumbling around the reactor, and as beams of light poked out from across the space, a ball of blue enveloped her. Though no voice or face could communicate it, she knew that this tangle of electricity and sparks was the final burst of Waris. She'd *sworn* she'd seen something like this in a movie. Something she'd streamed a few months ago, something where the effects were surprisingly good for being made in the early 1970s, but its name refused to materialize.

The bubble wrapped around, sealing her in silence so completely that whatever destruction was happening on the other side seemed a thousand miles away. Right before everything went black, the name of the film came back to her.

42

JAMIE COULDN'T GET THE words out of his head.

I'm sorry we didn't get to rob a bank together.

Zoe didn't say anything further and several seconds passed before Jamie's eyes fixed on an indescribable sight, a wave or a ripple or *something* he felt more than saw pulsed outward from the facility, as if the entire building let out a sigh of finality. That moment came silently, the din of people around him still filling his ears.

Windows lit up from behind, some breaking with flashes of explosions, some accompanied with tiny popping sounds; it moved from left to right, like a lit fuse ripping through the first and second floor of the facility. And then he heard the first moan of metal beams bending against their will. Soon followed heavy thunks of collapsing concrete and the sounds of glass shattering. All of the different individual sounds of destruction mixed together, creating a wall of white noise as devastating as it was inscrutable.

From there, it was plain to see. The facility's main tower, which had stood six stories high, with different balconies and exhaust pipes and communications wiring, looked like something simply removed all of its guts on the bottom floor. The second floor fell into itself, then the third, then on and on until the dirt and dust kicked up and rolled upward and outward. The clouds rolled slowly before thinning out and disappearing, leaving only a mountain of rubble about a third as high as it originally stood. It rested, like it had suddenly gained its footing, only for a massive explosion in its center to act as the knockout punch that brought it all down upon itself.

Behind him, Jamie realized that all of the police and media chatter paused, leaving only the sound of wind interspersed with crumbling debris in the distance. Different voices soon started from behind him, and Jamie gradually tuned in enough to realize that the media storm that they'd baited into coming was doing their job.

"Who is the woman you've arrested?"

"Where is the Throwing Star? Did she cause this?"

"Are extraordinaries out of control?"

Jamie pushed the headset's speaker against his ear. "Zoe? Zoe? Tell me you got out."

The sound of shoes grinding against dirt gradually approached until Jamie realized that someone now stood next to him.

He didn't have to look to know it was Chesterton.

"I, uh..." the detective said before leaving it to silence.

Thoughts raced, possibilities and hopes and fears and remembering to do a countdown, to *breathe* and ground himself until he might be able to do something.

Not just something. The *only* thing he could do.

Jamie sprinted across the parking lot to the perimeter of the debris and landed on one knee, hands outstretched. The sound of footsteps and jingling keys followed him, only Chesterton trailing him, but he kept a respectful distance. With eyes closed,

Jamie searched the space—up and down, left and right, anything to lock on to the distinct mind that was Zoe Wong.

Blank.

Nothing at all. No hint of a mind, no shadow or echo, simply a void. Even with hands out, fingers searching, all he got was emptiness.

He opened his eyes, the only thing left to do was to stare at the mountain of twisted debris while the morning sun poked its first rays out over the horizon. A crackling sound came from within the wreckage, and Jamie stood up, hope carrying him to his feet. Seconds later, a loud pop echoed through the air, bits of dirt and scrap landing on his face. He coughed, clearing the dust out when he realized something else was happening.

Something extraordinary.

He blinked several times to make sure the explosion hadn't caused him to see things. But no, it was there: a jagged piece of metal about the size of a hand somehow *hovering* in the air mere inches from his head.

Jamie turned around, mouth wide, only to find Chesterton standing still with his hand outstretched. His fingers flexed and the metal fell harmlessly to the ground, then he met Jamie's eyes.

"You did…" Jamie finally said. "I mean, that was…"

"It was going to hit you. And yes." He took a step forward. "I did that. I can do that."

"How…" Jamie hesitated, the implications flooding his mind with questions that tugged in every direction. "How long?"

Chesterton glanced back at the combination of police and media across the lot behind them, though their voices still carried out to this spot. "I don't think we've got time to go into that."

"Do they know? The police?"

"No. And best to keep that quiet. For both of our sakes." He brushed dirt and dust off his shirt.

Jamie turned, blowing out all of the remaining air from his

lungs, and as he did, Chesterton walked up next to him. "Did you…sense anything in there?" he asked.

"No. I didn't."

"Power is back on the city grid. A little messy, but things should calm down." Chesterton filled the silence by clearing his throat. "It, uh, could have been much, much worse."

A response failed to pop in Jamie's mind as the blend of dust and burning odors tickled his nose. "She did it," was all he came up with.

"It looks like it."

The shouting from behind grew louder, the voices taking on more intensity.

"You've arrested Kaftan?" Jamie asked.

"Yeah," Chesterton said.

"I'm not sure if you'll be able to contain her."

"She's coming willingly."

Jamie nodded, but chose not to concern himself with the possibilities surrounding that for now.

"I have to make a decision," Chesterton said. "About you. You robbed banks. Those are pretty major crimes."

A gust of wind kicked up, blowing ashes and debris over him. It crusted on his face, in his hair, stinging his eyes. "Not the best way to make a living."

"On the other hand, you helped save San Delgado. I can't even imagine the chaos if the entire grid was down for any longer. Even for a day."

The voices of uniformed officers shouted over the now-rabid media members, telling them to stay behind the line.

"There's cameras rolling," he continued. "I'm sure this is livestreaming a dozen places. You could do that *thing*—" he waved his hand in front of them "—you do. But not all of us. Not at once. Not while the world is watching." Escape was the last thing on Jamie's mind at this moment, so much so that when the detective mentioned it, the mere idea of it caught him by surprise.

"And handing you to *them*," Chesterton said, "I don't think that's the best idea." He huffed out a breath.

Jamie wanted to ask what that meant when Chesterton suddenly straightened and moved. "Come with me. We should do this quick."

Jamie gave a solemn nod. Those words *should* have given him a sense of the walls closing in, of claustrophobic entrapment. But they didn't. Instead, Jamie found that his eyes refused to stop staring at the smoldering rubble in front of him.

"Now's your time."

"Wait," Jamie said. His palm fell flat against the ground, fingers digging in. He didn't know why, it just seemed like the right thing to do, one final search for connection, a chance to find a light in the void. But nothing registered. "I just needed to try one more time."

They marched, walking stride for stride, and Jamie's thoughts returned to the present. What did the detective expect him to do? Give a Mind Robber speech, the full flair and bravado, complete with poor American accent?

A cacophony of sound swarmed him, voices meshing into each other until they became a single dense buzzing. Chesterton stopped next to Jamie, who was facing the line of reporters like a defendant awaiting a jury's verdict. Jamie opened his mouth to speak when Chesterton interrupted. "Everyone! Everyone, attention please. There are many questions about what happened here today and the police still have to sort much of it out. But one thing for absolute certain is that this man, Jamie Sorenson, is *not* the Mind Robber. It's true that the Throwing Star went rogue. She did some things that shouldn't have been done. Like forcing Jamie to help her. Her motives are mixed but what we do know is that we have one person in custody, and we believe the Throwing Star perished in the facility's collapse. Now, we'll be bringing Jamie back in for questioning in the days and weeks ahead. But for now, I think he deserves to get some rest."

As if a switch flipped, the reporters turned on him in unison, more and more questions fired at both him and Jamie. "Look," Chesterton said, "I know the conspiracy theorists will have a field day with this. But he's not the Mind Robber. Listen to him talk, he's got a totally different accent."

Jamie noted that his argument basically absolved all actors from being criminals, so it probably wasn't the best excuse. But he gave Chesterton marks for trying. At this point, he'd take it. Chesterton gave him a gentle push and then pointed toward his car. "Come on," he said. "I'll give you a lift home. You've probably got questions."

43

"IT WAS—" JAMIE SUCKED in a breath "—the night of the fire. At our old meeting place. The YMCA."

Murmurs and nods of agreement followed that statement.

"I know we all deal with our issue in different ways. It's easy to hide away, question who we are or what we were meant to do. Memory loss is not an easy thing. My friend Zoe. She shared on that night. And she helped people escape the fire. She had all these extraordinary things about herself and she wouldn't let herself recognize them. Because they were always obscured with these questions of who she was supposed to be. Because when you don't have your memories, what defines that?

"We both felt that way. But then we, um, took a road trip. Had a bit of an adventure together. And I watched her realize that your past doesn't have to define your present. Or your future. It's just your choices now that matter."

Three months. Three months had passed. Three months of the media dissecting that night, the security footage of the Mind Robber and the rough cell phone videos of the Throwing Star, even speculation about the intensifying rumors of extraordinaries in Hartnell City. Three months of everyone else trying to find the meaning of it all.

But for Jamie, three months of going back to the site and hoping that something would be different. A hint or a clue or *something* to give him something to cling on to.

In the end, there wasn't a trace. Not physically. Instead, the only thing that remained of the real Zoe Wong, not the media creation of the Throwing Star, was, ironically, in the memory of the Mind Robber.

"She's, um, gone now. Haven't heard from her in a bit. Because she decided to be everything that *she* saw in herself. Not the others. Not whatever past she presumed she did or didn't have. I think we can all strive to be like her."

Jamie's legs bumped into the chair's as he stood up. It nearly tipped back, but he reached behind him to steady it.

"And with that, I wanted to thank you all for being my support system. It's time for me to go somewhere now. Don't know when I'll be back in San Delgado, but this group, these people. It's where everything began for me."

Light applause filled the space, a private room in the local library branch—one that was more likely to be compliant with city codes than their previous spot. Jamie sat through the rest of the shares, though his attention kept wandering to the plane tickets in his bag, folded next to the pay-as-you-go phone that Chesterton gave him to stay in touch in exchange for his new official anonymity. Tickets, plural, because even though the final stop for him and Normal was Costa Rica, he had to stop somewhere first.

Jamie sat in the car, engine idling so the air-conditioning kept blowing. Behind him, Normal mewed in her cat carrier, standing and stretching before setting back down into a curl. He looked back to check on her, then returned his attention to the scene in front of him. Even though his white paper coffee cup was nearly empty, he still raised it up for a sip while he waited.

Several weeks of research led to this. Getting to the facts *shouldn't* have been that difficult, but the police shut down Telos almost immediately following the destruction of Project Electron. No Telos, no records. Instead, Jamie simply searched through a *lot* of people named Zoe Wong.

But that was the thing about the internet—look hard enough and you'll eventually find anyone.

The home was as expected, a two-story house in an upper-middle-class neighborhood. Multiple cars parked in front. Finally, someone in a polo shirt and slacks stepped outside. Jamie squinted and came to the conclusion that it must be Zoe's brother. They shared the same curve of their noses. Shortly behind came an older man in similar attire and an older woman in a plain blue dress that flowed past her knees.

Zoe's parents.

If Zoe had been here with him, perhaps he would have showed her how to deep dive into their memories, extracting whatever bits and pieces possible to fill in her blanks. But she wasn't there, she wasn't anywhere, and so digging up the past for details seemed irrelevant.

But giving the past a voice, that much he owed her.

He stepped out of his rental car. "Excuse me," he said, wind whipping his hair into a frenzy. The southwest sun burned his pale skin, and even the metal frames on his sunglasses felt hot. The three people in the driveway turned around, confused brows all around.

Jamie walked across the street. "Hello," he said when he got on the sidewalk. His feet planted still, and other than an awkward wave from Zoe's mom, no one moved. "You don't know me. But I was friends with your daughter. Zoe.

"I know you all felt like she was a disappointment. Hopeless. Completely ordinary. Status quo. When I knew her, she worked in food delivery and had trouble keeping a regular schedule. Sometimes she drank too much. Sometimes she was impulsive. Sometimes she quit on things." Jamie pointed at her dad. "You're nodding. I see that."

He pulled his sunglasses off the bridge of his nose and looked each of them in the eye.

"You shouldn't be. Because the Zoe Wong I knew, it didn't matter that she was sometimes impulsive or sometimes quit a little early. Because she always fought back. Do you do that?" He pointed at Zoe's brother. "Do you come clawing back when you've lost everything you've known?"

Months ago, someone might have mistook *that* question and *that* gesture as a snippet of the Mind Robber at a bank. This, however, was far from that.

The Mind Robber was all for show. This was real.

"Because Zoe did. Countless times. Against all odds. You were all wrong about her." Jamie took in a breath, not for dramatic pause as the Mind Robber might, but to let himself *feel* this moment. For her. "She may not have fit the mold of your family. But that's the thing you don't understand. Extraordinary comes in many forms. You never realized that, and that pushed her to find it elsewhere, and now she's gone. But *I* wanted to tell you. For her. For my friend."

Glances exchanged between members of the Wong family, eyes looking everywhere but at the stranger confronting them. They started to say something, all of them at once, but Jamie simply held up his hand.

"Now, if you'll excuse me, I have a plane to catch."

He turned and began walking, even while their voices echoed through the suburban neighborhood. He reached the still-idling car, the air-conditioning still keeping a comfortable temperature for Normal, and settled in. Normal mewed a greeting, and right when he clicked his seat belt into place, his phone buzzed.

It was a text.

From Chesterton, of all people.

Can we talk? I could use your help.

44

SHE AWOKE TO VOICES.

Not light, not heat, not touch. But voices. And the taste of dirt in her mouth.

"I can't believe this place is finally opening up," a woman said. "Who knew a park took this long to build?"

"You'd never even guess that old factory was here," another woman said. "Too bad we have to share it with everyone next week. Did you hear the mayor's going to do a ribbon cutting?"

"For a park? Jesus Christ."

The voices continued, eventually fading away, along with the sound of a low rumble.

Her fingers flexed, pushing through a mix of…well, everything and nothing. Nothing specific, but a cocktail of dirt, rocks, bits of metal. But not packed tight enough that they didn't shift as she began to tense and release, ebb and flow. Soon, little bits displaced and she had enough space to move her arm. A few centimeters at first, then a few inches, and within minutes, she began to tear through, clawing at the muck and grime layer by layer. First came the packed-in pieces around her, then maneuvering around tree branches, then the loose soil that practically felt like swimming.

How much time passed? Minutes? Hours? It was hard to tell, given her singular focus, though at some point, she did have enough self-awareness to consider that something really *fucked up* must have happened for her to be buried under all that. Also, how the hell was she alive?

Her focus returned, every moment solely about going farther and farther up, and though she didn't exactly have a compass pointing the right direction, the sounds of *everything* called to her: massive engines mixed in with birds chirping and the echoes of footsteps, even the rolling of bicycles. Somewhere there was even some running water.

Fistful after fistful came and went, pulling and digging until she hit something flat. Not totally flat, as her hands explored the surface to find crevices and edges.

A big goddamn rock.

"Are you serious?" she muttered to herself, and rather than just go around it, something tugged at her to form a fist and hit the rock as hard as she could. Surprisingly, her hand did *not* shatter, but parts of the rock did. She could feel chips of it stuck against her knuckles, but that wasn't enough to stop her, or even slow her down at this point. Not this close. She was getting through that rock to breathe air on the surface even if it obliterated her arm.

It didn't, though. Each successive punch seemed to tear further into the boulder until it had a clear splitting point. She thrust both hands through the middle, and tensed her shoulders, giving herself a quiet count to three before pulling as hard as she could.

Suddenly, light blinded her. Her hands fell on dirt, and after her eyes adjusted, she saw the large chunks that had once been a single boulder lying round. A glance down showed that she was waist-deep in earth, but with a few seconds of wiggling, she stood on firm ground.

"Holy shit," a man said, his mouth open.

She looked down at herself. Dirt fell off of her, catching in the light breeze, and beneath the layer of dirt appeared to be some kind of leather suit, black with silver zippers, with most of the left arm torn off.

Who would wear such an idiotic costume?

"Are you... I mean...is this—" the man sputtered.

"Where am I?" she demanded. The sun sat just above the horizon, purples and pinks beaming into the sky, but was it dusk? Morning? That remained unclear, and as the man stammered again, a weird glow formed around him. "Slow down. I'm getting my bearings here."

Then it hit her, a proverbial light bulb flickering to life in her mind. She spit dirt out and ran her fingers through her hair, pulling out two rusty nails that got tangled during the climb up.

"Are you...alright?" he asked.

She didn't know how to answer that question. Seriously, saying "I'm fine" after crawling from however-many-feet buried and punching through a rock didn't quite seem appropriate.

But she did know one thing, one solid thing that arrived seconds ago and infused every fiber of her being with certainty. And it was the *only* thing that mattered.

Her name was Zoe Wong.

45

JAMIE STOOD IN THE lobby of the bank, face hidden by a
San Delgado Barons cap while pretending to look at a brochure
for IRA investment plans.

In reality, he watched. Stretched out with his abilities, assessing the state of the room, from the tellers to the security guard
to the two people in line.

No threats.

Everyone here, it turned out, was a complete stranger to the
person he tracked, the man second in line for the tellers. Jamie
locked into his mind, staying present but keeping a distance to
not affect his actions. Simple observation of the man's memories, and as proof that he cleanly invaded the headspace, the man
even began to scratch the back of his neck.

"Next in line, please," a teller called, and this man walked up,
a casual step forward while he pulled out several checks and a
large wad of cash. He offered chatter, comments about how the
rain had been unusually heavy this season and did she hear the

latest news about extraordinaries in New Turning City, some even claiming to be magicians or wizards or something ludicrous like that. Smiles and nods, polite laughter and friendly replies, all of that going the way a simple bank transaction should have.

Except Jamie knew better. He had an inside peek.

As expected, the man's memories turned to the source of the deposits as he handled each item—a simple trick Jamie had discovered regarding human behavior in identifying critical memories.

And there it was: clear memories of skimming funds out of San Delgado's Police and Firefighter's fund. Step by step, everything lined up as expected, from cashing out dummy checking accounts to "losing" bits of cash here and there. All meticulously constructed into the lump sum represented by his deposit—and definitely not the first time he'd done it.

Got you.

Jamie pulled out his phone, holding it like he was texting but in reality snapping a photo of the man. The brochure now in his back pocket, he found the exit before the man even finished his transaction then walked across the street to a café where a different man sat, a man with large sunglasses and a hoodie framing his light brown cheeks and serious smile.

"You're right," Jamie said. "Lethbridge is dirty. I saw pretty much everything you suspected."

Chesterton nodded and said a casual, "That's all I need," before handing Jamie an envelope, the familiar thickness of cash slapping against his palm. The detective stood up and walked away before Jamie could reply.

Was he the only cop on the straight and narrow in San Delgado? Probably not, but he did seem to be the only one committed to rooting out corruption in the city. Or the only one with abilities. Maybe both. And "consulting" for Chesterton proved to be a much safer gig than robbing banks—and it came with another strange, completely unexpected perk.

Satisfaction.

Jamie started walking to the bus stop, taking a shortcut between buildings. As it started to drizzle, a sneeze echoed through the alley. Jamie stopped and swiveled, the words "Bless you" already spoken by the time he'd turned around.

But there was no one there.

Adrenaline coursed through Jamie's body, his senses sharpening in a way that had nothing to do with his mental abilities. He whirled around, looking back and forth in a constant motion, trying to locate the source of it.

Then it hit him, harder than an extraordinary punch. Of course there was no one in the alley with him.

Instead, Jamie looked up.

"Working with Chesterton now, huh?" a female voice called out. "Still wanna rob a bank?"

★ ★ ★ ★ ★

Acknowledgments

The bulk of this book was written and edited during a time of personal upheaval. A family medical crisis, seemingly endless home repairs and a day job transition all led to finishing edits while trying to homeschool during a global pandemic. It was, as you might imagine, not easy, and I am lucky that the day always started and stopped with my wife, Mandy, and my daughter, Amelia. They are the 100% most best, and there's no one I'd rather drink coffee and watch superhero shows with.

Every book has its own unique (and often twisted) journey, and this one is no different. Its genesis, in fact, started as a short story. Shortly after I'd signed with my literary agent, Eric Smith, he sent me an open call for superhero short fiction. I'd come up with a pitch about a superhero and supervillain who accidentally meet in an AA meeting. Sometime later, I wrote that short story with Jamie and Zoe, then titled *Anonymous*, and sold it to *Storyteller* magazine.

And when *Storyteller* folded, the rights for the story reverted back to me. Toward the end of edits on *A Beginning at the End*, I told Eric that I had an idea to take that short tale and go much bigger with it. Thus, *We Could Be Heroes* was born.

So this would not exist without Eric in many ways—not just him pitching and selling the book, but going all the way back to entering that contest that started this idea. And the other half of that is Margot Mallinson, my editor, who understands the fine line I'm walking between genres and pushes me to get better. Margot gets an extra shout-out for taking a chance on a story that's quite a bit lighter than my first two books.

This book wears its influences on its leather superhero outfit, and I'll be the first to admit that. In particular, this book would not exist without *Arrow, Jessica Jones, Daredevil,* and *Legends of Tomorrow*. In fact, I think Zoe and Jamie would fit right in with the Legends (my favorite show in recent years). And if you recognized the character names here, well then hello fellow classic *Doctor Who* fan.

Of course, writing requires a good team of trusted feedback and I'm lucky to be friends with amazingly talented people. Sierra Godfrey assured that the first act was off to a good start; Kat Howard gave really smart suggestions to rework the first half; and Meghan Scott Molin sped-read the final draft before I turned it in. Peng Shepherd contributed the very important names Tater Truck and Noodle Tent to the story's world as well as being part of the crowdsource group that came up with Zoe's ridiculous shuriken catchphrase.

Some noteworthy shout-outs: Jeff Kakes, who challenged me to get a Lobot easter egg in a book (see, I did it!); Richard Donelly, who earned a character name by providing a bunch of free plumbing advice as everything in my house was falling apart; and Matt Smith and Ming-Na Wen, who played Jamie and Zoe in the movie I saw in my head. My many writer friends who help my sanity and creativity on a regular basis, but especially Diana Urban, Wendy Heard, Randy Ribay and my TeamRocks tribe.

And my lovably clueless cat Nermal, who will now be immortalized for playing a cat named Normal in this book, down to the exact awkward mannerisms.

And finally, thank you to David Bowie for the absolute perfect title for this book. Your presence is in my family's life every day.